"Not generally. But I'll make an exception in your case."

Lyla shook her head. "Men like you don't even ask out women like me."

Wyatt frowned. "Men like me and women like you?"

"Hot guys who know they're hot," she clarified. "Don't you dare say you don't know you're hot. And I'm the opposite of hot."

"Oh, you're hot, all right."

And he so wished he hadn't blurted that out. He knew how to keep things close to the vest, and he darn sure shouldn't be saying something like that to Lyla. Especially since it was the truth.

WANTED

BY
DELORES FOSSEN

First published in Great Britain 2014
by Mills & Boon, an imprint of Harlequin (UK) Limited,
Eton House, 18-24 Paradise Road, Richmond, Surrey, TW9 1SR

© 2013 Delores Fossen

Published in Great Britain 2014
by Mills & Boon, an imprint of Harlequin (UK) Limited,
Eton House, 18-24 Paradise Road, Richmond, Surrey, TW9 1SR

© 2014 Delores Fossen

ISBN: 978 0 263 91346 0

46-0114

Harlequin (UK) Limited's policy is to use papers that are natural, renewable and recyclable products and made from wood grown in sustainable forests. The logging and manufacturing processes conform to the legal environmental regulations of the country of origin.

Printed and bound in Spain
by Blackprint CPI, Barcelona

Imagine a family tree that includes Texas cowboys, Choctaw and Cherokee Indians, a Louisiana pirate and a Scottish rebel who battled side by side with William Wallace. With ancestors like that, it's easy to understand why *USA TODAY* bestselling author and former air force captain **Delores Fossen** feels as if she were genetically predisposed to writing romances. Along the way to fulfilling her DNA destiny, Delores married an air force top gun who just happens to be of Viking descent. With all those romantic bases covered, she doesn't have to look too far for inspiration.

imagine a family tree that includes Texas cowboys, Choctaw and Cherokee Indians, a Louisiana pirate and a Scottish rebel who battled side by side with William Wallace. With ancestors like that it's easy to understand why USA TODAY bestselling author and Rita Award-winning Delores Fossen reckons... she were practically predestined to write... Along the way to fulfilling her DNA destiny, Delores married an Air Force top gun who just happens to be of Viking descent. With all those romantic bases covered, she chose to... forever at her imagination.

Chapter One

Marshal Wyatt McCabe adjusted his binoculars and studied the woman. Lyla Pearson. She was leading a roan mare into the barn just behind her small ranch house, and from what he could tell, she appeared to be talking to the horse. Maybe even singing to it.

She sure didn't look like someone on the verge of committing a felony.

Not yet anyway.

One thing was for certain—he'd never met her. If he had, Wyatt was pretty sure he would have remembered her even though there was nothing much about her that stood out.

Five foot seven or eight. Average build. Brown hair that she'd gathered into a ponytail.

She was wearing no-frills jeans and a weathered buckskin coat—practically a uniform for someone working with horses. Something he knew a little about, since he worked his own family's ranch.

Wyatt checked his watch. A little past seven in the morning, which meant Ms. Pearson would soon change her cowgirl *uniform* for her job as assistant director of the San Antonio Crime Scene Unit. He had every intention of following her there, too. In fact, he didn't intend to let her out of his sight until he figured out what the heck was going on.

He *would* get answers.

And those answers extended to the baby she was carrying.

There was no baby bump that he could see. Probably too early in the pregnancy for it, but Wyatt wasn't a baby expert. However, from everything he'd read about her, Lyla had wanted a baby for years even though she was single and not in a relationship.

What Wyatt needed to know was why she'd wanted *this* particular baby.

She disappeared into the barn, probably to stable the mare, and when she came out, she stopped and looked around as if she sensed someone was watching her. Wyatt ducked lower behind the pile of boulders, though he figured he was hidden well enough. He'd had a lot of experience doing surveillance duty in rural settings during his six and a half years as a marshal.

The sharp January wind slapped at her, and it was cold enough that when her breath mixed with the chilly air, it created a split-second foggy haze around her face.

Still, she didn't move.

She continued to glance around.

Even though she wasn't a cop, she had cop's eyes. Maybe a cop's instincts, too, which Wyatt hoped didn't kick in. He needed to figure out what she was up to before she even realized he was on her trail.

Finally, she moved, walking toward her house, and Wyatt was so caught up in watching her that he nearly missed the movement on the back side of the barn. It was just a blur of motion. Maybe a horse. But with everything else going on, that seemed too much to hope.

Wyatt volleyed glances between her and the barn,

and he saw it again. This time, he got more than a blurry glimpse. No horse. It was a man, and he was lurking behind the barn. Wyatt watched, wondering if Lyla knew about her visitor. Maybe he was even her partner in crime.

But the man didn't call out to her.

And she didn't seem to notice him.

Hell.

This was not a complication he needed right now.

If the guy wasn't her partner, then Wyatt needed to know why he was there. Because he figured someone skulking around a barn didn't have the best of intentions. Unless he was a lawman, that is.

Wyatt took a harder look. The guy was dressed in camouflage clothing. There was no sign of a lawman's badge, so Wyatt drew his Colt from his shoulder holster and eased onto the top of the boulders. Wyatt started hurrying toward Lyla. Anything he did right now was risky, but the risk went up a significant notch when he saw the man dart from the barn to the back of her house.

The guy was armed.

Lyla didn't appear to be.

And worse, she was smack-dab out in the open. If this wasn't her partner, then why was he there, and did that gun mean he was going to try to kill her? Maybe this was someone opposed to what Lyla had already set into motion, and if the man killed her, Wyatt would never know the full truth.

Plus, there were other reasons to keep her alive, and the biggest reason of all was that baby she was carrying.

"Get down!" Wyatt shouted to her.

She whirled around as Wyatt had expected her to do. And froze again. The gunman darn sure didn't freeze. He darted out from the barn and took aim.

At Wyatt.

Wyatt dropped to the icy ground. "I'm Marshal Wyatt McCabe," he shouted.

The guy ducked back behind the barn, but Wyatt didn't see or hear anything to indicate he was on the run. Too bad, because if there was a gunfight, then Lyla could be caught in the cross fire. Definitely not something he wanted.

Even worse, Wyatt couldn't call for backup. He'd checked his phone shortly after he'd parked his truck on the hidden curve of the road—not far away at all—and the whole area was a dead zone. No reception whatsoever.

"Get down!" Wyatt called out to her again.

Thankfully, this time she got moving and did as he'd ordered. Lyla landed on the dead winter grass, yards from her front porch and the safety of her house. There was nothing she could use to hide behind or for protection, and that meant Wyatt had to get to her, fast.

He levered himself up but kept as low as he could. He also kept his Colt aimed and ready. And he started running. He braced himself to dive back to the ground if necessary, but when the gunman peered out from the barn, he didn't fire.

"Drop the gun!" Wyatt ordered.

He was close enough to Lyla now that he heard her make a sound of surprise mixed with a whole lot of fear. Her reaction made Wyatt think she hadn't known that an armed man was less than thirty feet away from her.

An armed man who clearly wasn't listening to a thing Wyatt was telling him to do.

The guy didn't drop his gun. He stayed put, just tossing out the occasional glances. Once Wyatt had Lyla safely inside, he was going to do something about this nonlistening moron. That didn't mean killing him. No. That was the last thing Wyatt wanted, because he wanted answers from him, too.

"Don't move," Wyatt reminded Lyla when she lifted her head. She dropped back down but looked at him as if trying to figure out who he was.

Or rather, *pretending* to do that.

Since her pretense and the reaction to the gunman could all be a ruse, Wyatt kept his attention on both her and the gunman. He made his way across the narrow dirt road that stopped directly in front of her house. Each step was a victory because there were no shots being fired at them. He really wanted to keep it that way.

Wyatt hurried the last few yards to her, and he moved directly in front of her, making sure he was between her and the gunman.

"What's going on?" she asked, her voice shaking as hard as the rest of her.

"I was hoping you could tell me." He took aim at the barn and stood. "Is your front door locked?"

"No."

Good. Though he'd figured she hadn't bothered to lock it. Not usually much crime out in the rural part of the county. Of course, *usually* wasn't the norm right now.

"Stay behind me," Wyatt instructed. "We're going inside."

Where he hoped she wouldn't try to kill him. But then, he figured her plan didn't include murdering him. Nope.

She or someone else had put too much in motion to outright kill him.

Well, unless the plan had changed and someone was trying to cut their losses and make sure there were no loose ends with equally loose lips. If that was the case, then both Lyla and he could be targeted to die.

She didn't argue about going inside with him, and Lyla slid her hands over her stomach and practically pressed herself against his back as they inched across the yard. Wyatt could feel the tight muscles in her arms. Could feel her warm breath hit against his neck.

And he could feel her fear.

He shifted his position a little as they went up the steps. He had to keep Lyla shielded, but he also had to make sure the gunman didn't try to go in through the back of her house.

That led him to his next problem.

If someone was trying to nix a plan that was already in motion—like this one—there might be another attacker waiting inside. Or maybe this was all part of Lyla's plan—get him inside so she could move on to the next step.

Whatever the heck that was.

Despite the *don't be stupid* warning echoing through his head, Wyatt opened the door and stepped inside, keeping her next to him. His attention and gun slashed from one side of the living room to the other.

Nothing.

Well, nothing that he could immediately see anyway. It wasn't a large room, but there was a dark red sofa and two chairs. Not easy hiding places, but he checked anyway. Then he checked for what could pose the most immediate danger.

Lyla Pearson herself.

"Are you armed?" he asked, but didn't wait for her to answer. Wyatt shoved his hand inside her coat and gave her a quick pat down.

She gasped and tried to push him away, but Wyatt held his ground. "I don't carry a gun," she insisted.

"Maybe not, but you have one registered to you."

Her eyes widened. "How'd you know that?"

Wyatt just tapped the marshal's badge clipped to his belt.

Lyla still looked confused by all of this. Heck, maybe she was. After all, if she'd truly set up the gunman pretense, she would've had to have known that Wyatt would be there at that exact moment. He'd kept this visit secret. Not even his five foster brothers knew, and they were all marshals, too. He hadn't wanted to tell them anything until he'd figured out what was going on.

The figuring out started *now*.

"Back door locked?" he asked. He pulled her inside, keeping her against the jamb.

"I'm not sure."

"Stay put," Wyatt snarled, and he hurried into the kitchen. If anyone was hiding, they would have to be in the fridge, because the pantry door was wide-open and he could see inside. He turned the dead bolt on the door to lock it.

She didn't ask why he'd done that, but he could feel her fear go up a notch. Or maybe she was faking that, too. At any rate, she was breathing through her mouth, and the pulse on her throat was skittering a mile a minute.

Wyatt went back to her, waited. Listened. But he didn't hear anyone inside, or out, for that matter. So, he grabbed the cordless landline phone and handed it to her. "Call 9-1-1 and request backup."

Her hand brushed against his when she took the phone, and for just a split second, their eyes met. Hers were brown, just as her file had said, but what wasn't in her file was they were deep and warm.

Oh, man.

He didn't need to be thinking of her eyes. Or anything else, for that matter. She could be one of the most conniving criminals he'd ever met.

Or maybe an innocent pawn.

Until Wyatt knew which, her eyes and the rest of her were off-limits.

While she made the call, Wyatt got her all the way inside and kicked the door shut. He locked it. But he didn't move. He stayed put, waiting to make sure they were indeed alone. Waiting, too, to see if she'd make some kind of move.

She didn't. Lyla called 9-1-1 just as he'd asked.

The window on the east side of the room was both a blessing and a curse. It allowed Wyatt a decent view of the back side of the barn. The last place he'd spotted the guy with the gun. But that window was also a danger, since the gunman could see them and shoot right through the glass.

"A deputy's on the way," Lyla relayed once she'd finished the call.

Good. But the nearest town, Bulverde, was a good thirty minutes away, and he was on his own until then.

"Who's out there?" she asked.

"You don't know?"

Her breath rattled in her throat. "I have no idea." She shook her head and caught onto the door, maybe because she didn't look too steady on her feet. "He can't shoot me. I'm pregnant and he could hurt the baby."

If this was an act, she was damn convincing.

Wyatt glanced around, looking for the safest way to approach this—for both him and her. "Get down on the floor in front of the sofa."

It wasn't a perfect location. Not by a long shot. But it

would get her out of direct line of fire of that window, and with her on the floor, she wouldn't be able to attack him.

She moved to do just that but then stopped and stared at him. "What's going on?"

He didn't have to lie about this. "You're going to tell me that after I take care of the guy by the barn."

Her stare tightened into a glare, and with that glare aimed at him, she eased down onto the floor.

That freed him up to hurry to the hall entry, where he spotted three doors. Probably two bedrooms and a bath. All the doors were open, but unlike with the pantry, he didn't have a clear look inside any of them.

"Why are you here?" she asked. "How did you know there'd be a gunman at my house?"

Tricky questions, both of them. If she didn't truly know the answers, then they were both in some Texas-sized trouble.

"I'm involved in an investigation, and you might have something to do with it," he settled for saying.

"I don't understand. What investigation?"

Wyatt knew he couldn't dodge her questions for long, but he really had to make sure another gunman wasn't inside the house. "Don't get up," he warned her, and he hurried into the hall for a quick check of the bedrooms and bath.

"What investigation?" Lyla repeated.

Even though he'd stepped into her bedroom, Wyatt had no trouble hearing her. "Jonah Webb's murder."

She mumbled something he didn't catch, but Wyatt ignored her, had a look under the bed and in the closet. Everything was neat and in its place. Definitely no smoking-gun evidence that he could use to arrest her on the spot.

When he was satisfied they were alone and there was

nothing immediate for him to find, he hurried back to the living room and met Lyla's glare. It was worse than the other one she'd aimed at him.

"Jonah Webb," she repeated. "He was the man from the orphanage who was murdered years ago."

Sixteen and a half, to be exact.

She studied his face. Then his badge. "You're one of the marshals who were raised at the orphanage." Again, he couldn't be sure if her surprised tone was fake or not.

"Rocky Creek Children's Facility," he supplied.

He tried not to go back to those bitter memories. Failed. Always failed. But bad memories weren't going to stop him from doing his job. Wyatt went back to the center of the living room so he could keep watch to see what the bozo with the gun was going to do.

"Webb's body was found, what, about six months ago?" she asked.

"Eight. The Rangers are still investigating it." He paused, to try to figure out if this was old news to her, but he couldn't tell. "Webb's wife, Sarah, confessed to the murder, but she had an accomplice. Unfortunately, she wasn't able to say who her accomplice was, because she's in a coma."

And Sarah had been that way since she'd tried to kill his brother Dallas and Dallas's wife, Joelle. Dallas had had to shoot the woman, and she'd been in a coma ever since.

"Your foster father is a suspect," Lyla whispered. "I remember reading that in one of the reports."

Yeah. Kirby Granger was indeed that. And worse, he might have actually done it, though Wyatt never intended to admit that aloud.

Not to her.

Not to anyone.

Especially if it turned out that Lyla Pearson was living proof that Kirby was not just innocent but that someone else was willing to do pretty much anything to cover their own guilt.

"You're a suspect, too," Lyla added. Her breathing kicked up a notch, and she got to a crouching position. Maybe because she was just now realizing she could be in danger—from him. Heck, she might even be thinking of running.

Wyatt nodded, watching both her and the window.

She blinked, and he saw the doubt in her eyes. Lyla shifted her position again. Oh, yeah. Definitely planning to run.

"I'm not sure what's going on," he said. "But I suspect you know a lot more than you're saying."

The remark had no sooner left his mouth when Lyla leaped to her feet and started toward the hall. Probably to get the .38 that was somewhere in her bedroom. Wyatt hadn't seen the gun, but he figured it must be in the house.

Wyatt latched on to her, trying to stay gentle, but it was hard to do when she brought up her knee to ram into his groin. He had no choice but to drag her to the sofa and pin her body with his.

It didn't put him in the best of positions. He could no longer see the window or the gunman, but it stopped her from getting away.

Lyla frantically shook her head and tried to punch him. "Why are you doing this?"

He dodged her fist, barely. "Why are *you* doing this?" And Wyatt dropped his gaze to her stomach.

"I don't understand." The words rushed out with her breath.

Maybe she did. Maybe she didn't. But Wyatt decided

to test a theory or two. "I think you got pregnant so you could manipulate this investigation."

She stared at him as if he'd lost his mind. "My baby has nothing to do with Jonah Webb's murder."

"You sure about that?" he countered.

"Positive," Lyla mumbled, but there it was. The doubt that slid through those intense brown eyes. "Why would it? Why would my baby have anything to do with this?"

Wyatt took a deep breath. Had to. "Because that baby is mine."

Chapter Two

Lyla figured either Marshal Wyatt McCabe was insane, or someone had told him some huge lies. Either way, she had to get away from him.

She put her hands against his chest and gave him a hard shove. She might as well have been shoving a brick wall, because he didn't budge. He wasn't exactly what she would call muscle-bound, but he was solid.

"Please." Lyla tried to reason with him. "Let me go. Neither me nor my baby has anything to do with you or the murder investigation."

The marshal made a *yeah right* sound, but he did move off her. Not far, though. He levered himself up but continued to loom over her. Continued to volley glances out the window, too. Did that mean the man with the gun wasn't working with Marshal McCabe?

Lyla wasn't sure.

She wasn't sure of anything any longer except that she wanted to get away from both men. Her keys were already in her car, which was parked in the garage. If she could get to it, she might be able to escape.

Might.

But she couldn't risk getting shot. Of course, these men might have something much worse in mind than just hurting her. They might want to kill her.

But why?

She shook her head. Marshal McCabe obviously wasn't the only one with questions.

"Who's the gunman?" she asked him again. Maybe now that the facade of the helpful lawman was gone, she'd get some straight answers, because the ones she'd gotten from him so far hadn't made a lick of sense.

McCabe lifted his shoulder. "I don't know. Your bodyguard maybe?"

"I don't need a bodyguard." But she rethought that. "At least, I didn't until twenty minutes ago. Clearly, I need one now to protect me from you."

He studied her as if trying to decide if that was a lie or not. It wasn't. In fact, everything she'd told the lawman had been the truth, but he obviously didn't believe her.

Lyla tried to remember everything she knew about Marshal McCabe, but other than the sketchy details about the Webb murder investigation, she drew a blank.

"We've met before?" she asked, though she was certain they hadn't. McCabe was the sort of man a woman tended to remember. Tall, good-looking. Dark brown hair and gunmetal-blue eyes.

Yes, definitely the sort to be remembered.

"No," he answered. "But you know me."

"I don't," she insisted.

That baby is mine, he'd said, but he had to be wrong about that.

Well, maybe.

"I used in vitro fertilization to get pregnant," she explained, though judging from the flat look he gave her, he already knew.

"Yeah. At the Hanover Fertility Clinic in San Antonio," he supplied. "You had the procedure done two and half months ago, on your thirty-first birthday, and it worked on the first try. You got the news two weeks later that you were going to be a mom."

A chill went through her. It was downright creepy that this stranger knew such private things about her, but it chilled her even more to know he might have told the truth about the baby being his.

"The clinic assured me that the donor I used would be anonymous," Lyla explained. "In fact, I insisted on it, because I intend to raise this baby myself."

"Yeah," the marshal repeated. "Old baggage. I know about that, too."

Lyla snapped back her shoulders, ready to blast him for invading her life and privacy this way. It wasn't any of his business about her failed relationships.

She had to get her teeth unclenched so she could speak. "I want you to get out of here now. The deputy's already on the way, and if you don't leave, I'll have him arrest you. I don't care if you're a marshal or not."

"Oh, I'm a marshal, all right, and I believe you manipulated that in vitro procedure so you could force me to cooperate."

Lyla tried to throw her hands in the air, but McCabe pinned them to the sofa. "And how could I possibly have manipulated it?"

He glared at her. "By switching mine and my late wife's embryo with the one you should have received."

Oh, yes. He was crazy.

"I didn't switch anything. There was a slim-to-none chance that I'd get pregnant the old-fashioned way, because my body rarely produces eggs, even with fertility treatments. So, I used the donation the clinic gave me." She paused just long enough to gather her breath. "And what possible proof do you have that it was yours?"

"All the proof I need." But McCabe paused, mumbled

some really bad profanity. "Four months ago I hired a
surrogate to have a baby, using the embryo that my late
wife and I'd stored at a clinic. Not Hanover," he quickly
added. "Another one in San Antonio. But then the surrogate changed her mind and decided not to go through
with the pregnancy."

Lyla mentally went through all that. "And you think
I somehow got yours and your wife's embryo instead of
the anonymous one I requested."

"I know you did," he fired back. "Last month, the
clinic called me and said the embryo was missing. They
said maybe it'd been stolen or accidentally donated, and
I followed a very hard-to-follow paper trail that eventually led to you."

Oh, mercy. Maybe it was true, then, but Lyla wasn't
just going to take this man's word for it. "I want to see
this paper trail."

Marshal McCabe tipped his head toward the barn.
"After I hear what your gun-toting friend has to say."

"He's not my friend!" she practically shouted. "And
so what if the clinic accidentally gave me your embryo?
It doesn't matter. I don't want you in my life, and I don't
want you part of my baby's life."

Except there was the possibility about this being his
late wife's embryo. No. Did that mean he'd have some
kind of legal claim?

That couldn't happen.

"The switch wasn't an *accident*," he insisted. But then
he shook his head. "At least I don't think it was. I think
there's something bad going on here and that you're a
key player in this wrongdoing."

Lyla couldn't argue with the *something bad* theory.
He was there, right in her face. But she'd done nothing

wrong and had taken no shortcuts in getting pregnant with this baby.

"I don't know where you got your information about me, but there's no reason whatsoever that I'd want to have your baby." And she didn't bother to say it nicely, either. "I want you arrested and out of here. That'll happen as soon as the deputy arrives."

Soon couldn't be soon enough, though. Lyla prayed that whoever the sheriff had sent out was speeding to her ranch right now.

"If I explain to the deputy what I've learned, maybe he'll arrest you," McCabe threatened right back. "Because one way or another, you will tell me what's going on."

"I have no idea," Lyla insisted, but she was talking to the air, because the marshal's attention was fastened to the barn now. He practically jumped to his feet and snapped in that direction.

Alarmed at the concern that she saw in his eyes, Lyla jumped up, as well, and followed his gaze. There wasn't one man but two out there now. Both wearing camouflage fatigues. Both armed.

Oh, God.

Now she had three armed men on her ranch.

"Either your second bodyguard just showed up, or you've done something to piss off someone other than me," McCabe growled.

Even though she didn't trust the marshal, that didn't mean Lyla could ignore what he'd just said. Maybe she had riled someone. After all, she was the second in charge of a huge crime-scene-unit lab, and processed all kinds of evidence.

"You think those men are here to hurt me?" she asked, peering out at them.

"Hard to say."

She was tired of the vague answers. "Then guess," Lyla demanded. She pinned her attention to the gunmen, too. If they moved one inch, she'd have to move as well. She prayed they didn't start shooting into the house.

McCabe shook his head. "Maybe there's someone who doesn't want you involved in this."

Well, she certainly fell into that category. Lyla didn't want to be involved even if she had no idea what *this* was. Still, that was something she would have to work out later. After she had some way to protect herself.

Lyla moved, ready to race toward her bedroom to get the .38 she had in the back of her nightstand drawer.

"I don't think so," McCabe snarled.

He hooked his left arm around her waist, dragged her to him and anchored her against his body. She'd only known him a matter of minutes, and it was the third time he'd put his hands on her. Lyla wanted to do something about that.

Actually, she wanted to punch him and run.

But she couldn't risk hurting the baby. No. As angry and scared as she was, her best bet was to wait for the deputy and maybe try to reason with this man, who claimed to be the father of her child.

A father who might be a criminal.

Lyla tried to think back through their entire conversation. Not easy to do, with her heart and mind racing and with McCabe plastered against her. It was hard to think or breathe with him so close. Still, she forced herself to do just that, and she went back to the part of their conversation before he'd dropped the embryo bombshell.

"Why did you think I had anything to do with the Webb murder investigation?" she asked. Lyla also kept watch on the two gunmen.

"You don't…yet," McCabe said.

Despite the clear danger outside, that caused her attention to snap to the marshal. "What do you mean?"

"I mean you'll be put in charge of compiling the final investigation, the one that'll determine who's responsible for Jonah Webb's murder."

Lyla was shaking her head before he even finished. "Not possible. The Texas Rangers have their own crime lab, one of the best in the country."

"And soon the governor will say there's a conflict of interest, that the head of the Ranger lab once worked on a case with one of their prime suspects, Kirby Granger."

"Your foster father," she mumbled. "It's true?"

McCabe nodded. "True that they worked together. Not true about the conflict of interest."

That probably wouldn't matter. Appearance was everything in this sort of investigation. The sixteen-and-a-half-year-old murder had drawn national attention, and the governor and the Rangers would want to make sure the right people were held responsible for the crime.

Still, there was something about this that didn't make sense.

"Even if the governor transferred the investigation to the San Antonio Crime Scene Unit, they wouldn't put me in charge of the case. He'd choose my boss, Dean Mobley."

"Your boss will excuse himself and insist that you take over," McCabe said without hesitation or doubt.

Not likely. Mobley and she didn't see eye-to-eye on much. "Why would he do that, huh?"

"I don't know, but he will."

Lyla huffed. "He won't." And she would have added more to that argument if she hadn't heard a welcome sound.

A police siren.

Thank God. The deputy was nearly there. And she hoped he had plenty of backup.

McCabe cursed again, and for a moment she thought it was because of the siren. Maybe it partly was. But he didn't even spare the front of the house a glance, despite the fact that the police cruiser would soon arrive there. He still had his attention on the two men by the barn.

"Stay inside," McCabe ordered, and he started for the back door.

Lyla didn't intend to let him leave. She wanted him arrested. She reached to latch on to his arm, but then she saw the movement.

The two gunmen.

They were no longer behind the barn. They were running. Getting away.

McCabe threw off her grip, and with his gun aimed and ready, he hurried to the back door. Lyla followed him, but there was no way she could stop him. Not with that rock-hard strength.

He'd barely made it to the door before one of the men stopped. Pivoted.

And fired.

Chapter Three

The sound of the bullet blasted through the house.

"Get down!" Wyatt shouted to Lyla.

Wyatt got down, too, but he stayed near the back door so he could keep an eye on the gunmen. One was already racing across the pasture, away from the house, and the other didn't even take aim before he fired another shot and then took off running, as well.

Hell.

Wyatt couldn't let them get away, but he also couldn't risk one or both circling back around and coming after Lyla. He had no idea if she was innocent or not, but by damn, he was not going to let her get gunned down.

"What's happening?" Lyla asked. She was on the floor, thank God, one hand over her head and the other over her stomach. He hoped she stayed that way, though her hands would be a paltry shield for bullets.

"Someone's trying to kill me," Wyatt relayed to her. "Or maybe you."

But there was something off about this attack, if it was indeed a murder attempt. For one thing, the men had waited way too long before shooting. In the twenty minutes or so that Lyla and he had been in the house, two gunmen could have torn the place apart with a shower of bullets.

Maybe that meant they'd wanted her alive.

Or scared.

If so, they'd succeeded in doing both. Lyla was trembling on the living room floor, but she hadn't been hurt, and that meant the baby was safe.

Wyatt tried not to think about that. Tried not to think about the deception that had gone into creating this child. He just focused on the job, and right now the job was keeping Lyla and the baby safe and stopping those gunmen.

The moment that Wyatt heard the cop car brake to a stop in front of the house, he bolted out the back door. Not because he was afraid of being arrested. No, he could handle that. But now that Lyla had someone else to protect her, it was time to see what he could do about the gunmen.

Wyatt had to go after them.

Both of the men were running, their backs to Wyatt. He considered shooting but dismissed it. If he hit one, the other could return fire, and he was still too close to the house to risk that.

Wyatt leaped off the porch and hit the ground running. Not the easiest thing to do in cowboy boots and winter gear, but the men were weighed down by equipment belts, which no doubt held extra ammo. Maybe extra weapons, too. They'd obviously come prepared for an attack that they'd barely carried out.

The pasture wasn't that deep, unfortunately, and behind it was a fence and then a heavily treed area. He wanted to stop the men before they could disappear into those woods, but they had too much of a head start on him. When Wyatt saw the first man reach the fence, he knew he had to do something.

"Stop or I'll shoot," Wyatt called out.

Still not listening, they didn't stop. Both of them continued to run, and the one in the lead latched on to the top rung of the wood fence and started to hoist himself to the other side.

Wyatt fired at him.

The shot was off because he hadn't stopped and aimed, but it got their attention. The guy on the fence turned and fired right back. Wyatt saw the bullet slam into the ground and kick up dirt. Much better than it going toward the house.

Wyatt fired another shot. Ducked. But the one on the fence didn't take the bait this time. He scrambled over the top and disappeared into the trees.

Wyatt turned to fire at the other one, but the shots began to blast through the air. Obviously, the gunman on the other side of the fence hadn't run away and left his partner after all. He was trying to save his sorry butt, and to save his own butt, Wyatt had no choice but to dart behind an old cast-iron bathtub that'd been turned into a watering trough.

He cursed, waiting, but knowing this would allow the second man to get away. Wyatt lost count of the number of shots fired, all of them smacking into the trough and the ground around him.

But they stopped just as quickly as they'd started.

Wyatt waited another second or two and then took off running again.

Neither man was in sight now, and since he didn't know the area, Wyatt couldn't even predict which direction they'd gone. Maybe he would be able to find their footprints and follow them.

"Stop!" someone yelled from behind him. Not Lyla. A man, probably the deputy.

Wyatt spared him a glance over his shoulder. Yep, a

deputy in uniform, all right, and he was standing with his gun drawn on the back porch. It was a risk, because the lawman might shoot him in the back, but Wyatt was so close to the fence now that he took his chances. He barreled over it and dropped to the ground.

There were footprints. Plenty of them, and some had bits of dried leaves and twigs in them, which could mean they were several days old. Later, he'd need to ask Lyla about who had access to this part of the property, but he was betting these weren't the footprints of a neighbor.

Someone had been watching her for a long time.

He lifted his head and listened for any sound of footsteps. Nothing. Just the wind. But he soon heard something he didn't want to hear.

An engine starting up.

Wyatt raced toward the sound, weaving his way through the trees and scraggly underbrush, and it didn't take him long to get to a clearing with a trail. He caught just a glimpse of the black SUV as it disappeared out of sight. He didn't even have a chance to get the license number.

Oh, man. He didn't need this.

Without thinking, he yanked out his phone, and he got a quick reminder of why he hadn't already called one of his brothers. Still no service out in this rural area. That meant he needed to get to a landline ASAP.

He also needed to face that gun-pointing deputy.

Wyatt meandered his way back to the fence and was about to climb over it when he spotted something.

A camera mounted on one of the trees.

He followed the angle of the lens—it was aimed directly at Lyla's house. Yeah, someone had been watching her.

But who?

Wyatt figured the camera might give him some clues about that, so he ripped it from the tree and climbed back over the fence. The deputy was still on the porch, but there was no sign of Lyla, who was hopefully still inside and on the floor. That was because the gunmen might make a return visit and this time launch another attack.

"Marshal McCabe," the deputy said as Wyatt got closer. He was a pencil-thin man with pink flushed cheeks and nearly white blond hair. "I'm Deputy Walter O'Neal."

"I hope you called for backup, because the shooters got away in a black SUV. They used what appears to be an old ranch road."

The deputy nodded. "Got two other deputies on the way. You can give us a description at the sheriff's office, 'cause I need to take you in for questioning."

Yeah, Wyatt had figured that, and he had no plans to resist. Or even argue. The sooner he finished his business with the deputy, the sooner he could have the camera analyzed and figure out the identities of those gunmen.

"Lyla said you accused her of some wrongdoing," O'Neal added when Wyatt made it to the porch.

"I did." He held up the camera. "And this might prove it." However, it was more likely to prove her innocence, since she had no reason to put her own house under surveillance, unless it was part of some security system to make sure no one got too close.

Like him.

"I did nothing wrong," he heard Lyla repeat, and she stepped onto the back porch to join them. But not for long.

Wyatt took her arm and put her right back inside. "She shouldn't be out in the open, because of the gunmen."

And he turned to the deputy. "You need to bring her to the sheriff's office with us."

"She insisted on coming," the deputy said, sounding a little uncertain about that. Or maybe his uncertainty was just for Wyatt and the shots that'd been fired. "Though I did suggest she see a doctor while I deal with getting your statement."

"The men really got away?" she asked, her eyes wide. Lyla grabbed her coat and purse from the peg next to the door that led to the garage.

Wyatt nodded and held up the camera. "Any idea who's been watching you?"

That didn't help ease the look of concern on her face. "No."

He hadn't expected any other answer from her, but then she stopped. "Three days ago someone from the electric company showed up and said he needed to do some repairs on the lines. He seemed, well, a little suspicious. Like he was nervous or something."

That was a start. "I'll make some calls and see if he was legit or not. Also, if there's a surveillance disk in here, we might get a better look of the gunmen's faces." Of course, there probably wouldn't be a disk. It likely had some kind of wireless feed to another device.

One that the gunmen had almost certainly taken.

Wyatt doubted they were so incompetent that they would have left something like that behind. Still, he might get lucky. He would have a closer look later.

"I take it all of this is part of some official investigation?" O'Neal asked.

"An investigation, yes," Wyatt answered. "Official, no. Not yet anyway. I'm here for personal reasons."

He waited to see if Lyla had told the deputy about the in vitro switch, but she didn't say a word. Wyatt figured that would change, though, when they got to the sheriff's office. Lyla was a crime scene analyst, bound by the law, and she no doubt trusted this deputy more than she trusted him.

Yeah, she'd tell, all right.

"I'll let you keep your gun," O'Neal said, leading them out the front and to his patrol car. "For now."

Wyatt didn't like the guy's attitude, but he had to admit it was a generous concession. If their situations had been reversed, Wyatt wouldn't have let him stay armed.

Since there was a bulky equipment bag in the front passenger seat, Lyla and Wyatt got into the back. She didn't say a word to him, but she did shoot him another glare. Wyatt gave her one right back. So far, the evidence was pointing to the fact that she might be a pawn, but until Wyatt knew for sure, he intended to be as wary of her as she was of him.

"What will happen now?" she asked, directed not at Wyatt but rather the deputy.

"We'll start with your statements," he answered, his attention shifting all around. Wyatt was doing the same thing, looking for those gunmen. "I guess neither of you recognized those two men?"

"No," Wyatt and she answered in unison. That seemed to annoy her, too. "But the marshal probably thinks I'm lying about that."

"The marshal figures she's telling the truth," Wyatt countered. "About that anyway." He looked at her for the rest of the explanation. "Those bullets were real, and I don't believe you'd put the baby at risk by hiring idiot gunmen to shoot at or near you."

"I wouldn't." Her chin came up. Her voice was strong. "This baby is my life, and..." She snapped away from him.

Wyatt could finish that for her. *This baby is my life, and you have nothing to do with it.*

Or something along those lines.

She'd already said she didn't want a baby daddy. Wyatt had to make sure that was the truth. Then he'd figure out what to do with that truth and everything else that seemed to be hitting him at once.

"Call ahead," Wyatt instructed the deputy, "and arrange for Lyla to be checked out by a doctor. Just in case."

He expected her to argue with that, too, and maybe it was on her mind when she opened her mouth. But then she just slid her hand over her stomach.

"Thanks," she said under her breath, and the deputy made the call.

While he did that, Wyatt checked his own phone. He finally had service, so he made a call and asked one of his foster brothers, Marshal Declan O'Malley, to find out if the utility company had sent someone to Lyla's house. With one thing down, he mentally went through the long list of other calls he had to make.

But the ringing of Lyla's phone stopped him.

"Mr. Mobley," she greeted the caller. Her boss. "I might not be in this morning. I'm on my way to the Bulverde sheriff's office....Oh, you heard about the shooting." She paused. "No, I'm fine."

Lyla opened her mouth to say more, but Wyatt heard the chatter on the other end of the line. He couldn't tell what her boss was saying, but it had captured her complete attention.

"What?" she finally said, quickly followed by "Why?"

More chatter, and Wyatt still couldn't make out enough of it to tell what was going on, but he hoped like the devil it wasn't more bad news. He'd had enough of that already.

"We'll talk when I get to the office," Lyla snapped, and she ended the call. It took several moments, though, for her to look at Wyatt. "Mobley excused himself from the Jonah Webb investigation, and the Rangers want me to take over."

Not exactly a surprise. "I hate to say I told you so, but I did."

"It could mean nothing," she concluded, but the worry in her voice said it was a whole lot of something. "Mobley got another job. A civilian company with much higher pay. They want him to work with a legal watchdog group that's retesting evidence from old criminal cases."

"The timing's suspicious, but it gives me another lead. The person who offered Mobley the new job could be behind the rest of this."

She swiveled around to face him. "What exactly is the *rest of this?*" She glanced uneasily at the deputy and moved closer to Wyatt. "If this is some kind of plan to get me to falsify evidence, it won't work," she whispered.

"It might be that." But he just didn't know.

"The in vitro could have been just an honest mistake," she whispered a moment later. "Mobley's new job could be a coincidence."

"And the gunmen? The camera?" Wyatt pressed. "More coincidences? Because when there are that many of them, we call that a pattern."

He almost told her about the information trail that had led him to her, but his phone buzzed. Declan.

"First of all, the utility company didn't send someone to Lyla Pearson's house," Declan said the second Wyatt answered. "And second, what the hell's going on?"

Considering that Wyatt had been about to ask his brother the same thing, this wasn't a good start to what he needed to be a good conversation. "Are you referring to something specific? Because there's a lot going on."

"The Rangers got an anonymous tip that you're trying to influence the Webb murder investigation."

Ah, man. He didn't need this. "No, someone else is trying to influence it." And maybe already had. "Look, this is too complicated to get into over the phone—"

"Does it have anything to do with Lyla Pearson, the assistant director of the San Antonio CSU?"

That sent an uneasy feeling knifing through him. "It does. Why? Other than the fact that she didn't get a real service call from the electric company, what do you know about her?"

"According to the criminal informant I just talked to, she's in big trouble, Wyatt, and you should avoid her at all costs."

"Too late."

Declan cursed. "You're with her?"

"Yeah. Now why don't you tell me why that's a bad idea?" Wyatt insisted.

"Because according to the informant, by going to her, you just signed her death warrant."

Chapter Four

Death warrant.

Those two words kept going through her head, and each time, they robbed Lyla of her breath. Not that her breath was anywhere near steady yet, despite the several hours they'd spent at the sheriff's office and hospital getting her checkup. All was well with the baby, thank goodness, but it might be a while before she could rein in this feeling of panic. Her racing heartbeat, too. And the adrenaline crash.

Yes, she had that going on, as well.

Despite the clean bill of health from her obstetrician, none of this stress could be good for the baby. But then, neither were those bullets.

It was the too-fresh memory of those bullets and those two words, *death warrant,* that had made Lyla get in the truck with Wyatt after they'd finished giving their statements to the deputy.

Now she was debating that decision to allow him to place her in his protective custody. She wasn't thinking straight, but what she did know was that Wyatt seemed to want to keep her alive and safe. And he seemed capable of doing that.

Capable of wrecking her life, too.

But maybe once she got all of this sorted out, there'd

be no need for protection. No need to dodge gunmen lurking on her ranch.

"You're sure this criminal informant was telling the truth about the death threat?" she asked. "Because if he's a criminal, how can you trust him?"

"He's getting paid to spill his guts, and if what he spills is a lie, then the payments dry up." He paused, mumbled some profanity. "Unfortunately, this guy's reliable, and he said somebody's got their eye on you."

"But he didn't know who." It wasn't a question. Lyla had already pressed Wyatt on that when he'd first told her about the threat. "Then how could the criminal informant know anything about the other details if he doesn't even know the person's identity?"

"Bad people talk. Sometimes too much, and this guy plays a fly on the wall so he can make money. He says someone's going to force you to cooperate with altering evidence, and if it doesn't work out, then you'll be eliminated. *Dead,*" he clarified.

Even if the informant had lied, she wasn't immune to just the threat of it. Mercy, how had things gotten this far out of control?

"I should be in San Antonio P.D.'s protective custody," she tossed out there. "Not yours."

He spared her a glance with those intense blue eyes but kept his attention on the rural road that would take them to his family's ranch.

Which she was certain wasn't a good idea at all.

"Those guys took shots at me, and that makes this federal now."

It was weird. Though he'd practically barked that at her, his voice was far from a bark. Everything that came out of Marshal McCabe's mouth seemed smooth as silk.

And genuine. Yes, he was a charmer, all right. Even when he was accusing her of assorted crimes.

Like stealing the embryo that belonged to him and his late wife.

"You can't possibly want me at your family's home," she reminded him.

"I don't. But I don't want you dead, either. And right now, I'm your best shot at not being dead."

Even that came out as an easy drawl, but it still slammed into her. She couldn't die. Couldn't be shot. Because anything that happened to her, happened to her precious baby, as well. But somehow, someway, she had to distance herself from this silver-tongued cowboy lawman. Once she was at the ranch, she'd need to start making calls to arrange for some private security. And a bodyguard or two.

"I'm sorry, by the way," he added a moment later. "If I hadn't uncovered what was going on, the person behind this wouldn't have ordered a hit on you. At least not until you'd done everything they want you to do."

None of that was reassuring, especially the last part. "But what do they want me to do?"

"I don't know yet. But it won't be legal, and doing it won't necessarily keep you alive. Right now, I'm your best shot for staying in one piece."

Again, not reassuring, since it was obvious he distrusted her. Probably hated her, too, because he still had his doubts about her involvement in all of this. She wasn't sure if she even wanted to address that or just make those calls to get her out of there.

Wyatt took the turn toward the ranch, and moments later the house came into view. Except, *house* didn't seem the right word to describe something that size. She'd heard of Kirby Granger's spread, of course, but she hadn't expected this. Miles and miles of pastures. Hundreds of Angus cows. And she spotted four barns, along with a small house and another massive brick one that looked as if it'd recently been built. Yet another one was under construction.

Heaven knew how many people and buildings were on the parts of the property she couldn't see.

Wyatt pulled to a stop directly in front of the main house, where there were several ranch hands milling around, all armed. A middle-aged woman with graying red hair stepped out.

"Declan called," she greeted them, the worry obvious in her voice. "He said someone shot at you."

But Wyatt just shrugged. Like his voice, it seemed to be an easy drawl, too. There was certainly no crazy panic in his body language, but Lyla was sure there was plenty in hers.

"The others call Wyatt a bullet magnet," the woman added, glancing at Lyla.

Lyla's gaze whipped to him. "Why do they call you that?"

Wyatt frowned. "Why do you think?"

"Oh, God," she mumbled.

"God's probably the only one who hasn't taken a shot at me yet."

The woman gave him a scolding look. "His brothers say he's a bullet magnet because someone's always trying to mess up his pretty face. But they don't say that around me. They know I don't like joking about stuff like that."

She came closer when Lyla and Wyatt made it onto the porch, and she slipped her arm around Lyla's waist. "I'm Stella Doyle, a friend of the family. I take care of Wyatt and the others when they let me."

"The others?" Lyla asked.

"Wyatt's foster brothers. Dallas, Clayton, Harlan and Slade. Mine and Kirby's own son, too—Declan. They're all marshals like Wyatt here, and they're all my boys."

Wyatt brushed a kiss on the woman's cheek. "Where's everyone?"

"Dallas took the womenfolk and Clayton's baby to his and Joelle's place." She tipped her head in the direction of the new house, which Lyla had noticed. "He said he talked to you about that."

"He did. I just thought it'd be better if there were fewer people here tonight. Is Harlan with them?"

Stella nodded. "Slade, too. You're expecting some kind of trouble?"

"Trying to prevent it." Wyatt glanced at the curvy dark-haired woman who was sweeping the porch. A maid, no doubt. "When'd you hire her?" he asked Stella.

"Last week. Why?"

"I just want the ranch on lockdown for a while. Give her and any other new help a few paid days off. That includes ranch hands."

Stella gave an uneasy nod, and she wasn't the only one who was uneasy. It hit Lyla then. If someone had been watching her, then maybe they'd done the same to Wyatt. With all the activity going on, it would be easy to get someone onto a ranch this size.

"And now I need help with our guest," Wyatt continued. "This is Lyla Pearson, and she'll be staying with us for a while."

Stella volleyed glances at both of them. "Your girl?" she asked Wyatt.

"Yes," Wyatt said at the exact moment that Lyla blurted out, "No."

Lyla was about to ask why he'd told such a lie, but

Wyatt just shot an uneasy look at the woman sweeping, took Lyla by the arm and got her inside.

"Later," he added to her in a whisper when Lyla opened her mouth to ask about that whopper. He looked at Stella again. "I need a couple of the ranch hands to go out to Lyla's place and take care of her horses."

"I can do that myself," she insisted.

"Those gunmen might return." And that was all he had to say to put her heart in her throat. She loved her little house. The only home she'd ever had, and now she couldn't go back.

Maybe ever.

It might never feel safe there.

"Her address is in the glove compartment of my truck," Wyatt explained to Stella. "But tell the ranch hands to go there armed. Just in case."

Stella's eyes widened a little, but Lyla didn't think it was so much from surprise as from fear or dread. Heaven knew how many incidents like this the woman had gone through, living with six active marshals and a retired one.

"Come on," Wyatt told her. And it took Lyla a moment to realize he'd shifted the conversation to her. "You're staying with me until further notice."

Wyatt didn't give her time to disagree with that order. With his grip still firm on her arm, he ambled them through the maze of halls and to a home office. His, judging from the way he ushered her inside, closed the door and eased down in the seat behind the desk.

"Right about now, you're thinking of running," he said, and he proceeded to go through some emails on his laptop. "But you can't."

Lyla huffed. She was tired of this knight-in-shining-Stetson routine, especially since Wyatt didn't seem the knight type. More like a pirate. A hot one.

Something she wished she hadn't noticed.

Hard not to, though, with those rock-star looks and that devil-may-care attitude. This was exactly the kind of man she avoided.

But was attracted to anyway.

Lyla shoved that attraction aside, put her hands on his desk and leaned in to get right in his face. "I want answers, and I want them now."

He held up his finger in a *wait a second* gesture and finished reading the email. "All my brothers are tied up with this shooting and the investigation. My brother Declan sent the camera to the crime lab," he said when he finished reading whatever was on the screen. "I was right about it not having a memory card, but we might get some prints or trace. Plus, Declan might be able to track down who bought it. It's not something available at the corner store."

Good. That was a start, to find out who was behind this, but Wyatt went on to the next email, ignoring the fact that she was right in his face and wanting an explanation about his *yes* answer to Stella about her being his girl.

And why he believed she was carrying his child.

"My other brother Clayton is looking into who just hired Dean Mobley for his new civilian job with the watchdog group," Wyatt went on. "But his new employer is actually a dummy corporation. A good front, though, and it won't be hard to break through the layers, especially since it was probably set up just to hire him. It'll disappear as soon as they're finished with Mobley and you."

She thought about that a moment. "How'd you know my boss would be offered this new job?"

"Criminal informant. The same one who said I'd signed your death warrant."

The new info whirled through her head like a tornado, and even though Lyla wanted to appear strong and resolute, she wasn't. To make matters worse, she had a sudden dizzy spell and would have sagged to the floor if Wyatt hadn't caught her.

But he didn't just catch her.

He scooped her up in his arms and deposited her on the leather sofa positioned in front of a massive wall of books.

"You need me to call a doctor?" he asked, going to the small fridge in the corner. He brought her back a bottle of water, and he opened it for her. The man certainly knew how to take control.

Something she had to put a stop to.

"No doctor. I just get dizzy sometimes."

She wouldn't mention the occasional morning sickness and these strange hormonal changes in her body. Sometimes she felt like crying her eyes out, and other times she felt like a randy teenager.

Heck, she hadn't been a randy teenager even when she was in her teens.

Her body was playing one of those stupid hormone tricks on her now. Probably because Wyatt was there, just inches away, with his drop-dead-hot face looking down at her.

Like her earlier thoughts, she pushed that hormone surge aside, too.

She had help with that. Also practically right in her face was the photo on the end table. A beautiful woman in a wedding dress. Smiling from ear to ear, and her dreamy smile was directed to her equally dreamy husband.

Wyatt.

"My wife," he explained, following her gaze. "Ann passed away two years ago from a rare blood disorder."

"I'm sorry," Lyla said, because she didn't know what else to say. Words wouldn't help the hurt that she still heard in his voice. But since he'd brought up his wife, it was time to start addressing the thousand-pound gorilla in the room.

"Why do you think I got your embryo?" she asked.

He did another of those effortless shrugs. "It went missing, and the theft was well hidden. The clinic didn't discover it until last month. Since then, I've tried to locate every woman in the state who used a donor embryo to get pregnant. Only twenty-three."

"That you know of," she argued. "Maybe some clinics keep that private, since the law requires it."

He gave her a flat look. "I am the law, and I was looking for something that belonged to me."

Yes, and he'd obviously been tenacious. "There's no proof I'm carrying your baby."

"You're the only one who makes sense. There was the wife of a high-level D.A. looking for a donor embryo, but the Webb investigation couldn't have been shifted to him. You're the only one who could affect the outcome of this case."

She shook her head. "That still doesn't prove it."

"No, but a test would, and we're lucky that you've already had an amnio."

Lyla flinched. "How'd you know that?"

Another flat look. "I had someone look into your medical records."

"You hacked them."

"Yeah," he readily admitted, and he wasn't apologizing for it. "You had one done three weeks ago to rule out a uterine infection. You didn't have an infection, but at your request the doctor didn't provide you with other info."

"I didn't want to know if it was a boy or girl."

"That's fine. That's not important anyway, but what is important is that test would have given me confirmation that you're carrying my child."

It would. And that suddenly terrified her. If this was his baby, there was no chance this man would just back away. "I can call the doctor and ask for the results." Even though that was the last thing she wanted to do.

She really had to get out of there, and she reached in her purse for her phone.

Wyatt stopped her again. "Your test results were stolen."

Lyla looked up at him, blinked. "Wh-what?"

"Stolen," he repeated. "The doctor hasn't told you yet because I'm not sure he knows. The results went missing from the lab, but there's another sample of the amniotic fluid. The thief didn't manage to get that, because it was stored at a different location in case the doctor wanted it retested."

Oh, God. All of this had gone on, and she hadn't even known about it.

"I'm having that second sample of amniotic fluid tested," Wyatt explained. But he wasn't so calm and cool right now. A muscle flickered in his jaw. "And I should have the results in a day or two."

"*I* should be the one to get those results," she challenged.

But that was as far as her challenge got, because his phone rang. Maybe because he thought she might bolt, Wyatt kept his eyes on her while he took the call.

"Declan," he greeted, and even though she couldn't hear what his brother was saying, it caused his forehead to bunch up. "I'm putting you on speaker so Lyla can hear this."

Please, not another death threat or news of some other violation to her privacy that she was just being informed about.

A moment later, his brother's voice began to pour through the room. "As I said, the lab lifted a print off the camera, and we got a match. Nicky Garnett. He's got a record a mile long."

Lyla shook her head. The name meant nothing to her. "You know him?"

"We know him," Declan confirmed. "He works muscle for a rich rancher, Travis Weston. No record for him, but that doesn't mean he shouldn't have one. The man's dirty and with plenty of money to cover his dirty tracks."

Another head shake. "What does this Travis Weston have to do with me?" she asked.

Declan didn't jump to answer that time. "I'll let Wyatt finish the explanation, and I'll get started on bringing Travis in for a little chat."

"Do that," Wyatt agreed, and he ended the call and looked at her. "Travis and Jonah Webb were old friends."

Oh, she didn't like the direction this was going. She'd just been put in charge of the evidence gathered from Webb's murder, and now his old friend had ties to a man who'd not only spied on her but had fired shots at Wyatt?

"Webb used to send some of the boys from Rocky Creek to work on Travis's ranch," Wyatt continued. "Including me. At best the arrangement was shady, probably illegal, and there were rumors that Travis used some of the boys to move illegal weapons in and out of Mexico."

She pulled in her breath. "He used you for that?"

Wyatt shook his head. "Probably because Kirby was looking out for me. Kirby was a marshal at the time. A good one. And they wouldn't have wanted him to have an insider like me in on their schemes."

Lyla tried to make sense of all of this, but she couldn't. "So, maybe Travis wants to make sure I help prosecute his friend's killer? Maybe he doesn't want me dead after all."

Wyatt made a soft grunt. "Webb and Travis had a falling-out. No one's sure about what exactly, but they were bitter enemies before Webb was killed." He paused. "Travis is a suspect in his murder, and the Rangers have been questioning him along with keeping any evidence they might have against him close to the vest. I'm sure Travis would like nothing more than the head CSI to clear him of any possible charges."

She swallowed hard. Lyla had thought it would help if she had a name to go with this mess, but from the sound of it, that wasn't a name she wanted associated with her.

"Travis is a killer?" she risked asking.

"Oh, yeah. If he hasn't killed already, it's only because he hasn't had to. He usually hires muscle like Nicky Garnett to kill for him."

It felt as if a chunk of ice had settled in her stomach, and Lyla pressed her fingertips to her mouth to try to steady the trembling. "How do we get out of this?"

"For starters, we lie. And not some little white lies, either. Big ones. We turn this con right on them and eliminate their reason for wanting you involved in any of this. That'll keep you and the baby safe."

Maybe it was the dizziness, but Lyla wasn't following him. "How do I do that?"

Wyatt stooped down, going onto one knee so they were literally eye to eye. "You'll marry me—*today*."

Chapter Five

Wyatt had expected Lyla to be shocked. And to argue, of course. But what he hadn't expected was to see the color drain from her face.

Clamping her hand over her mouth, she motioned toward the side door. "Is that a bathroom?" she asked.

He nodded, got up and opened it for her before Lyla ran inside. And she did run, fast, kicking the door shut behind her just seconds before he heard her throw up.

Wyatt wasn't sure if that was a major insult or if it was part of the pregnancy. Either way, it was a reaction he hadn't counted on. He needed her tough, asking all the questions that needed to be asked so they could move on to the next step in what he hoped wasn't a stupid plan.

Too bad it was the only plan he had.

"You okay?" he asked.

"Morning sickness." And he heard the toilet flush before she turned on the water in the sink. She splashed water for what seemed an eternity before she finally came back out. She was drying her face with a hand towel.

"You've lost your mind," she said, brushing past him and heading back for the sofa. She gulped down some of the bottled water.

"Wouldn't be the first time."

Her left eyebrow came up. "You make it a habit of proposing to strangers?"

"Not generally. But I'll make an exception in your case."

A burst of air left her mouth. A laugh, but not from humor. She shook her head, pushed away the strands of hair that'd slipped onto her face. "Men like you don't even ask out women like me. So, needless to say, your proposal is more than a shock."

Wyatt frowned. "Men like *me* and women like *you*?"

She made a sound to indicate the answer was obvious. It wasn't. Of course, maybe he'd missed something.

"Men like you," she repeated, waving her hand over his face. Then his body. She stopped waving when she got to his zipper area, probably because now that she was sitting down, it was sort of in her face.

He stepped back.

"Hot guys who know they're hot don't ask out bookworm tomboys like me," she clarified.

Wyatt was flattered. Then riled.

Then confused.

"Don't you dare say you don't know you're hot," she added.

He had to shrug. Yeah, women seemed to find him attractive. The wrong women anyway. The only one he'd had any luck with was Ann, and the luck hadn't lasted long. They'd had only three years of marriage before she'd passed away.

Lyla waved her hand over her own face. "And I know I'm the opposite of hot."

"Oh, you're hot, all right."

And he so wished he hadn't blurted that out.

He wasn't a blurter. Or someone who used the word *hot* to describe a woman. He knew how to keep feelings under wraps, and he darn sure shouldn't be saying something like that to Lyla. Especially since it was the truth. They had enough to work through without adding "hot" labels to each other.

Oh, man.

She glanced at his zipper again. And that stupid, brainless part of him decided it was time to give him a reminder that'd it had been way too long since he'd had a woman in his bed.

Well, he wasn't getting this woman there.

Except the plan was for him to do just that. He wouldn't be in his bed with her, of course. And that was no clearer than it was right now with them staring at each other and with the heat rising in the otherwise cool room.

"I think it's time for a change of subject," Lyla said, holding the damp towel against her throat.

Wyatt couldn't agree more, and it wasn't as if they didn't have a whole boatload they had to discuss.

"I've done some damage control," Wyatt started. "There are no official records around to prove you received a donor embryo."

Her eyes narrowed a bit. "Do I want to know how you discovered that?"

"No." And he waited to see if she'd challenge it. She didn't, so he continued. "Of course, whoever's behind this knows, because that's the person who likely set it all up. Unless you did it."

She huffed. "Why would I do that? I don't even know you, and I don't have a personal stake in this investigation. Well, I didn't until the shooting this morning."

Oh, yeah. It was personal now. "The only reason I could come up with was because you might be working with the person who wants the evidence altered."

Her eyes narrowed. "I don't break the law."

Admirable, but as Kirby always said—never mistake the law for justice. Over the past couple of days, Wyatt had done a lot of law *bending,* but he'd done it to make sure justice was served.

"So you're not in on the plan," Wyatt concluded, taking her glare as proof of her innocence. Besides, she didn't feel guilty, and while a gut feeling didn't sound good in a report, Wyatt always trusted his gut. "It means soon someone will contact you about what you're supposed to do."

"And according to you, they'll kill me if I don't cooperate. Then they'll kill me once they're finished with me."

Wyatt didn't have any doubts about that. "It's why we need a fake relationship. And a legal marriage. I already have the license." Best not to tell her how he'd come by that, but it'd required some string pulling, too.

"A license already?" she challenged. "But why? You thought I was guilty before you showed up at my place. Heck, you still don't trust me."

"I can't let my trust issues keep you in the path of a killer. And you're right—when I came to your place, I didn't know if this was your plan or not. I don't think it is," he quickly added when her eyes narrowed, this time to slits.

"How generous of you. Yet the point is, you didn't trust me, but you got the license."

"Just in case. I was trying to plan for any contingency." Because the stakes here were sky-high. "And I have a justice of the peace waiting for my call. As soon as you say yes, he'll be out here to marry us. Once we have this dirtbag behind bars, then we can get a quick annulment."

She looked at him as if he'd grown an extra nose. "How will saying *I do* possibly stop this?"

"Being married to me will exclude you from taking over the evidence in the investigation."

Ah. She got it. The light went through her eyes. Followed by some expected darkness. "Because you're a suspect in Webb's murder."

"My whole family, including a couple of sisters-in-law, are all suspects. No way would the governor allow you to stay on the case if you're my wife. And if we can convince everyone that we made that baby the old-fashioned way."

She glanced at his zipper again. "No one will believe we're lovers."

He had to disagree. "They will if we're married. Maybe not so much if we just lie and say we're together. That'd be a little harder to pull off, but marriage should convince even the person behind this."

"How?" she repeated.

"By planting so-called proof of our secret affair. Hotel receipts, doctored photos. Remember that trip you took to Dallas last month?"

She nodded. Then frowned. Probably because he'd invaded her privacy again. Of course, he'd invaded it so many other times that she should be getting used to it by now.

"Well, I can come up with a witness who'll verify we were in Dallas together." She opened her mouth to object, but Wyatt moved on to the next point. "You didn't tell anyone at work about the donor embryo."

"No." She pulled in a long breath. "I'd planned to tell them once I started showing."

"Then lucky for us you're not showing. Right now, the only people who know are us, your doctor—and he's agreed to keep it quiet—and the person who orchestrated all of this."

She stayed quiet a moment. "And for him or her to dispute what we're saying, they'll have to come out in the open."

Bingo.

Well, the person could just try to kill them because he or she was now riled that their plan hadn't worked, but Wyatt kept that to himself. Lyla had enough to deal with already. And besides, a marriage would give him a good reason to keep her right by his side so he could protect her.

The problem would be first and foremost the danger. It might not immediately go away. The next problem was this blasted heat. Lyla darn sure didn't look like a tomboy bookworm, and an unwanted attraction created a distraction that could get them killed.

"If this person only wanted my cooperation with the evidence in the investigation, then why try to kill me?" she asked.

"I don't think it was a planned attempt to kill you. The guy was probably supposed to keep an eye on you, to make sure you didn't try to talk to me or any of the other suspects who could be burned by falsifying evidence. Then, when I showed up, he panicked and started firing."

Lyla stared at him. "What stops them from *panicking* again?"

"Me." Yeah, it sounded cocky, but he would do whatever it took to keep her safe.

She groaned, wiped her face again. "You can't possibly want to go through with this marriage."

"I don't. But it'll cover several hot spots. Other than saving you and the baby, you can't be compelled to testify against me."

That got her attention. "Testify against you? For what?"

"For all the corners I cut while trying to figure out what's going on. Corners I'm cutting now to protect you."

With that tossed out there, Wyatt waited for the rest of her argument. And there would be more. From everything he'd learned about her, Lyla was a cautious woman, and she wouldn't just jump into this.

And that meant he had to push.

"You're doing this for the baby," she said. It wasn't a question.

"The baby's a big reason. I want him or her safe. For that to happen, I have to keep you safe, too."

Ah, her eyes narrowed again. "Even if I have no intentions of sharing this baby with you."

"Even then." Though he'd have something to say about that sharing if the amnio results proved he was indeed the father. If he was, he'd challenge her for full custody.

And he'd win.

No way would he let someone else raise his and Ann's child. But that wasn't the reason he wanted this marriage. He had to put an end to the danger.

"There isn't much time," he pressed. "The sooner we get out the word that we're married, the sooner you'll be pulled from the case and the sooner this bozo will back off."

She didn't jump to agree. In fact, she didn't jump to do anything, but he could see reality creeping into her eyes.

"Is there another way?" she asked.

"I haven't been able to come up with one." And he'd tried hard. Despite his player reputation, he didn't take marriage vows lightly.

"We could pretend to get married," Lyla suggested.

"I considered it, but it doesn't take care of your testimony against me. Besides, if the governor finds out it's fake, you could be charged with obstruction of justice."

She groaned, but he talked right over the sound. "There's also the concern that the person behind this could use a fake marriage to manipulate you."

And that wasn't exactly a long shot.

After all, the person had manipulated this pregnancy and had spent some big bucks to put all of this in place with Lyla's boss's new job, the surveillance and the gunmen. The only way to neutralize all of that was to take Lyla completely off the playing field. The culprit had to believe not only that she was involved with Wyatt, but that she was committed to him.

"You have to think of the baby," he reminded her.

"I know!" she practically shouted. That seemed to sap the rest of her energy, and she looked up at him.

On the verge of saying yes. Wyatt was sure of it.

But his phone buzzed. Wyatt looked at the screen to see if he could let it go to voice mail, but the name that popped up had him doing a double take.

"Billy Webb," he mumbled.

Lyla looked as confused as he was by this call. "Connected to Jonah Webb?"

"His son. And another suspect." Well, in some people's eyes. Billy's dad had been an abusive jerk when he'd been the headmaster at the Rocky Creek Children's Facility. Webb had beaten Billy enough times that if he'd retaliated against his father, Wyatt wouldn't have exactly called it murder.

More like doing the world a favor.

Still, they were back to that justice-and-the-law conflict, and in the eyes of the law, Billy was a suspect. One who happened to be calling Wyatt.

"Marshal McCabe," he answered. Best to keep this

professional. And quick. He still had some convincing to do in the marriage department.

"I tried Dallas first, but he was out of cell phone range, so I decided to call you. I'm out at the Rocky Creek facility going through some of my mother's things."

Because his mother lived in the cottage on the facility grounds. Well, she had before she'd gone into a coma after being shot.

Wyatt froze.

"Did your mother come out of the coma?" he asked. That was the only reason he could think of that Billy would be calling him.

"No, but she's improving. She's even opened her eyes a couple of times and said something to me."

"What'd she say?" Wyatt demanded.

"Just gibberish. Something about a tape, but I don't remember her mentioning anything about a tape before she went into a coma."

"Could she have recorded something? Like maybe a conversation?"

"Maybe. But if she did, the tape's not at her cottage. I looked right after she mentioned it but didn't find anything. I finally gave up the search and figured I could ask her once she wakes up for good. The doctors don't think it'll be long before that happens."

Wyatt didn't know whether to be happy about that or not. Sarah could clear him and everyone in his family.

Or she could name one of them as her accomplice.

Even worse, it was possible she had a taped conversation to prove it. Of course, the woman might be talking out of her head. After all, her injuries had put her in a coma. Injuries she'd gotten while trying to cover up the fact she'd murdered her husband.

"I didn't call about my mother," Billy went on. "I

thought you should get out here and see what's going on. There's a new team of CSIs out here, and one of them found something."

Though he wasn't sure he wanted Lyla to hear this, she apparently did. She got up and came closer. Very close. And that was when Wyatt hit the speaker button.

"They found old blood spatter on the wall in one of the rooms. Not my dad's office. But in Stella's quarters."

Hell, that was not what he wanted to hear. Stella was like a mother to him. But yeah, she had motive. Because she'd lived and worked at the children's facility when a lot of the abuse was going on. Along with Sarah's help, Stella could have indeed killed Jonah Webb.

"Describe the spatter," Lyla said, and she didn't sound scared anymore. She sounded like the CSI that she was.

"Who is that?" Billy demanded.

"A close friend," Wyatt lied. "We can trust her."

He hoped.

Billy hesitated, and for a moment Wyatt didn't think he'd add more. Finally, he cleared his throat. "Someone had painted over the spatter, but they saw it with some kind of special light."

"A UV light," Lyla provided.

"You should get out here," Billy insisted. "Because I'm thinking they'll try to use this to arrest Stella." And with that, Billy hung up.

Wyatt stared at the phone and tried to work through what Billy had just told him. There wasn't much to work through, though. He needed to know exactly what'd been found in that building.

He grabbed his keys from his pocket and then looked at Lyla. It was risky, leaving her, but he didn't want to pull his brothers away from what they were doing.

"You can stay with Dallas and the others at his house,"

he let her know. It wouldn't be comfortable. Sort of a baptism by family fire. "But don't talk about the baby or the proposal. I need to tell them in my own way."

A way he hadn't quite figured out yet.

"I want to go with you," she insisted. "I want to get a look at that spatter. It happens to be my area of expertise, and I can help you determine what happened. Or if it's been staged. Considering everything else that's going on, someone could have planted the blood there."

He was shaking his head before she finished. "This isn't your fight."

"To heck it's not. Someone's trying to kill me because of this *fight*. I'm not asking your permission. I want to see that crime scene, even if I have to hire a bodyguard or two to go with me."

Wyatt jammed his thumb against his chest. "I'm your bodyguard. And there's that little thing about conflict of interest."

"I'll be an observer. I won't touch the evidence or even talk to the investigators. But I want to see what they've found. And if it's legitimate, I want to stop anyone from tampering with it."

It was a good argument, but he had a better one. "Until we're married, you're in danger. I don't want you out there."

She looked at the marriage license. Then at him. "You're sure that's the only way to keep me and the baby safe?"

"Yes." And Wyatt prayed that was true. If this gamble failed, the consequences could be fatal.

Lyla pulled in a long breath. And nodded. "All right. Let me get a look at that blood, and then…" She stopped, gathered more breath, as if she might choke on the words. "I'll marry you."

Chapter Six

Lyla's heart dropped when she heard what Wyatt said to the person he'd just called. Justice of the Peace Elliot Stowe.

"Meet us at the Rocky Creek Children's Facility," he told the man. "I have the bride and license. You can marry us at the end of the road that leads to the facility. We'll be there in twenty minutes."

"We're doing this now?" she asked the moment Wyatt ended the call.

Wyatt didn't take his eyes off the road or their surroundings. As he'd done since their quick departure, his gaze kept darting to the side and rearview mirrors of the SUV he'd taken from the ranch.

"I'm not taking you inside Rocky Creek until we're married," he insisted. "It's the only way to ensure your safety."

"But there are CSIs and probably cops out in the building. You'll be there, too. Heck, it's probably one of the safest places in Texas right now."

He looked at her, those sizzling eyes showing some anger. "You agreed to this."

"Yes, but I thought I'd have some time to adjust."

And change her mind along with coming up with a different plan.

Mercy, this was happening too fast. She needed some downtime so she could think. But then Lyla remembered the sound of those bullets tearing into her place. Any one of them could have hit Wyatt, her or the baby, and she couldn't risk that again.

"Swear to me there's no other way," she said.

But he didn't swear. Well, he swore some profanity, but he didn't give her a charming or terrifying spin on why this had to happen. Right now, she needed some logic to hang on to.

"Consider this," he finally answered. "I think you're carrying the baby that I've wanted for the past five years. Heck, all of my life. I'll do whatever it takes to protect you. That includes putting my life on the line to save you."

Oh.

Well, that was something to hang on to, all right. Heaven help her, she believed him. About that part anyway.

"Swear on your wife's grave that this isn't an attempt to get custody of this baby when he or she is born."

No profanity this time. No quick answer, either. And that didn't do anything to steady her nerves.

Lyla groaned.

"I won't use the marriage to try for custody," he finally said, "and that's the only promise I can make."

She studied his expression, especially his eyes. Well, as much of them as she could see, considering he was still doing lookout. Lyla groaned again when she realized this argument was over. Both the physical one and the one inside her.

She was going to marry Wyatt McCabe.

A man she hardly knew.

She hoped this wasn't the worst mistake of her life.

She'd made some doozies in the past, but this could top them all.

But it could also save her baby.

Right now, that seemed the only thing that really mattered. That, and putting an end to the danger. Things couldn't continue this way, because the stress could cause her to miscarry.

That thought crushed her heart.

She'd planned and waited so long for this baby, and here someone might snatch it away from her.

Lyla spent the rest of the drive nibbling on her bottom lip and trying to work through the panic she was starting to feel again. How could her life have changed so much in just a few hours? And it might continue to change, for the worse, if they couldn't put a stop to this nameless, faceless person who'd want to manipulate her by using an unborn child.

Wyatt took the turn to the Rocky Creek facility, but there was a car on the road between them and the building. He reached for his gun, causing her heart to thud against her ribs, but he reholstered when the ginger-haired man and elderly woman stepped from the vehicle.

"Slide over toward me," Wyatt instructed her. "That's Elliot Stowe and his secretary, Adele Bedford."

"How did they get out here so fast?" Lyla thought she'd have a least a few more minutes.

"Stowe's a justice of the peace in the town just a few miles from here. He brought his secretary because we need a witness."

Wyatt had thought of everything, but when their gazes met, Lyla could have sworn she saw some uncertainty there. It vanished, however, when the JP and his secretary got into the backseat of the SUV. Because Lyla still hadn't moved yet, Wyatt unhooked her seat belt and slid her closer. Until she was tucked into the crook of his arm.

"Make it fast," Wyatt told the man.

Lyla doubted Stowe could do anything slowly. His muscles were tight and wired. Ditto for his expression. His Adam's apple was bobbing. Clearly he wasn't comfortable with this, either. However, his secretary just seemed puzzled about the whole ordeal.

Wyatt handed the man the license, and without even making introductions, Stowe started the vows. "Do you, Lyla Marie Pearson, take this man, Wyatt David McCabe…"

Lyla heard the words, saw them form on the man's mouth, but she was still dealing with the shock when it came time for her to say *I do.* Wyatt gave her a nudge on the arm, and she mumbled the words that she prayed she wouldn't regret.

"I do."

A few moments later, Wyatt repeated the words. And Stowe pronounced them husband and wife. He scrawled his signature on the license and handed it to his secretary to do the same as the witness.

"You so owe me for this," Stowe said to Wyatt.

Wyatt nodded and mumbled a thanks. "Make those calls I asked you to make."

Stowe returned the nod, and just like that, the couple exited the SUV, got back into their car and drove away.

The ceremony had lasted less than five minutes. Heaven knew how much time it would take her to get the annulment when this was over. And there would be an annulment. No way would she stay married to this stranger.

"What phone calls did you ask him to make?" Lyla wanted to know.

"He'll get the gossip mill going about our marriage. I want everyone to hear about it so the danger will end."

Maybe that wouldn't take long, and while she was hoping, Lyla hoped she could get close enough to that blood spatter to learn something. Because if Wyatt's plan failed, then her best shot was learning the identity of Webb's killer. And she was betting it was the same person who'd put her in harm's way.

Wyatt reached in his shirt pocket and extracted a simple gold wedding band.

Lyla was sure her mouth dropped open. "You took the time to buy me a ring?" But then she had a horrible thought. "It's not Ann's?"

"No. It belonged to Kirby's grandmother. I asked him if I could borrow it. Didn't say why, but I'll owe him and the others an explanation soon."

So, it was a family ring for something that usually meant the start of a new family. Too bad they'd made a mockery of the vows. But then she mentally shrugged. After two failed relationship, including one where she'd become a punching bag for her moronic ex, she'd given up altogether on the notion of marital bliss.

She was pretty sure there'd be no bliss in the sham one, either.

"Put on the ring," Wyatt instructed. "And make sure everyone sees it." Once the JP's car was out of the way, he started driving toward the facility. "We'll have to try to make people think we're newlyweds."

Lyla was almost afraid to ask what that might involve. And she was equally riled that her body seemed somewhat amused at the idea of playing a wife to Wyatt.

Get a grip.

Yes, he was attractive. Literally, he was the best-looking

man she'd ever laid eyes on, but she had to get her mind on ending the danger and not focus on the physical attributes of her fake husband.

Wyatt pulled to a stop in front of the building, where a group of vehicles were parked. One was the county CSI van. She knew the people who worked there, so she might see a friendly face. The sheriff's cruiser was there, too, along with a sleek silver car.

The moment they stepped from the SUV, a lanky dark-haired man came out of the building and started toward them.

"Billy," Wyatt greeted.

Billy Webb. The son of the man who'd been murdered. He no doubt knew he was a suspect, and that Wyatt might not trust him, because he lifted his hands to show them that he had no weapon.

Well, no visible one anyway.

His coat was plenty big enough to conceal a weapon or two.

"This is my wife, Lyla," Wyatt said, making introductions.

Billy tipped his head. "Mrs. McCabe."

She flinched before she could stop herself, but she didn't think Billy noticed, because he was already turning to go back inside. If he had any reaction whatsoever to the marriage, he didn't show it. Maybe that meant they could rule him out as a suspect in this manipulation-of-evidence plot.

Of course, maybe he was just a good actor.

"You remember the way to Stella's room?" Billy asked Wyatt.

Wyatt's gaze slid over the dingy walls and floor. "I remember everything about this godforsaken place."

Billy made a sound of agreement. They went through the main area and up the stairs and into a wide side corridor. "And now I'm betting someone is trying to set Stella up for Dad's murder," Billy added.

"You don't think she did it?" Lyla asked, earning herself a glare from Wyatt.

Probably because he didn't want her to say anything that would connect her with the Webb investigation. Then again, this was Wyatt, and even though she barely knew him, he'd probably planned out every step of this visit. And this conversation.

"No. I don't think Stella's guilty," Billy answered, and he didn't hesitate, either. "I think it was someone associated with my dad's side businesses. In fact, I think that's the person who talked my mother into putting the knife in my dad's chest."

From what Lyla had read and what Wyatt had told her, Sarah Webb did have an accomplice, but the woman herself had instigated the killing. Of course, anything was possible, especially since Sarah was emotionally unstable. The product of years of physical abuse. Lyla had gotten only a taste of it, and she knew how it could batter a woman's soul and confidence.

"By side businesses, you mean the gunrunning your father was doing with Travis Weston?" Wyatt asked.

"Yeah. But there doesn't seem to be any proof to link Travis to the crime."

Wyatt didn't say anything about the gunman who was connected to Travis, so Lyla didn't bring it up, either.

"What about the boys your father used?" Wyatt continued.

"The Rangers have checked. No records for that, of course, and the only names I could remember were Dakota Cooke and Spenser Cash. Dakota died a few years ago in a car accident. Spenser has dropped off the radar."

That sounded some alarms in her head. Wyatt had called these events a pattern, and she was beginning to agree. It seemed awfully suspicious that one possible witness was dead and another missing.

They turned down another corridor, where there was a string of doors, all closed except for one, and a Texas Ranger was standing guard outside it.

Stella's room, no doubt.

"Who all lived here in this wing?" she asked.

"The help. Stella, the cooks and the housekeepers." Wyatt pointed to the doors at the end. "That was the Webbs' quarters at the time of the murder." He pointed to the door near it. "And that was his office."

Where it was believed the murder had taken place. Well, until now anyway. If Lyla remembered correctly, there'd been some spatter detected there, too, but it hadn't been enough to determine that Webb had actually died there.

"Stella has motive?" Lyla asked Wyatt.

"Yeah. I guess. Declan's her son, and Webb had beaten the hell out of him that day."

"He'd beaten a lot of people that day," Billy mumbled a split second before they stopped in front of the Ranger.

"Tucker McKinnon," the Ranger said. "You're Marshal McCabe, and I can't let you into this room."

Wyatt nodded. "This is my wife, the new director of the San Antonio Crime Lab."

"Your wife?" the Ranger questioned. His forehead bunched up. "Until I get word otherwise, I can't let her in, either."

But Lyla didn't need to get in. She just needed a look. And she got an eyeful. The UV light was still on the blood spatter that someone had tried to cover with paint, and the other tech was photographing it.

It certainly looked like a cast-off pattern to her, but there wasn't a lot of it. And the pattern would indicate only a single blow from the killer.

"Tell me about the spatter found in Webb's office months ago," Lyla said to no one in particular.

It was Billy who answered. "There was blood on the windowsill, the nearby wall and the floor. It appeared as if someone had tried to clean it up."

Interesting. Two areas of spatter and maybe someone had tried to conceal both. "Could the spatter have been caused by someone of your mother's height?"

Billy hesitated, then nodded. "She's about as tall as you are. Maybe a little shorter."

"Well, I don't think that's consistent with your mother's height." She tipped her head to the droplets on Stella's wall. "Or with Stella's. Of course, I can't be positive without actually examining it, but it looks as if this cast-off was created by someone taller. Someone at least six feet."

"Did you find any blood on the floor?" she asked the CSI who glanced in her direction.

He was young, and she didn't know him, but maybe because she was standing in between a marshal and a Texas Ranger, he answered anyway with a head shake. "In fact, this is the only blood we've found in the room," he added.

Since no one objected, Lyla tried a different question. "Can you determine how long ago the paint was put over the blood?"

"My guess is shortly afterward. It has the same amount of dust as the rest of the walls."

So, if the blood was from the time of the murder, then

someone had likely done a quick cover-up. Of course, that wouldn't have been hard to do. From what she'd read, no one had reported Webb missing for a full day. Plenty of time for a paint job.

She looked back at Wyatt. "How many of your suspects are over six feet tall and how many of them would have had access to this room?"

"Not Stella. But Kirby. With the exception of my youngest brother, Declan, the rest of us were already that tall."

"I was, too," Billy volunteered. "A lot of the boys were. But they wouldn't have come here often unless they were going to my dad's office. We weren't allowed in the staff's rooms."

That didn't mean it hadn't happened. A lot of rules had been broken here. "How about suspects who weren't residents? How many fit the height description?"

"Travis Weston," Billy and Wyatt said in unison.

Mercy, the circumstantial evidence just kept coming. But circumstantial wasn't going to hack it in this case, because they had volumes of it already. What they needed was to pinpoint a single, solid suspect so they could focus on stopping him.

She moved back from the Ranger, and both Billy and Wyatt followed her to the other side of the hall. "If that turns out to be Webb's blood," she whispered, "and none is found on the floor, then the investigator will likely conclude that the attack started in this room."

Wyatt glanced around, obviously considering that. "And then Webb went to his office, where Sarah finished the job?"

"Maybe." It was impossible to tell without testing both areas of spatter, something she was itching to do.

"There were traces of blood here on the floor." Billy

motioned from his dad's office to the stairs. "It appeared that he was dragged."

Not good. "The drag marks from his office could have obstructed or even destroyed the ones leading from Stella's room to his office." It was a wide hall, but two people dragging a body would have taken up most of the floor space.

Wyatt mumbled some profanity. "So, you're saying that maybe Sarah didn't have an accomplice for the actual murder, just someone after the fact to help her dispose of the body."

"That's exactly what I'm saying. And whatever investigator they name could likely say the same."

That, in turn, would implicate not only Travis but Kirby, too. Along with Wyatt and the majority of his brothers. Anyone could have helped Sarah drag her husband from the office and out of the building.

"There were no surveillance or security cameras, right?" she asked.

Wyatt shook his head. "And the visitors' log is missing. Which points to an outsider. Like Travis."

Kirby, too. But she kept that to herself. Wyatt already knew anyway.

However, Wyatt had a point about this maybe being an outsider. *If* the missing visitor's log was indeed connected to the murder. After all, the children who lived there wouldn't have signed in and out. But someone like Travis would have, and if he'd visited Rocky Creek at the time of the murder and if his name had been in the log, he would have made sure it disappeared. Which meant it wasn't just missing.

It'd likely been destroyed.

"What about this tape or recording your mother mentioned?" Wyatt asked Billy. Wyatt turned to her. "Sarah's been coming in and out of a coma, and she mumbled something about a tape."

"Still no sign of it," Billy insisted. "But she keeps talking about it. In fact, it's the only thing she has said so far. She opens her eyes, asks me about the tape, and then slips back into the coma."

That also got Lyla's attention. "What specifically does she say about the tape?"

Billy lifted his shoulder. "Only those two words— *the tape*."

So, not enough to tell them what the woman meant, but it had to be important for her to use what little conscious time she had to bring it up.

The Ranger's phone rang, the sound shooting through the hall. Seconds later, Wyatt's phone rang, too. And so did one of the CSIs'.

That put Lyla on instant alert, and she watched and waited as Wyatt looked at the screen. "Declan," he answered a moment later.

She couldn't hear what his brother said to him, but she had no problems hearing the Ranger. "Get out!" he shouted. "Someone just reported a bomb in the building."

"It's probably a hoax," Wyatt added. But he took her by the arm and got them running back toward the stairs. Billy and the others were right behind them.

"The evidence," Lyla reminded the Ranger. This could be an attempt to get them away from that blood spatter so that someone could tamper with it.

"I'll secure the building once everyone is out," Ranger McKinnon assured her.

They barreled down the stairs, with Wyatt still gripping on to her arm, but he stopped when he got to the front door, and he looked out. Only then did Lyla realize this could be a trap to lure them out into the open.

"Stay behind me," Wyatt insisted, and he drew his gun.

He maneuvered them to the porch and then made a beeline for his SUV. The others scattered toward their vehicles, as well. However, they'd barely made it inside the SUV when there was the horrible sound that shook not just the truck but the ground itself.

The sound of the blast.

"Get down!" Wyatt ordered, but he didn't wait for her to do that. He pushed her onto the seat and followed on top of her, shielding her with his body.

Lyla caught just a glimpse of the explosion as it ripped through the building and sent a spray of bricks and debris right at them. It pelted the SUV, but somehow the window held.

Cursing, Wyatt took out his phone while he kept his gun ready. "You need to get the fire department and bomb squad out here now," he said to whoever he'd called. No doubt one of his brothers. "Someone just blew up Rocky Creek."

Lyla lifted her head a little, praying that some part of the building was intact. And it was. But it wouldn't be for long.

The blast had made a gaping hole in the center of the bottom floor, but it'd also created a fire, and it was spreading fast. The fire department could likely save some of it if they got there in a hurry. But the smoke and the blast would almost certainly destroy or compromise any evidence inside.

"We're getting out of here." Wyatt moved back behind the steering wheel and started the engine.

He spun the SUV around and hit the accelerator. Lyla looked behind them at the wreckage, and her heart sank.

Not for the lost evidence, but for how close they'd come to dying. *Again.* They'd barely made it out of that building before the blast.

Wyatt hit Redial and then the speaker on his phone, and she heard Declan answer. "Who phoned in the bomb threat?" Wyatt asked.

"Anonymous call to the marshals' service from a disposable cell. Did everyone get out all right?"

"I think so. Who knew about the evidence that'd been discovered?"

"I'm checking on that now. You're thinking that was the motive?"

But Wyatt didn't answer. His attention was fixed on the road ahead, and when Lyla followed his gaze, she spotted the truck.

Not the justice of the peace.

But judging from Wyatt's profanity, it was someone he recognized. And didn't want to see. His grip tightened on his gun.

"I'll call you back," he said to Declan. "Travis Weston just showed up at Rocky Creek."

Oh, mercy. Travis was their prime suspect in this mess of an investigation.

Lyla studied the man, but she didn't think she'd ever met him. Tall, wide shoulders, and even though his hair was iron-gray, he didn't look old.

He looked formidable.

Wyatt brought the SUV to a stop because he had no choice. There were deep ditches on each side of the road, and Travis had parked his truck at an angle so they wouldn't be able to get by.

"Stay down," Wyatt warned her.

But he didn't take his own advice. With his gun ready,

he stepped from the SUV and took aim at Travis. "What do you want?"

Travis pulled back the side of his coat to reveal a gun in a shoulder holster. "Marshal McCabe, I understand we have a score to settle."

Chapter Seven

The last thing Wyatt wanted was this confrontation. Yeah, he would love to interrogate Travis and force him to talk, but he sure as heck didn't want to do that with a bomber in the area.

Especially since Travis or one of his cronies could be the one who'd set the explosive that'd been used to blow up Rocky Creek.

Wyatt kept cover behind the open door of the SUV, and he aimed his gun at Travis. "Why are you here?"

"A little bird told me this is where I'd find you. Since I didn't figure your ranch hands would let me near you, I decided to take a little drive so we could have a chat."

"Better make this conversation fast," Wyatt warned him. "Pretty soon this place will be crawling with cops and firemen. And Ranger McKinnon will want to *chat* with you, as well."

"The Ranger can wait. This is between you and me."

Wyatt first checked on Lyla to make sure she was staying down on the seat. She was, though she had that look of terror on her face again. He hated that there was nothing he could do about it. Two attacks in one day weren't going to give her any peaceful memories.

He tipped his head to what was left of the building behind them. "Your handiwork?" Wyatt asked Travis.

"Hardly." If he was insulted by that, Travis didn't show it. "I've got no reason to blow up things."

"Really?" And Wyatt didn't bother to take the sarcasm out of it. "Because I'd think finding new evidence would make you do something desperate. And you're here. Makes me wonder if you wanted to see your handiwork in action."

Travis shrugged as if he didn't have a care in the world. But obviously he did, otherwise he wouldn't be here. "If I was guilty of anything, I'd be desperate. But I'm not."

"You sure about that?" Wyatt pressed. "Because it seems pretty desperate to me that you'd drive all the way out here just to talk to me."

"I consider it a necessary chat. I'm here to tell you to call off your lawmen dogs. I got people digging through my bank records, looking for a connection to some idiot who apparently took shots at you."

"Nicky Garnett," Wyatt supplied. "But, of course, you know that because he's your hired gun."

"I haven't worked with Nicky in ages, and he was never my hired gun. I just used him as a bodyguard a time or two. Call off your dogs," Travis repeated.

"Not until they find whatever's needed to put you behind bars." In the distance, he heard the sirens. Soon, both Travis and he would have to get off the road so the fire department could get to the scene.

"Marshal, I figure it won't be long before you're a wanted man," Travis taunted. "If you're not already. And I'm not talking about your pretty face and how the women fawn over it, either."

"Is there a point to this?" Wyatt snapped.

"There is. You bent some rules, huh? And the truth is, that so-called new evidence inside Rocky Creek was just as likely to implicate Kirby, Stella, you or any of your brothers as it was me."

Wyatt hoped that wasn't the case, but it could be. Especially Stella, since the blood had been found in her former quarters.

"If you're not behind these threats, then who is?" Wyatt asked. "And don't name Kirby, Stella or anyone else related to me. I want the name of a real suspect."

"Hey, I can give you two. Sheriff Zeke Mercer and his business partner, Greg Hester."

They certainly weren't new names to Wyatt, and this wasn't the first time Wyatt had heard of them being associated with Webb's murder. They had already been questioned, of course, but there'd been no red flags.

"Why those two?" Wyatt pressed.

Travis made a sound to indicate the answer was obvious. "What better person to help cover up a crime than the sheriff, and Zeke was the first lawman on the scene after Sarah reported her husband missing."

"But Webb and Zeke were close friends," Wyatt pointed out.

"Friends don't always do friendly things," he mumbled. "The way I remember it, Zeke was mighty riled when he learned Webb was doing business with me."

"Riled because the business was illegal, like gun-running?"

"Or maybe just 'cause it was cutting in on the illegal junk Zeke had Webb doing for him."

Wyatt tried not to look too surprised. "You're saying Zeke's dirty?"

"Hell yeah. I'm the one everybody suspected of doing something wrong at my own ranch, but doing something wrong is a heck of a lot easier if you're wearing a badge."

Wyatt huffed. "You want me to believe that Zeke set up the gunrunning at your ranch?"

He gave Wyatt a flat look. "Now, for me to admit to that, I'd have to admit I knew it was going on. And even if I learned it after the fact, I'd have to try to explain why I didn't report it. So, Marshal, I'm not admittin' anything."

"Then you're wasting my time." Wyatt started to turn and leave.

"No. Not if you hear what I'm saying, and I'm telling you to look at somebody other than me. Trying to pin Webb's murder on me is just plain dangerous. Not just for you but for your new bride, Lyla Pearson." Travis's eyes narrowed. "Yeah, I heard about your marriage already."

"That little bird you got is awfully chatty," Wyatt growled. And soon to be silenced, if Wyatt found out who it was. He didn't mind the marriage news being spread around—he wanted that—but Wyatt didn't want the same for Lyla's and his whereabouts.

"I figure you broke a few more laws to make those vows happen," Travis challenged. "Again, that's dangerous."

Now it was Wyatt who narrowed his eyes. "Is that a threat?"

"It's a warning for both of you." Travis turned to get back in his vehicle.

"The Ranger will want to talk to you," Wyatt reminded him.

"He knows where to find me. I'll be out at my ranch."

"Tell everyone that Lyla's out of this game," Wyatt called out to the man. "She has nothing to do with this investigation."

Travis stopped, spared him a glance. "Now, who would I tell that to? Just because you married her, it doesn't mean she's your wife. At least, not in the way that truly matters. And it doesn't mean she'll get a free pass on this."

The man smiled before he got into his truck.

Wyatt wanted to punch that smile right off his face. But he had enough to do without adding a fistfight. Too bad, since he knew he'd win. He never lost fistfights.

Travis drove out in reverse to get back onto the main road. Wyatt had to jump in his truck and do the same.

"You think he set that explosive?" Lyla asked the moment they drove away.

"Maybe. Or maybe he's just a jerk."

Unfortunately, Wyatt might not even get a chance to question him. But Ranger McKinnon would, and Wyatt hoped the lawman was good enough to spur some kind of confession.

But there was another possibility here.

Billy.

Wyatt didn't like the timing of the man's visit to Rocky Creek and the discovery of that blood evidence. Had Billy known all along it was there, because his mother had told him? If so, Billy could be using it to try to clear his mother's name and pin the murder on Stella. After all, Billy had said his mother might be coming out of the coma soon, and he wouldn't want her going to prison for the rest of her life.

"What about the other two Travis named, Sheriff Zeke Mercer and Greg Hester? Are they really suspects?" She shook her head. "I don't remember anything about them in the files I read."

"Because there wouldn't have been much to read. Webb and the sheriff were friends, and Greg Hester has been in business with Sheriff Mercer for the past decade or more. They're cattle brokers." And both very well-off. Brokering has made them rich men.

Unfortunately, rich men could buy hired guns like the ones who'd been out at Lyla's place. They could also hire someone in the medical field to steal an embryo and make sure it got in the person who could do them the most good.

Even though Wyatt needed to keep watch, he glanced at Lyla to make sure she was okay. She wasn't. There wasn't just the fear and the adrenaline on her face this time, but no doubt the realization that she'd made a huge mistake going through with this sham of a marriage.

She drew in a long breath, then another. "Travis made it sound as if our marriage wouldn't get me out of danger."

He had. And Wyatt wasn't sure what Travis had meant. But he'd find out.

"Keep watch around us," Wyatt told her, and while he did the same, he took out his phone to call Declan.

"What did Travis want?" Declan immediately asked. "Are you all right?"

"We're fine. He just told me to back off. No fists or bullets exchanged." Wyatt didn't spell out Travis's warning, but Declan no doubt picked up on it. "He said we should look at Sheriff Mercer and Greg Hester. Anything come up about them recently?"

"Not that I know of, but I'll check."

"Thanks. But maybe Travis is just blowing smoke." Or setting bombs.

"Is it true?" Declan said before Wyatt could continue. "Did you really get married to the new director of the San Antonio CSI?"

"I did. Her name is Lyla Pearson." And while Wyatt

needed to explain why he'd done what he had, he didn't want to do it over the phone. "We'll talk soon."

"Better be sooner than soon," Declan warned. "Stella and Kirby know. Saul, too. In fact, he was just talking to me about it when you called."

Well, good news did travel fast. That was good, *if* it stopped the danger. Saul was the head marshal, and Wyatt's boss, and he was also someone Wyatt would have liked to have told in person. Later, he was sure his boss would have a ton of questions, as would Wyatt's own family.

"What'd you need me to do?" Declan asked.

Wyatt mumbled a thanks to his brother for not pressing him on the marriage details. Because there were plenty of other things on their plate. "Ranger McKinnon needs to know about Travis's visit to Rocky Creek. He was there the same time as the explosion, which automatically makes him a suspect in the bombing. See if the Ranger will let Saul interview Travis."

Saul was maybe someone that the Rangers and governor would trust to do a simple interview. That way, Wyatt or one of his brothers could observe and even feed their boss some questions. That wouldn't necessarily happen if the Rangers ran the show.

"Billy needs to be questioned, too," Wyatt added. Even though Wyatt had no idea why Billy would destroy evidence that might help his mother's case. Unless… "Maybe you can find out if Billy had some kind of rift with his mother before she went into that coma."

"I'll try. Where you headed now?"

"The ranch." Wyatt paused. "Lyla's with me."

"Good." Declan paused, too. "Look, I don't know the reasons you married her, but there could be a problem.

Saul's already gotten a phone call from the governor about it."

Whoever was behind this had some serious contacts. Something that Wyatt needed to give some additional thought. "What'd the governor have to say?"

"Well, he wasn't pleased." Declan mumbled some profanity. "He wants Saul to find out if the marriage is real. And if it's not and if you did this to somehow manipulate whoever will be doing this investigation, then the governor wants you arrested for obstruction of justice. Not just you but Lyla, too."

Now it was Wyatt's turn to curse.

"So, my advice is this," Declan went on. "When you get to the ranch, you introduce everyone to your new bride. And make it convincing."

Oh, that should be fun. Lying to his family while pretending to be a happy couple.

"The best way for you two to stay out of jail is to convince everyone that you're real honest-to-goodness newlyweds," Declan added. "Put Lyla in your bed and keep her there."

Chapter Eight

Lyla was past having second thoughts about this so-called marriage, and those doubts got even worse when she stepped from the bathroom and spotted Wyatt. Before she'd left him to take a shower, he'd warned her that he wasn't going anywhere, that they'd be sharing his bedroom until the danger was over.

Well, he was true to his word.

He was on his bed, lying sideways. Still dressed.

For the most part anyway.

He'd taken off his holster and put it on the nightstand, but he'd unbuttoned his shirt while he talked on the phone. Something he'd been doing almost nonstop since they'd arrived at the ranch. He was obviously getting updates on the investigation, but those calls had done something else. They had prevented him from having more than a brief conversation with his family.

And with her.

However, he had taken the time to relay to her what Declan had said. That Wyatt should put her in his bed and keep her there.

Lyla hoped that wasn't a suggestion for them to have sex.

But then she rethought that.

Seeing Wyatt's bare chest and handsome face was

enough to spur her imagination in a really bad direction. He was certainly an eyeful. The stuff of fantasies and dreams, with that toned body. Not muscles from gym equipment, either. That was a cowboy's body.

If this marriage had been real, they'd be on a honeymoon, and she'd be on that bed with him. Her body went all soft and warm, clearly trying to push her to do just that.

She pushed back.

Consummating this marriage would be a disaster. Yes, it would no doubt be good.

No doubt.

But Wyatt and she had enough complications in their relationship without adding that. Besides, the attraction was probably one-sided on her part. Yes, she'd seen some heat in his eyes when he'd looked at her, but she figured a man like Wyatt looked at every woman that way.

He finished his call and sat up, his gaze zooming right in on her. First her face. Then, the bulky T-shirt she was using for a gown.

His T-shirt.

When she'd first put it on, she felt as if it swallowed her, but now she felt as if it skimmed way too much of her body.

Wyatt continued that sliding glance from the shirt to her bare feet and legs. "Tomorrow, I'll have someone pick up your things from your house."

She nodded and wished that she had a chastity belt for someone to retrieve. Or body armor. But even that might not be enough to stave off this heat.

Darn hormones.

He got up from the bed as if he didn't have a care in the world. Easy and slow. The movement caused his shirt to shift, and she got an even better look at his chest. Like his face, it was a winner. Toned and tanned and sprinkled with dark coils of chest hair. Until that moment she hadn't realized just how attractive that sort of thing was.

Of course, maybe it wasn't, on any other man.

Her body seemed fixed on this one.

"Nerves?" he asked.

And it took her a moment to realize she was nibbling on her bottom lip along with staring at his chest.

She nodded. "Sharing a bed isn't a good idea."

He lifted his shoulder, shifting the shirt again. Mercy. He had a great stomach, too, but then what had she expected? The man probably didn't have a flaw.

Well, not a physical one anyway.

But he had come up with a plan that basically sucked. Even he would probably agree with that right now. Because despite that calm exterior, he had to be thinking of the logistics of close quarters with a woman who was clearly attracted to him but wanted no part of him.

Yes, this would be an interesting night.

"I agree," he said. "Sharing a bed probably isn't wise." His voice, like his motions, was slow and easy. But maybe that was her imagination. Everything about him suddenly seemed way too interesting.

Wyatt tipped his head to the floor on the other side of the bed. Lyla had to step around to see the pillow and covers he'd put there.

So, no bed sharing.

That was good, even though her own body seemed to have a different notion about that, too.

"Any updates on the bombing?" she asked. Best to get her mind on something other than Wyatt, and it wasn't as if they had nothing to discuss.

"All of this is just preliminary, but it appears the device had been set outside the building on an exterior wall just below Stella's room. It was on a timer so it could have been put there hours earlier. Or days."

Lyla tried not to groan. "Are there security cameras?"

Wyatt shook his head. "No guard, either. The building was locked, though."

Of course, that hadn't stopped the bomber. "What about the evidence? Any idea yet how much was lost?"

His mouth tightened, and she knew the answer before he even said it. "The CSIs got out with the photos they'd taken, but pretty much everything else is gone. The building collapsed shortly after the fire department arrived."

Mercy. That meant the explosive device had been extremely powerful, and she shuddered to think how close they'd come to dying.

"Yeah," Wyatt said. He went closer, touched her arm with just his fingertips and rubbed gently. "But Declan thinks the bomber was the one who phoned in the threat."

So, he'd wanted them to get out. But why?

"More questions, few answers," he said when she made a sound of frustration. "I'm getting a little tired of that, too."

He drew back his hand from her arm, and Lyla hated that she was disappointed. Touching, even as a comforting gesture, was a big no-no with this sexual energy sizzling through the room.

"What about our situation?" Lyla asked. She saw the flicker of heat go through his eyes and realized she should clarify. "The possible charges for obstruction of justice?"

"Oh. That." Another shrug. "As long as we appear to have a marriage, there isn't much the governor can do. There's no physical evidence to link me to information

I found out about you. There are no records of the donor embryo or the theft at the fertility clinic storage."

"You destroyed it?" she asked.

"No. But someone else did."

Lyla pulled in a hard breath. What the heck was going on?

Wyatt made a sound, as if agreeing with her reaction, and he checked the time. "I need to grab a shower. The door's locked, and the security system's on." He pointed to the windows of the second-floor room. "Even the windows are wired for security, and if someone manages to get close enough to break the glass, the alarm will sound."

Good. Even though Lyla hated that these precautions had to be taken.

"When I'm in the shower, I want to leave the bathroom door open," Wyatt added. "Just in case."

Just in case there was an attack.

He didn't wait for her to agree, probably because he knew she had no choice, and he gave her arm another of those fingertip brushes before he headed into the bathroom.

And yes, the door stayed open.

Lyla made sure her attention was anywhere but on Wyatt undressing, but her imagination was too good tonight, and she saw him anyway. Not just the undressing. But as Wyatt stepped into the shower and let the steamy, hot water slide over his body.

Get a grip.

Her heart was racing. Her breath thin. All normal reactions if this were a real honeymoon night.

She snatched up her phone to get her mind on something else. No messages, but there were plenty of emails. Work was stacking up, but she'd already called the captain at San Antonio P.D. and explained why she couldn't come into the lab. Of course, he'd already heard about the attacks.

Had no doubt heard about the governor's concerns, too.

So, no one was pushing her to return to work, but soon a decision would have to be made. Either her cases would have to be reassigned or she would be replaced.

That felt like a fist around her heart.

She'd been a crime scene analyst since graduating from college seven years ago. She loved what she did, helping to solve cases that would clear the innocent and help convict the guilty.

But all of that could be taken from her.

She heard Wyatt turn off the shower and purposely kept her back turned, though she could hear him dressing. Except, he didn't really dress, Lyla soon learned when he stepped back into the room. No shirt, bare feet and he had on a pair of gray boxers that dipped precariously low on his waist.

Her mouth went dry.

Which was good, since she couldn't blurt out something stupid about his making a top-notch underwear model. Except somehow, wearing just the boxers, he still managed to look like a cowboy lawman.

Probably because of the scars.

She counted three. One on his upper right forearm. Another on the left side of his chest. And the other on his hip bone.

"Sorry, but I don't own pj's," Wyatt said.

Lyla tore her gaze from him and focused on her phone, which in no way needed her attention. There was nothing new left to see there, but it beat gawking at Wyatt.

"Are the scars from gunshots?" she asked.

"Yeah. There's another on the side of my head. Just a graze that my hair covers."

Four wounds. Good grief. Stella had been right about the bullet-magnet label. She wondered if that was because he was truly unlucky or if he'd just stepped up to take more dangerous assignments than most. Considering the way he was protecting her, she figured it was the latter.

Wyatt did a phone check, too, but he'd no sooner glanced at the screen when it rang.

"Hell," he grumbled. "Sheriff Zeke Mercer."

One of their suspects, and considering it was past eleven in the evening, his call probably wouldn't be good news.

"It's late," Wyatt snapped when he answered. Thankfully, he put it on speaker so she could hear what the man had to say.

"Yeah, but I figured you were up, being a newlywed and all." His voice was like gravel, and he sounded riled to the core.

So, Zeke knew about the marriage, too. Probably the baby, as well. Which was a reminder of something else hanging over their heads. The lab test that Wyatt had ordered on the amniotic fluid. The test that would determine if she was truly carrying his child.

"Travis told you I got married?" Wyatt asked.

"Who else? That man's got a ten-gallon mouth. Said he mentioned my name to you when you asked who'd blown Rocky Creek to smithereens."

"Your name came up. So did your business partner, Greg Hester."

Zeke stayed quiet a moment, as if surprised by that. "Because Travis is trying to cover his own hide, that's why. But you and I both know I had no reason to want Jonah Webb dead."

Lyla thought of the gunrunning deals that had gone on years ago. The ones Travis hinted that Zeke had orchestrated. But she doubted the retired sheriff would admit to a crime like that. Still, there might be some old records to link him, and she made a mental note to do some checking. Sometimes, evidence from gunrunning turned up in other cases, and maybe she could cross-reference that. Of course, that would first mean having access to the crime lab and files. Lyla wasn't sure how much longer she'd have that.

"What about Greg?" Wyatt pressed. "Did he have a reason to kill Webb?"

"You'd have to ask him, wouldn't you? But if I did the math right, Greg would have been just a teenager back then. Of course, that doesn't rule him out. You and your foster brothers were teenagers, and you're all suspects."

Wyatt huffed. "Is there a purpose to this call? Because as you pointed out, I'm a newlywed with better things to do." And he slid her a glance that caused her skin to flush.

"There's a purpose. Travis's hired gun, Nicky Garnett, was holed up in a dirtbag hotel over in San Antonio. I called the locals. Doing my civic duty. But they got there too late. Or else there's some kind of leak that alerted him."

Lyla knew of no such leak, but it was possible. Equally possible that Garnett had just gotten lucky and evaded the police.

"Next time I spot Nicky, I'll be calling you," Zeke said to Wyatt. "You got a hell of a big reason to bring him in, since he's the one who took shots at you."

"I'd appreciate any tip I can get." But Wyatt didn't

look or sound very appreciative. It was clear he didn't trust this retired lawman. And Lyla didn't trust him, either. Still, if he could deliver Garnett to them, then the gunman could tell them who'd hired him to come after Wyatt and her.

"Be talking to you then," Zeke added before he ended the call.

Wyatt stared at his phone for several seconds. "There's only one of our main suspects who hasn't contacted me personally," he mumbled. And he made another call. "Declan," he said a moment later. "I think it's time we talk to Greg Hester. Can you set up something for first thing in the morning?"

Unlike the other call, this one wasn't on speaker, but Wyatt rolled his eyes. "All right, but not too early, for appearance's sake."

Oh, because Wyatt and she were on their honeymoon and they needed to continue that facade until the culprit was caught.

Wyatt ended the call with his brother but kept hold of his phone and went across the room to the light switch. "Need anything before we pretend to get some sleep?"

Lyla couldn't help it—she smiled. It was the second time Wyatt had managed to do that, and she realized it'd been a while since a man had brought a smile to her face. Of course, Wyatt seemed to have her number.

"You can turn off the lights," she told him, and she climbed into the bed. Lyla pulled the covers up to her neck despite the fact the room wasn't chilly. She needed all the protection she could get between her and Wyatt's half-naked body.

He groaned when he got on the floor, and she nearly asked if it was hard. But best not to bring up that word, either. Still, it was difficult to avoid it when she heard him toss and turn, no doubt trying to get into a more comfortable position.

Lyla hoped she didn't regret what she was about to offer.

"It's a king-size bed," she pointed out. "One of us could sleep on top of the covers."

He didn't wait even a second to debate that. Wyatt grabbed his pillow, put his phone on the nightstand by his holster, and he dropped down onto the mattress. There was at least three feet of space between them, but Lyla figured that was still much too close.

"Now we can pretend to sleep and not notice each other," Wyatt mumbled.

Just like that, he eased the tension rising in her body. The heat was there, too, of course, but it actually helped to get everything out in the open. They were attracted to each other, and they shouldn't be.

Lyla closed her eyes, praying for sleep, since she was past the point of exhaustion, but barely a minute had gone by before the phone rang. Not Wyatt's.

Hers.

Wyatt scrambled across the bed, and they looked at the screen together. Unknown caller.

Not a good sign.

"Answer it on speaker," Wyatt instructed, and he turned on his own phone's recorder function.

Lyla waited until he had his phone right against hers before she hit the answer button.

"Lyla," the man said, his voice practically echoing through the room. "You've probably been waiting to hear from me."

Wyatt and she exchanged glances, and there was just enough light filtering from the windows that she could see the lift of his right eyebrow, no doubt asking her if she recognized the voice. But she had to shake her head.

This was a stranger.

Or perhaps one of the hired guns. She hadn't heard either of them speak, so she couldn't tell if this was one of them or not.

"Who are you?" Lyla asked.

"My name's not important. The only thing that's important is for you to listen. Did you really think marrying Wyatt McCabe would stop me?"

"I don't know what you mean," she answered.

"Sure you do. You married him to get yourself taken off the case."

"We got married because we're in love," Wyatt lied.

The caller made a *yeah right* sound. "Well, you and your new bride have a decision to make. Except, it's not really a decision. Lyla still has access to the crime lab and all the files on the Webb murder investigation."

It wasn't a question. "My marriage to Wyatt will disqualify me from working that case."

"I don't want you to work it. I want you to remove anything that implicates an accomplice. *Any accomplice,*" he emphasized.

"Why?" Lyla demanded. "From what I can tell, the evidence doesn't point to a clear-cut suspect, and who knows, there could be something in the case files to establish your innocence. If you're innocent, that is."

"Since you're likely recording this, I'll neither confirm nor deny that. But since you're recording this, it means there'll be no misunderstandings about what you're to do. Only keep evidence that proves Sarah Webb acted alone when she murdered her abusive husband. Destroy everything else."

Her heart rate doubled. Wyatt had been right about

someone wanting her to tamper with the evidence. But Wyatt had thought their marriage would prevent that from happening. Not according to the caller, though.

"And if we choose not to break the law?" Wyatt snarled.

"That's easy. You'll both die."

And with that, the man hung up.

WYATT COULD FEEL the throbbing in his head before he was even fully awake. He blamed that on the hour or two—at most—of sleep that he'd managed to get after Lyla's and his lives had been threatened.

These continued threats riled him to the core. But there'd been nothing he or his brothers could do to end this latest one, since there was no way to trace a call made from a disposable or burner phone.

Declan had the recording—Wyatt had given it to him the night before after the last call—and Declan would use it to try to get a voice match, but Wyatt figured that it hadn't been their would-be killer on the phone.

No way.

He would have used a peon for that call so that his voice wouldn't be recognized.

Wyatt forced his eyes open and came face-to-face with a sleeping Lyla. She was close to him. *Very* close. She was on her side, her left leg slung over his. Her leg was bare, and the new position hiked up her T-shirt so he could see her panties.

Pink.

He hadn't taken her for the girlie-underwear type, but it probably wouldn't have mattered what she was wearing. She could have had on granny panties, and his body would have still reacted. And he reacted, all right.

He went rock hard.

Great. Just what he didn't need this morning.

He glanced at the clock on the nightstand. It was barely six, but he needed to get up and check for updates on the case. Wyatt inched away from her. Or that was what he planned to do, but the slight movement must have startled her.

Her eyes flew open.

And suddenly he was looking right into all those shades of brown.

"Oh," she mumbled as if remembering where she was. But she didn't back away. Lyla just lay there with her leg still positioned over his.

As the seconds crawled by.

Wyatt couldn't be sure what she was thinking. However, it was pretty clear what was on his mind, and her gaze drifted in the direction of his erection, which was now pressed against her stomach.

She opened her mouth as if she might say something, but she clearly changed her mind. Wyatt changed his, too. A couple of times.

Should he kiss her? Should he do the smart thing? Smart would be, well, smart. But he decided to go the stupid route and kiss her anyway.

Wyatt slid his hand around the back of her neck, pulled her closer and put his mouth on hers. He didn't push things by deepening the kiss, figuring Lyla would stop this. And maybe slap him straight into the next county.

But she didn't.

No stopping.

Definitely no slap.

He remained firmly in the county, pressed against her and kissing her.

She made a sound of pure pleasure. A pink girlie

sound that went through him like a lightning bolt. And Wyatt put that fire and heat into the next kiss.

Oh, man. She tasted good. Not like morning, but like something forbidden and hot. Which she was. His mouth didn't let him forget that, and neither did the rest of his reckless body.

He pulled her closer, deepening the kiss even more. Deepening everything else, as well, since her leg had stayed on top of his, and the new position put his erection right against those pink panties.

Not good.

Because he already had some raunchy thoughts. Morning sex was usually the best. But sadly, he didn't think time of day had anything to do with it. He just needed Lyla badly, and he did some bad things because of that need.

He ran his hand between them and under her shirt. Touching her. On her stomach and then making his way up to her breasts. No bra. Just his bare hand on her bare skin, which was warm and well past inviting.

The kiss continued. So did the touching, but Wyatt wasn't the only one playing this game. Lyla touched, too. Her hand sliding over his chest. Her finger, easing through his chest hair. He'd never considered that a sensitive spot on his body, but he had to rethink it. Her touch was fanning the flames and making him crazy.

She made that sound again. A silky moan of pleasure mixed with some surprise.

Yeah, he was surprised, too.

Surprised this was turning into full-blown foreplay. Surprised that it felt far better than it should have.

And it was that last thought that kicked him in the head and caused him to back off and think. They couldn't keep this up. Not with so little clothing between them, a good bed and semisleepy brains. It was a perfect storm for what would be great sex.

That both of them would regret.

It wouldn't take long for that regret to set in, and Wyatt tried to focus just on that. And not on what would almost certainly be the pure pleasure leading up to the regret.

Her breath was gusting now, and she was staring at him as if trying to figure out what to say or do. She started to defuse things by slipping her leg away from his. That helped a little, but her scent was still on him, and he could still feel the sensation of his fingers touching her.

"Sorry." Lyla had to clear her throat and repeat it for the word to have sound. "It's the pregnancy. My hormones are all messed up."

Wyatt glanced at her tightened nipples, which were highly visible with the cotton shirt pressed against them. "Hormones caused that?"

"And you." She added some mumbled profanity. "That's not a compliment. I'm always attracted to the wrong man. Two failed engagements prove that."

It stung a little to hear himself called the wrong man. Even if it was the truth. But the rest of what she said wasn't true at all.

"I think the only thing your two failed engagements prove is that you were smart enough to end things before they went too far."

Of course, here she was married to him. Temporarily anyway. But in her mind, things had probably already gone too far in a really bad direction. That's why she'd lumped him in there with the two other wrong men.

Wyatt suddenly wanted to punch both of those men. And he didn't know why.

There was just a lot of dangerous energy simmering

inside him, and he didn't know where to aim it. He definitely couldn't aim it at another make-out session with Lyla, because this time he might not have the willpower to pull away from her.

"What about you?" she asked. "Other than your late wife, have you had any serious relationships?" But she frowned, moved away and pulled the covers over her. "Don't answer that. A few kisses don't obligate you to tell me your life story."

No, but it felt as though they did. If not his life story, he wanted to share something with her. "I haven't been involved with anyone long-term since Ann."

Her chin came down a fraction. Her eyebrows came up. "If that's true, it's not for lack of opportunities."

He thought maybe that was a compliment to offset the wrong-man zinger. "There have been opportunities," Wyatt admitted. "But I gave up casual sex about the same time I grew chest hair."

She laughed. It was smoky and thick, and it slid through him just as fast as the fire from that kiss. Still smiling, she climbed off the bed and started for the bathroom, but she came to a quick stop.

And glanced at the front of his boxers.

"Need a cold shower, or can I go first in the bathroom?" she asked.

"Go ahead."

Once she was out of his sight, his other *problem* might take care of itself. And if that didn't work, his conversation with Declan was sure to do the trick. Because by now Declan had no doubt set up the interviews with their suspects. In a few hours, Wyatt would need to face down the person who wanted Lyla and him dead. That was a surefire way to kill some of these lustful urges.

He hoped.

So far, nothing else was working.

Wyatt got up, grabbed a pair of jeans from his closet and pulled them on. A shirt, too. Best not to be half-naked when Lyla returned. But before he could even zip up, his phone rang. Probably one of his brothers, but considering the hour—and the fact that all but Declan thought he was on his honeymoon—this was no doubt something important related to the investigation.

Maybe they'd gotten lucky and the bomber had been caught. While Wyatt was wishing and hoping, he added that maybe this idiot who'd set the bomb had made a full confession so that the danger would be over.

But it wasn't one of his brothers' names on the phone screen. It was his boss, Saul Warner. Hell. Was Saul calling to say he was on the way to arrest him?

"We got a big problem," Saul greeted before Wyatt could even say a word.

"What's wrong?" And Wyatt wasn't sure he wanted to hear the answer. He was sick and tired of bad news, and especially bad news that put Lyla in more danger.

"Wyatt, there's been another murder."

Chapter Nine

Lyla followed Wyatt down the stairs while he continued his latest call, this one to the medical examiner. There'd been a flurry of them since his boss had phoned to tell him the bad news.

That Sarah Webb had been murdered.

The news hadn't just shocked Lyla, it had terrified her. This wasn't some bomb set to destroy evidence in an abandoned building. Sarah had been murdered while in a coma in her hospital bed. A place most people considered safe, but obviously the killer had gotten to her.

And silenced her for good.

Since Sarah had confessed to murdering her husband—along with having an accomplice—that information was now dead along with her.

"We must be close to learning the truth," Wyatt said when he finished his call. He shoved his phone back into his pocket. "Or the killer wouldn't have murdered Sarah."

True. Plus, Billy had said that Sarah appeared to be coming out of the coma. Her accomplice wouldn't have wanted that if he or she thought that Sarah would implicate them in the murder. The penalty for assisting in a murder was the same as doing the act itself. So, the accomplice was looking at a life sentence, or maybe even the death penalty if premeditation could be proven.

"Does this rule out Billy?" Lyla asked. "Because I don't see him killing his own mother, and I don't see Sarah naming him as her accomplice."

Wyatt made a sound of agreement and continued toward the back of the house. "But that doesn't get the others off the hook."

No. In fact, it made their three suspects, Sheriff Zeke Mercer, Greg Hester and Travis Weston, look even guiltier.

Of course, the same could be said for Wyatt's family.

And speaking of family, Lyla hadn't expected to find them all there in the massive eat-in kitchen.

They were everywhere.

At the table. The stove. Leaning against the counters. Even though they all seemed to be doing something, they all stopped and turned to look at Wyatt and her. It didn't take long for a collective hush to settle over the room.

A long hush.

Since Declan was the only one who knew the marriage was a sham, they were probably all thinking that either Wyatt had lost his mind or she'd somehow trapped him. After all, she couldn't be his usual type. They were probably used to him bringing home beauty queens and model types.

Lyla resisted the urge to make sure her ponytail and clothes were straight, but she wished she'd at least put on some makeup.

"Anything on the caller who threatened Lyla?" Wyatt asked Declan.

"Nothing." Declan made an uneasy glance around the room, as if bracing himself for someone to demand to know more about the marriage. When no one did, Declan cleared his throat and continued. "There's nothing in his voice or the background noise to indicate who he is or where he was when he made the call."

"You'll have to excuse our manners, but this is how crazy things get in the middle of an investigation," a very pregnant blonde said, walking toward Lyla. The woman hugged her. "Welcome to the family. I'm Jo-elle." She tipped her head to the lanky dark-haired man on one of the bar stools, who was talking on his phone. "Married to Dallas."

Wyatt continued the introductions from there. "Everyone, in case you haven't heard, this is Lyla, my wife." He hooked his arm around her as if remembering at the last minute they were playing the part of honeymooners.

There were several more moments of pin-dropping silence. A few odd looks, too. Even a whisper between one of the couples. Then, the chatter and activity continued as if a marriage announcement wasn't that unusual.

And maybe it wasn't.

Because Stella was the only one in the room who wasn't wearing a wedding ring.

Stella took a skillet of sizzling bacon off the stove and came over to give her a hug, too. "That's Harlan and Caitlyn," she said, pointing to the couple at the table. The woman was also pregnant and sitting so close to her husband that she was practically in his lap. They both added a welcome after looking up from papers they were studying.

"That's Lenora and Clayton," Stella continued. "And their precious little boy, Clay, Jr." She motioned toward the woman helping her in the kitchen and then to the man seated at the table next to Declan. Clayton was holding a sleeping baby only a few months old on his lap, and he glanced up from his computer, mumbled a welcome.

Declan managed a smile when he looked at Lyla. Forced, no doubt. And brief. He put his attention back on the laptop screen positioned in front of him.

"That's Kirby." And Stella's smile was genuine when her attention landed on the man in the wheelchair at the head of the table. Even though it was obvious that the man was recovering from a serious illness, he didn't look nearly as weak as Lyla had imagined he'd be.

"Welcome," Kirby greeted. He, too, had some papers on the table. "Wish it were under better circumstances. Still, we'll have time to celebrate soon."

Yes, soon, if they managed to identify and catch this killer. And after that, there'd be no need to celebrate the marriage, because Wyatt and she would be able to either tell them the truth or get an annulment. First, though, they had to stop kissing and doing other things that would lead to sex. Because even though she had no legal training, Lyla was pretty sure that sex would nix an annulment.

It would certainly make it harder for her to walk away from Wyatt, too.

"Slade, his wife, Maya, and their two boys will be here soon," Joelle finished. "And Declan's fiancée, Eden, is in her office, working. She's a P.I. and is trying to use her contacts to get a lead on the gunman Nicky Garnett."

Joelle leaned in closer to Lyla. "Bet you're wondering how we all fit in this room, huh? Especially with all the babies and pregnant bellies?"

Even though Joelle probably meant it as a joke, it had crossed Lyla's mind. This massive dose of *family* was past being overwhelming, especially since she'd been an only child, and her parents had passed away a few years earlier.

"You okay?" Wyatt whispered to Lyla the moment Joelle stepped away to join her husband at the breakfast bar. "You're looking a little pale."

"I'm okay," she lied. And she prayed the smell of that

bacon didn't trigger a bout of morning sickness. That would add another level of discomfort to this family gathering, and it would be darn hard to explain, since they didn't know about the pregnancy.

"What about Sarah's death?" Wyatt asked. "I was trying to talk to the medical examiner earlier, but he was tied up. Do we know yet how she was killed?"

Declan scrubbed his hand over his face. "No marks on her body, but something was injected into her IV. They're examining it now."

"Looks like it could be snake venom," Clayton said, reading from his computer screen.

"Sweet heaven," Lyla said under her breath. Some of the others responded with profanity, including Wyatt.

It was a first for Lyla. In all years of crime scene investigation, she'd never seen a case where snake venom had been used as a murder weapon.

"Once they know specifically what kind of venom was used," Clayton continued, "then we might be able to find the source."

True. There weren't many places in the state where someone could buy it. Of course, the killer could have hired someone else to do the job. If so, there wouldn't be a record, and judging from the dire expressions on Wyatt's brothers' faces, they had already come to that conclusion.

"What'll you have to start you off? Coffee or tea?" Stella asked in an attempt to change the gruesome conversation.

It might seem too obvious if she asked for milk, something she'd been drinking a lot of lately. "Tea, thanks. Black." Maybe she could hold that down.

"I'll get that for you. And if you're hungry, just help yourself to the bacon and eggs on the stove."

Lyla smiled. Thanked her. But Lyla knew she wouldn't be touching anything on the stove.

"Saul just got us the surveillance feed from the hospital," Declan said, drawing Lyla's attention back to him. "I'm looking at the hour and a half before Sarah's murder. Clayton's looking at the hour and a half after. If we don't find anything, we'll widen the time frame. It's possible her killer sneaked in earlier in the day."

And it was just as possible that it was a killer they wouldn't know, since he could be just another hired gun. For that matter, the person could have even used a disguise. She doubted anyone was bold enough to walk into a room and murder a woman when there was a good chance that someone would recognize him.

"Was there a camera outside her room?" Wyatt went for the coffeepot and poured himself a huge cup. He gulped down some, as if it were the cure to the headache he no doubt had. He also snatched a piece of bacon piled high on a platter.

"No camera there," Clayton answered. "The only ones inside the hospital are in the pharmacy and the emergency room."

Both places where crimes were the most likely to occur. "What about the exterior?" Lyla asked.

Declan nodded. "And that's what we're focusing on now. There are two cameras that cover both the back and front parking lots and all the entrances except for several of the clinic doors on the west side of the building."

"Anyone can go through those doors?" she pressed.

"No," Wyatt answered. "But anyone could break into them, especially since Sarah was killed after regular clinic hours."

Lyla groaned. It wasn't much of a stretch to believe a killer would also resort to breaking and entering to get to his soon-to-be victim. Added to that, it wouldn't have been especially hard to conceal a syringe filled with venom. It could easily fit into a pocket, unlike a gun that might be noticed.

Stella brought Lyla a steaming cup of tea, and even though there were empty seats at the table, she stood. Wyatt stayed next to her, though he continued to check his phone for updates while he wolfed down more bacon, which he sandwiched with some toast.

"I'm going over the report from the bombing," Harlan volunteered. "The bomb squad says it was almost certainly a professional job. They're hoping once they reconstruct the device, they'll be able to tell us who made it."

The bomb's signature. Lyla wasn't an expert in the area, but she knew someone who was. She nearly reached for her phone to call him but then remembered she wasn't in a position to be asking favors from former coworkers. In fact, she wasn't sure exactly what position she was in when it came to work, but she doubted it was a good one.

"So, what are we gonna do about this caller who threatened Lyla and Wyatt?" Kirby asked.

She looked at Wyatt, even though Lyla already knew the answer. "I won't tamper with evidence," she insisted.

"Wouldn't do any good anyway," Kirby concluded. "There's little chance this guy would just let you live afterward. You'd be a deadly loose end for him."

Mercy. She'd known that, of course, but it was hard to hear it said aloud. It didn't matter which way she went, she was in danger. And that included this marriage arrangement with Wyatt.

"I figure we'll just need to keep Lyla safe here at the ranch," Wyatt explained. "Of course, that means everyone else should stay away just in case."

Just in case bullets start flying.

Clearly that bothered Joelle, because she snuggled closer to her husband. Even though Dallas was reading something, he idly looped his arm around her and kissed her. The idleness vanished when he looked at her, and he kissed her again.

Lyla quickly glanced away. It was too private a moment. Except, her attention landed on Caitlyn and Harlan, and they were kissing, too.

"Ignore them," Wyatt whispered, following her gaze. "They've had the hots for each other since they were teenagers. Dallas and Joelle, too."

"What about them?" She tipped her head to Stella and Kirby, and even though they weren't kissing, Stella had leaned in, her mouth close to Kirby's ear as she whispered something.

"Them, too." Wyatt cursed under his breath. "It's possible we're the only ones on the ranch not having sex."

Lyla didn't dare laugh, because in this case, the truth hurt. Despite all the danger and the trouble that sleeping with him would cause her, her body was still aching from the memory of Wyatt's kisses.

"You should try to eat," Wyatt suggested, and he led her into the kitchen. Nothing looked good, and her stomach felt ready to clench at any moment, so she settled for a piece of dry toast that was sitting in the toaster.

"Bingo!" Declan said, getting up from his seat and turning the laptop to face their direction. The others quickly gathered around.

Lyla saw the image that was frozen on the screen, and it appeared to be the back parking lot of the hospital. It was littered with cars, but there was only one person visible in the shot.

A man wearing jeans and a white cowboy hat.

"Sheriff Zeke Mercer," Wyatt provided. "He was at the hospital."

Declan nodded. "And from the time stamp on the surveillance, he was there about one hour before Sarah was found dead."

That meant the former lawman had motive and opportunity. All that was left was the means, and to do that, they'd need to connect him to the snake venom.

"You got Sheriff Mercer," Harlan said. "Well, I got his business partner, Greg Hester." He turned the screen toward them, and Lyla saw the short blond-haired man getting into a black car.

"Greg didn't come with Zeke," Harlan added. "Because this footage was shot after Sarah had already been found dead."

"Run the footage," Wyatt insisted.

Harlan rewound and then hit Play, and it didn't take her long to see Greg coming out, not through a side entrance but the front. And he wasn't just walking. He was hurrying. Like a man on the run.

"Hell, what were they both doing there?" Wyatt asked, but he didn't wait for an answer. "Maybe they were in on it together."

"Maybe," Lyla agreed. "But wouldn't they have known about the security cameras?"

"They haven't been up in the parking lot that long," Declan explained. "Just a few months. Before that, there were only cameras in E.R. and the pharmacy."

She thought about that a moment. "What about Billy? Any sign of him?"

"Not so far," Declan said, and Harlan mumbled something similar.

"If Travis Weston shows up on that footage," Dallas said, "then they'll all claim they were set up."

They'd probably claim it anyway. And at least one of them would be lying. Well, unless Billy had somehow managed to do the unthinkable and kill his own mother.

"It's time one of you talked to all the suspects," Kirby advised. "You, too." His weathered eyes landed on Lyla. "If one of them is behind the threats, then it might do them some good to see you and Wyatt together. That way, they'll know he and all his brothers will be protecting you."

Lyla hadn't thought of things from that angle, that it might get the killer to back off if he thought she was well protected by a family of federal marshals.

Was that why he'd gone after Sarah instead?

Because she'd been vulnerable?

Or maybe he'd even wanted to send Lyla a message—that she could be next. Whatever his motive, she didn't want to be away from Wyatt anyway since he seemed bound and determined to protect her and the baby.

Lyla was counting heavily on that.

She wasn't a coward, had always fought her own battles, but fighting this one alone could cost her the baby. She'd rather rely on Wyatt than risk that.

"I'll make the calls," Dallas volunteered, "and have the suspects come to the marshals' office. Declan's arranged for Greg to be there, so we might as well get three birds with one stone." He checked the time. "Does an hour or two from now sound okay?"

Wyatt didn't agree right off. He looked at her, as if debating what Kirby had suggested.

"You want me to stay here while you talk to them?" she asked, knowing that wasn't going to happen.

"I'm not letting you out of my sight," Wyatt verified. "We'll just have to be smart about this. I don't want to take you into town unless I'm sure I can keep you safe."

And he moved away from her to start coordinating things with Dallas.

Lyla intended to stay out of the action, but both Caitlyn and Joelle came toward her. "They'll be a while," Joelle said, taking Lyla by the arm. "It'll give us a chance to talk."

That put a knot in Lyla's stomach, and she looked back at Wyatt to see if he could stop this, but his attention was on whatever Clayton was showing him on the computer screen.

Joelle and Caitlyn led her through the kitchen, snagging some food along the way, and they sat at a small breakfast table that faced the massive manicured backyard.

"All right." Caitlyn dished up some of the bacon and eggs for the three of them. "Spill everything. How'd you manage to snag Wyatt?"

Lyla realized she should have expected the question, but she didn't know how to answer it. Anything she could say would be a lie.

"Wait." Caitlyn shook her head. "I didn't mean it like that. *Snag* makes it sound like you tried to deceive him in some way. It's just that Wyatt never said anything about being involved with anyone, much less being in love."

"He's not exactly the baring-his-soul type," Joelle continued, "but we're surprised we didn't get a hint about the marriage before he just sprang it on us."

"It happened very fast," Lyla settled for saying.

Caitlyn smiled. "Love at first sight. The best kind. It's what happened with me when I first saw Harlan."

"Same here with Dallas." Joelle leaned in, lowered her voice. "But with the exception of Ann, Wyatt just hasn't jumped into any relationships. Before Ann, he was definitely the *love 'em and not hang around for long* type."

Lyla didn't doubt that. "How long have you known him?"

"About eighteen years," Caitlyn answered, and Joelle bobbed her head in agreement. "We all grew up together at Rocky Creek."

"I'm pretty sure you're the first woman he's brought home since his late wife," Joelle continued. "Of course, that's what happens when you're in love." She glanced over at him. "And it's pretty clear that he's crazy about you."

Lyla frowned and looked at Wyatt to see if Joelle and she were seeing the same thing. Obviously not. The only thing she saw on Wyatt's face was worry and concern while he was talking on his phone. If there was any craziness involved, it was only his obsession to keep her safe.

An obsession she was thankful for.

"So, when will you tell everyone you're pregnant?" Caitlyn asked.

Lyla's mouth dropped open. Either Wyatt and she were giving off some kind of weird vibes or else these two were mind readers.

"Uh, excuse me a second," Lyla said, hoping to get her out of answering that question. But she also wanted to see what had put that look on Wyatt's face.

He ended his call, but he stared at the phone for several seconds before his gaze met hers. There was something in his eyes that she couldn't interpret.

Wyatt didn't hurry when he came toward her, but as Joelle had done earlier, he gripped on to her arm and took her not just out of the breakfast area but through a formal dining room and to the other side of the house. He finally stopped when they reached the foyer, and he looked around to make sure they were alone.

They were.

"What happened?" she asked, and Lyla tried to brace herself for another death threat. Or worse, another murder.

Wyatt dragged in a long breath. "The test results are back."

With all the talk of the crime scene and bomb, it took her a moment to realize which test results he meant.

The one from her amniocentesis.

A test that would tell them whose baby she was carrying.

Chapter Ten

Wyatt hadn't thought beyond the test results. Hadn't even considered how to tell Lyla. But judging from the way she staggered back and caught onto the wall, she already knew what he was about to say.

"The baby's mine."

The jolt went through him. So did the memories of how Ann and he had planned and hoped for this baby. Of course, they hadn't planned on *this*.

But then neither had Lyla.

She'd planned to have her own baby. One that she wouldn't have to share with a birth father.

"You're sure?" she asked, but then she waved him off, and she moved away from him when Wyatt tried to take hold of her. She didn't look too steady on her feet.

And wasn't.

Groaning and with her back still pressed against the wall, she sank down to the floor and put her hands over her face.

Wyatt had no idea what to say to her. Not *I'm sorry,* because that would be lie. He'd desperately wanted this child to be his, and it was. But there was no joy in seeing Lyla fall apart like this.

"Everything you told me has come true." Her words didn't have much sound, and she was on the verge of crying. "The threats, the attempted blackmail." She paused, her mouth trembling. "Now the baby."

Wyatt stooped down and tugged her hands from her face so he could make eye contact. Why, he didn't know. He was probably the last person on earth she wanted to see right now, but he had to try to make this better.

Even if that was impossible.

Yeah, there were tears, all right, and even though Lyla was blinking them back, one still spilled down her cheek. Wyatt brushed it away with his thumb, but another quickly followed.

"I love this baby," she whispered on a hoarse sob.

"So do I." And that was a massive understatement. For both of them.

Lyla wanted this child enough to carry it and become a single parent. Definitely not an easy lifestyle choice. It'd be easier for him because he had a huge family ready and willing to help, but Wyatt didn't think Lyla would appreciate his bringing that up now.

She finally met his gaze. "You'll challenge me for custody." And it wasn't a question.

He would.

Except that didn't feel right, either.

After all, Lyla still had over six months to go to carry this child. He seriously doubted her love for the baby would lessen during that time. Just the opposite. And she'd be the one taking all the risks that came with the pregnancy.

"Maybe we can work something out," he offered.

"Shared custody." She shook her head. "You really want this baby starting out his or her—" Lyla stopped, froze, probably because she saw the look on his face. "The test would have given you the sex of the baby."

He nodded.

Wyatt didn't get to do or say more than that, because he glanced over his shoulder at the sound of footsteps behind him and he spotted Declan making his way toward them.

"Everything okay?" Declan asked.

Neither Lyla nor he answered, but Wyatt did help her to her feet.

"Two of our suspects are on their way to the marshals' office," Declan continued, studying Lyla. He'd no doubt noticed the tears she was still trying to wipe away. "Zeke and Travis."

Even though it was hard, Wyatt forced himself to think of the investigation and not the life-changing news he'd just delivered to Lyla.

"Did Zeke happen to say why he was at the hospital right before Sarah was murdered?" Wyatt asked.

"Not yet, but no one's there to question him yet, since Saul's had to leave town to testify at a trial over in Eagle Pass. It's just Zeke, Travis and the dispatcher until Harlan gets there. He just left. Ranger McKinnon's on the way, too, but he's still a half hour out."

Great. It wasn't a good idea for Zeke and Travis to be alone together, since they were both accusing the other of being involved with not just Webb's murder but the recent attacks. They might try to kill each other, and while Wyatt didn't care if they inflicted some bodily harm, he wanted them both alive so they could answer questions.

"Dallas and Clayton are staying here with the family," Declan continued. "Just in case." He didn't spell out there could be an attack, but all of them knew it. "Slade's out of pocket because he just got called out to pick up a fugitive. I'd like to head over to the crime lab so I can push for some headway on this bomb and study the other reports coming in."

All of that was necessary, but it left Wyatt to assist with the interrogations. Well, unless Saul pulled the plug on them before Wyatt could try to get whatever information he could out of Zeke and Travis.

"We should go," Wyatt told Lyla. "I don't want Harlan to have to tackle this by himself."

She nodded. Her crying had finally stopped but that was probably because Declan was there. Later, the tears would come and so would the inevitable discussion they'd need to have. He was betting that wouldn't lead to another round of kissing.

But Wyatt did brush a kiss on her forehead.

He wasn't sure it gave her much comfort, but it certainly helped him.

"Let me get my purse," she mumbled, and headed toward the stairs, leaving Declan there to stare at him.

Make that a glare.

"Are you trying to make this harder than it already is?" Declan asked. "Because there's no reason to do a loving-couple act around me."

"It's not an act." Wyatt winced at that. Then, cursed. "I mean, I'm attracted to her."

Declan's hands went on his hips. "Not exactly a news flash, brother. But what do you think this is doing to her, huh? She's already having to play the part of your wife, and if you find out the baby is yours—"

"It is."

Declan's glare melted away, and he squeezed his eyes shut a moment. "Like I said, don't make this harder on her than it already is."

Darn good advice. Wyatt hoped his body would listen. And his heart. Because with Lyla carrying his baby, it tore down even more walls between them. He wasn't ready for that to happen yet. Maybe never would be.

"Did something happen?" Lyla asked from the top of the stairs. She volleyed glances at both of them.

Wyatt shook his head and got them moving out the front door and into his SUV. He wanted to hurry so he didn't have to keep thinking about paternity tests and feelings. Better for him to concentrate on learning about what was going on. But he also had to be careful about another attack, so he watched their surroundings when he drove away from the ranch.

"What did Caitlyn and Joelle have to say to you?" he asked.

Lyla didn't jump to answer, and she gave him the same kind of look she'd given him when she'd seen him talking with Declan. She no doubt figured he was hiding something. And he was. He was hiding the fact that the baby news had clouded everything in his head, and the warning from Declan had just added to his confusion.

"Caitlyn guessed I was pregnant," she finally said.

That was not something he'd expected to hear. "How?"

Lyla shook her head. "I didn't say a thing, but maybe it takes one to know one. Or something like that." She groaned softly. "All of this pretense is a lot harder than I thought it would be. And pretty soon you'll have to tell them the truth about the marriage. About the baby."

Yeah, he would. Especially if his brother's wife had already figured out part of it. Still, it wasn't something he just wanted to blurt out, and he didn't want it to come in the middle of this dangerous mess. Of course, one way to end the mess was to get a confession from the person who'd orchestrated it.

Maybe Zeke or Travis.

But he didn't want those answers at Lyla's expense.

"You've already taken on enough stress," he told her

as he pulled into the parking lot of the marshals' building. "It's not good for you or the baby to add more, so you can wait in Saul's office while Harlan and I talk to these guys."

She didn't argue, didn't even make a sound, but then the same thoughts whirling through his mind were no doubt whirling through hers.

They went inside and through the security check, but before they even got up the stairs to the offices, Wyatt heard the yelling. When Wyatt stepped into the squad room, he saw Travis and Zeke with Harlan between them. His brother was definitely having to stave off a fistfight.

Wyatt grabbed Zeke by the collar just as Zeke brought up his fist, and Wyatt slung the man out of the fray. He didn't get any thanks from Zeke though for stopping him from trying to land a punch.

"He set this up!" Zeke threw off Wyatt's grip and jabbed his index finger in Travis's direction. Zeke's face was bright red, veins bulging on his neck, and his breath was coming out in ragged spurts.

Unlike Travis.

He didn't appear to be ruffled at all, but Wyatt figured that was just to rile Zeke even more.

"What'd he set up?" Wyatt demanded.

"Nothing," Travis answered, but Zeke had a different notion.

"He had some woman leave a message on my phone," Zeke fired back. "A woman pretending to be Sarah Webb. I kept the message, so you can listen for yourself."

"I already did," Harlan explained. "It's a woman, all right, and she called about an hour and a half before Sarah was murdered. But it could have been anyone. Her voice isn't louder than a whisper."

"Exactly the way a woman would sound if she'd just

come out of a coma." Zeke gave Travis another finger jab. "And he's the one who had her call me and ask me to come to the hospital, saying she had to talk to me right away. He knew I'd go running to the hospital and that it'd set me up for her murder."

Interesting. Wyatt wondered if Greg had gotten the same message. Of course, even if he had, it didn't mean Zeke and he were innocent. Because they could have had someone call them and leave the message so they'd *look* innocent.

Or maybe Sarah really had come out of the coma.

If she had, then the woman could have used the phone in her hospital room. It was a long shot, but Wyatt needed to see if there was a way to trace a call from there.

"The same woman called me," Travis volunteered. "I didn't save it, and I damn sure didn't go to the hospital. I figured it was some kind of setup."

"Yeah, because you're the one who set it up," Zeke snarled.

Since this argument could go on for a while, Wyatt looked back at Lyla. "Why don't you go ahead into Saul's office?"

"Your bride should stay," Travis insisted. "She might learn something to make you back off from trying to pin this on me."

"I'm not trying to pin anything on you," Wyatt insisted. "I'm trying to learn the truth."

Lyla did go to Saul's office, but she didn't close the door.

"If you want the truth," Travis went on, "then try this theory on for size. Years ago, Webb asked me to let some of the boys from Rocky Creek work on my ranch. But what he had in mind was gunrunning with his old friend, the sheriff here."

"You're admitting to this?" Harlan asked Travis.

"Just a theory." Travis's tone became even more smug. "And continuing that theory, something went wrong with the arrangement, and Webb and Zeke had a fallin'-out."

"You're a lying, worthless snake," Zeke argued. "And you're the one who had the fallin'-out with Webb, because he didn't know about the gunrunning. You set it all up, and when Webb confronted you about it, you helped Sarah kill him."

Travis just smiled. "Prove it. Oh, you can't, can you? Because you got no evidence."

"Other than your connection to the gunman who took shots at Lyla and me," Wyatt reminded him.

Oh, that narrowed Travis's eyes, and it got worse when Zeke chuckled.

Travis turned those narrowed eyes on Zeke. "It's not me on that surveillance footage. It's you." And Travis's smug look returned. "And I'm thinking you murdered Sarah because she might spill her guts and tell everyone you helped her kill her husband."

No angry outburst this time. Zeke just shook his head. "Sarah was my best friend's wife. I wouldn't have hurt her."

"But you think I did," someone said.

Wyatt cursed because he hadn't heard the footsteps behind him. Cursed even more that Greg, a suspect, had managed to waltz right in with Lyla so close.

"I don't think that," Zeke told Greg. He tipped his head to Travis. "I believe he set us up."

"Well, someone did." Unlike the other men, Greg was wearing a dark blue business suit. He definitely didn't look like a cattle broker. "I got a call asking me to come to the hospital." He pressed the speaker function on his phone. "Listen for yourself."

It only took a few seconds for the voice to pour through the room. "It's me, Sarah Webb," the woman said in a hoarse whisper. "I need to see you. I'm scared. Please don't tell anyone I'm out of my coma, because someone wants to keep me silent. Come to the hospital now but don't let anyone see you going into my room."

Wyatt checked the time of the call. A good half hour before Sarah had been found dead. "How'd you get into the hospital without being seen?"

"Clinic entrance," Greg said without hesitation. "One of the doctors was working late, I guess, because I saw a patient leave through that door, and I went in." He paused. "By the time I got to Sarah's room, she was already dead."

Wyatt studied Greg's body language but couldn't tell if he was lying. In fact, he couldn't tell much of anything, because Greg seemed completely unruffled by any of this.

"Did you see anyone?" Zeke asked him. "Like Travis, maybe?" He didn't wait for Greg to answer. "Because he could have gotten in the same way you did."

"I wasn't there," Travis insisted.

"I didn't see him," Greg said at the same time. "But that doesn't mean he wasn't there."

Lyla came out of the room, and even though Wyatt gave her a warning glance to go back, she stayed put.

"Why would Sarah have called you?" she asked Greg, taking the question right out of Wyatt's mouth.

"Greg's known Sarah for over a decade," Zeke answered. "Ever since we've been in business together. I took him with me more than once whenever I drove out to Rocky Creek to check on her."

Wyatt kept his attention planted on Greg, who suddenly looked uncomfortable. Or something. "That's true?" Wyatt motioned for Zeke to keep quiet.

"I knew Sarah," Greg finally said. At first, he dodged Wyatt's gaze, but then met him eye to eye. "Remember the two boys who Webb sent out to work on Travis's ranch?"

"Don't do this." Zeke tried to take hold of Greg's arm, but Harlan blocked him. Zeke continued to warn Greg, but he obviously ignored him.

"The ones he had gunrunning," Greg continued.

Wyatt nodded. "Dakota Cooke and Spenser Cash. Cooke's dead and Cash is missing."

"He's not missing," Greg said, and then he hesitated. "He's standing right in front of you."

Travis went closer, his attention pinned to Greg's face. "Well, I'll be damned. It's you, ain't it, boy? You're Spenser Cash."

Judging from Zeke's profanity, not only did he know it, but it was something he'd wanted to stay hidden.

Wyatt stared at Greg, trying to pick through the features to see if it was a face he remembered. He could see it now but only after the fact. Of course, he hadn't expected Spenser to change his appearance and identity, and Wyatt had even considered the guy might be dead.

"I've had a few surgeries. Changed my hair," Greg explained. "After Webb disappeared, someone tried to kill me. At first, I figured it was his gunrunning friends trying to tie up loose ends, so Zeke helped me change my identity."

"You knew all this time?" Harlan demanded, looking at Zeke.

The man nodded. "Greg was a good kid. And Kirby's not the only one who wanted to protect some of the boys there. I got Greg out of harm's way, and the person causing that harm is standing right there." He pointed at Travis again.

"I didn't try to kill him," Travis grumbled. "I didn't even know he was still alive until just this minute. And besides, I got no reason to want him dead."

"No reason other than trying to cover up the gun-running," Zeke argued. "Or covering up your part in Webb's murder."

"It might not have been Travis," Greg said, drawing everyone's attention back to him.

His remark also caused Zeke's eyes to narrow. "Think before you say anything," Zeke warned him.

But Greg didn't even pause. "I saw something at Rocky Creek that night Webb went missing. Something that made me a target for a killer."

Wyatt got an uneasy feeling in the pit of his stomach. "What'd you see?"

Greg swallowed hard. "The person who helped kill Jonah Webb."

Chapter Eleven

A dozen questions went through Lyla's mind, but first and foremost—was Greg telling the truth? And if so, why was he coming clean now? Still, those were questions that might have to wait to be answered because of the last bombshell that Greg had just dropped.

"Well?" Travis snapped. "Spill it. Who'd you see? And if that lie comes out of your mouth saying it was me, you'll regret it."

Greg ignored the threat and looked at Wyatt. "It was Kirby."

Wyatt started cursing, and because she wasn't sure what he was going to do, Lyla put her hand on his arm to try to steady him.

"You didn't see Kirby kill Webb because he didn't do it," Wyatt insisted.

"I didn't see him put the knife in Webb," Greg explained, "but I did see him leave Webb's office that night."

Wyatt cursed some more. "Kirby could have been there for a variety of reasons. Webb had beaten up Declan that day. He'd hit one of the girls, too."

Both good reasons for Kirby to have paid a visit to the headmaster, but obviously he hadn't told Wyatt about it.

"What exactly did you see?" Lyla asked Greg. And

she tried to make note of not just his body language but Travis and Zeke's. That might help her figure out what was really going on here.

"I was in the storage closet just down the hall from Webb's office." Greg's voice was low and strained. He glanced at the floor. At her. Even at Wyatt and Travis. At everyone but his mentor, Zeke. "I used to go there sometimes when I wanted to be alone."

"Go ahead," Zeke pressed when Greg paused. "You opened this can of worms, and it's too late to stop now. Tell them *everything*."

And either Zeke was acting, or else he truly hadn't wanted this to come to light. But she couldn't imagine why. Because if Greg was telling the truth, this took the blame off everyone else, including Zeke, and put it on Kirby.

Greg bobbed his head but still didn't look at Zeke. "I heard someone arguing in Webb's office. A lot of arguing," he corrected. "First, with Stella. She was upset about the way Webb had hit Declan." His gaze came to Wyatt's. "Webb slapped her."

Because she still had hold of his arm, she felt Wyatt's muscles turn to iron, and it took a while to get his teeth unclenched. "You should have come and told me."

"And me," Harlan added.

"You both would have killed him."

Harlan's expression took on a dangerous edge that matched Wyatt's. "Damn right."

Greg shook his head. "I was only sixteen, but I wasn't stupid. I could see what was going on, and I knew it could turn deadly if the wrong people found out what Webb had done to her. Anyway, Stella and he argued for a while, and then she stormed out."

"And Webb was alive when she left?" Lyla pressed.

"Oh, yes. He got other visitors after her." He paused again. "Zeke came."

Travis's face lit up, and he made a sound to indicate this wasn't a surprise to him. "This just keeps getting better and better."

"I already told the sheriff and the Rangers that I was there that night," Zeke readily admitted. "Webb and I were friends, and he called me after his little run-in with Stella. She'd told him she was reporting him to the state officials, and I tried to calm him down so he wouldn't do something he'd regret. Like fire her. Because that would have only made her go after him even harder."

Lyla figured this was difficult for Wyatt to hear. Stella was like a mother to him, and she had put herself in danger by going up against Webb like that.

"Stella never told you about this run-in with Webb?" she whispered to Wyatt.

His jaw muscles stirred again, and he shook his head. "That doesn't mean she's guilty."

No, it didn't, but Lyla did have to wonder why she'd kept it secret all these years. Of course, maybe Stella hadn't wanted to add any more horrible memories to the ones that her *boys* already had.

"After Zeke left Webb's office," Greg continued, "Sarah went into the room. A few minutes later, Kirby arrived. They argued, too. I couldn't hear about what exactly, but their voices were raised. And then everything got quiet. Kirby left, and he shut the door behind him. Sarah stayed inside, but I don't have any idea when she came out, because I fell asleep."

"That doesn't mean Kirby helped kill him." Wyatt scrubbed his hand over his face. "Besides, the blood spatter found at Rocky Creek points to the initial attack happening in Stella's quarters."

Greg shook his head again. "I'm not sure why that blood was there. I'm just telling you what I saw and heard. And because of it, someone tried to kill me."

"What you *saw and heard* doesn't make sense," Wyatt snarled. "If Kirby didn't know you were in that closet, then how would he have known to *silence* you?"

"Maybe you should ask Kirby." Greg checked his watch. "He should be here any minute."

"What?" Wyatt snapped. "Why would Kirby come here?" And now it was Wyatt's eyes that took on a dangerous edge.

Harlan's, too. He grabbed his phone. No doubt to call the ranch.

"I called Kirby," Greg explained. "Told him I was coming here and told him what I was going to say."

"That you were going to accuse him of murder," Wyatt snapped, and he looked at Harlan, who only nodded.

"Kirby's on the way," Harlan verified. "And Stella didn't know. Now she's on the way, too."

"Well, well," Travis mocked. "Soon the whole gang will be here, and this is one show I don't want to miss."

Wyatt gave him a glare that could have withered every blade of grass in Texas. "Who's with Kirby?" he asked his brother. "And can you stop him from coming?"

"Cutter's bringing him, and they're already in the parking lot."

"Cutter?" she whispered to Wyatt.

"He's a ranch hand," Wyatt explained.

And that in itself told her that Kirby had sneaked away not just from Stella but the rest of the family, as well. Probably because he knew they would have stopped him.

But why was he coming?

Hopefully to explain the accusation Greg had just made. Of course, it wasn't so much an accusation. More of an observation, and it certainly didn't prove Kirby was a killer. So, why had he felt the need to come here? Apparently, they wouldn't have to wait long for that answer.

"Excuse us for a second," Lyla said, and despite Wyatt's attempts to stay put, she led him into Saul's office. She didn't shut the door, but she maneuvered him to the other side of the room so they wouldn't be heard.

"I won't let them railroad Kirby." And he tried to get around her. But Lyla held on, pinning him against the wall. Of course, he could have thrown off her grip at any time, but he didn't. He continued to curse and mumble for several more seconds before he stilled and looked at her.

"Kirby's getting better, but he's still weak from the cancer treatments," Wyatt said. "We came close to losing him."

Lyla heard the emotion in his voice. Saw it more in his eyes, and she slid her arms around him and pulled him to her. "I'm sorry for all of you."

"For us," he corrected. Still looking as if he wanted to battle something, anything, he brushed a kiss on her forehead. "You're caught in the middle of this, too. You and the baby."

But then the intense warrior look changed. Maybe because of the baby. He was no doubt still coming to terms with the fact that the child was his.

Lyla was certainly struggling with it.

Wyatt gently pushed away a strand of her ponytail that had slipped onto her neck. The back of his fingers brushed against her skin. And just like that, she got the jolt of heat.

So did he.

Because he kissed her again.

This time on her mouth, and he lingered a bit, adding more and more to that heat. Maybe because he wanted to escape for just a few moments. Lyla understood that. She was escaping, too, except it felt like a lot more than that.

He slid his hand between them. Over her belly. "I don't want any of this to hurt you."

She was pretty sure he wasn't just talking about the danger now. Or just the situation they had to work out with the baby. But it was already too late for avoiding hurt. She was well on her way to getting her heart crushed.

Again.

Apparently, she hadn't learned anything when it came to love.

"Kirby's coming into the building," Harlan called out.

Wyatt didn't rush out, and she looked up at him, dreading what she had to ask. "Did Kirby help kill Webb?"

His mouth tightened, the response he usually had when anyone questioned Kirby's innocence, but then he shook his head. "I honestly don't know. In fact, the only person in my family that I'm positive is innocent is me."

That was what she was afraid he was going to say, and that could mean this meeting with Kirby could have devastating consequence. Because she doubted any of their other suspects were on the verge of a confession. They were still too busy blaming each other.

She followed Wyatt back into the squad room, and he went into the hall to wait by the elevator near the stairs. No doubt where Kirby would be making his arrival. But even though they had only a few moments, Lyla decided to keep digging for information that Greg might or might not have.

"That night when you were in the storage closet, did you hear a noise, like a body falling to the floor?" she asked the man. "Because it would have made a heavy, thudding sound." And if he'd been able to hear voices as he'd claimed, he wouldn't have missed that sound.

"I heard some things. Maybe not a thud exactly, but more like someone moving furniture or something."

So, maybe after being stabbed, Webb had fallen onto a chair or some other piece of furniture. Without Sarah alive to tell them, they might never know. Well, unless they got a confession from her accomplice.

Or her killer.

Of course, that could be the same person, but clearly Wyatt didn't believe it was his foster father.

"You shouldn't have come here," Wyatt immediately said when Kirby rolled into the room in his wheelchair. "And you shouldn't have brought him," he added to the ranch hand who stayed in the hall.

"When I saw him gettin' into his truck, or rather tryin' to do that, he told me he'd drive here on his own if I didn't bring him," Cutter protested.

"And I would have," Kirby insisted. "I'm not an invalid, and I can speak for myself." His gaze softened a little when he looked at Harlan, Wyatt and her, but there was no soft look for Greg. "Greg, aka Spenser Cash, called and said he was about to implicate me in Webb's murder. As far as I was concerned, that was throwing down the gauntlet."

"A gauntlet you should have let Wyatt and me pick up," Harlan insisted.

Kirby shook his head. "Like I said, I'm not an invalid, and I wasn't going to sit by at the ranch while Greg spins a web of lies."

"No lies. I was just telling them what I saw and heard," Greg argued. "I'm sorry if that points to you being Sarah's accomplice."

"I doubt you're sorry," Wyatt snapped. "And you're

just spilling all of this now?" He didn't wait for an answer. "Why didn't you speak up all those years ago?"

"Because he was a scared kid," Zeke said.

Wyatt shot him a *back off* glare. "I'd like to hear it from him."

Greg took a moment, gathering his breath. "Because I wasn't sorry that Webb was gone. I didn't know he was dead. I just knew he wasn't around to beat us anymore, and I didn't really care who was responsible for that." He paused. "Well, not until the threats started."

"What threats?" Lyla asked. Again, she watched the body language. Travis was enjoying this far too much, but he was the only one.

"They started within days after Webb disappeared," Greg continued. "Notes telling me to stay quiet about what I saw. The notes escalated to the tires on my foster parents' car being slashed."

"That's when I stepped in," Zeke explained. "I told him he'd never be safe if he didn't disappear, too. I helped him get a new identity, and eventually we started a business together."

"You withheld information pertinent to a murder investigation," Lyla accused.

That earned her a hard look from the retired sheriff. "I didn't know Webb had been murdered then. Thought he'd just walked out on Sarah and turned his back on Rocky Creek. I didn't know he was dead until his body was found eight months ago."

"Right," Travis snarled. "He was your so-called friend, and you didn't think it strange that he hadn't contacted you in nearly seventeen years?"

Zeke turned that frosty look on Travis. "One breath you accuse me of wrongdoing. The next, it's Kirby or Greg. The only person you're not accusing is yourself."

Travis smiled. "Because I wasn't there that night that someone put a knife in Webb's ribs. Unlike others." His gaze landed on Kirby. "So, are you here to confess, Marshal?"

"No," someone said.

Everyone turned in the direction of the doorway, to find Stella standing there. She was breathing hard, probably because she'd run to get into the building.

"Kirby's not here to confess," Stella insisted. Her narrowed gaze landed on Travis. "But I am."

The room went totally silent, but it was the calm before the storm. Wyatt went toward her, but Kirby was closer, and he whirled his chair around to face her.

"You're not doing this," Kirby insisted, and both Harlan and Wyatt echoed the same. "You're not lying to protect me."

Stella lifted her chin. "Not to protect you. And I'm not lying, because it's true." Her determined gaze came to Wyatt. "You need to arrest me because I'm the one who helped Sarah kill her husband."

Chapter Twelve

The day was still going at breakneck speed, but one look at Lyla, and Wyatt knew he had to slow down this pace. At least temporarily so he could get her back to the ranch.

She was literally asleep at his desk.

Worse, Wyatt wasn't sure how long she'd been that way. He'd gotten so caught up in trying to help Stella and dealing with the investigation that he hadn't realized just how late it was. Half past three, which meant she'd spent the better part of the day at the marshals' building. Considering she'd slept very little the night before, she had to be exhausted, and that wasn't good for either her or the baby.

"I'm getting Lyla out of here," he told Declan. Like Wyatt, his brother had been on the phone for hours, still was, but he gave Wyatt a go-ahead nod.

Leaving didn't mean Wyatt wouldn't continue to help. All of his brothers had pitched in to try to stop Stella's arrest, but so far they were batting zero. Mainly because Stella wasn't cooperating. She'd lawyered up and was refusing to talk to any of them.

That didn't make her guilty.

Well, guilty of murder anyway. No. She was almost certainly doing this to protect Kirby. Unfortunately, Greg's statement, which he'd now officially made and signed, put Stella at the crime scene, and that slap from Webb gave her a motive.

"How about you?" Wyatt asked Kirby. "Want a ride back with us?"

But he knew Kirby's answer before he'd even asked the question. Kirby just shook his head.

On a weary huff, Wyatt grabbed their coats, went to his desk and gave Lyla a gentle tap on the shoulder. She snapped to a sitting position, but then she looked around as if trying to figure out where she was.

"Oh, sorry," she mumbled. "I didn't mean to fall asleep." She yawned and rubbed her eyes.

"Don't be. You needed the rest, and I should have gotten you home by now. To the ranch," he corrected when he realized what he'd said.

It wasn't Lyla's home, and he was reasonably sure she didn't want to be there. But that didn't matter. He wasn't letting her out of his sight.

She stood, wobbling a little, and he resisted the urge to scoop her up into his arms and carry her down the stairs. Four of his brothers were in the office. And his boss. Along with Kirby, who was refusing to leave. Best not to have to explain to his family yet why he'd be carrying a perfectly healthy woman. But he'd have to explain things soon.

Once they had Stella's confession nixed.

Lyla glanced around the room as they put on their coats and headed out. "Please tell me that Travis, Zeke and Greg haven't all been released."

"Travis has. No grounds to hold him, since we still haven't made a concrete connection between him and the missing gunman. Greg's in the interview room, finishing up his statement with Ranger McKinnon, and Zeke's in another room, waiting his turn to be interviewed."

"And Stella?" she asked hesitantly.

"In Saul's office with her lawyer. Unless something drastic happens, Ranger McKinnon will take her into custody when he's finished with Zeke."

That sounded about as unright as anything could sound. Stella was going to be placed under arrest, and so far there was nothing he could do to stop it.

Wyatt paused at the front door, looked out. He half expected Travis to be there, waiting to add some wise-cracking remark that would make Wyatt want to break his face. But no Travis. No sign of a gunman, either. So, Wyatt got her moving to his SUV.

The clouds were iron-gray, and the temperature had dropped. There'd been no time to check the weather, but it looked as if a winter storm was moving in. The way his luck had been running, they'd get a blizzard.

"What else did I miss when I was asleep?" she asked once they were on the road.

A lot. But Wyatt wouldn't tell her about the family debate on how to handle Stella's confession. It hadn't been pretty and had involved a lot of emotion. All of them had agreed to try to have the confession tossed out, but none of them had come up with a reasonable way to make that happen.

Though some unreasonable ways had been bantered about.

Kirby had wanted to hog-tie her.

No need to go through all of that again, so Wyatt stuck to the investigation itself.

"It was rattlesnake venom used to kill Sarah," he explained. "But it's a dead end because it was such a small amount that the killer could have gotten it from dozens of places around the state."

She groaned softly, obviously disappointed about that.

"What about the surveillance footage? Anyone other than Greg and Zeke on it? Or should I say Spenser and Zeke?"

She said Spenser's name as if it were profanity. Wyatt felt the same way. He sure as hell didn't like that the man had waltzed in after all these years and implicated Kirby.

Which was probably the reason Stella had confessed.

"Neither Travis nor Billy popped up on the footage." But Wyatt had to shake his head. "Of course, they could have come in earlier and just waited around."

"Or they could have just hired someone," she added. "Someone whose face wouldn't have stuck out on the security cameras."

Yeah. And that, too, was something that Wyatt had already considered. But it didn't rule out any of their suspects. Even Greg and Zeke. Because one of them could be behind this and still have shown up at the hospital to make himself look as if he'd been set up.

"There was a landline in Sarah's room," Wyatt continued, "and it was off the hook, as if someone had just used it."

"You mean Sarah?"

Wyatt lifted a shoulder and made another check of the mirrors. No one else was on the road. "Her prints are on it."

"That's not proof. The prints could have been planted there by simply taking her hand and putting it on the surface. But if I could take a look at it, I might be able to determine pressure points. If someone was holding her hand on that phone, sometimes the grip pattern is off."

"Giving you access to the evidence might be hard to do." He figured that would get her looking in his direction, and it did.

"I'm officially off the case?"

He nodded. "The governor's assistant called and made

it clear that we weren't to have any part of this. But that doesn't mean we can't continue to investigate on our own. Maybe after you get something to eat, then you can call one of your CSI friends who can in turn contact the lab and make sure they're doing a check for the grip pattern on the phone."

"Of course." He heard the disappointment in her voice. They'd known they would be taken off the case, but it felt like being fired for doing something wrong. Well, he'd done wrong, all right, but it'd been for the right reasons.

To keep Lyla safe.

And if necessary, he'd continue to do wrong.

"I spoke with Sarah's doctor," Wyatt went on, "and he said she had been responding more lately and that he thought she might be coming out of the coma."

"Billy was right," she mumbled.

About that anyway. But since this whole mess with Greg, Zeke and Travis, Wyatt wasn't ready to completely eliminate Billy as a suspect in either his father or his mother's murders.

Lyla stayed quiet a moment, obviously giving that some thought. "Is it possible that Sarah came out of the coma but then pretended to still be in one?"

"It's possible." Wyatt had asked the doctor that, too. And if that's what had indeed happened, then she could have made the calls herself.

But why?

Could Sarah have done that to get her accomplice to come to her room, or had she made the calls because she'd been genuinely afraid for her life? Unfortunately, the answer to that might be buried with her.

Wyatt took the final turn toward the ranch when he heard the sound. A loud popping noise. The steering wheel immediately jolted to the right, followed by a much louder sound as if a helicopter were hovering overhead.

No helicopter though.

"The tire blew out," he told Lyla.

Not the best time for something like this to happen, but at least they were close to the ranch. The white fence surrounding the pasture was just ahead and to his right. Rather than take the time to change the tire himself and risk being out in the open with Lyla, he could just call one of the ranch hands to come and get them.

Lyla grabbed on to the dash. Just in time. Because there was another hard turn of the steering wheel, followed by the grinding noise of his tire rims scraping over the asphalt. He had no choice but to bring the SUV to a stop on the shoulder.

Everything inside Wyatt went still.

What were the odds that he'd have two blowouts within seconds of each other when he hadn't seen any debris on the road?

Slim to none.

"Get down!" he ordered Lyla.

But his warning was already too late. The bullet blasted across the top of the SUV.

LYLA DIDN'T HAVE TIME to react. But Wyatt sure did. He shoved her down on the seat, covering her body with his, and in the same motion, he drew his gun.

Just as another shot slammed into the SUV.

The fear was instant. So was the burst of adrenaline. Followed by the absolute terror that her baby and Wyatt could be harmed. They had to get out of there because the bullets just kept coming.

Despite the panic crawling through her, Wyatt seemed

to stay calm, though every muscle in his body had turned to iron. Still, he grabbed his phone and made a call.

"Get someone out here to the east corner of the ranch," he said to whoever answered. "Someone's firing shots at us, and we're pinned down."

That made the fear even worse, but Lyla tried to concentrate on getting out of this deadly situation.

"Did he shoot out all the tires?" Lyla asked.

"I don't think so. But the front two tires are both flat. I think it was some kind of explosive device."

Mercy. That meant this wasn't just some loosely planned attack on a rural road. The device had likely been set earlier. Maybe even while they were in the marshals' building. Of course, there'd been plenty of opportunity, since they'd been there for hours. It could have happened when she'd fallen asleep, and Lyla cursed herself for that lapse in attention.

"I should have kept watch when we were in town," she mumbled.

"Whoever's behind this would have found a way to make an attack happen," he mumbled right back.

That was no doubt true, but knowing the truth didn't make this situation less dangerous. Why had the killer come after them now and like this? The blood evidence at Rocky Creek had been destroyed, and Stella had confessed to being Sarah's accomplice. Not that she'd actually done it, but why would that matter to the real killer?

Unless there was something else out there that needed to be concealed or destroyed.

Still, that didn't answer her question as to why someone had come after Wyatt and her again.

"The shooter's on the driver's side," Wyatt told her. "Probably in those woods, and he's using a rifle. But I don't think he wants us dead. If he did, he could have set a bigger explosive device on the SUV."

True, and that only caused her heart to race even more. "So, this is a kidnapping attempt?"

"Maybe. Or maybe he only wants you alive."

So he could force her to tamper with evidence. Except, that didn't make sense, since she was officially off the case. Unless this person believed she'd still have access to the evidence.

And she probably could get access.

But not without compromising the entire investigation.

Which might be exactly what the killer wanted to happen. After all, it wasn't just one murder now. With Sarah's death, it was two.

"Hold on," Wyatt told her, and that was the only warning she got before he threw the SUV into gear, caught onto the steering wheel with his left hand and hit the accelerator.

The SUV lurched forward, and despite the two flat tires, somehow Wyatt managed to turn them in the direction of the white fence. It was at least eight feet high. Too high to climb with the bullets flying, but if they could somehow manage to get over it, there were some trees on the other side that they could use for cover.

Maybe.

Unless there was someone waiting for them there.

What they needed was backup, and it was no doubt already on the way thanks to Wyatt's call. Lyla wasn't sure how far they were from the ranch, but she thought it was only a mile or two. However, that was way too much, considering they were in the sights of a shooter.

The muscles in Wyatt's face and arms strained to keep the SUV aimed at the fence, and even though he'd told her to stay down, she had to do something to help. She reached around, gripping the steering wheel with him. It was like pulling at dead weight, but they continued toward the fence.

Wyatt didn't hit the brakes as they got closer. The SUV plowed right through it, sending the wooden planks flying and battering into the vehicle. Finally, he brought them to a stop next to a pair of oaks. All in all, it was a good position, because the SUV would block the shooter's view once they were out the passenger's side door.

"Get behind the tree," he insisted. "But stay low and move fast."

Even though her hands were shaking like crazy, Lyla managed to get the door open, and she practically dove out of the SUV. She landed on her feet behind one of the oaks, and she made room for Wyatt so he could join her.

But he didn't do that.

His phone buzzed, and he hit the answer button. Lyla couldn't hear any of his conversation because of the gunfire, but when he finished the call, Wyatt glanced at her.

"Get on the ground and crawl to that next tree," he ordered.

She did, scrambling to put some more distance between the shooter and her.

Wyatt, however, didn't do the same.

"Come on!" she shouted to him.

But Wyatt only shook his head. He took aim at the shooter from the driver's side window and fired.

"Go with him," Wyatt insisted.

It took Lyla a second to figure out what he meant. Then she heard the sound of a horse's gallop and spotted the ranch hand on a pinto.

"Go!" Wyatt repeated.

Lyla shook her head. "Not without you."

Wyatt's gaze met hers. "Think of the baby."

That was playing dirty, but she couldn't ignore the risk to the baby. Even if the shooter somehow managed to kidnap her, heaven knew what would happen to them. And to Wyatt.

"Go ahead," Wyatt added. "I'll be right behind you."

"Move now!" the ranch hand called out to her.

Lyla couldn't take the time to debate this any longer, so she darted through the trees toward the pinto. The moment she reached them, the ranch hand caught her by the arm and levered her onto the back of the saddle before he got the pinto moving.

Fast.

She tried to get one last glimpse of Wyatt, but the hand immediately maneuvered them into yet another group of trees. Away from the danger.

Away from Wyatt.

And even over the sound of her heartbeat crashing in her ears, Lyla heard the shots slam nonstop into the SUV.

Chapter Thirteen

Wyatt sent another shot in the direction of the gunman, who was obviously trying to kill him. But at least Lyla was out of harm's way.

For now.

The ranch hand, John Busby, had worked on the ranch for years and was someone Wyatt trusted. Busby would get her back to the house and guard her until Wyatt managed to join them. And when Wyatt's phone buzzed again, he hoped it was news that would speed up his doing just that.

"Almost there," Declan greeted him. "Dallas, too. He's coming from the other direction. He didn't want to leave until he made sure the others were locked in and safe."

Wyatt couldn't blame him. Both Caitlyn and Joelle were pregnant, too, and plus, Slade's and Clayton's infant sons were there. That was a lot of people who had to be protected on the ranch. Normally, the doors wouldn't be locked, but they would be until the danger had passed.

The second that Wyatt pushed the end-call button, he heard the sirens. Declan, no doubt. And his brother's loud approach got the results Wyatt needed.

The gunman stopped firing.

Wyatt immediately grabbed his phone and called Dallas. "The shooter's getting away. Get someone to that old ranch road on the west. That's probably his escape route."

"Will do," Dallas assured him. "Now get back to the main house. Lyla's worried about you."

That worry had to be pretty extreme for Dallas to even mention it, so the moment Declan pulled to a stop on the road, Wyatt kept low but made his way to the truck. Declan didn't waste any time getting them out of there.

"You okay?" Declan asked.

Wyatt nodded, but he was far from okay. "How was Busby so close to us when the shooting started?"

"He was out riding fence, and I had Cutter call him."

So, they'd gotten lucky. Wyatt hated that it'd taken something as random as luck to keep Lyla and the baby from being hurt. Or worse.

"I think someone was trying to kidnap Lyla," Wyatt told his brother.

Declan cursed, pushed the accelerator even harder and sped toward the ranch. Busby was on the porch, his rifle ready and aimed, and Wyatt spotted Lyla in the window. Despite Busby yelling for her to stay inside, she threw open the front door, barreled down the steps and landed right in Wyatt's arms.

It didn't feel like a hug from a fake wife. Neither did the kiss she planted on his mouth. Or the tears that were in her eyes. Those were caused by genuine worry and fear. Of course, it didn't mean her reaction was more than that. And Wyatt didn't want it to be. However, it gave him some reassurance, too, to have her in his arms.

"You weren't hurt?" she asked, her voice trembling.

"No." And Wyatt got her moving back toward the door, because he didn't want her out in the open with the rifleman on the loose. He looked at Busby. "Come in and stand guard. I want someone else watching the back of the house."

Busby nodded, took out his phone and followed them in.

"I'll help Dallas look for this guy," Declan offered. "But everybody should stay inside with the doors locked."

Wyatt did exactly that, and he set the security system once he had Lyla and Busby in the foyer. He didn't arm the security just for the house but for the sensors that were scattered over the property. It didn't mean someone couldn't get through, but at least they'd have a warning if that happened.

"Busby said no one else is here," Lyla told him. "They're all at Dallas and Joelle's house."

"I brought her here because it was closer," Busby explained.

A wise decision.

"Thanks for getting Lyla out of there," he told the man.

Busby just nodded. "You think the shooter's coming back for another round?"

"I think we're okay for now." But it was a lie. Wyatt had no idea what would happen other than he would do whatever it took to keep Lyla safe.

"Grab a chair from the den if you want," Wyatt offered the man. "You might be here a while. And once the other ranch hand's here to guard the back, let him in, but then make sure the security system is reset."

"Will do. I'll give a yell if I see or hear anything."

And Wyatt would do the same. Once he had Lyla settled.

But he debated where to take her. There were too many windows in the kitchen and the den.

In most rooms, actually.

Plus, she was shaking all over now and likely ready to crash. But he still needed to be where he could monitor the security sensors and camera. So, he led her toward the ranch's main office on the side of the house. Too bad he couldn't offer her some whiskey to settle her nerves, because she was going to need something.

The room was much larger than his own office, and while it wouldn't be as comfortable as one of the bedrooms, it'd have to do. Keeping an eye on her, Wyatt booted up the laptop on the desk that Kirby had used daily before he got sick. These days, it fell mainly to Wyatt and his brothers.

"People keep shooting at us," Lyla said under her breath.

Wyatt considered a bullet-magnet joke, but the fear was still too fresh and too raw for that. He had her sit on the leather sofa, and even though it wouldn't do much in the nerve-steadying department, he handed her a bottle of water.

"You need to see a doctor?" he asked, praying that she didn't. It might not be safe to get a doctor out here with a gunman on the loose. Still, he'd make it happen if she needed medical attention.

But she didn't answer. Lyla took the plastic bottle of water as if it were fragile and might crack in her hand, and she set it aside on the table. With that same level of fragility, she stood and buried her face against his shoulder.

"We can't keep going through this." Her breath broke, and Wyatt braced himself for the tears to start. But there were no tears in her eyes when she pulled back and met his gaze.

"I want to get this bastard," she said. "I want to stop him before he hurts us."

Wyatt wanted the same, with another demand tacked on to hers. He wanted to make this jerk pay for putting Lyla through another ordeal.

She eased back even farther, looking a little stronger now, and tipped her head to the laptop. "We need to watch to make sure the gunman doesn't try to get on the ranch."

"If anyone comes across the fence or the road, it'll trigger a sensor that'll give us a warning beep." But just in case the shooter figured out some way to jam that specific sensor, Wyatt turned the laptop in the direction of the sofa. The security system had cameras so even if they lost the warning sensor, they should still be able to see what was going on. He had Lyla sit again so she could watch.

But she didn't sit by herself.

She caught onto his hand and pulled him down beside her.

"I can't imagine going through this alone," she whispered.

He heard every ounce of raw emotion in that. Saw it in her eyes, too. And silently cursing the gunman and the person who'd hired him, Wyatt put his arm around her and drew her closer.

Lyla looked up at him. "This is a mistake. I'm sure of it."

Wyatt had to shake his head because he wasn't sure what she meant.

Until she kissed him.

But she didn't just *kiss* him. She coiled her arms around him, put her mouth on his and kissed him the right way. Well, the right way if this had been a real make-out session and not just some reaction to the shooting. Everything else about it was wrong, especially the timing.

"You could cost me everything," she said with her mouth against his.

She was talking about the baby now, something Wyatt wasn't sure they should discuss. Not with too many other things unsettled. But the one thing that was settled was this blasted attraction between them.

It was getting stronger with each passing second.

Of course, that kiss sure as heck hadn't helped.

Neither would what he was about to do. He was about to take one wrong kiss and turn it into an even bigger one. One that he was certain they'd regret, but even knowing that didn't stop him.

Cursing himself and cursing her, Wyatt latched on to the back of her hair, not gently, either, and he hauled her even closer until they were tangled against each other. The kiss continued. Raging like the fire building inside him. Man, he wanted her.

And he did something about that.

He pulled her onto his lap so he could kiss her neck. And so he could kiss lower, too. He was still too rough and tried to slow down. Tried to take things easier. But Lyla clearly wanted no part of easier, because she pulled him right back to her when he tried to ease away.

She was wearing a stretchy sweater top, and with one tug he shoved it up and had access to the tops of her breasts. He kissed her there. First one, then the other. And his own body reacted to the breathy little moan of pleasure she made deep in her throat.

So, Wyatt ignored the big warning in his head and pretty much gave in to what a different part of him was demanding. Of course, that part often came up with stupid demands, but he'd already crossed so many lines with Lyla that it didn't take much to keep crossing more.

He shoved down her bra, and her breasts spilled into his hands. Oh, man. She was perfect.

And he was toast.

He didn't stop. Wyatt kept touching her. Kept kissing her. Until the ache inside was well past the point of no return.

"I can't catch my breath," she said, and went after his mouth again.

Great. She was acting just as reckless as he was, and Wyatt had counted on her to stop this.

It had to stop.

But it took him several moments to remember why exactly that had to be. And the reason was his wife, Ann. Except, Lyla was his wife now.

In name only.

Of course, they were blowing that big-time. If these kisses and touches kept up, this marriage would be consummated the old-fashioned way. With a great round of sex.

And he was sure it would be great.

With this much fire and energy between them, there was no chance it would be bad, which meant once they'd finished this mistake, he would almost certainly want to make another one with her.

Lyla stopped so she could drag in some air, and when she came back with one of those deep, mind-blowing kisses, she turned, easing back onto the sofa and pulling him down with her.

Or, rather, on top of her.

Probably the worst place for him to be, but Wyatt went there anyway until he knew the next step would involve clothing removal.

And it would have if not for the buzzing sound.

Because he had only one thing on his mind—sex with Lyla—it took him a moment to realize it was a phone.

Hell. This could be critical. There was a gunman on the loose near the ranch, and Wyatt had gotten so caught up with Lyla that he'd forgotten everything that he sure as heck should be remembering.

"Hold that thought," he told Lyla, moving her hand from his zipper. Though he should have been telling her to forget all about it. Not that he could do that, but maybe she'd see this from a different angle.

The right one.

He got up. Not easily. He could barely stand, because he was hard as stone. And he looked at the name on the phone screen. Not one of his brothers, thank God, with bad news about the shooter.

It was Billy.

Of course, this could be bad news of a different kind. Lately, no one had been calling him just to chat, and he figured that wasn't happening now.

"I'm sorry," Billy said the moment Wyatt answered.

Wyatt groaned. An apology wasn't a good start to a conversation. "Sorry for what?" And he was certain he wasn't going to like this answer.

"I know why someone just tried to kill you, Wyatt. And it's all my fault."

EVEN THOUGH WYATT didn't have the call on speaker, Lyla could hear what Billy said, and she immediately got to her feet and fixed her clothes. Obviously, the kissing session was finished.

Or at least delayed.

Because it was clear that Billy had something important to tell them.

Lyla motioned for Wyatt to put the call on speaker, and he did, just as Billy's voice poured through the room.

"I wanted to find out who killed my mother," Billy said. "So, I lied. I made some calls and put out the word that she'd kept something from the night my father died. Something she gave me so that it could be analyzed."

"What are you talking about?" Wyatt asked, taking the question right out of Lyla's mouth.

"I lied," he repeated, but that didn't explain anything. "I told some people that I found the tape that my mother had mentioned. I said it was scratchy, very poor quality, but it was a recorded conversation between my mother and the person who helped her kill my father."

Oh, mercy. Lyla's heart started racing. "You said you gave it to me to be analyzed, didn't you?"

"Yes. You were the only person I could think of, because you work with evidence like that and crime scenes. And I told the people I called that I didn't want the Rangers to know the results yet just in case the evidence pointed to someone I wanted to protect. Like one of the kids from Rocky Creek."

Wyatt started cursing. Lyla wanted to do the same, but she couldn't muster the breath.

"Who did you tell, Billy?" Wyatt snapped.

"All of them." He hesitated, mumbled something that she didn't catch. "Kirby, Stella, Zeke, Greg and Travis. I called them and told them one by one. Well, except for Stella, and I told Kirby to tell her, because she didn't answer her phone."

Now Lyla cursed. Billy had put her directly in the path of a kidnapper, at best.

A killer at worst.

Because the accomplice would no doubt do anything

to keep her from detecting his or her voice in what would essentially be a murder confession.

"I thought the person would give us some warning so we could trap him," Billy quickly added. "Or I thought maybe he'd try to work out some kind of deal to get back the tape. I didn't think he'd try to shoot you."

"Well, you thought wrong." Wyatt's voice was a low, dangerous growl, and Lyla thought if he could reach through the phone and grab Billy, he would. That was what she wanted to do.

"I know, and I'm sorry. So sorry. I'm going to try to fix this."

"No—" Wyatt practically shouted, but he was already too late. Billy had ended the call. "He'll get himself killed."

Or get someone else killed—like Wyatt or her. Either way, he had to be stopped.

Wyatt called Declan, and while Lyla paced, he filled his brother in on what Billy had done.

"I'll see what I can do to stop him," Declan promised. "But in the meantime, I've got more bad news. We didn't catch the gunman. I saw him get away. I'm on my way back to the marshals' office now to see what I can do about talking Stella out of this stupid confession."

"I'll come with you."

"No, you won't. Not after what just happened to Lyla. It's not a good idea for you two to be out and about."

Wyatt looked at her, and she saw the debate in his eyes. A very short one. "You're right. But call me the second you find out anything."

He clicked the end-call button but stared at the phone as if he was trying to will someone to call with good news. Lyla wanted that, too. Desperately.

"How could Billy have been so stupid?" she mumbled.

"Desperate people do stupid things." And Wyatt looked at her, probably because Wyatt and she had just gone in a stupid direction with the kissing session.

Except it hadn't felt stupid.

It'd felt right. And comforting. And somehow perfect, even when it was far from it.

"So, what do we do now?" she asked, even though she already knew. There was nothing they could do.

"I can't take you out of this house," he said. A reminder she didn't need. "Declan and the others will find a way to fix this."

She figured that was possibly another lie and almost certainly for her benefit. Maybe it was the renewed fear from Billy's call. Or from the realization that she could do absolutely nothing to stop what he'd already set into motion, that they could only wait and see what would happen.

Heck, maybe it was just hormones.

But despite everything they'd just learned, despite another layer of danger, her body was still humming, not for news, but for Wyatt.

And that made her one sick puppy.

She forced herself to take a deep breath to try to clear her head. It didn't work. But she did manage to put a few steps between Wyatt and herself when she went to the other end of the desk. Distance might help.

Or not.

Lyla groaned because she wasn't sure anything would help at this point.

He looked at her, ducking down so that he forced eye contact. One glimpse at her, and he blinked. "Oh. You really held that thought."

Lyla knew exactly what he meant. He was talking about that scalding-hot making out that'd been going on before Billy's call. She'd not only held it. Lyla was still feeling it.

He lifted his shoulder, but there was nothing casual about the gesture. She could feel the intensity coming off him. "We have time to kill." Then he shook his head. "Except you and I both know this isn't about killing time."

Yes, they did. It was about this attraction that was begging to be satisfied.

She was absolutely positive that she shouldn't consider doing this, but Wyatt and she hadn't acted reasonably since they'd first laid eyes on each other. She went to him, ready to kiss him again, but he beat her to it.

Wyatt slid his hand around her, hauled her closer and brought his mouth to hers.

Even though he'd kissed her only moments earlier, this was different. The heat was there. That was a given. It was always there. Along with the need clawing away inside her. She'd given up trying to figure out why she was so attracted to him. Why she let her need for him override common sense, her past.

Override everything.

And Lyla let herself melt against him.

The kiss didn't stay on her mouth. He dropped that heat to her neck. And it didn't stay simple, either. Everything felt as if it were spinning out of control, and the only thing Lyla could do was hold on to Wyatt and let him take her.

"You know we shouldn't be doing this," he said a split second before his hand went underneath her top. He touched her breasts, causing the fire to roar even hotter.

His gaze met hers, maybe to give her a moment to back away again from this. But they were past the point of no return, and Lyla maneuvered him not away from her, but back toward the sofa. Along the way, Wyatt had the good sense to lock the door. Something she hadn't even considered. Again, this wasn't a situation involving reason or logic.

Still kissing, still touching, they landed on the sofa.

Lyla felt the cool leather surface against her bare skin and realized that Wyatt had already shoved up her sweater. But he didn't stop there. He pulled it off, dropped it to the floor and kissed her breasts through her bra.

The heat soared.

And the bra didn't last long, either. He quickly rid her of that and went after the zipper on her jeans. Lyla tried to help him, but she got caught in some kissing and touching of her own. The man tasted as good as he looked. Not just his mouth, either, but his neck, and she figured the rest of him would be equally nice to sample.

Too bad they were already past the foreplay, the sampling stage. Probably because they'd been skirting around this since they'd first met. Not love at first sight. But definitely lust.

Everything was frantic now. The need pushing them to finish this, and Lyla did her own share of pushing them to that finish. Somehow, even though she was dealing with the effects of his clever mouth on her breasts, she managed to get his shirt unbuttoned. He was already so many steps ahead of her, and she wanted to catch up.

She wanted to seduce him as much as he was seducing her.

But she was doomed to fail. Obviously, Wyatt was a lot better at this than she was, and before Lyla managed to locate his zipper, he was already shimmying her shoes and jeans off her.

"You have on too many clothes," she said through her rough breathing.

She did something about that. She shoved his shirt off him and then his jeans. Stripped off his boxers, too. And Lyla got one of those *wow* moments. She'd known that Wyatt looked amazing, of course. Everything about him was past the hot stage, but she realized he was hers.

Well, for this moment anyway.

He couldn't be more than that, but for now, this was enough. It had to be.

"What?" he asked, looking down at her.

Since he seemed to be in tune to everything happening in her body, he'd probably felt the hesitation. But it wasn't a hesitation at all. "I'm just admiring the view."

The corner of his mouth lifted with a smile that only heightened the heat, and his gaze skimmed along her body. All of it. "Yeah, my view's pretty damn good, too."

That just about stole the rest of her breath. As did his next kiss. It wasn't a no-nonsense kind of kiss but one that signaled to her body that this was happening *now*.

He adjusted their positions again, catching onto the back of her knee and anchoring her leg against the outside of his hip. There wasn't much room to maneuver on the sofa, but Lyla forgot all about that when he pushed inside her.

The pleasure exploded in her head.

And through the rest of her.

She gasped. Definitely not in pain. From the pure pleasure. But Wyatt's gaze met hers again. Obviously checking. She assured him that all was perfect by pulling him down to her for a deep kiss.

Everything was deep, too. The way he moved inside her. The grip he had on her leg and the back of her neck.

Lyla wanted it to last, but she knew that wasn't possible. Something burning this hot couldn't last.

She felt the climax ripple through her and tried to hang on to every moment, every sensation. But the pleasure took over, consuming her until there was only one thought, just one word, repeating in her head.

Wyatt. Wyatt. Wyatt.

Chapter Fourteen

Wyatt felt the jolt go through his body. The release that made him mindless, numb and satisfied all at the same time. It was a good way to finish what that kissing session had started.

He buried his face against Lyla's neck. Drew in her scent. And let that and the other sensations slide through him. The feel of her bare skin against his. The soft rhythm of her breath.

Those little aftershocks from her climax that kept gripping on to him.

Yeah, that was a good sensation, all right, and a nudge to his body that it would be ready to take her again soon.

But *soon* was going to have to wait.

He would have preferred to stay there with her arms around him, still deep inside her, but with everything going on, it wasn't a good idea to lie around naked.

Of course, it hadn't been a good idea to have sex with Lyla, either, but that hadn't stopped him. Before he could talk himself out of it, he groaned and started to move off her.

But Lyla slid her leg over his and held him in place. Not that he fought her hard. He was a more than willing captive.

"What, regrets already?" she asked. "I thought it'd

take at least five minutes or so before the panic started to set in."

"Not panic." Because her mouth was so close and she smelled like every good thing rolled into one, he brushed a kiss on her lips.

"But regret," she clarified.

"Some." He hadn't meant to admit that and spoil the moment, but Lyla seemed to be clued in to what was going on his head. "But probably not nearly enough. For what it's worth, I'm sorry that I just complicated the hell out of this."

She lifted her shoulder. "I was an equal participant in the complication." She held the stare a moment longer, and he saw the realization go through her eyes.

Not regret, exactly.

But she had to be mentally playing this out. It would affect everything they did in the future.

Everything.

Now she groaned.

And that was Wyatt's cue to get up and start dressing.

"I didn't even ask you if it was okay for you to have sex," he said, aiming a glance at her stomach.

"Probably because it was hard to ask anything with those French kisses."

He couldn't help it. Wyatt smiled, leaned down and gave her another kiss. "You're being, well, rational about this."

And he wasn't. Especially when his gaze landed on her butt-naked body. Mercy, he wanted her all over again, and he'd just had her. What the heck was wrong with him?

"On the outside I'm being rational," Lyla started. "Inside…"

Wyatt put on his boxers, stared at her, waiting for her

to finish. But she didn't. "You're panicking?" he finished for her.

But she shook her head. "Not exactly. I think I'm feeling panicky because I'm not panicking. That doesn't make sense, I know."

Yeah, it did. Too much about this had felt much better than it should have, considering they both had a baggage-filled past. And then there was the baby.

The ultimate complication.

And yet, it was perfect. Of course, Lyla might dispute that when they sat down to work out custody. Sooner or later, they'd have to do just that.

However, before he could say anything about custody or what'd just happened, his phone buzzed. He had to rifle through the heap of clothes on the floor and locate his jeans and his phone in the pocket. But his heart practically skipped a beat when he saw the name on the screen.

Kirby.

He showed the screen to Lyla, and she immediately got up and started dressing. Like him, she was no doubt bracing herself for more bad news.

"Anything wrong?" Wyatt said the moment he answered, and he put the call on speaker.

"Not with me, but I heard from Declan about the shooting and what Billy did. You and Lyla okay?"

"Yeah." Better than okay. And worse. But Wyatt was going to have to deal with the *worse* later, too. "Billy said he called you and all the other people he considers suspects."

"He did, and it was a stupid thing to do. He could have gotten Lyla and you killed."

Wyatt couldn't argue with that. "I don't think it'll make the killer come after Stella or you. If the killer continues to believe Billy's lie about that tape, then Lyla will remain the target. But take some precautions just in case I'm wrong. Maybe keep Declan or one of the others with you."

"Yes." And that was all Kirby said for several long moments. "Stella's getting out of lockup. For now, I've had her confession suppressed."

Well, that was good news, especially since he hadn't picked up on anything good from Kirby's gloom-and-doom tone. "How'd you manage that?"

"By riling her to the core, that's how. I convinced Saul that she's having some mental issues because of everything going on."

Oh, mercy. Yes, that would have riled her. "But she's coming home?"

"She is. Maybe soon she'll quit glaring and start speaking to me again."

Wyatt actually felt sorry for Kirby, because he knew how much his foster father cared for Stella. But Kirby also cared enough not to see her go to jail for something that she hadn't done.

"Anyway, we'll be on our way back soon," Kirby continued. "Me, Stella and Declan. Dallas, too. He's turned over the hunt for your attacker to the Rangers."

"Smart idea. There's been enough danger for this family." Too bad that danger was just going to continue until they caught the person behind this.

Kirby didn't answer, and that put a tight grip on Wyatt's stomach. "Is something wrong?" Wyatt asked. "Something other than the obvious, I mean?"

"We need to have a family meeting." And with that, Kirby paused a long time. "Call the rest of your brothers and have them come to the main house so they'll be with Lyla and you. I'll bring Billy with me. I've put the ranch hands on alert. All of them are armed and ready in case something goes wrong. I even asked some of them to patrol the fence and road."

That didn't help ease the knot forming in his stomach. "I don't think that's wise to bring Billy here."

"Declan's already disarmed him, and we'll all keep an eye on him."

That still didn't help, since Billy had nearly gotten them killed. "What's this meeting all about?" Wyatt came out and asked.

"It's time," Kirby said, pulling in a weary-sounding breath. "All of you need to know the truth about Jonah Webb's murder."

LYLA STOPPED in the doorway of the family room and studied the crowd that'd gathered. The tension was so thick she could feel it, and it didn't seem to improve when some of Wyatt's family looked at her. Probably because they thought she didn't belong there.

Or maybe it was just because she seemed to be turning into a bullet magnet like Wyatt.

Caitlyn and Joelle offered thin smiles, but the others just couldn't muster it.

Even Stella. Kirby had been right about her glaring, because she was doing it now.

So, maybe this didn't have anything to do with her, but with the possible bad news that was hanging like a dark cloud over the room.

"I can wait upstairs while you have the meeting," Lyla whispered to Wyatt. Not the first offer she'd made. In fact, she'd made several of them shortly after Kirby had called for this family meeting. Emphasis on *family,* and she was pretty sure a fake wife didn't count.

"You should be here," Kirby said, probably because he saw the hesitancy all over her face. "You're right smack-dab in the middle of this mess now, and you should hear what has to be said."

"The baby's in the middle of it, too," Wyatt volunteered. "Yeah, Lyla's pregnant, and it's my baby."

Caitlyn, his brother's pregnant wife, made an *I told you so* sound.

"I don't want her or the baby involved in anything else that's dangerous," Wyatt added.

He probably hadn't meant to make her feel like a gestational carrier. In fact, she was sure he hadn't meant it. But the truth was—it was his baby, not hers. And soon his family would know that, too.

Then how would they react?

Of course, they weren't her biggest worries when it came to this baby. It was Wyatt himself. And now that she'd slept with him, it was going to make their entire situation that much harder.

She heard someone unlocking the front door, and Wyatt eased her behind him. But not before she got a glimpse of the men who came in. Declan and Harlan. Busby, the ranch hand who'd rescued her in the pasture, and he had a firm grip on Billy's arm. He led Billy into the family room.

"Billy's not armed," Declan told everyone. He closed the door, locked it and rearmed the security system.

Billy didn't look exactly happy about being frisked and locked in with a group of people who were riled at him, but Lyla was glad Declan had done it, since Billy might be able to help solve this mess of a puzzle. She was equally glad that Wyatt and all his brothers were wearing their weapons just in case Billy was there to do more than help.

"So, what's this meeting about?" Billy asked.

Lyla wanted to know the same thing. She'd heard what

Kirby had told Wyatt. That they all needed to know the truth about Webb's murder, and that could mean some-one in the room was about to make a confession.

Kirby stood. Not easily. Clearly, he was still weak, and he held on to the back of the chair for support. That softened Stella's glare a little, but she didn't get up from the reading chair on the far side of the room. She stayed seated, her gaze fixed on Kirby.

"Since Webb's body was found," Kirby said, "we've all been trying to protect each other. None of you wants Stella and me to go to jail, and we feel the same about you." He looked around the room the way a loving fa-ther would.

Until his gaze landed on Billy, that is.

"It's time for the truth," Kirby said to him. "Did you help kill your daddy?"

Billy didn't jump to respond to that, but for several seconds his mouth flattened into a line. "No. And if that's why you brought me here, to try to pin his murder on me, then I'm leaving." He turned to walk out.

"It's not why I asked you here," Kirby insisted. "I just need to get to the truth. I've nearly lost my boys and their wives. Wyatt nearly lost his wife and baby today. This can't go on."

Billy stopped and eased back around. "I didn't help my mother kill him," he finally answered.

Kirby nodded—though it was hard to tell if he be-lieved him—and he looked at Stella. "I won't ask if you did it, because you'd just lie to cover for the rest of us. But you might not need to cover for us. We have to get this out in the open so we can deal with it."

Stella swallowed hard. Nodded. "I didn't help with the murder, but if any one of us is going to jail for it, it'll be me."

"Admirable," Kirby mumbled. "But not very smart. By giving that false confession, it allows the real killer to hide behind it. And the hiding has to end tonight."

It should end with the truth, but Lyla wasn't certain they were anywhere near that point yet. Still, she had some questions that might clear up some things.

"I saw the blood spatter on the wall of your former quarters before the bomb destroyed it," she said to Stella. "There wasn't a lot of blood, but it was something you would have noticed."

Stella gave a weary sigh. "The attack probably did happen there. Or at least I think it could have started there anyway. But I'd moved out of that room earlier in the day because a water pipe had burst and flooded the floor and damaged part of the wall."

Lyla looked at Billy, who confirmed that with a nod. "There was a leak, and Mom told me that Stella had moved rooms." He paused. "But I didn't know if the leak was just an excuse so that no one would see the blood."

"It wasn't an excuse," Stella insisted. "Not on my part anyway. I'd been in the clinic with Declan after Webb had beaten him, so I have no idea what went on in my room. I just know when I tried to get back in, the door was padlocked and my stuff was in the hall."

"And you didn't get suspicious?" Lyla pressed.

"Of course I did. Just hours earlier Webb had beaten my son within an inch of his life. And he'd slapped me when I confronted him about it."

Declan went to his mother, slipped his arm around her shoulders. "It's okay," he murmured to her.

Stella's eyes were filled with tears when she looked at Lyla. "I hoped someone had murdered Webb, and I didn't want to ask questions."

"Because you thought one of us had done it," Declan finished for her. He shook his head. "I didn't kill Webb."

"I didn't, either." Harlan spoke up.

Clayton echoed the same. Then Dallas. Slade, too. Joelle and Caitlyn, who'd lived at Rocky Creek at the time of the murders, added their "I didn't" responses.

"I didn't kill him," Wyatt added, "but I'm not sorry he's dead."

And all eyes turned to Kirby.

Lyla hadn't realized she'd been holding her breath until her lungs started to ache, and she forced herself to breathe. Some of the others in the room seemed to have the same trouble—all of them waiting for Kirby to respond.

"I'll confess to the murder," Kirby finally said.

"No, you won't!" Wyatt snapped, but his wasn't the only voice in the room. All his brothers and their wives protested, as well.

"I won't let you sacrifice yourself," Stella insisted. The glare and anger were completely gone from her expression, and she left Declan to go to Kirby's side.

Kirby gave her a flat look. "You were willing to make a false confession for the family."

"Did you kill Webb?" Wyatt demanded. His hands were on his hips now, and his jaw muscles were stirring.

Lyla held her breath again. It seemed everyone in the room did.

Kirby shook his head. "I would have killed him, though, if I could have found him. I went looking for him after I saw what he'd done to Declan, and the bruise on Stella's face. But Webb wasn't anywhere around, and Sarah said she didn't know where he was."

Lyla could practically feel the relief go through every one of them.

"But none of this matters," Kirby continued. "I'm not letting any of you go to jail for killing that piece of scum."

"And you're not going to jail, either." Wyatt's gaze swept around the room. "There's another way. One that'll put the right person behind bars. Yeah, whoever it was did us all a favor by killing Webb, but he's not doing us any favors now. He's trying to kidnap Lyla to force her to falsify evidence."

"Evidence that I faked," Billy mumbled.

"We can use it," Wyatt said. "Because the killer doesn't know it's fake. We can use it to trap him."

"I'm listening," Kirby said. Everyone was. Including Lyla. She was willing to try anything that would get Wyatt, his family and the baby out of harm's way.

"We can leak that we have the tape that Sarah gave Billy. The one with the killer's voice," Wyatt continued. "We can say it's going to a specific crime lab for expedited analysis. And we can make sure the lab is well guarded. When the killer or his henchman shows up, we can arrest him and force a confession."

"Using the fake tape worked before," Billy added. "Well, it worked in the wrong way, because it sent the killer after Lyla, but this time we can leave Lyla completely out of it."

"I have the contacts to leak this," Lyla argued. "I can make it sound official so the killer believes that the recording truly exists and will be tested for voice identification."

Wyatt was shaking his head before she even finished. "You're not getting in the middle of this."

"I don't have to. The killer just has to think that I'm involved. We could arrange for a CSI vehicle to come out here under the guise of picking up the tape."

Wyatt stared at her, obviously processing that, and he finally nodded. "Okay to the CSI pickup and to you making the call to get things started, but no to any involvement on your part after that. We could use the marshals' official communication channels to set up the leak. Maybe the sheriff could even be the one to let it slip."

"I can work on that," Declan volunteered. "I can have Sheriff Geary put in a request for extra security to accompany the tape to a lab, and that's what we can leak."

"What if we say we're transporting the recording to the lab in San Antonio?" Lyla asked. "And that Wyatt and I will be going with the CSIs in the evidence van so we can get the results as soon as they're done?"

"That's good," Declan said. "And I won't create the leak until the van is out here. That way, it won't get attacked en route, and the killer won't have time to plant someone on the vehicle."

A good precaution for the CSIs. But it wouldn't end the danger for Wyatt's brothers and the sheriff. Lyla realized a second too late where this conversation was about to head.

"No," Declan said before Wyatt could speak. "You should stay here with Lyla." His gaze dropped to her stomach. "She's been through enough." He tipped his head to Dallas and Harlan. "You should stay with Caitlyn and Joelle, too."

Slade stood. "I'll do protection detail." His wife, Maya, didn't look pleased about that, but she didn't try to stop him. Maybe she understood this was a risk that the entire family had to take.

"And I'll join you," Declan insisted.

They all looked around as if waiting for someone to bring up a major hitch in this impromptu plan. When no one did, Kirby continued. "Dallas and Harlan should take everyone else to Dallas's house. Everyone except Lyla and Wyatt. That way, they could appear to get into the CSI van, just in case someone has the ranch under long-range surveillance. As backup to the security system, Stella and I can stay here with them and keep watch out the back of the house from my room. They can keep watch out the front."

"That means the CSI van and the route to San Antonio has to be heavily guarded," Wyatt insisted. "And when the van arrives, it can park right next to the house so that no one can tell who's getting inside it."

Again, no one objected, though Stella did look at all of them. "Everyone has to be careful."

And with that, they got moving. Dallas and Harlan started ushering family out. Lyla took out her own phone. She called the lab in San Antonio and requested a pickup for evidence surrendered to her in the Webb murder case.

That would get them moving fast, especially since she'd been removed from the case.

"Bring some security with you," she added, "because it's possible someone might not want this evidence to reach the lab."

Of course, there'd be no such danger until the leak happened, and Declan wouldn't create that until the van had actually arrived.

Everything inside her felt like a huge, tight knot. She'd just made Wyatt and herself bait. His brothers, too. So, this had to work.

But Lyla did think of a potential problem.

A leak of a different kind so that the killer could learn what they were actually going to do.

"Could the killer have hired someone to blend in with the ranch hands or someone else on the grounds?" she asked Wyatt.

"Normally, yes. We don't usually have this high of security, but everyone hired within the past three months was given paid time off. Like the new horse trainer Dallas had hired and the maid who was sweeping the porch when I first brought you here."

Yes, she remembered. It was a good precaution to keep them away just in case they had some kind of connection to the killer. Of course, that didn't mean the killer hadn't managed to somehow get to a trusted employee. But Lyla wasn't going to borrow trouble.

Especially since they had enough of it already.

"What now?" she asked Wyatt.

He pulled her to him, brushed a kiss on her forehead. "We wait."

Chapter Fifteen

Wyatt watched the feed from the security cameras on his laptop and tried not to let Lyla see the hurricane of emotions going on inside him. Declan and Slade were out there, headed toward San Antonio in a CSI van. Maybe on the verge of being ambushed, if this plan turned deadly.

Still, having no plan at all could end up getting them killed, too.

That was why both Dallas and another of the ranch hands were monitoring the feed from the security cameras. Wyatt wasn't only watching the feed, he was also keeping an eye on the front windows in case someone managed to sneak on the ranch. Kirby and Stella were doing the same through the window that faced the backyard.

If something moved out there, they needed to be able to respond immediately. Ditto for anything that could happen to the CSI van. The sheriff and his deputies were following it. Not too closely, though. Because they wanted the killer to make his move.

Which made Slade and Declan bait.

That caused him to feel the rapid pump of his heart.

"You should rest," Lyla suggested again.

But she wasn't taking her own advice. Yes, she was

on the bed while he was at his desk in the corner. And she actually had her head on the pillow, but she'd yet to shut her eyes. Probably wouldn't, either. Because Wyatt figured she had the same worries and doubts he did.

He could have used a drink to steady his nerves but didn't want a cloudy head just in case he had to hurry out to help his brothers. Of course, that would only happen if everything else failed.

Because he couldn't leave Lyla alone.

His other brothers were already tucked away at Dallas's place, and some of the ranch hands were there standing guard. The others were watching the main house and pastures. There was a lot of ground to cover, but Wyatt kept reminding himself that the security system would alert them if anyone tripped any of the sensors. The killer couldn't get onto the ranch without them knowing.

And besides, the highest probability was that the killer would go after that van. To steal the evidence that didn't exist.

Billy had left to go to the sheriff's office in town so he could monitor things from there with the night deputy. It wasn't ideal, especially since Wyatt wasn't sure he could completely trust Billy, but that was the reason he hadn't wanted him to stay at the ranch. There was enough to stretch his attention without adding Billy to the mix.

Outside, the winter wind was slapping at the windows. No snow, but it felt as if it were on the way. Hopefully that didn't mean there'd be ice on the roads. Declan and Slade had enough on their plates without having to deal with Mother Nature.

Wyatt glanced at his phone. No calls yet. Not that he'd expected any. It was too soon to hear from Declan, but *soon* couldn't come soon enough.

"I think Kirby and Stella have resolved their differences," Lyla said. Probably an attempt to make small talk since he no doubt looked ready to come unraveled.

"Yeah. They're in love." Which meant settling differences was a given. He looked at Lyla, at the way she had her hand on her stomach over the baby. "Sometimes, settling differences has to happen even when there isn't love."

That probably wasn't a good thing to toss out there like that, but it was better than small talk. And it was something Lyla and he wouldn't be able to avoid much longer.

Her forehead bunched up, and she eased to a sitting position. "You'll challenge me for custody."

It wasn't a question. And he didn't want to answer it anyway. They needed to discuss this, not start a raging argument.

Since he'd still be able to hear the security system from the bed and glance out the window, Wyatt went closer and sat next to her. She was fully clothed in her jeans and sweater. Barefoot, though. And maybe it was her bare feet that reminded him of the rest of her that'd been bare.

Who was he kidding?

He didn't need to see her feet to think of that. Sex with Lyla seemed to be permanently on his mind now, and it didn't help that he'd had her only hours earlier.

Wyatt leaned in. Kissed her. And because he liked that little purring sound she made, he kissed her again.

"When you look at me," she asked, "do you think of your late wife?"

"No." He only saw Lyla here, and that created a new flurry of guilt inside him. He'd loved Ann for so long. For years. And he still loved her. However, he could feel a tug in his heart telling him it was time to let go.

But he couldn't.

Letting go hurt too much.

Lyla took his hand, put it on her belly. "What about the baby? Does that make you think of Ann?"

Not nearly enough. In fact, he was having a hard time wrapping his mind around anything but Lyla and this child. Still, Wyatt shook his head. Best not to share that with Lyla.

"The baby's like a gift from Ann," Lyla continued. "A gift for both of us. We'll both get the child we always wanted."

He knew where this was going—back to the subject of their wanting this child so much that they'd end up fighting for custody.

"We can stay married," Wyatt suggested, cutting her off at the pass while he continued to glance at the window and the security screen. "Raise this child together."

She stared at him. What she didn't do was jump to take him up on that offer.

"Earlier, before Billy called, you said you were about to tell me what you felt on the *inside*," he reminded her. Maybe that would get her to consider his offer.

More staring. "I'm falling in love with you." And with that bolt from the blue delivered, she got up and moved away from him. She didn't look at him. Lyla kept her back to him. "I don't want to feel it. You don't want me to feel it, either. But I can't seem to stop it."

Well, hell. It had to stop.

Didn't it?

Part of him realized this would be a good thing for the baby. But sure as heck not for Lyla. Or even for him. Because he wasn't sure he could ever love her in return. That would make for a very uncomfortable arrangement.

"I'm offering to be your husband," he settled for saying. "And a full-time father for this child."

She looked over her shoulder at him. "It's not enough, Wyatt."

For such simple words, they packed a punch. A hard one. "Are you saying you'll leave?"

"I won't continue this sham of a marriage after the danger's over."

There it was. The threat he'd been trying to dodge since he learned the baby was indeed his. Because if she walked out, the baby went right along with her. Yeah, he could fight her and win. But the cost of winning would be pretty damn high.

A beep pierced through the room, and Wyatt pushed the conversation aside so he could hurry back to the window and the laptop. He didn't see anything unusual outside so he searched through the images on the screen, but he saw only the ranch hands.

And a blank spot.

Where there should have been some camera feed.

Wyatt's phone buzzed, and Busby's name popped up on the screen.

"What happened?" Wyatt immediately asked the ranch hand.

"Not sure, but I'm taking two of the men with me, and we're going out for a look at the west fence. That's where the sensor was tripped and the camera's out."

"Let me know if you spot anything."

There weren't any other precautions to take. The blinds were closed, and he'd already warned Lyla to stay away from the windows. Still, Wyatt turned off the lights and kept his gun ready.

Lyla's breathing had kicked up a significant notch by

the time she made it to him, and she watched the screen over his shoulder.

But there wasn't much to see.

There was no movement around Dallas's or Harlan's house. Still no one visible in any of the pastures, except for the ranch hands. There was one man standing guard on the back porch and another on the front. Both men were bundled in heavy coats and were carrying rifles to protect their home.

Home.

She probably thought of this place as the opposite of that. Nearly every minute she'd been here, Lyla had been in danger or in bed with him.

And she was still in danger.

She'd already said she would leave when it was safe to, but Wyatt knew she wouldn't just leave. She'd try to run, and even though he couldn't let her do that, he would have tried to do the same thing in her position.

It didn't take long for Busby and the two hands to disappear from view and into that blank space. Wyatt held his breath. Prayed. And he wished he could somehow divide himself and be out there to help them while protecting Lyla, too.

Even though Wyatt had been expecting the call, the buzzing sound from his phone still shot through him, and he immediately jabbed the button to answer it.

"False alarm," Busby said. "A tree limb fell on the camera and took it out. Looks like it's too damaged to fix."

Normally, that wouldn't have given Wyatt much cause for concern. After all, it was winter and downed tree limbs were common.

But this situation was far from normal.

"You're sure the limb wasn't tossed there?" Wyatt asked.

"Can't be sure of that at all, but I don't see anyone out here."

"Okay." That helped ease the tension a little. "Come on back to the house," Wyatt told Busby. "But keep watch." He didn't have to tell the man that this could turn into an ambush.

Or even something worse.

"I'll call Dallas, too," Busby offered, "and let him know what's going on. Keep watch on that computer screen."

"I will." In fact, Wyatt didn't intend to take his eyes off it.

Lyla sat on the edge of the desk, her attention nailed to the laptop, as well. Her breathing was way too fast, and Wyatt touched the back of her hand in an effort to soothe her.

"Are Kirby and Stella watching this?" she asked.

"Probably."

There was another laptop in Kirby's room where they were waiting and keeping watch. And if they were indeed seeing what was going on, Kirby would call Dallas for an update. Even though Kirby and Wyatt hadn't talked about it, his foster father knew that Lyla would be in the room with him. Listening to every word. Kirby would want to do whatever it took not to add more stress to what had already been too much for Lyla and the baby.

Wyatt was torn between staying put with Lyla so he could keep watching out the window or going to Stella and Kirby. Maybe if something did go wrong, he'd get enough of a heads up so he could hurry to them while still protecting Lyla.

The seconds crawled by with no sign of Busby and

the other men. Wyatt knew they probably weren't moving fast because they'd want to be able to hear if anything went wrong around them, but the wait was almost unbearable.

Finally, Wyatt saw the men come into range of a working camera. He had a clear view of them thanks to the lights they had fixed onto their hats. They weren't too far from the house now, and each step put them closer to being out of the line of a possible attack.

"Maybe it really was just a fallen limb," Lyla whispered, releasing the long breath she'd been holding.

Wyatt released a breath, too, but then he saw something that tightened every muscle in his body.

The shadows.

Not in front of the men. But behind them where their lights didn't reach.

There was just enough of a moon for Wyatt to make out the trees and underbrush on the camera feed.

"It could be the wind moving the tree branches," he said, hoping. Praying even more.

But then he saw something else. Another shadow, and it didn't mesh with the movement of the trees.

Without taking his eyes off the screen, Wyatt called Busby. "We might have a problem," he said the moment that Busby answered. "I think there might be somebody trailing along behind you."

"You're sure?"

"No—"

But Wyatt had to take back that answer. Because the shadows moved again. Thanks to the wind fanning the branches, he got a glimpse of something he sure as hell didn't want to see.

Two men dressed all in black.

And they were armed.

Chapter Sixteen

"Get out of there now!" Wyatt ordered Busby.

Lyla's throat snapped shut.

No. This couldn't be happening.

The killer was supposed to go after the fake evidence in the CSI van. He wasn't supposed to send his henchmen here to the ranch. But Lyla couldn't think of who else would be out skulking around on a bitter winter night. And there was no doubt about it—those men *were* skulking.

Wyatt had no sooner hung up with Busby when his phone buzzed again, and it was Dallas's name on the screen.

"I see them," Dallas said the moment Wyatt answered and put the call on speaker.

Busby and the two ranch hands pushed their horses in a gallop, racing back. The two men behind them, however, didn't run. They just continued to move through the pasture, using whatever they could for cover.

Making their way toward the house where Wyatt, Kirby, Stella and she were.

"I'll make sure Kirby and Stella stay down and take cover on the side of the fireplace in his room," Dallas offered. "And that all the ranch hands are inside. I can be there in five minutes."

"No," Wyatt said, surprising Lyla that he'd turn down backup. "This could be some kind of trap. They aren't shooting at anyone, so it could be a ploy to lure you away from the others."

"But Lyla and you seem to be the target," Dallas argued.

"And they could use any one of you to draw us out."

Mercy, she hadn't thought of that. There was no way Wyatt would sit still if his family came under attack.

"Besides, I don't want anyone out in the open right now," Wyatt added. "Just stay where you are and keep watch."

Wyatt was right. Dallas could be shot if he tried to get to them, and it would leave his own family more vulnerable. Heaven knew what they were all going through right now, because they had to be watching this possible threat unfold on the security screen.

"What do we do?" she asked Wyatt, and cursed the fear crawling through her.

He opened the desk drawer, took out a gun and handed it to her. "If they come closer to the house, you'll need to go in the bathroom and get in the shower."

It was lined with river rock similar to the fireplace that Stella and Kirby could use for cover. An attractive feature, but in this case, both could be good shields against bullets.

"You'll go in the shower with me," she said, and she tried not to make it sound like a question.

"I'll stay safe," he promised her, but there was no way he could guarantee he'd keep that promise.

Wyatt pulled her down for a kiss. Much too quick. But he had to keep his mind on the screen. Kisses, even those just to help keep her calm, were a big distraction.

Lyla said a prayer of thanks when Busby and the

ranch hands made it back to the house. Busby unlocked the front door, disarming the security system just long enough so they could get inside the foyer. The other hand went to the back and inside an enclosed porch.

So, everyone was safe and inside.

Well, inside anyway.

"There are three of them," Wyatt said.

It took her a moment to understand, and see, what he meant. The third man came into view of the camera. He was also dressed in black, his face was covered with something and he was armed.

Was this the killer? And had he sent his henchmen on ahead of him? If so, why?

The approaching gunmen were clearly outnumbered. Stella and Kirby were no doubt armed. Wyatt and she were. Ditto for the ranch hands. That meant it was seven-to-three odds. Knowing that should have eased some of the tension that was rifling through her body.

But it didn't.

Wyatt and she exchanged a glance, and she saw on his face the same concern she felt. Maybe there were more than three possible attackers, but there was no one else they could call for backup. At least no one that could make a fast response. The sheriff and one of his deputies were with Declan and Slade, and that probably left only one other deputy to protect the town. And he was with Billy.

The phone buzzed again, and even though Lyla had been expecting a call from one of his brothers, the sound still caused her to gasp. However, when she looked at the screen, her stomach dropped.

Unknown caller.

Someone had blocked the number and name, and she doubted they'd done that for any good reason. It wasn't one of the three men in the pasture, either, because Lyla could see them on the security camera, and none was on the phone.

"Marshal McCabe," Wyatt answered.

It seemed to take an eternity for someone to speak on the other end of the line, but finally she heard the voice. "It's me," the man said.

Lyla shook her head and looked at Wyatt to see if it was someone he recognized. It wasn't.

"Who the hell is this?" Wyatt demanded.

"Nicky Garnett."

The gunman who'd shot at them at her house. A very dangerous man and someone almost certainly connected to the men in the pasture.

Men who were now running.

What was happening? Was this the start of the attack that they'd been dreading?

"What do you want?" Wyatt asked Nicky.

"To give you a little warning." There was no urgency in the man's voice. In fact, he seemed pleased about the threat Lyla was sure was coming. "If I were you, I'd get my bride and anyone else out of the house."

"And why would I do that?"

"Remember that maid you put on paid leave?" Nicky didn't wait for Wyatt to respond. "Well, she had some family problems that required her to come up with a big chunk of cash. Cash that my boss gladly provided her for services rendered."

Lyla pressed her fingers to her mouth to stop the gasp, and everything inside her went completely still.

Wyatt's grip tightened on the phone until his knuckles were white. "What the hell did she do?"

"For one thing, she put a tiny camera with infrared technology on one of the outside windowsills. It made it pretty easy for us to know that you and Lyla aren't in that heavily guarded van heading to San Antonio."

Sweet heaven. That meant Nicky and his boss would know exactly who was in the house. And the infrared would pick up on their specific location. It would make it easier for them to target them with long-range rifles.

Like the ones the men who were nearing the house had.

Wyatt and his family had been so careful making sure the place was secure, but it would have been easy to miss a small camera. Now they might pay a high price for that.

"One more thing," Nicky said, his voice still calm but yet cold as ice. "We had the maid set a bomb, too. A bomb with a timer like the one we used at Rocky Creek."

Lyla could have sworn her heart stopped for several seconds, and then it slammed against her ribs.

"Where is it?" Wyatt demanded through clenched teeth. "Where's the bomb?"

"Very near to you. And if my calculations are right, you've got less than five minutes before you're all blown to smithereens."

"WHERE IS IT? Where'd she put the bomb?" Wyatt shouted into the phone. But he was talking to himself because Nicky Garnett had already hung up.

Hell, no. This couldn't be happening.

"What do we do?" Lyla asked, the terror spiking her voice.

Wyatt tried not to panic. Tried to think. This could all be a trap to get them out of the house, but he'd seen the destruction the bomb had done at Rocky Creek. If one that size detonated here, the house could be destroyed and everyone inside killed.

"Come on." Wyatt drew his gun and got them running

out of the room and down the stairs. He slapped off lights along the way so they couldn't be pinpointed by a shooter using a long-range rifle. Of course, if Nicky had told the truth, they were being tracked with infrared, which allowed them to be tracked no matter where they went.

"We have to get out," Wyatt told Busby and the other ranch hand in the foyer. "The place might blow up."

Wyatt had a split-second debate with himself about having them come with Lyla and him, but the nearest vehicle was his truck, and there wouldn't be room in the cab.

"Go to the mare's barn," Wyatt told the men. That was at the front of the property by the road, and they'd be able to see if anyone drove up. "But watch out for those guys moving in the pasture. They're armed."

That was the only warning he had time to issue. While they hurried to Kirby's room, he phoned Dallas to fill him in. "Nicky Garnett just called. There could be a bomb."

Dallas cursed. "He's probably lying through his teeth."

"Yeah, but I can't take that chance. It's me, don't shoot!" Wyatt called out. He threw open the door to Kirby's room and spotted Stella and him, both armed, huddled by the fireplace. He motioned for them to get to their feet. "Nicky said they have infrared, and if they do, they know exactly what we're doing now. But I can't see them. The laptop will lose the internet connection once I'm out of the house."

"I'm on my way," Dallas said, repeating his earlier offer.

Like before, though, Wyatt had to turn him down. "Too risky. If they'd wanted us dead, they would have just blown us up. They wouldn't have given us a warning or time to get out."

So, what did they want?

Wyatt figured it had something to do with that fake tape. He'd been so sure the killer would follow that trail.

But he'd been dead wrong.

And in doing so, he'd put Lyla and the baby in grave danger again.

"Stay where you are and keep monitoring the security systems," Wyatt told Dallas. They hurried through the house and toward the back. "I'm taking Stella, Kirby and Lyla to the truck. I left it parked right out by the back steps. And we'll come to you. That way, I can drop them off and face down whoever's out there."

"No!" Lyla insisted. "You can't sacrifice yourself for us."

Yes, he could. For them and the baby, he would do whatever it took. But it wasn't a sacrifice he had in mind. "I'm a good shot," he reminded her. "And unlike those men, I know every inch of this ranch. I can stop this."

"And you could be taking the danger to Dallas and the others. I'm the one who's drawing the trouble here. I'm the one they want."

Probably. But Wyatt didn't have time to argue with her. "The bomb could hurt the baby," he said. "Or worse."

Yeah, it was brutal, and even in the darkness he could see the color drain from her face. But it worked. It got her moving, which in turn got Stella and Kirby moving. Kirby was still a little shaky on his feet, but Stella looped her arm around his waist and helped him walk. Wyatt grabbed the keys from the peg near the door and hurried with them onto the back porch.

"Run," Wyatt told the ranch hand. "Go to the hay barn and keep watch from there."

The guy frantically bobbed his head and practically sprinted away.

Wyatt moved fast, too, and crammed the others into the truck. They were nearly on top of each other, but it wouldn't be a long drive to Dallas's place.

"Maybe they set more than one bomb," Stella said, looking up at the house and then the grounds.

"They don't want us dead," Wyatt repeated, and he prayed that was true.

He threw the truck into gear and gunned the engine. Just as his phone buzzed.

"Answer it," he told Lyla. And she somehow managed to get it from his pocket.

"It's me, Busby," Wyatt heard him say the moment Lyla put the call on speaker. "We got a problem, boss. I just had a look through the binoculars. The ones with night vision. And I can see at least three men on the road that leads to Dallas's house."

Wyatt's heart went to his knees. "Where exactly?"

"They're not on the ranch grounds, which explains why they didn't trip the sensors. They're just on the other side of the fence. And they appear to be carrying long-range rifles."

That was not what Wyatt wanted to hear. Especially since that was the direction they were headed. Wyatt slammed on the brakes.

"Change of plans," Wyatt said to Busby. He was aware that Stella and Lyla were terrified, but he couldn't take the time to assure them now. "I'm heading to the barn behind the house. Call Dallas and tell him what's going on."

Wyatt didn't wait for Busby to agree. Without pushing the end-call button on the phone, he hit the accelerator and got them heading toward the barn. He had to put some distance between the house and them in case of an explosion. They were still close enough to be hurt.

"Hold on," Wyatt told them. "And get as far down on the seat as you can."

The barn doors were closed. There were no animals inside because it was used for storage during winter months. And so that he wouldn't have to get out, Wyatt planned to drive through the wooden doors.

Lyla, Stella and Kirby were still scrambling to get down when the truck slammed into the doors and sent them flying off their hinges. The air bags deployed, slapping into them. But even over that noise and the roar of the engine, Wyatt heard something he damn sure didn't want to hear.

Someone fired a shot.

Chapter Seventeen

The fear jolted through Lyla.

Because she knew what that sound meant.

They were under fire again.

She looked up just as a bullet came through the back window of the truck. It went straight through, shattering the windshield. The glass cracked and webbed and made it impossible to see.

However, she had no trouble hearing.

Not just the second shot, either, but also Wyatt's profanity when he shoved her back lower onto the seat. There wasn't much room, with the four of them and the air bags, but he squeezed them as low as he could manage.

What she didn't hear was an explosion, and they were still plenty close enough to the house that if there'd been one, she would have known about it. Of course, they didn't know yet if Nicky had lied to them, to get them out of the house. But it could have just as easily been a real bomb, so Lyla didn't regret their decision to leave.

Well, not yet anyway.

They had to make it out of this alive first.

"Find out where the shooters are!" Wyatt shouted, and it took her a moment to realize he was talking to Busby and not one of them.

She couldn't hear what the ranch hand said, but Lyla figured the shooters weren't the ones Busby had spotted near the road leading to Dallas's house. No. These shots had almost certainly come from the trio they'd seen earlier on the security cameras. They could have easily made it to the area by the barn by now.

The shots kept coming, and Wyatt crawled over her to shield her with his body. She hated that he was taking the risks. Hated even more that there was nothing she could do about it. They had to protect the baby and that meant protecting her.

One of the bullets slammed through the back of the truck and into the dashboard. The air bags stopped any debris from flying at them, but whoever was shooting was literally tearing the truck apart.

"We have to move," Wyatt said, taking the words right out of her mouth. They'd die if they stayed put.

The truck was in the open doorway, and they needed to get to the side of the barn. Unfortunately, if the shooters were using infrared, they would still be able to target them, but maybe they could use something as a shield until someone could stop the gunmen.

With the engine still running, Wyatt turned the steering wheel to the left, maneuvering them out of the doorway. It took some effort, and it didn't help when the bullets continued to come at them nonstop. Clearly, these men had come prepared to kill them.

Maybe.

Like the other attack, most of the shots were going into the top and sides of the vehicle. Only the one to the dash had come close, and it was possible that it'd been misfired.

Did that mean this was another kidnapping attempt?

If so, then she was no doubt the target.

Not exactly a comforting thought, especially since these goons were likely prepared to kill everyone else to get to her. And why? At this point if she got anywhere near the real evidence, it could be discredited.

Maybe that was the point.

She could taint it by association.

The second that Wyatt had the truck maneuvered out of the entrance, he threw open his door. "Come on."

And that was the only warning Lyla got before he took hold of her arm and pulled her from the truck. They landed in an open stall that was strewed with hay. Kirby and Stella piled in right behind them.

The cold was instant and sent her teeth chattering, a reminder that she hadn't grabbed her coat when they'd run. Of course, staying warm hadn't exactly been a high priority with the bomb threat.

"We should get into the tack room," Kirby insisted. Like her, he was shivering. Stella, too. And with everything Kirby had been through recently, that couldn't be good. This might cause him to have some kind of relapse in his recovery.

The shots didn't stop. They continued to pelt the truck, but thankfully none of them were coming in their direction. Not yet anyway. But it seemed to her that the shooters were moving, probably coming closer to them.

Wyatt tipped his head to a walled over area in the center of the barn. "The tack room," he told her.

Not the standard place to keep tack, but the barn was far bigger than most and clearly used for storage now since inside there were some all-terrain vehicles, a boat and even a travel trailer. None of it would give them much protection, but what it did do was give them plenty of places to hide. And with only one way in, that meant the shooters would have to come to them.

"Let's go," Wyatt ordered.

They stayed close to the side of the barn, out of the path of the gaping hole in the door, and once they made it to the room filled with saddles and other riding gear, Wyatt got them inside.

Not himself, though.

He leaned out, looking for those shooters.

"I still don't see them," he said to Busby, and waited while the man spoke. "Well, find them."

Wyatt hit the end-call button and rammed his phone back in his pocket. "The gunmen took out the security cameras. We have no way to monitor them."

Sweet heaven. That meant they could be anywhere, but she was betting they were sneaking up on the barn. Those shots were definitely getting closer.

"Stay back," Wyatt warned her when she tried to pull him deeper inside with the rest of them.

And without warning, the shots stopped.

Because she had her hand on Wyatt's left arm, she felt his muscles freeze, and his breath seemed to stop for a second. Only then did he ease back, and he put his finger to his mouth in a *stay quiet* gesture.

Lyla heard another sound.

Footsteps.

The gunmen had arrived.

She tried to level her breathing. Tried not to move. So she wouldn't do anything to give away their position. Beside her, Stella and Kirby did the same, but if any of them made a sound, the gunmen would hear them.

The room was much larger than the truck, but Wyatt was blocking the doorway. Again, protecting them. However, it prevented any of them from moving beside him and taking aim. Something he almost certainly didn't want them to do anyway, but Lyla hated that all she could do was sit there and wait for this nightmare to play out.

Judging from the sound of the footsteps, the men kept coming closer. Wyatt held steady. Definitely not shaking like she was, and he leaned out just a fraction.

And fired.

The sound blasted through the barn. Through her, too. There was a groan of pain followed by the sound of someone thudding to the ground.

Wyatt had obviously managed to take out one of the men. Lyla was both relieved and thankful.

But not for long.

"Marshal?" someone shouted. And this time she recognized the voice. It was Nicky again. "I think it's time we had a little talk."

Wyatt didn't answer, but the smugness in Nicky's voice had her heart racing. He didn't seem like a man who had any doubts about this plan he'd just put into place.

"Who hired you to come here?" Kirby shouted. "Was it Travis Weston?"

"No. I don't work for him. Got me a new boss now, who pays a lot better."

Maybe a lie, but it could be the truth. From everything she'd heard Wyatt say about him, Nicky wasn't the sort to stay loyal. He was a follow-the-money kind of hired killer.

"Why don't you tell them you're here?" Nicky said.

Wyatt glanced at her to see if she knew what he meant, but Lyla had to shake her head.

"Go ahead," Nicky said. "Why don't you show the marshal what you got there?"

"I'm sorry, Wyatt," she heard another man say.

Billy.

Good grief, what was he doing here?

Like her, he sounded terrified. Of course, he could be faking it if he was the mastermind behind this plan.

"I'm sorry," Billy repeated. "But this is something you have to see."

Despite the hold she had on his arm, Wyatt leaned out just slightly.

And he cursed.

Lyla desperately wanted to see what had caused Wyatt to react that way, but she stayed put. And quiet.

"It's a detonator," Billy said, his voice barely audible over the sudden howling of the wind.

Oh, God. A timer for what? Was there actually a bomb after all?

"I got it mixed up a little when I told you the maid had set a bomb," Nicky mocked. "She did. But not at the ranch. It's beneath Dallas's house, where most of your family is holed up. Get out here now, or the bomb goes off, and everyone inside that house dies."

WYATT HAD FELT FEAR before, but this was a whole new level. He thought of his brothers Dallas, Clayton and Harlan. All in the house. Their wives, too, along with Slade's wife and Declan's fiancée. And the children.

All babies.

And now they were in danger.

Well, they were if Nicky was telling the truth.

"Billy?" Wyatt called out. "Is there really a detonator?"

"Afraid so. I didn't mean for this to happen. They grabbed me when I got to the sheriff's office and then forced me to call the deputy to tell him that I'd changed my mind about staying there."

So, this plan had been in motion for several hours. Before the CSI van had even arrived.

"Step out!" Nicky insisted. "Or I push this little button and a whole lot of marshals die tonight."

It was a huge risk, but Wyatt had no choice. "Stay put," he warned Lyla and the others.

"No!" she practically shouted. She tried to stop him, but Wyatt stepped out anyway.

Yeah, it was a detonator, all right.

And it was clipped to Nicky's belt like a badge.

If Billy was in on this little plan, then he was giving a fine acting job, because thanks to the headlights on the truck, Wyatt could see that the man was pale and shaking. He was also cuffed, with his hands in front of his body.

Nicky looked as calm and cocky as he'd sounded on the phone. He was also armed and had his gun pointed at Wyatt. He had his other hand on the detonator. In fact, his index finger was poised right over the button.

Wyatt glanced at the hole where the door had once been, and he spotted one of the gunmen. His rifle was pointed right at Billy. The other gunman was dead on the ground.

"Don't give me a reason to press this button," Nicky warned.

"Who's behind this?" Wyatt asked before Nicky could say anything else.

"Maybe I am."

"Not enough brains. And no motive. The person behind this wants to hide their involvement in Webb's murder."

A flash of anger went through Nicky's eyes. That *not enough brains* insult had pushed his buttons, and even though Wyatt didn't personally know the man, he appeared to have a short fuse. Not good, since he controlled the detonator.

"Well, I hope you're getting paid enough," Wyatt added, "because attempted murder is going to send you away for a long, long time."

"Only if I'm caught, which I don't intend to happen. Now shut up and listen to how this is going to work. You and Lyla will come with me, and Kirby will get the detonator. Your brothers and their families will be safe."

"But not my wife," Wyatt argued.

"She'll be safe as long as she cooperates. And all she has to do is alter the voice on the tape that's being delivered to the lab as we speak."

Wyatt didn't believe Nicky for a minute about Lyla being safe after she cooperated. She would be a loose end, and while they might not kill her instantly, eventually the killer would want her eliminated.

"Why didn't you just go after the CSI van?" Wyatt asked.

"Too risky. Lyla's a better bet, and she'll probably be happy to cooperate rather than risk endangering that baby's she's carrying."

Wyatt didn't have to see Lyla's face to know that it sent a shock of fear through her. It went through him, too. And not just fear. Pure, raw anger. How dare this SOB threaten his unborn child?

"How'd you know about the baby?" Wyatt snapped. "Are you the one who stole the embryo?"

Nicky chuckled. "Wish I could take credit for that, but, no, my boss hired someone else to do it."

Another lackey. What Wyatt needed was the identity of the person responsible for all this chaos.

"Let's get in your truck," Nicky instructed. "Me, you and Lyla. And one of my helpers, who's waiting outside, will climb in the back with Billy. The other helper will stay here with Kirby, Stella and the detonator."

"Why take Billy?" Wyatt asked.

"Because I know too much," Billy answered. "Or so he thinks. He believes that I listened to the tape recording of the murder. I didn't."

"Yeah. Because he says it's fake," Nicky grumbled. "Like we're gonna believe that."

Well, he should. It was the truth, but Wyatt seriously doubted he could convince Nicky or his boss of that now. And it meant Billy was soon to be a dead man, too—unless he was the person behind this. But that didn't make sense, because Billy knew the tape wasn't real.

Wyatt had to figure a way out of this. But how? If he dove at Nicky, the guy with the rifle would just shoot him, and that would leave Lyla and the others without anyone to protect them. It was entirely possible that Dallas and Slade were on their way to help him, but Wyatt prayed they'd somehow gotten news of the possible bomb and were evacuating.

"Get moving now!" Nicky ordered.

Billy's gaze met Wyatt's, and even though he wasn't sure what Billy intended to do, the one thing that couldn't happen was for the killer to get his hands on Lyla.

Wyatt gave Billy a slight nod, and he braced himself for whatever was about to happen.

And it happened fast.

Despite the cuffs, Billy grabbed on to Nicky's hand, snapping it away from the detonator. Wyatt didn't waste a second. He pivoted and aimed at the man with the rifle and fired before he could.

The man went down.

Wyatt hoped he was dead or at least incapable of

firing that rifle, because he didn't have time to disarm him. He launched himself into the fray with Billy and Nicky, but he had to drop his own gun to use both hands to try to restrain Nicky and to keep his finger off the detonator.

He sensed the movement behind him and cursed. Lyla was out of the tack room, trying to take aim at Nicky. But Wyatt didn't want her out in the open.

With a firm grip on Nicky's left hand, Wyatt managed to punch him. Hard. It was enough for Nicky's head to flop back, and Wyatt reached for the man's gun.

But the sound stopped him cold.

"Hold it right there, Wyatt," someone said. "Move another inch, and you're a dead man."

Chapter Eighteen

Even though she was only inches away from grabbing Nicky's gun from the barn floor, Lyla froze. Because the man who'd spoken that warning meant business.

It was Sheriff Zeke Mercer.

And he had a semiautomatic pointed right at Wyatt.

With just a glance of his narrowed gaze, Zeke issued a firm threat. If she tried to help, Wyatt would pay the price. And Zeke would shoot him, because in his mind, Wyatt was likely expendable.

All of them were.

Well, she would be after she faked that evidence. After that, she and her baby would be expendable, too.

"Get up," Zeke ordered Wyatt. "And move away from Nicky. Our ride should be here any minute now, and we'll be leaving."

Wyatt did get up, slow and easy, and he volleyed glances between Zeke and the detonator. Nicky got up, too, retrieved his gun and pointed it not at Wyatt but at her. He knew that was the only way to keep Wyatt from going after him again.

And it worked.

She saw the fear, and the frustration, tighten Wyatt's entire body.

"Told you I had a new boss," Nicky bragged. "No

way would I go back to work for Travis. Not with what Zeke pays me. And besides, me working for Zeke puts the blame right back on Travis. That's why Zeke even pretended to rat out my location when he called you. But before he made that call, he had me in some place where the law would never get to me."

"Shut up," Zeke told the man, and he looked at Wyatt. "Now call Dallas and tell him to stay put," Zeke instructed. "Not just him, all of them. Because we'll detonate the bomb if any of them show up here. Oh, and put the call on speaker and don't mention my name or the bomb. Because I will kill you if you do. And then I'll kill all of them."

That wasn't a bluff. Neither was the bomb. That was probably why Wyatt made the call. "Stay away from the barn," Wyatt told his brother. "I want the ranch hands kept back, too."

"What's going on?" Dallas demanded.

"Something that I have to ask you and the others to stay out of." And with that, Wyatt put his phone in his shirt pocket, his gaze fixed on Zeke. "There's no need for this."

Zeke shook his head, and despite the cold wind battering him, he stayed put in the shattered doorway. "Yeah, there is a need."

"Because it'll be your voice on that tape," Lyla continued when he didn't add more. "Except there isn't a tape."

"Oh, there is. Sarah made one. She used to threaten me with it whenever she thought I might tell anyone what'd happened that night. It's the reason Billy's coming with us. I'll let Nicky get the truth out of him, because I'm betting Sarah put copies somewhere. And I have to find those copies and destroy them."

If Sarah had indeed done that, the copies hadn't turned

up, and Billy genuinely didn't seem to know where they'd be. Of course, that didn't matter. He'd die because of this after they tortured him to get information that he didn't even have.

"Sarah could have been bluffing," Lyla pointed out. "In fact, it could have been her insurance policy to keep you from coming after her."

That realization flashed through Zeke's eyes. Not a good realization, either, because he had to be thinking this was all for nothing.

"You killed my mother," Billy said. His voice wasn't too steady. Neither was he, and he looked ready to launch himself at Zeke.

"No, I did," Nicky volunteered. "Sneaked into the hospital and then had my girlfriend call those other idiots and set them up. It was Zeke's idea to go to the hospital, too, so he wouldn't look guilty."

"But you are guilty," Wyatt stated through clenched teeth. "Let me guess. You and Webb had a falling-out over a business deal, and you were more than happy to help Sarah kill him."

Zeke didn't say a word. He only glanced behind him, no doubt looking for the vehicle that would come and collect them. Once they were away from the ranch, it was likely that the bomb would be detonated anyway.

Too many potential witnesses to leave behind.

"Webb got greedy. He wanted more of the cut they were making from the gunrunning that they were doing with some of the boys from Rocky Creek," Nicky said, ignoring the glare that Zeke shot him.

Zeke suddenly didn't seem nearly as confident and cocky as his hired gun, and he kept glancing back, looking for the vehicle.

Maybe one of the ranch hands or Wyatt's brothers

had managed to stop it. She hoped so, because once the vehicle arrived, their chances of escaping dwindled considerably.

"And what about Travis and Greg?" Wyatt asked. "Did they have anything to do with this?"

"No, but I wish Travis had," Zeke mumbled. "I would have loved seeing his arrogant butt behind bars."

"That's the pot calling the kettle black. You killed my father for money," Billy spat out. "You had no right to kill him. No one did."

Zeke huffed. "You remember how he used to beat on you? And on you?" he added, tipping his head to Wyatt.

"I remember," Wyatt answered, "but that isn't why you killed him. It's because he wanted a bigger cut of the illegal money you two were making."

"I'm not admitting to anything," Zeke snarled.

No, but the admission was there and unspoken. There would have been no reason for him to kill Sarah unless it was to cover up the fact that he was an accessory to murder.

"Did you ever see the recording that Sarah made?" Lyla pressed, though it was too late to convince Zeke that the recording didn't exist. Still, she might be able to distract him in some way.

"No. But she said she had it hidden away where I could never find it. She said she recorded the tape during one of our conversations and that I'd mentioned something about my business dealings with her husband."

"But not his murder," Lyla pressed.

His forehead bunched up, and Zeke stopped, looking even more uneasy about all that he'd set into motion. He glanced up the road again. "The van's here. Time to leave." And he motioned for Lyla to come closer.

Wyatt stepped in front of her. "Webb deserved to die, but we don't. Not just to cover up your crime."

"You're wrong. I'm not going to jail for anything. I'll cover my tracks any way I need to."

"That included having your goon kill my mother." Billy's hands tightened into fists.

Zeke didn't seem to notice Billy's reaction. The lights of the vehicle slashed through the hole and into the barn, and Zeke had to turn his eyes away. It was just a split-second distraction.

And the only one necessary.

With a feral sound screaming from his throat, Billy dove toward Zeke, crashing into the man and knocking him to the ground.

Nicky reacted, fast, moving toward his boss to protect him. But Wyatt reacted, too. He lunged forward, trying to catch onto Nicky's arm before he could press the detonator.

Lyla started to move, too, but she didn't get far before the sound stopped her.

A shot blasted through the barn.

WYATT PRAYED THAT the bullet hadn't gone anywhere near Lyla, but he couldn't look back to see if it had. Suddenly, he was in another fight with Nicky, and the man was still trying to hit that damn button on the detonator.

Nicky outweighed him by a good forty pounds, but he didn't have nearly the motivation that Wyatt had. Lyla, the baby and his family were in danger, and he had to stop this dirt wad from killing them all. Of course, that wouldn't stop the danger if he couldn't do something about Zeke.

But one fight at a time.

Wyatt took hold of Nicky's left hand, but the man kept

a death grip on his gun. Wyatt's own weapon was just out of reach, and he could let go of Nicky to get it. Lyla must have realized that because she rushed forward to help.

"Stay back," Wyatt yelled.

She didn't listen. Of course. Later, he'd chew her out for that. But she kicked the gun closer to his hand just as Nicky punched him so hard that Wyatt swore he saw stars. Before Wyatt could snatch up his gun, he heard the blast.

It was too close.

Maybe right at Lyla.

God. His heart skipped some beats, and he looked back, expecting to see the worst. But instead he saw Kirby. He was standing in the tack room door, his gun aimed at Nicky. He'd been the one to fire the shot and looked ready to fire a second.

But it wasn't necessary.

Nicky was dead.

"Get the detonator," Wyatt told Lyla. "Then stay down on the ground. There'll be gunmen in that van." He grabbed his Colt and raced toward Billy and Zeke, who were still in a scuffle on the floor.

"You need to tell Dallas to evacuate," she called out to him.

"Dallas knows. I left my phone on after Zeke had me make that call. Dallas would have heard everything."

He hoped. That was the plan anyway when Wyatt had risked not pressing the end-call button. If Zeke had noticed, he probably would have killed him.

And that's exactly what he was trying to do to Billy now—kill him. Zeke had managed to hang on to his weapon and was trying to aim it so he could shoot Billy.

Outside the barn, Wyatt heard familiar voices. Busby, Dallas and Slade. He maneuvered himself around Billy and Zeke so he could stop the gunmen in the van from coming inside after them. But he looked out in just enough time to see Dallas slam one of the men against the van.

"Is everyone out of your house?" Wyatt asked him.

"Yeah. Thanks for the heads-up."

Later Wyatt would say *you're welcome*. But for now, all hell was breaking loose, and Wyatt had to make sure that no one fired any shots near Lyla. He tried to take aim at Zeke, but his and Billy's bodies were in such a tangle that Wyatt didn't have a clean shot.

So, he waited, watched. With his heart pounding in his throat and with every inch of his body on alert. Finally, he saw an opening in the scuffle, and when he got the chance, Wyatt leaned in and bashed the butt of his gun against Zeke's head.

It worked.

The man stopped struggling, his hand dropping limply on the ground.

But Billy didn't stop. He latched on to Zeke's gun and came up, ready to fire. He took aim at Zeke's heart.

"This is for killing my mother," Billy said, putting his finger on the trigger.

"Don't," Wyatt warned him. Though he wasn't sure what to say to stop Billy. Zeke had killed both of his parents and was planning to kill him. Still, at the moment, Zeke was unarmed.

"You're not a murderer," Wyatt told Billy.

"But I want him dead. You should want him dead, too. He nearly killed Lyla and your baby."

"I know." And Wyatt had to tamp down the anger. No, it was rage. But the rage faded considerably when he felt Lyla's hand brush over his arm.

"Zeke will get his punishment in prison, Billy," Lyla

said. Her voice was soft. Almost soothing. He wasn't sure how he managed it, because when he looked into her eyes, Wyatt saw the aftermath of the fear that was no doubt mirrored in his.

"If you think this ends anything," Zeke snapped, "it doesn't." With venom in his eyes, he looked at Kirby, then Wyatt. "When I give my statement, I'll just tell everyone that you helped Sarah and me hide Webb's body."

"Then you'd be lying," Kirby said.

"Would I?" The corner of Zeke's mouth lifted into a twisted smile. "Something like that can follow a man around for a lifetime. Wouldn't hurt Kirby much, since he's retired, but all his boys would have to listen to the whispers about taking the law into their own hands. But if you convince Billy here to pull the trigger, then I'll have no statement to make."

Wyatt wanted his name cleared. His family's too. But not at the cost of coaxing Billy to kill an unarmed man.

"Not all lawmen are capable of murder," Kirby told Zeke.

Zeke chuckled. "Yeah. You are. So, what will it be? If I'm dead, there'll be no one to point a finger at you and these boys you've worked so hard to protect. And as for me, death would be welcome."

Yeah, because Zeke wouldn't end up in prison with men he'd help to put there. Even if they couldn't pin accessory to Webb's murder on Zeke, he would still be charged with orchestrating Sarah's murder and the attacks on Lyla and him. That would be a life sentence, at least, and with no possibility of parole.

The next moments crawled by. Billy, with the gun still ready to end Zeke's life. Zeke, staring up at them and not offering one bit of remorse or regret for anyone but himself.

But it didn't matter.

The realization hit Wyatt. It didn't matter why Zeke had done what he'd done. It only mattered that Lyla and his family were safe.

Wyatt extended his hand. "Billy, I need the gun." And he made sure he sounded like the lawman that he was. The one that Kirby had trained him to be.

With all eyes on him and with his hand shaking, Billy finally gave Wyatt the gun.

Wyatt released the breath he'd been holding, and while Kirby held Zeke at gunpoint, Wyatt pulled Lyla into his arms. The embrace didn't last long, and he barely had enough time to check and make sure she was okay.

There wasn't a scratch on her.

That was another prayer answered. There'd been a bunch of those tonight.

"These are the guys who were on the road near my place," Dallas explained, and Wyatt went out to help him contain the men who'd been in the van. "Sheriff Geary's on his way back to help us arrest every one of them. Zeke, too." He said the man's name as if it was profanity. "I want him taken to the marshals' office and thrown into jail."

Wyatt looked around. "We need to get a bomb squad out here to sweep every inch of the ranch." Which would mean they would all end up in town at a hotel for the night.

"You should see to Lyla." Dallas tipped his head toward her. "She doesn't look too steady on her feet."

She didn't. And even though there was plenty that Wyatt needed to be doing to get these gunmen off the property, he went to her.

Yeah, definitely not steady.

He hooked his arm around her and moved her against one of the barn posts. "What's wrong?"

She shook her head. "I just realized it's over."

Wyatt got the feeling she was talking about more than just the danger.

Lyla pulled away from him, dodged his gaze. "I can go home now."

Wyatt hadn't expected that to come out of her mouth. Not this soon. Only minutes earlier they'd survived a life-and-death situation, so he'd figured there'd be a little downtime to come to terms with everything that had happened.

Apparently not.

He was trying to figure out what to say, when his blasted phone buzzed again. Wyatt considered ignoring it, but then he saw his boss's name on the screen.

"We're making the arrests now," Wyatt answered, hoping to put a quick end to this.

"Good. But that's not why I'm calling," Saul answered back. "You should get down here to the marshals' office as soon as you can. There's something you and the others need to see."

Chapter Nineteen

Wyatt was a hundred percent sure he didn't want to deal with anything else tonight. Well, nothing that didn't involve talking to Lyla to figure out how he could fix this.

First, though, he needed to figure out what *this* was, exactly.

And it would have to wait until he found out what had arrived at the marshals' office. With the rotten luck he and his family had had lately, Wyatt prayed this wasn't another dose of bad news. They'd had enough of that to last a couple of lifetimes.

Wyatt pulled into the parking lot of the marshals' building. Not alone, either. Lyla and Stella were with him in his truck, and Kirby, his brothers and their families were in assorted vehicles that pulled in right behind them. Billy, too, had come along with them.

Saul probably hadn't intended the entire family to come to the office, but since they were all going to check in to the hotel just up the street, it wasn't exactly out of the way. Besides, none of his brothers probably wanted to be away from their wives and children.

Danger had a way making a person realize just what was important.

And in Lyla's case, apparently it had clarified for her

that she wanted to go home. Away from him. Away from the chaos that'd been her life for the past couple of days.

They huddled together against the cold and made their way into the building and up the stairs. Soon, there'd be reports to write up on the shooting, the deaths of the gunmen and Nicky Garnett. Reports of what Zeke had and hadn't confessed to. But Wyatt hoped that wasn't the reason Saul had called them all in.

After one glimpse of his boss's face, and hands, Wyatt knew that it was more than that. Saul was wearing gloves, the kind a marshal used when handling evidence.

Saul wasn't in his office but rather at Dallas's desk, which was toward the center of the sprawling squad room. "This arrived by courier about an hour ago."

There was a shipping box, and Saul reached inside and took out an old-fashioned cassette tape player.

"Sarah," Lyla mumbled.

Saul nodded. "Apparently, long before she went into a coma, she'd put this in a safe-deposit box in San Antonio and left instructions that it was to be delivered here in the event of her untimely death."

Well, it'd been untimely, all right.

"Nicky Garnett confessed to killing her, and he was working for Zeke," Billy said, walking closer. "So, there really was a tape?"

"Yeah. And I figured we'd all listen to it together."

Hell. They weren't out of the woods yet. Because if that was Sarah or Zeke on the recording, either one of them could implicate Kirby. Or one of the rest of them. It wouldn't even have to be true, but as Zeke had said—it could put a shadow over them for the rest of their lives.

Wyatt felt Lyla's arm go around his waist, and just that simple gesture felt far better than it should have. His brothers' wives did the same, despite the fact that Clayton's wife, Lenora, was holding their son. Slade and his wife, Maya, each held their babies.

"I want you to marry me," someone said out of the blue.

Kirby.

And he was looking directly at Stella.

Judging from the mumbles and sounds of surprise, no one in the room had been expecting that. And Wyatt hadn't expected Stella's reaction.

"You're proposing now?" Her hands went on her hips. "Why, because you think some lies on that tape will send one or all of us to jail?"

"I don't care what's on that tape," Kirby insisted. "It won't change how I feel about you. About any of you." He motioned around the room and then pried Stella's left hand off her hip so he could hold it in his. "I love you, and asking you to marry me is something I should have done a long time ago."

Stella's mouth opened as if she might question that. But how could she? Every one of them knew what Kirby had said was true. He'd been in love with her for years.

"You'd better say yes," Declan volunteered. "I'd like to attend my parents' wedding, and I'm sure your other sons and daughters-in-law feel the same."

No more sounds of surprise. Just nods and mumbles of approval.

There were tears in Stella's eyes now, and she went into Kirby's waiting arms. "Yes, I'll marry you."

Wyatt smiled in spite of Kirby's rotten timing. Except, Kirby had managed to inject some genuine happiness in what had been a hell of a bad day.

The hugs and well-wishes came. Lots of them. Everyone went over to hug their parents. It didn't matter that Declan was their only biological son—Kirby and Stella had been Mom and Dad to all of them. The only person who stayed back was Billy, his attention focused on the tape recorder on the desk.

"Should we listen to this tape now?" Saul prompted.

It was time.

But it wasn't.

Wyatt glanced around the room at his family's faces and knew there was something missing. Lyla. Who'd already told him she intended to go home.

"I want this to be your home," Wyatt blurted out to her. He said it a little louder than he'd intended. Actually, a lot louder, because suddenly everyone was looking at them.

"Not the marshals' office," he clarified, feeling very tongue-tied. "I want the ranch to be your home." He motioned around the room as Kirby had done. "And I want this to be your family."

Like Stella, she didn't jump to say yes. In fact, Lyla just stared at him. Then shook her head.

Damn. She was going to say no, and Wyatt didn't want that. So he stopped her with a kiss. In hindsight, it probably shouldn't have been so long and deep, but it hushed her, all right.

And left them both a little out of breath.

"I want you to marry me," Wyatt insisted.

"Uh, you're already married," Declan pointed out.

Yes, but in name only. Well, except for the one time they'd made love. But Wyatt wanted more. More than in name only. More than what he had with Lyla now.

"The baby is Ann and Wyatt's," Lyla said. Apparently, Wyatt wasn't the only one in a blurting mood.

"They know." Declan, again. "I told them."

"And we're all happy for Wyatt and you," Kirby said, coming to her and pulling Lyla into his arms. "We loved

Ann, but we love you, too. And we'll welcome you to this family with open arms."

Lyla still looked a little stunned but nowhere on the verge of saying yes.

"The tape?" Saul prompted again.

"Play it," Wyatt answered, but he took Lyla by the arm and marched her out into the hall.

She stared at him as if he'd lost him mind. Maybe he had, but he wasn't dropping this.

"What's on that tape could be important," Lyla said.

"Not more important than this."

She huffed. "You've made it clear. You want me to stay married to you. You want us to raise this baby—"

"I'm in love with you."

Like the earlier kiss, that stopped her. She stared at him, her expression softening. Well, it softened for a few seconds before she shook her head again.

"You haven't gotten over your wife's death," she added. "And until you do, you shouldn't be asking me or anyone else to marry you."

"I'll never get over that," he answered honestly. "She'll always be part of my life. But a part that I've put behind me so I can move on. With you and the baby."

She just stared at him.

"This would be a good time for you to realize you're in love with me," Wyatt tossed out there. He didn't expect much but hoped for the best.

Actually, he hoped for a miracle.

And he got one.

The corner of Lyla's mouth lifted. Barely a smile, and it didn't have time to grow into something bigger. That was because of the footsteps he heard heading right toward them.

Sheriff Geary was leading a handcuffed Zeke up the stairs and no doubt to a jail cell.

With her still in his arms, Wyatt ushered Lyla back into the room, where they got congrats and well-wishes, which were cut off when Zeke was brought in.

Zeke aimed glares at all of them, but that glare morphed to pure shock when he saw the tape recorder on the desk.

"Anything on there will be a lie," Zeke snarled.

As if to prove him wrong, Saul pressed the button on the recorder.

Just like that, the happy moment was gone, and they all seemed to hold their breaths. Even Billy.

"This is Sarah Webb," the voice said. And it was indeed Sarah, all right. "I'm making this tape because I believe my life's in danger. If something happens to me, then the person responsible is Sheriff Zeke Mercer."

There it was. Exactly what Wyatt had wanted to hear. But the tape wasn't over. She could still drag Kirby and the rest of them into this.

"Sheriff Zeke Mercer walked in on a fight between Jonah and me. We were in Stella's room because of a broken pipe, but Stella wasn't there. Jonah hit me, and in the heat of the argument, I grabbed his knife and stabbed him. Zeke's the one who pulled the knife out of his ribs."

That explained the castoff and why it didn't match a woman of Sarah's size.

"Jonah ran down the hall to his office and was going to get a gun and kill me," Sarah continued. Even though her voice was soft, it seemed to shout through the room. "I tried to wrestle the gun away from him, but he backhanded me. I fell, hit my head on the desk and lost consciousness. When I came to, Jonah was dead, his chest covered in blood, and Zeke helped me bury his body."

That was it, the end of the tape, and Wyatt mentally went through the explanation he'd just heard.

"The stab wound Sarah gave him didn't kill Webb, did it?" Wyatt asked Zeke.

Zeke just resumed his scowl.

"You killed him after Sarah was knocked out cold and then let her believe she'd done it."

Bingo. Wyatt saw the slight reaction in Zeke's eyes, letting him know he'd hit pay dirt.

"It doesn't matter if you don't confess," Kirby pressed. "You're already going down for Sarah's murder and for being an accessory. Plus, a whole boatload of other crimes that involve attempted murder of federal marshals. You'll get the death penalty whether you man up to this or not."

A muscle flickered in Zeke's jaw. "I'm more of a man than you'll ever be, Kirby Granger."

"Really?" Kirby challenged. "Then prove it. Man up."

The muscle flicked harder, and Zeke cursed some raw profanity. "Yeah, I did it. I killed Webb." And that was all he said for several long moments. Wyatt was worried his fit of temper had come and gone.

But it hadn't.

"Webb was blackmailing me for a business deal where he'd arranged to move those guns from Rocky Creek to Mexico, and he would have ruined me. That's why I went to see him that night, to try to reason with him, and I walked in on Sarah stabbing him."

"She didn't kill him," Billy mumbled.

"No. Barely made a cut, with the puny way she lunged at him with that knife. It only pissed him off, and he would have killed her if I hadn't stabbed him and finished the job."

Wyatt shook his head. "You didn't kill Webb to save Sarah. You did it because he was blackmailing you."

Zeke lifted his shoulder. "Doesn't matter none now, does it? It was easy killing him. And when Sarah came to and saw him dead, she just assumed she'd done it. I helped her bury the body."

"When did she tell you about the tape?" Lyla asked.

"A couple of days later. She said if anything happened to her, then everyone would learn that I'd been an accessory to murder."

None of them said anything, but Wyatt could feel the stunned silence. Zeke hadn't been just an accessory. He was the one who'd killed Webb.

"You nearly killed us, too," Lyla said, "when you had the bomb go off at Rocky Creek."

"That wasn't meant to kill you. If it had been, you'd be dead. It was to destroy that damn blood spatter that the CSI geeks found. I cut my hand when I pulled the knife from Webb, and I figured some of my blood could be mixed in with the castoff. I made an anonymous call to report the bomb so you could get out in time."

Wyatt had figured as much. At that point, Zeke would have still wanted Lyla alive so he could force her to manipulate any evidence that might incriminate him. That didn't mean, however, that they couldn't have died in that explosion.

"You're the one who had the embryo stolen," Wyatt said. He was certain of it, but he wanted the admission from the man who'd made their lives a living hell.

Zeke nodded, grumbled something under his breath. "You hadn't exactly kept it a secret that you wanted a kid, and, yeah, I figured you'd try to protect Lyla once she was pregnant. But I also figured you'd be so anxious to protect the baby she was carrying that you'd tell her to do whatever it took—and that included fixing any evidence against me."

It turned Wyatt's stomach to hear a fellow lawman accuse him of something like that. It was true that he would have protected Lyla and the baby, but Wyatt would have never forced her to tamper with evidence. He would have looked for another way. And had found it. That's why Zeke was under arrest right now.

"I'm bringing in your business partner, Greg," Saul informed Zeke.

"He did nothing wrong. Was just a kid when the killing happened, and he heard just enough not to have heard anything that would point to me. A lot of people had a beef with Webb that night."

"But you kept Greg close," Lyla said. "All these years you kept him by your side, in your business, in case he remembered the wrong thing."

"Maybe. But it doesn't matter now."

"It could," Lyla argued. "We got a call from an unknown name and number, It wasn't your voice, but it could have been Greg's. That would make him an accessory to your crimes."

"It wasn't Greg. I hired someone, a lackey, to make that call. I wouldn't have dragged Greg into this when it was easier to pay someone."

That was true, and it would have turned Greg into another loose end that Zeke might have to tie up.

Sheriff Geary started to lead Zeke toward the jail cell, but the man stopped directly in front of Kirby. "Jonah Webb got exactly what he deserved," Zeke snarled.

Kirby nodded. "Now you'll get what you deserve, too."

Zeke was still mumbling profanity when the sheriff hauled him away.

Despite the profanity and the somber mood, there was relief, too. And something else. The realization that for the first time in nearly seventeen years, there was no dark cloud hanging over his family.

But it was more than that.

Lyla was there. Part of it. And Wyatt pulled her back into his arms. "In the hall, I said this was a good time for you to realize you're in love with me."

"I'm in love with you," she whispered.

Now it was Wyatt's turn to lose his tongue. Yeah, it was exactly what he wanted her to say, but he sure as heck hadn't expected it.

"Say it again," he insisted. Because he had to make sure his ears weren't playing tricks on him.

"I'm in love with you," she repeated, and she kissed him.

Wyatt kissed her right back. In fact, he upped it a significant notch until they were breathless, giddy and probably stupid.

But it was the good kind of stupid.

"I want it all with you," he told her. "A family and home. I want you."

"And I want you," she answering, pulling him into another kiss.

That one, too, would have gone on a lot longer than planned if several of his brothers hadn't cleared their throats. Saul, too.

"That's the end of the tape," Saul said, giving them a flat look. "That means you lovebirds can head out and, well, celebrate or something."

Wyatt had the idea of hauling Lyla off to bed to celebrate. Apparently his brothers, Kirby and Stella had a similar thing in mind, because there was a lot of kissing going on in the room.

"Let's get out of here," Lyla said. "Take me home."

And this time there was no doubting what she meant. Wyatt scooped her up in his arms and headed *home*.

* * * * *

"Strip."

"I beg your pardon?" Her shock erupted as a nervous laugh.

The same cute sound, from early that morning, that had been so damn attractive. *Stow it, Marine.* One more time, he debated sharing why it was important to wait on the supplies he needed. He'd be prepared this time.

"I'll wash your clothes while you shower. How did you think we were going to clean up?"

"I… That can't possibly be a good idea—what if they come here and I'm—"

"Soapy?" He laughed, unable to stop himself. The look on her face was priceless. "We weren't followed. Promise. If you're worried about getting on the road, you should probably get moving."

She stood and Dallas jumped off the couch to follow. Bree picked her up and Jake held out his hands to take her.

"The paramedics warned me about an infection." He pointed to his bullet graze. "Do it for me. After all, I did save your life."

THE MARINE'S LAST DEFENCE

BY
ANGI MORGAN

All rights reserved including the right of reproduction in whole or in part in any form. This edition is published by arrangement with Harlequin Books S.A.

This book is sold subject to the condition that it shall not, by way of trade or otherwise, be lent, resold, hired out or otherwise circulated without the prior consent of the publisher in any form of binding or cover other than that in which it is published and without a similar condition including this condition being imposed on the subsequent purchaser.

® and ™ are trademarks owned and used by the trademark owner and/or its licensee. Trademarks marked with ® are registered with the United Kingdom Patent Office and/or the Office for Harmonisation in the Internal Market and in other countries.

Published in Great Britain 2014

Published in Great Britain 2014
by Mills & Boon, an imprint of Harlequin (UK) Limited,
Eton House, 18-24 Paradise Road, Richmond, Surrey, TW9 1SR

© 2014 Angela Platt

ISBN: 978 0 263 91346 0

46-0114

Harlequin (UK) Limited's policy is to use papers that are natural, renewable and recyclable products and made from wood grown in sustainable forests. The logging and manufacturing processes conform to the legal environmental regulations of the country of origin.

Printed and bound in Spain
by Blackprint CPI, Barcelona

Angi Morgan writes Mills & Boon® Intrigue novels "where honor and danger collide with love." She combines actual Texas settings with characters who are in realistic and dangerous situations. Angi has been a finalist for the Bookseller's Best Award, *RT Book Reviews* Best First Series, Gayle Wilson Award of Excellence and the Daphne du Maurier Award.

Angi and her husband live in North Texas, with only the four-legged "kids" left in the house to interrupt her writing. They recently began volunteering for a local Labrador foster program. Visit her website, www.angimorgan.com, or hang out with her on Facebook.

Dallas and Valentine—two sweet puppies who gave love every minute they were here. THANKS, Steve, for your quick responses to my many questions and your many years of service as a police officer. AND THANKS, Jen—we both know this book wouldn't have happened without you.

Prologue

Six Months Ago

"Keep the girl alive. I'm telling you it would be less complicated," Griffin Tyler said. "More money for us, too."

"You don't tell us nothin', Tyler."

Sabrina Watkins flattened herself to the hall paneling. *They wanted to kill her?* She'd been three years behind Griffin in high school, been in youth group with this man who had become her business partner. And recently she'd thought of him as a very close friend. Their mothers even still went to the same church every Sunday morning.

"She has too many friends," the unknown voice continued. "Too many that will believe her when she claims she's innocent. If we leave her alive to chat 'em up, everybody gets sympathetic. It's better to kill her. Make it look like a suicide and then evidence comes out proving how guilty she is. We lose a little money framing her, but overall the operation survives. You set up shop somewhere else. Insurance, no one's the wiser."

She didn't know the second voice. Average tone, not deep or high. She didn't think he'd ever boarded a pet with her. She'd only seen the back of the man's head as she'd rounded the corner from the offices into the clinic. She had no description for the police and didn't even know his hair color since he was wearing a ball cap.

"Whatever," Griffin said, not trying hard to sway his partner. "Suicide works. She's surrounded herself with the business for the past two years. Everything she has is tied up in it. When it goes up in flames, our hometown will think she was too depressed to start over." He put his hands on his hips, a gesture she'd seen a thousand times when he was ready to move on from a subject. "When will you do it?"

Oh, my Lord, they really are going to kill me, she thought, panicking. *Why? What did I do?*

"Listen, Tyler, you're the one who screwed up. Too many fingers in the pie. You should never have involved the local cop who's getting greedy. The higher-ups want them both gone, along with all traces of the connection to us. You're damn lucky they don't want you gone."

Who have you gotten involved with, Griffin?

Sabrina's heart pounded faster than Tweetiepie, the miniature Chihuahua she'd groomed at the truck stop that afternoon. Her hands shook even while she was plastered against the wall. She wanted to close her eyes and have someone explain why this was happening. Could someone wake her up from this nightmare so she could go back to her simple life of boarding pets?

Her thoughts drifted through her last conversation with Griffin. As far as she knew there had been no indicators that he was upset with her. But, then again, how did your best friend speak to you three hours before casually mentioning no one would miss you if you were dead?

Wait. Flames? Had he said flames?

Was Griffin speaking in metaphors or were they really going to burn the clinic down? "Gone...all traces." She had to get to the police. No. The stranger had mentioned involving a cop. Which one? They didn't mention anyone by name. Who could she trust? But they couldn't all be bad. Right?

What could she tell them if she did trust them? She'd overheard her business partner plotting to kill a "she," but unfortunately there were a lot of "shes" in Amarillo, Texas.

She'd look like an idiot. Griffin continued his discussion with the stranger. She couldn't distinguish their words as they walked to the rear exit. She dropped to the floor and crept around the corner into the operating room.

Griffin was right about one thing—she had no other life outside the clinic or pet sitting. He was also right that every dime she had was tied up in her half of the business.

But right now, she needed help.

No one worked in the clinic on Sundays. She made a special trip with the house-call van once a month, working with truck drivers. It was five o'clock and she'd spent the afternoon grooming dogs at the I-40 truck stop and let Amber borrow her car for a baby shower. If she hadn't finished an hour early, decided to restock the van while waiting on her assistant's return, she wouldn't have a clue about their plot to kill her and burn the clinic.

She'd been so dumb. Well, not anymore. It was time to get closer, find out what they were doing.

On her hands and knees, she scooted across the painted concrete floor. Staying close to the counters and then behind the stainless steel exam table, she was careful not to knock any of the rolling trays full of instruments. She'd never felt comfortable in this room. It wasn't organized and certainly didn't function effectively according to what she'd seen over the past two years.

There were many times she'd wondered how Griffin made any money. Now she knew. He made it illegally. She dared to look around the side of the table. There wasn't enough light in her section of the room for her to be seen, but she was still very careful.

"So we're agreed. Tonight," the stranger said. "Get your cop friend to patrol nearby. I'll nab the girl before the fire's set and make it look real enough."

"You think it's necessary to burn the place with the animals inside?"

"You want the fire to look genuine, don't ya?"

The stranger was near the back door. She caught a tilt to his lips when Griffin's back was turned. Her stomach twisted in fear. Whoever this stranger was, he enjoyed killing. Animal or human, that smile indicated he looked forward to it.

She swallowed the bile in her throat and hid behind the island table again. *Oh, God. Oh, God. Oh, God. They were going to kill her.*

What should she do? Remember his voice. Remember that deadly smile and his thin, flat lips. She had no evidence, no proof that someone wanted her dead. And from what she'd overheard, they'd planted evidence that she was responsible for something. Dear Lord, she didn't even know where to start. She knew nothing about police procedures except that they needed more information than she had to begin an investigation.

Fading daylight briefly filled the room as the back door opened and closed. The sound of the dead bolt turning echoed through the cold room. Oh, no, the van was parked out front now. How long had they been here? Would they notice? Would they come back?

Silence.

She sank to the floor. There was nowhere to hide and if they did return, what could she do?

The faint whine of an abandoned pup bolted her into action. No one was going to kill the animals left in her care. She tugged on one of the rolling tables and opened a bin. She yanked a scalpel, wielding it like a hunting knife. She could defend herself a little, maybe deter them long enough to race out the front door.

Explanation or no, she could get to the police to save her own life. Panda and Pogo barked.

The animals. She had to get them out of the building. She took a peek through the windows and didn't see any cars. She ran through the clinic to the back of the boarding kennels and unbolted the door, slightly propping it open for quick access. Then another dash through the building and out the front, moving the van to the back.

Thank goodness she didn't have a lot of animals at the clinic or being boarded for the weekend. The three dogs and kitty would fit inside the van and be safe. She closed the van door with a sigh of relief, dropping her forehead to the cooling metal. She could meet Amber at the house and have her drive the animals to their owners.

Then she would drive her car directly to the police station and take her chances. Crazy sounding or not, she had to report Griffin to the authorities.

"Back early?"

She yelped like one of the puppies. "Oh, Griffin. You scared the living daylights out of me." Her partner jerked her away from the van in a constricted grip. "You're hurting me."

"Don't play dumb, Sabrina. I saw you loading the animals. You heard us inside and are moving them before we torch the place."

She pulled. His grip tightened. "I don't understand any of this, Griffin. What's going on?"

"Get inside." He shoved a gun in her ribs. "Now."

"Don't do this. Don't kill me, please. Whatever the problem is we can work it out." She stumbled as he propelled her through the door. "I'm sure the police can sort through everything."

"No, they can't. I don't give the orders. I follow them. My office."

The gun was securely in his hand and she shuffled through the kennels sideways, unwilling to turn her back to him. What if he had the same maniacal smile as the stranger?

Had Griffin shot someone before? He couldn't have. He wasn't the man who drowned kittens—he was the veterinarian who saved them. Right? But he was an excellent marksman, who wouldn't miss when he fired.

How am I ever going to get away from you? she wondered.

"Is it drugs? Money laundering? Who are you working for?" she asked, stalling. *Think, think, think.* She couldn't allow herself to be trapped in his office. There was no way out. Only a slit of a window, high above her head.

"None of the whys or whos matter anymore, Sabrina. There's nothing you can do."

"Doing nothing is exactly what I did for the past two years while you plotted to set me up to commit suicide." She stopped at his office door, so close to her own.

Unfortunately, her box of an office would be just as bad as his. The window was just as high. There weren't any weapons inside. The can of pepper spray her father insisted she carry was on her key chain, in the van. Her only path out of the building was blocked by Griffin.

"I didn't think they'd really kill anybody. You were supposed to take the blame, but they never said they'd kill you. But it's you or me and I won't let it be me. I'm lucky I came back for my *insurance* before they torch this place. Otherwise, we'd both be dead by morning."

The light in his office was already on. The door was ajar

enough to see an open briefcase overstuffed with paper. His insurance?

"I can't believe you're going to just kill me." But she knew he meant what he said. What if *she* got his "insurance"?

Tears of fear trickled down her cheeks. She covered her face with her hands, leaning close to the picture of puppies they'd rescued last year. But she wouldn't voluntarily move another inch to her death so she spread her feet for a stronger fighting position.

He'd relaxed, leaned lazily against her office door. If she could just delay him long enough to grab the briefcase and get to the van…she might have a chance.

"It's no use," he said. "You might as well stop stalling."

Sabrina looked up, plucking the scalpel from her pocket. "Would you stop?" she shouted, lunging at his leg, stabbing him as deeply as she could.

He screamed. Fell. The gun went off. She darted into his office, grabbed his briefcase of "insurance" and ran for her life.

Chapter One

Present Day

"I didn't complain when I was a private. I didn't complain while serving three tours in Afghanistan. These guys have no clue how to make life miserable for someone like me. I can take a few icy sidewalks and midnight shifts."

Jake Craig skidded on the slushy cement. Digging his steel-toed boots into the ice, he balanced on the slippery incline before he embarrassed himself by slamming to the ground. His partner—sitting in the nice warm car—probably had his smartphone ready, just waiting for him to fall flat on his butt so he could record it all.

The cold of the early morning felt good compared to the many long, hot desert memories he had from six years of war. North Texas cold didn't compare to the bitter mountain freezing when he thought he'd lose his toes. Yeah, he could take his turn walking in the cold. At least this time he didn't have seventy pounds of gear to carry.

On the Dallas P.D. a little over a year, he'd recently transferred to the homicide division. The promotion raised more than a few eyebrows when he jumped from rookie to detective—skipping everything in between, including the right to do so. Not too amazing for former military personnel. His fellow P.D. officers knew about department politics where qualified ex-military got bumped to the head of the list. It didn't keep them from resenting him or make being the butt of their jokes any easier.

Just like now when he'd been directed to search for a dead body. An anonymous 911 call claimed there was a dead woman at the lake moving around in the bushes. He'd asked dispatch to repeat and again the claim was that a dead woman was moving around in the bushes.

"You go see if you can find that ghost," his partner had ordered when they'd arrived. He'd leaned his head against the headrest and shut his eyes. "I'm going to keep the heater running on these old bones, *partner*. You love the cold, don't cha, *partner?*"

"Sure, Owens. I could stay out here all freakin' day." Okay, maybe his reply had been a slight exaggeration. Then again, he hadn't actually replied, just mumbled after he'd left the car. He would continue to accept the late shifts, practical jokes and crank calls, just like he had this morning.

"I'm a freakin' machine." No one could break down the machine at work.

The ghost was probably a drunk trying to get out of the snowfall, but it had to be checked out. What if the call was just a staged joke? Could Owens have arranged for a "ghost" to be at the spillway?

It was the perfect setup. Someone could pop out of the bushes, try to surprise him, and he might even lose his footing. "I will not fall and have that humiliation blasted across the internet. I'll never hear the end of it." Those guys knew he'd be the one out here verifying ghosts don't exist. And he wouldn't put it past any of them to have cooked up this entire charade.

As long as they dished it out, he'd take it. The cold,

searching for a ghost, whatever, he'd keep at the job. He wanted the job. He had nothing else but the job. He wouldn't let it slip through his fingers like the rest of his life.

An early morning search of the underbrush around White Rock Lake beat picking up Friday-night drunks from Deep Ellum any night of the week. Homicide detectives wore civilian clothes, a definite improvement from the street cops. Man, he was glad to be out of a uniform. Any uniform.

His years as a marine MP didn't seem to make a difference to his coworkers. Maybe they thought he was more qualified to deal with drunks than legitimate homicides. If they only knew what he wanted to forget.

The beam from the flashlight reflected off a pair of red eyes. The animal didn't bolt. Jake took a step closer to the fence and heard the low whine of a dog.

A black Labrador was under the brush on the other side of the six-foot security fence. Located just below a large yellow-and-orange danger sign, warning that the lake's spillway was nearby.

The leash must have tangled around a limb, pinning the dog to the cold February ground. The pup yelped, whining louder, visibly shaking from the cold. He dropped back to the ground, obviously tired from his struggle for freedom.

"Hang on, now. How'd you get over there?" Just to his right the section of fence was raised off the ground, easy enough for a dog or person to crawl under.

Jake clicked off the light and dropped it in his pocket. Going over the icy fence was a lot cleaner than crawling under like the dog had. He shook the chain-link fence, verifying it could hold his weight, and scaled it in a few seconds, landing on the spillway side with both feet firm in the melting snow.

"So you're the ghost those drunks reported?" He knelt and offered his hand for the Lab to sniff. It quickly licked his fingers. "You're friendly enough. What are you caught on?"

The stubborn dog refused to budge even with encouragement and a gentle tug on his collar. His young bark did some tugging of its own on Jake's heart—he hadn't thought he had one left—earning a smile from a jaded soldier.

He pushed farther into the bushes, conceding that the only way to get the dog loose was to get wet himself. The poor mutt shivered hard enough to knock his tags together. Jake could relate, having been there a time or two.

Working his tall frame closer, his slacks were soaked as the slush seeped through the cloth. The snow that dropped on the back of his neck quickly melted from his body heat and dampened his skin. He slipped his hand around the dog collar and tugged again, receiving a louder howl and whimper.

"Are you hurt, boy? Is that why you can't move? All right, then. I might as well send my coat to the cleaners, too." He stretched onto his belly, sliding forward until he could reach the hindquarters of the dog, which had gone completely still. "What's wrong besides me calling you a boy when you're clearly a girl?"

Nothing felt out of place or broken. The pup's whine was consistent. The harder he pulled her toward freedom, the more the dog pressed backward.

The leash was caught on something or the pup was injured. He pulled hard and he still couldn't get the leash free. Blindly he followed the leather to an icy death grip of fingers, causing him to instantly retreat. His jerky reaction scared the dog, causing her to struggle harder in the dark.

"It's okay, sweetheart. Take it easy and I'll get you out of here." Jake kept a firm grip on the collar, snagged the flashlight from his pocket and flipped the switch to take a closer look at the body.

The glassy look of the dead took him back to Afghanistan. He'd experienced that look more than once in his military career. Male or female, it always twisted his gut.

Then it hit him. The smell of death. Faint, most likely because of the cold, but there wafting into his brain and triggering more memories that he wanted to forget. Once experienced, he could never forget.

The call hadn't been a prank. The woman's coat was covered in white. She'd been there all night. He'd flattened the crime scene getting to the dang dog, which wouldn't or couldn't leave her side.

"Hold on there, girl. I'm not going to hurt you. Give me a second here." He couldn't remove the leash from the body. So he'd have to disconnect the dog.

Expensive leash with a word etched into the wet leather. "Dallas? That your name or just a souvenir?" He kept a grip on the Lab with his left hand and unsnapped the leash from the dog harness with his right.

He crooned, attempting to calm the shivering mass of fur. He peeled his jacket off in the cramped space, the sharp broken twigs poking him with every shrug. He draped Dallas and shoved his coat under the dog's legs. He took one last look into the frozen face. There was something about her, or the situation.

Something he couldn't put a name to. Or maybe just a habit he'd started with the first investigation he'd had as a military cop. He didn't want to make the vow. He had a clean slate but couldn't stop the words. "Whoever did this won't get away. And I'll take care of your pup, ma'am. That's a promise."

Unable to move, Dallas didn't struggle much covered in his jacket. Jake pulled her free, shimmying under the fence instead of scaling it, dragging the pup under after. Then he sat on a fallen tree, holding Dallas in his lap. He began to feel the cold as the wind whipped through the secluded jogging path that viewed the spillway overlook and hit his wet clothes.

Dallas made a unique noise halfway between a howl and whine.

"It'll be okay, girl. We'll find you another owner before too long." He stroked the pup's head and she quieted just a bit. Her tags indicated a rabies vaccination and that she'd been chipped, but they'd need Animal Control to access the information.

Jake tried his radio. Nothing. He took his cell from its carrier on his hip. Nothing. He moved up the hill until he had reception and dialed.

"Dallas 911. What's your emergency?"

"This is Detective Jake Craig, badge 5942. I have an expired subject. Bus required at Garland and Winstead parking lot WTR 114 marker."

"An ambulance has been dispatched to your location. Do you need me to connect you to Homicide?" the dispatcher asked.

"Thanks, but we're already here."

"Understood, Detective Craig."

Protocol required him to ask for an ambulance, but he knew it wasn't necessary. The woman frozen to the ground a couple of feet away was dead and had been most of the night. He'd seen the dead before. Many times over and under too many circumstances to remember them all. He didn't want to remember.

Life was easier when he didn't.

The pup tipped her soggy face up at him, and then

rested on his thigh. Jake looked around the crushed crime scene as he dialed his partner's cell. "I don't know about you, Dallas, but it's going to be a helluva long day."

Chapter Two

This murder should have been Jake's. He'd discovered that body—and ruined the crime scene. No one razed him or admonished him for being so stupid.

All of the men thought the dog was great. But it was still his job to control it—not an easy task without a leash. He'd found a silver emergency blanket in the trunk and had fashioned a makeshift rope by slicing the end off.

No words saying he should have left the pup there. Nothing except "four black coffees, Craig," turning him into a glorified errand boy. He had to remember that it was the appropriate place for the rookie team member. He walked to the car with a few laughs and snickers behind his back. His partner hadn't offered the keys. No way he was going to beg, but he could keep the pup warm inside the car while he walked across the street.

A local diner was on the opposite corner. He could handle the errands and understood they came with being the newest team member. He'd dumped enough rookies into the same position himself over the years. He was just ready to move forward, to investigate. He hated being stuck with unimportant things. It gave him too much time to think about the life he'd wanted while in Afghanistan that seemed so far out of his reach.

The tremor he'd forgotten started his hand twitching.

He fisted his fingers and shoved it in his pocket. Out of sight, out of his thoughts. Right along with the dreams he'd had from another time.

"Man alive, it's cold out here." A man waited on the corner to cross Gaston Boulevard, jumping in place to keep warm. "You a cop?"

Jake gave a short nod, not in the mood for curious on-lookers. Even those dressed all in black, sturdy shoes and expensive leather gloves. Why was this guy walking anywhere in this weather? *Not everyone's a suspect,* he said, to quiet the suspicions forming in his head.

This wasn't the Middle East, where he couldn't trust a kid crossing the street or even a middle-aged man dressed in black. The light turned red, the walk light blinked on and they both crossed. The man continued to the convenience store next to the diner, probably after cigarettes, since he'd reeked of nicotine.

Jake entered the old-fashioned diner and stuffed his gloves in his pockets. The place was basically empty except for a pretty raven-haired woman in the back booth. As soon as he looked in her direction, she dropped her lips to the edge of the mug and blew, gingerly sipping and not making eye contact.

Nothing suspicious in a young woman wanting to be left alone by a man covered in mud.

A robust man dressed in a bright red-and-black shirt hurried out of the kitchen. He only needed a white beard to look exactly like an off-duty Santa Claus. "Have a seat anywhere," he said, wiping his hands on the bottom of his flannel plaid shirt.

"I just need five coffees to go, Carl." The Santa named Carl looked surprised to hear his name until Jake pointed at his dangling nameplate stuck on his sleeve. "Don't lose that in someone's breakfast."

The woman in the corner laughed, barely, but it was a sweet sound compared to the silent razing he'd been taking for wrecking the murder scene. Sweet, and it brought a smile to his frozen face.

"I was wonderin' how you knew." Carl reached for the cups and coffeepot. "You want cream or sugar?"

"Blacks all round. Thanks."

"Hey, you with the cops at the lake? A guy came in earlier and said you found a body by the dam."

"Detective Jake Craig, Dallas P.D.," Jake acknowledged, trying to dissuade him from asking more questions. It didn't work.

"So was it a woman, like they say? Was she really all in white? Murdered? Froze to death?"

Everyone, including himself, wanted those answers.

"How long have you been at work today?" he asked. If the counter guy wanted to be chatty, might as well point him in the right direction.

"Been here since 'bout midnight, I think. Took a while in this weather with the roads the way they were. I skidded through two different red lights. Glad you weren't around then."

"How about her?" Jake asked about the woman in the corner.

"Bree? She's been here since I came on board."

"That's a long time to nurse a cup of java."

"Nah, happens all the time. And I think that's her fourth or fifth hot chocolate. She nods off every once in a while."

There was a rolling suitcase against the wall next to her. "She homeless?"

"Naw, nothin' like that. Lost her car, broke down a couple of months back, and she walks everywhere. Does jobs for people in Lakewood, picks up an extra shift around here sometimes. Manager don't mind her sitting there when we ain't busy."

"You said she's been here since midnight?" His victim had already been killed by then.

"Yeah, let me get you a carrier for these. I got a new box of 'em in the back," Carl said, putting the last lid on a large cup.

"How much do I owe you?"

"On the house for cops."

After leaving a five, Jake put his wallet away and leaned against the counter, watching the busy intersection. Predawn joggers, walkers with dogs, people driving by and going about their ordinary day. Busy, yet not a single witness. He took the lid off one cup and poured a good amount of sugar in. He'd need the extra calories today.

While he sipped, he watched, honing his skills, making mental notes. Passing the time like he had for so many years.

The woman Carl called Bree shifted in her seat, looking nervous. She'd obviously overheard the conversation with Carl. Most people were more curious for details. When he came across someone who turned away, covered their face and tried to act casual about doing so…it normally meant they were hiding something.

Or was he just being overly suspicious again, wanting to investigate a murder instead of paying his dues by getting coffee?

Stick it out. They'll come around soon enough.

Carl loaded the coffees into the cardboard.

"Thanks, man."

"No problemo. Come back when there's not a murder. Gotta get ready for my breakfast regulars." Carl waved and returned to the kitchen.

"I'll do that." Jake leaned his shoulder against the door,

pushing it open for a fraction of a second. Hit by a blast of frigid air, the coffee carrier tipped toward his filthy coat. He let the door slam, successfully catching the coffees and balancing them against his chest. A tiny giggle from the corner. He looked up and locked eyes with Bree. The woman had a beautiful smile. No matter how brief or even if she was laughing at his near disaster.

She quickly hid her eyes by resting her forehead on her hand. Her reaction made him more than a little curious. He set the container down on the first booth's table and deliberately meandered past the booth that separated them. *Speak.* He stood there, waiting. Expecting…he didn't know what. Anticipation took over his vocal cords, refusing to let them work. He didn't want to ask her why she looked suspicious. He didn't want her to be a suspect or a witness. What he wanted was her phone number.

Naw, he couldn't do that. At least not as a police officer. He hadn't asked for any phone numbers or called any that had been offered to him in the year since his divorce. Dang it. She was a potential witness. He should ask for her information, since she'd been here all night. *Man, that is so weak. Just say something.* His hand had reached inside his coat for his notebook before he realized he needed a pen.

Then her spine straightened, her hands dropped to her lap and she tilted her face up at him. Strikingly magnificent amethyst eyes. He'd never seen that color before.

"Do you need something, Detective?"

"I was…" The pen had been with the notepad earlier. He patted every pocket on his coat. "Can I borrow your pen?"

She didn't turn away, just slid her larger spiral notebook in front of her and handed over the pen from between its pages.

"Thanks."

"If you need one for the crime scene, I'm sure Carl has an extra. That ink's actually pink."

The old saying of a smile lighting up a room popped into his head. He would swear the entire diner had brightened when the corners of her mouth rose, silently amused that he'd be writing with her girlie-colored pen. He shook himself and wrote Carl's name and then *Bree*.

"Ma'am, sorry to disturb you. Carl mentioned you walked here. Did you come through the park?"

"No, not last night. Was someone really murdered?" She visibly relaxed when she answered.

"Unfortunately, yes." Sort of an odd physical reaction to the word *murder*. *Don't read anything into it*.

"That's so sad."

"Yes, ma'am. Did you see anything unusual? Anyone running from the park or a car speeding away?"

"No. But I slept some after midnight."

"I'd like your name and phone number, just in case we have new information and need to pursue it with you. You never know what detail might help."

"It's really hard to see out of these windows at night, Detective. I really don't think there's a need to put me in a report."

He looked up to see the reflection of a man covered in mud—even on his face. He looked like an extra in a disaster movie. He agreed that from the booth you couldn't really see much outside.

"Not for the report. It's only in case I need to get in touch again. I'd prefer your cell number, if possible. Carl said your name was Bree?" He concentrated on the tip of the pen where it met the paper. Not on the disconcerted twitch that occurred at the corner of her eye when he said he wanted information about her.

"Yes. Bree Bowman. And I don't have a phone, but you

can reach me at 214-964-79— Well, shoot, I always get those last numbers confused." She opened the spiral and removed a yellow flyer. "Here."

"Jerome's Pet Sitters. You work here?" He stuffed the paper in his pocket.

"I fill in when I have time. Jerome takes messages."

"Is Bree short for something?"

"No."

She shifted on the bench, looking as uncomfortable as he felt awkward. He knew cops who used the addresses and numbers of pretty girls. That wasn't his style. He couldn't legitimize pushing for her address. He'd get it if he really needed to get in touch.

"That should be enough for now." He set her pen on the table, watching it roll to the edge of the spiral. "Thanks for your cooperation."

"No problemo," she said, imitating Carl.

"Right. Thanks again." He scooped up the coffees, including his own, and headed for the door.

"Wait. Let me help." Bree's voice came from just behind him. "I can get the door so you don't have a disaster with those cups." She darted around him, pushed the door and kept it open while he passed through.

"Thanks for the help."

"You're very welcome."

Like an idiot he stopped and took another look at her. And like someone who hadn't flirted in a decade—which he hadn't—he said, "You know you have the most beautiful eyes I've ever seen."

She inhaled sharply and pressed her lips together. Maybe embarrassed. Maybe flattered. Maybe like she received that compliment a lot. "Thanks, Detective. But it's really cold out."

"Yeah, sorry. Have a nice day."

"You, too."

Just before the door closed, he heard another sweet giggle.

You're such an idiot.

DAWN CAME AND WENT along with the ambulance and dead woman's body. She'd had no identification, no keys, and to their knowledge, no one had reported her missing. Dallas howled endlessly as her owner was removed by the medical examiner.

The obvious assumption was that the victim had been mugged while walking her dog. Locate where the dog lived and they'd discover the identity of the owner.

Simple.

No one was pursuing it. They'd wait on Animal Control to call with the chip's registered address.

After contaminating the scene, Jake had been told he was lucky to be holding the dog. Coffee run completed, he'd waited in the car. Warmed the dog. Fed the dog his sandwich from home. Watered the dog. Pacified the dog. Everyone else finished up, the crime scene had been released, and he was now letting the dog do his business near a tree.

"Hey, Craig," his partner called to him from across the lot, laughing and slapping the back of another longtime detective. "Make sure you wait around for Animal Control to get that mutt. They're expecting you to be right here, so you should probably walk the dog in circles until they show." He laughed some more and threw the car keys. "I'm catching a ride back to the station."

Jake caught the keys and didn't have a chance to ask his partner what they all found so hilarious before the car pulled away. He stood there holding the pup's makeshift leash, fearing the joke was on him. Yeah, he was darn certain that around the station he'd graduated from the position of rookie to leash holder.

The last patrolman headed to his car, pointing at the ground. "You got a bag to clean that up, man?"

Jake shrugged, then shook his head.

"Seriously, man. You can't leave that on the ground like that."

He shot him a look, hoping the patrolman would back off. "I'll get something from Animal Control."

"You gotta set a good example for the kids over there. Leaving it in a park's against city ordinances. You're a cop now."

"Sure. I got it." And he did…get it. The marines were behind him and he was on his own, alone in a city where he barely knew anyone. He'd wanted that after the divorce. No one around to remind him of the six years of humiliation.

Jake sat in his car and started the engine, thinking of amethyst eyes. A better memory than the wasted time he'd invested with his ex. Should he call Bree Bowman?

And then what? Say what? Do what? Ask her to meet for coffee? Maybe he'd make it a habit to have breakfast at the diner and try to catch her there again. And breakfast to boot. It wasn't too far out of his way. Then he might be able to offer a ride sometime. That was a plan he could live with. Slow. No commitment.

Another twenty minutes went by and more kids on bikes gathered in the parking lot. It looked like they wanted his car out of the way so they could take advantage of the ice and snow.

He moved to the far edge of the lot to give the boys room. Some of the tricks they performed were amazing. It wasn't too much longer before Dallas began whining again, soon howling loud enough to attract attention.

This time she clawed at the window as one of the boys

slowly approached from the curb. Dressed in a ski cap, a huge coat that wasn't zipped, and straddling a bike designed more for tricks than street cruising, the teen waved and gestured to roll down the window.

"Hey, Dallas. You get lost, girl?" the teen crooned to the big pup and stuck his gloved hand through the window to stroke the silky ears. "Whatcha doin' way over here?"

"Do you know this dog or the owner?" Jake asked.

"Sure, this is Dallas. She belongs to Mrs. Richardson. I ride past her house every day. Weird that she ran away. She sticks pretty close to home even when she gets loose." The teen continued to pet the pup through the open window. "You a cop? One of the other guys said a drunk froze to death. He got a look at the body bag."

"Would you happen to know her address?"

"It's five or six houses up on Loving Street. The one on the hill. I can take her back if you want. She's run next to my bike before."

"Thanks, but I better hang on to her. What does the house look like?"

He shrugged. "We can show you. Nothing to do around here anymore. It's getting too wet."

"Thanks. There's no rush. Make sure to use the crosswalks."

"It's the second street, mister." The teen turned and tapped the hood before peddling off through the snow. "Try to keep up."

Jake pushed the button to roll up the window and put the car in gear. Dallas turned three circles on the passenger seat before settling. She dropped her head in the crook of Jake's elbow and looked up with dark brown sad eyes.

"It'll be okay, sweetheart." He scratched the pup's snout and then picked up the car radio. "You'll be okay. Somebody with a great yard will snatch you up quick."

One by one the boys followed each other, skidding through the parking lot, enjoying the snow and slush. Sometimes, being a kid had its advantages. No worries and no past.

"Dispatch, Craig to Loving and Winstead. Cancel the Animal Control pickup at White Rock Lake. I'll call back if needed later." He turned on the second street, following the kid he'd spoken with while the others continued straight.

"Detective Craig, no record of a request for Animal Control. Your location is noted."

The other detectives were probably having a big laugh at breakfast with this joke. He'd been left holding a dog leash, waiting for the past two hours on Animal Control when they'd never been notified. Some joke.

But he'd take the hazing. This time it might just work in his favor. When he'd spoken his opinion that the dog had a connection to the murder victim, his partner had put him in charge of the animal.

He'd either return Dallas to her owner without anyone the wiser or call in the identity of the dead woman. Maybe he'd get the last laugh after all.

Chapter Three

Two weeks in one bed. Sabrina could barely believe how much she looked forward to having the same pillow under her head for that long. Living out of a suitcase, shuffling from house to house or a couple of nights in a hotel room had gotten old after the fourth or fifth time. Six months later and she wasn't any closer to discovering Griffin's connection to whoever had ordered her death or who they'd referred to as the "higher-ups."

She was ready to give up her search and her nomad existence. Griffin had accused her of not having a life. Well, he'd been wrong. Her life had been full of people and pets and things to care about. It was living like this that wasn't really living. If that even made sense. A solitary life void of friends and fun. Shoot, she didn't even have a car.

And to top it off, the first inkling of an attraction she'd had was for a cop. A detective she'd nearly given her cell number to. Yes, she'd lied to the detective about owning a cell. What if he'd actually called? What a stupid move that would have been. But he'd seemed so...so shy.

She lifted the suitcase out of the slush as she crossed the last street.

Walking through a little snow wasn't hard for a girl born and raised in the Texas Panhandle. No, sir, a little snow and ice didn't slow her down at all. She walked the four blocks from the coffee shop to her next pet-sitting job, pulling her handy-dandy suitcase. Barely any cars passed by. She'd taken the long way around to avoid the park just in case the detective was still nearby. From her view at the diner, it had appeared empty with the exception of one car and the local kids on their bikes.

Dallas with a layer of snow was a lot different than Amarillo in the same condition. Back home on a Saturday morning all the kids would have been on that hilltop, sliding until their fingers were frozen from grabbing the edge of their plastic or even cardboard sled. She couldn't let herself think of home.

Thinking of the people she'd hurt by running away wouldn't help her get home any sooner. At first, she hadn't contacted her parents because she hadn't wanted anyone in danger from the men working with Griffin. She soon realized being dead made getting around much easier. Law enforcement wasn't searching for her.

Even if the police weren't looking, it didn't mean she could see the handsome detective. That would be thumbing her nose at the good fortune she'd had for the past six months. Sooner or later her luck would run out.

Each day she hoped her family would forgive her when she finally proved her innocence and could go home again. There were three more names to check out and then she'd have to turn herself in to the police. Or use the stolen money to hire a detective to clear her name.

She couldn't do that. The money was evidence. If she'd used it, she could have gone anywhere, hired that dang detective months ago, slept in a nice hotel instead of those shelters the first week. Other than the three hundred dollars she'd been forced to use, over ninety thousand dollars—in very large bills—was now hidden in the liner of her toiletry bag. She'd only grabbed one bundle and hidden the rest with her uncle, who'd helped her leave Amarillo.

Sabrina peeled off her gloves and found her keys in her jacket pocket. She pushed the handle of the suitcase down. The huge monster was wearing out along the bottom faster than the first one she'd bought secondhand. Obtaining another needed to be added to her list of things to get done soon.

Think about that in two weeks. Maybe living out of a suitcase won't be necessary then.

Stomping her wet tennis shoes on the welcome mat, she wished again she had her favorite snow boots. She tried to get as much snow off them as possible before entering Brenda Ellen's immaculate domain and just pulled them off instead, along with her wet socks. She turned her key in the kitchen door, dropping the set into her pocket.

Backing inside, she lifted her case over the threshold, bracing for Dallas's welcome. The big, rambunctious pup could knock her down when she caught her off guard.

No Dallas.

She whistled while shrugging out of her coat and dropping it along with her shoes on top of the suitcase. She clapped. Still no sound of nails clicking on the hardwood floors.

"Dallas," she called. "Mrs. Richardson? Brenda Ellen?"

Had her trip been delayed again because of the snow? Dirty dishes sat on the counter and stove. Weird, because Brenda Ellen Richardson practically ate over the sink when she bothered to eat at home. The loaf of bread was open. Grease in a frying pan where eggs had been cooked. Blood near a block of cheese on the counter.

"Oh, God."

Was that Brenda Ellen's blood? Or had someone else made themselves at home?

Brenda Ellen didn't eat eggs and never fried anything. Had they found her? *No! No! No!* Don't panic. Maybe Brenda Ellen had forgotten to text her that the flight had been delayed. Maybe she'd had company overnight. *That* potential scene was embarrassing but held much less panic.

But where was Dallas? Even if she was locked out of Brenda Ellen's bedroom, she'd be greeting any visitor at the door.

Something was wrong. Brenda Ellen was a business-woman and wouldn't have forgotten to cancel her dog sitter. Should she leave? *Yes, turn and run this minute!* Grabbing the suitcase and running down the sidewalk was the safest thing to do.

And then what? She could go…where?

If someone was here, they'd heard her come inside, heard her whistle for Dallas. They'd follow her down the street. What if they were waiting for her to search the house? What if Brenda Ellen was tied up or…or…worse?

I'm so tired of being afraid, she said to herself.

It was time to stop being afraid and confront the fear. Take action. Do something proactive and not just run. Dial 911 and then leave.

Her cell was packed. Fortunately, or it would have been in plain sight for Detective Jake Craig. *Then get to the landline in the living room, and get help for Brenda Ellen, then leave.* That was a plan. She'd taken self-defense classes. She could get to the phone on Brenda Ellen's desk.

As quietly as possible, she rolled open the drawer that contained the meat mallet. The knives were tempting, but much bigger than the scalpel she'd stabbed Griffin with.

Attempting to get to Brenda Ellen's phone was risky. But she couldn't leave without trying, without knowing if her employer needed help. If Brenda Ellen was in trouble, it was Sabrina's fault and she had to do whatever she could.

Mallet in hand, she knelt at the doorway, trying to see if anyone waited in the living area. Surely, if anyone were there, they would have already come to see who had whistled and clapped. There wasn't anything to be frightened of. Unfortunately, she couldn't stop shaking or thinking about the different possibilities. Overreacting had become the new normal for her.

"There's nothing there." Sabrina stood and shook the tension from her arms but kept the mallet in her hands.

She rounded the corner, prepared to whack any intruder or at least throw the mallet at their head. Nothing. The pillows were out of place, the cushions were crooked and the glass top on the coffee table was shattered.

It might look like an accident had happened, but she knew Brenda Ellen. The woman had given her a five-minute lecture when she hadn't vacuumed one morning.

She froze. Had that been wood creaking? Barely a sound from the carpeted stairs, but she recognized it. Being in the house alone with Dallas, she'd heard it many nights as the pup had gone downstairs to bark and howl. She swallowed hard, the simple silent sound reverberating in her head like a shout. She held her breath.

Was it the man from the clinic? The one who looked like he enjoyed killing? His horrible smile haunted her nightmares where she was endlessly being chased.

Whoever was behind her on the stairs knew she was in the house. She couldn't make it across the room to the phone. She couldn't unbolt the front door without her keys, which were in the pocket of her coat. Out the kitchen door was her only choice.

So she ran. She hated turning her back, afraid the crazy-smile guy would shoot her between the shoulders. Unlike her dreams, where she ran all night, just out of his reach.

He heard her. She could hear his heavy, fast-paced steps.

The lamp from the sofa table toppled to the floor behind her as she skidded around the corner of the kitchen.

Don't look. Don't look. Don't look.

She slid to a stop, yanked the door open as far as her suitcase allowed and jumped the two steps to the driveway.

"Hi, Bree, looking for Dallas?"

It took a couple of seconds to shove her heart from her throat to her chest again. It was just a neighborhood kid she'd met plenty of times while walking the dogs. "Get out of here, Joey."

"It's okay. This cop found her at the lake. I guess she got out after Mrs. Richardson left."

"Cop? Where?" She grabbed his bike handles and pulled. "Come on, Joey. I said to get going."

"What's wrong?" he asked, dragging his feet through the drifting snow.

The door swung open. She caught a glimpse of a barrel, a man in a mask. "Get down!"

Sabrina jerked the handle bars sideways, knocking Joey to the ground and jumping on top of him. A beige blur pulled her sweater and shoved her facedown into the snow next to the street.

"Hold it," a deep voice boomed from above her.

"He's…he's in the house with a gun," she explained, spitting the snow from her mouth.

"You okay, kid?" the voice asked. Nothing like the voice from the clinic. The tones floating to her ears were deep and rich with a natural Texas twang she recognized.

Jake Craig.

She watched Joey's head bob up and down and then an excited gleam dart into his eyes at the thought of danger. *Give it up. It ain't anything like you think it might be, kid.*

"Stay here," the voice commanded as he ran toward the door.

They'd do no such thing.

She was getting Joey as far away from the house as possible. "Get behind that car," she told Joey, who seemed mesmerized.

"But he said—"

"I don't care. Get up and move."

Faster than she thought possible, they were sitting with their backs against the tires. She expected gunfire to explode around them at any moment. The more seconds that ticked by, the easier she breathed, and the more she realized she needed to sneak away before the cop returned.

Her feet were stinging from the cold. Could she get somewhere safe without any shoes?

Scratching against glass. She heard a familiar bark and whine. *Dallas.*

The pup was in good hands. The cop would take care of everything. She could leave without him ever really seeing her face. She shivered from the cold, wiping melting snow from her skin. She could get another used coat when she picked up a new suitcase.

Oh, no! The money!

Whether it was her exasperated cry of utter disappointment or her slow recovery from having been scared to death, Joey responded with an awkward pat on her shoulder.

"Was there really someone inside with a gun?" the teen asked, unable to hide the excitement in his voice. "Was she, like, being robbed or something?"

He started to stand and she tugged him back to her side.

"How did Dallas end up with a policeman? What's going on?"

"See, we was, like, going down to do some stunts in the empty lot and instead there was a lot of cop cars. They hauled somebody off in, like, a real body bag and everything. Then we notice this guy and he had Dallas. So I went over and asked him why."

During the explanation, her heart ventured into another part of her body again. "Do you know who died?"

Dallas barked, pawing at the door.

"You're Mrs. Richardson?" the detective asked, coming around the end of his car. "Is this your dog?"

"Nope, this is Bree. She's the dog sitter," Joey answered.

Jake had a strange look on his face. He listened intently the entire time and never took his eyes off her. Sabrina knew he was tall. He'd towered over her at the diner, but from a sitting position on the ground, he was frighteningly tall. It didn't help that his wary approach seemed ominous. She knew he was legit and not a part of the higher-ups, but she couldn't stop shaking.

"Can I go now?" Joey asked, touching her hand.

She hadn't known she still held the teen's arm. She released him and the cop came closer. He didn't slide around on the quickly defrosting ice. But his clothes looked like he'd already taken a couple of bad spills. She'd seen them in detail at the diner.

"Thanks for the directions, kid."

"I gotta go tell everybody what happened," Joey said. He was down the hill and nearly around the corner by the time she turned to face Jake.

Jake? Detective Craig! The same detective who does not need your phone number, she realized. *Oh, my gosh.* She was even rambling nervously in her thoughts.

"Hold on a minute, sweetheart."

"What?"

He reached past her and stuck his arm inside the car, then swung the door open and Dallas leaped out. The pup joined her, crowding her face with a cold nose. She automatically began running her fingers across the pup's sides. While her chin was being licked, Bree shifted her gaze from the ground, connecting with the detective's curious observation.

The images of a gun, body bags, jail… They all circled her head, making it swim. *Brenda Ellen would have been walking Dallas last night.* She felt desperately ill and dropped her face into the black fur.

"You didn't catch him?" she asked.

"I didn't find anyone, no."

"Is she…? Is that why you were bringing Dallas home?" *Oh, my gosh, she's dead.* Sabrina could tell she was right by the detective's sympathetic sigh and awkwardness.

"I need to ask you a few questions, Miss Bowman." He extended his hand to help her stand.

Sabrina had no choice. Because of her, Brenda Ellen had died. Perhaps she should be arrested and leave the investigating to professionals. She placed her cold fingers within his warm grip and stood. She didn't want to go to jail. "I'm Bree."

"Yeah, I remember."

He kept hold of her hand, steadying her. Gone was the shyness, the awkward bit of flirtation from the diner. They stood there for several seconds until Dallas whimpered and pawed at her legs.

"Maybe we should go inside?" he asked.

"Can we? After that guy was there? I mean, don't you need fingerprints or something? He killed Brenda Ellen."

"Did you actually see someone?" He shoved into her hand some silver material that he'd used for a leash, then tugged her to the sidewalk, protectively pushing her a couple of feet behind a giant sycamore. She winced as the snow covered her feet.

"He pointed a gun at Joey out the door. The kitchen's a wreck and you said someone killed her."

"I didn't say anything."

"Didn't you?"

"No."

"But you found a body and Dallas was at the lake. There's eggs and grease and a mess." She wasn't making sense and, from his curious expression, could tell he was confused.

"Did you actually see someone in the house?"

"Yes. He chased me outside and was going to shoot us, but then you got here."

"What makes you think that? What did he look like?"

"I don't know. He had a mask and a gun. I saw the gun." Her hands shook. She hadn't been this frightened since stabbing Griffin with a scalpel. "She never, ever eats fried food."

"Ma'am, I'm having a hard time following. You aren't making much sense. I didn't find anyone inside, but I can check it out if you want to wait in the car."

"HE KILLED HER, didn't he?"

Bree Bowman was losing it and sort of melted onto the sidewalk along with the snow from the night before. He didn't believe she'd actually fainted but it was close. Jake did the only thing he knew how to do…

He grabbed the leash and lifted Bree. She was a tiny thing, fitting easily into his arms. She was crying hard, and was half-frozen from being outside without a coat or shoes. Her tiny feet were a bluish color, waving in the air. His only option was the house. Crime scene or not.

The door banged half open again. He took a second to look this time at what it hit. He recognized the suitcase from the diner—so she was a house sitter, not only a dog walker. The bottom of the case was still wet, so she hadn't been there long. She clung to the dog leash and Dallas pulled them a couple of steps forward. Jake whacked his hip on a drawer.

"I'm so sorry. I needed the meat mallet in case someone attacked."

"Drop the leash, Bree."

"I can't." She locked her arms around his neck, pulling herself closer. "She'll run through the house, maybe destroy evidence. She's certain to get into things and someone was here. They chased me."

"I've got it. You can let go." She searched his eyes and then let go as instructed.

When he set her on her feet, he kept an arm around her waist to steady her. Dallas continued to tug and beg to be free.

"What makes you think your boss didn't just have an overnight guest who didn't clean up after himself and maybe thought *you* were the intruder?"

"Brenda Ellen was scheduled to leave for Seattle yesterday. Her flight was canceled and she was rescheduled for eleven o'clock this morning," Bree whispered. "She wouldn't have left anything out of place. She never does."

Jake searched the kitchen. It was immaculate compared to his apartment. "Look, even if someone was here earlier, they're gone now."

"How do you know they aren't hiding? Where'd they go? All the doors are still closed. What if someone was with the man with the gun?"

"I checked out the perimeter and backyard." He needed to follow procedure and begin from the beginning. But instead, he broke protocol and placed his hands on Bree's shoulders, trying to reassure her it would be okay.

Great, he hadn't even called the location into his partner or captain yet. If someone had been there, they were long gone. He had little hope of a BOLO. Bree inhaled and opened her mouth to speak again. He covered her parted lips with a finger. Her warm breath escaped, but she didn't utter a sound.

"I'm going to call for backup. You're going to stay here with Dallas. Try to keep her quiet. Nod if you understand?"

She barely moved. He wanted to dab her wet lashes and give her a long hug. Why? Maybe it was the sympathy he felt for the dog spilling over to this petite, caring woman. Or the way she'd giggled at him in the diner. He didn't know and squashed the urge.

"One thing first. What did Brenda Ellen Richardson look like?"

"Dark brown hair, about my length, slender, average height."

"What color were her eyes?"

"Were? She's…then she *is* who you found at the lake. They're brown."

She described his murder victim. With his luck, he'd be destroying more evidence by searching the house, but he needed to secure it. He pulled his cell from its belt holster. "Wait here."

Jake called for backup and moved methodically through the rest of the house. Once he was in the front room, he saw a picture of his murder victim, laughing with an older couple. Most likely her parents. And then another of her with a golden retriever. He called his partner, giving him the name and address, and hung up before the old goat could gripe at him for being inside the house.

The furniture was nice, no dust on the shelves, a variety of books in the hallway case. From his point of view, barely anything was out of place. Breakfast dishes, a drop of blood from slicing cheese and a cracked coffee table that could have happened when the dog ran through the house. It didn't look like there'd been an intruder.

But he entered each room as if an AK-47 was on the opposite side of the door. He couldn't help it. Old habits were hard to break. His last partner had laughed a couple of times, but it had quickly become a routine for them. Better safe than sorry.

A dress was lying on the bedspread—could have been worn Friday or laid out for today, he couldn't tell. Two nice suitcases sat in the corner by the master bath, giving credence to Bree's story.

The house was clear. His backup should be here in a few minutes. Time to get some information from his witness and get himself back on this case. He headed downstairs and Dallas greeted him halfway up. "So you got loose. Overanxious?"

He hooked his hand in the leash and spent a couple of minutes coaxing the pup to go with him.

"I need to ask you a couple of questions now." He entered the kitchen, but his witness was no longer there. Gone, along with the coat and suitcase.

He'd fallen for her act, hook, line and sinker.

Chapter Four

"Dark hair, amethyst eyes, about five-three or -four. Looks a lot like the victim from the back. Nothing like her up close. Probably about twenty-five." If Jake went into detail about the heart shape of her face, the petite bone structure or how he'd noticed the way her nose curved at the tip and had five distinct freckles, his partner would think him nuts. Or might believe Jake had let her go deliberately.

As it was, the razing hadn't ceased since Detective Elton Owens had shown up to continue the investigation. More precisely, the murder investigation that didn't involve Jake. Owens stood there, checking his notes, treating Jake like a suspect. Or worse, like a naive rookie.

"You say you saw her at the diner this morning? And you didn't think to mention this when you returned with coffee?"

"Come on, Owens. There was no way to know she was the victim's house sitter. You'd still be waiting on Missing Persons or the chip information about the dog if I hadn't followed the kids here." And Animal Control, if it hadn't been for the kids. He knew he was acting defensively and was just tired enough not to care.

Owens ignored him and asked the crime scene investigator some questions.

Jake knew he'd been a good police officer over the past

year. He'd accepted being the low man on the totem pole in Homicide, accepting the grunt work, not caring how many hours he worked without pay. He didn't have a life outside of the job and didn't want one. Working over Christmas had kept him from a face-to-face meeting with his parents, siblings and other relatives.

Being around his family made him uncomfortable. Being grilled by his partner was almost as bad.

His family had never asked if the accusations his ex-wife had made were true, but they'd also never said the words were lies. Maybe they interpreted his embarrassment for being blind to his wife's indiscretions, somehow making him the guilty party. After a while, it just didn't matter. It was easier to let sleeping dogs lie and avoid confrontations about his disastrous marriage. He was moving past his first wife and the war.

Thing about it—he *was* past his ex. And that was the hardest part for his parents to understand. Sad, but whatever had been there in the beginning of his marriage had slipped away after spending months and thousands of miles apart over the past six years.

When the position opened in Dallas—three hours from his hometown in east Texas—he jumped at it. He needed a new start and it was easier that way. A year later and he was working in Homicide. Exactly where he wanted to be.

Now his partner assumed he'd made mistakes instead of decisions. He'd like someone—anyone—to trust his judgment. No one really had since he'd left the corps. Well, he couldn't actually blame them. He'd let the witness escape. Bree had turned on the waterworks and he'd been suckered in, big-time.

Bamboozled. That's right, Craig, teased the devil sitting on his shoulder.

Owens removed the picture from the frame. "Definitely

our victim. Looks like we need to find her parents to notify. The dog sitter, this Bree woman, you say she seemed more frightened that someone was in the house than that Mrs. Richardson had been murdered."

"I didn't say that, Owens. She was visibly upset about both instances." *I think.*

"When you get back to the station, you can spend the day looking through mug shots. We'll be taking a hard look at Richardson's finances, see if we can find payment to this mysterious dog sitter. Right now, she's our only lead." He closed the notebook, returning it to his jacket pocket. "You sure she was a dog sitter?"

"Joey knew her and seemed to trust her."

"No last name on the kid or any of the other kids?" he asked, but barely paused. "I'll get a sketch artist to the diner and an officer moving house to house. Shouldn't be too hard to locate this chick. Oh, and the captain wants to see you when you return."

"I figured."

Owens left the house, laughing as he stood on the porch talking to the first responding officer—as luck would have it—the same guy who had told him to set a good example for the kids at the park.

"It'll get easier, you know," Shirley, the crime scene analyst, interrupted his self-deprecation.

He stopped himself from asking what she referred to by compressing his lips together. He knew the answer, just didn't want to have the conversation.

"The ribbing goes away. This is how they treat all the new guys."

"Find anything?" He'd rather hear about the case—even if he wasn't officially a part of the investigation.

"It will all be in my report. I'd rather not take wild guesses."

"Hey, this is Jake Craig, the detective who's not officially on the case. Can't you give me the unofficial version? It won't go any further. Promise." He flashed her a smile, hoping it did the trick. Blatant flirting never hurt.

"Okay. It looks like she was killed at the park. Only a drop of blood in the kitchen and no real struggle other than in the living room."

"Any fingerprints? The dog sitter said the victim kept things clean and lived alone."

"The table does appear to have been shattered today. Very few of the pieces were ground deeply into the carpet. The prints left around the house are fresh and easy to find. We'll rule out the victim's easily enough."

"So it was wiped clean?"

"I don't think so. I agree with the missing dog sitter. I believe the victim did like things clean and took care of it almost daily." His confusion must have appeared on his face since Shirley continued. "Look around you. The owner of this house had a black dog and white carpet. Either the dog didn't live inside, or someone was meticulous about cleaning."

"Got it. What about the footprints in the backyard?" he asked as the analyst gathered her gear. "Anything there?"

Jake stuck his hands in his pockets. He caught a glimpse of his tattered appearance in the mirror and pushed his shoulders back, standing tall. His mother had taught him he looked defeated when he slouched. He wouldn't let this situation defeat him.

The marines corrected the high school self-consciousness of being six inches taller than everyone else around him. But his first week out of uniform, faced with a divorce, living with his parents and not having a future had his mother badgering him to stand up straight on more than one occasion.

"With the layer of snow and ice, it's impossible to gather

anything. Let's just say the little bit of evidence I've collected won't be the strongest lead for solving this homicide." She slipped into her coat.

"Did you catch what the medical examiner surmised was the cause of death?" Definitely strangulation in his opinion. He'd seen the same bloodred eyes on a marine killed by a local militant.

"This isn't official, mind you, but the M.E. noted the subconjunctival hemorrhages before they moved the body." With the last of her winter wear in place, she lifted her cases and flashed him a smile. "In layman terms, she was strangled."

He followed her to the front door and held the outer one open, lowering his voice. "Sounds premeditated if they made it look like it happened while walking her dog and then came back here to cook themselves breakfast."

"Came back is right. They estimated her TOD sometime between eight and eleven last night."

Premeditated and yet the death wasn't violent like a lovers' quarrel. The guy had probably strangled her while she was walking the dog.

Heartless? Had they left the pup to freeze or not killed the dog because they liked animals? Premeditation bugged him. It didn't fit. The murderer seemed to be waiting around for something—or somebody—*after* the murder. Had the dog sitter taken them by surprise or had they been lying in wait?

Exactly who had she been running from when he drove up and why had she run when he was upstairs?

"Shirley?" He caught up with her on the front walk. "I need a favor." Jake handed her his business card. "Can you send the results from the fingerprint search to me? Specifically the one you lifted from the kitchen drawer. That's my cell."

"Sure, but I thought Owens said—"

"Yeah, the favor is you're not going to tell him I know."

"Oh, that won't be a problem. So you think we'll find a match." Shirley stashed his card in her pocket.

"She was too scared for her knees to work. And there is the fact that she ran without putting on her shoes." As indicated by two sets of bare footprints that led into the street.

"It would seem so." Shirley smiled and picked up her case. "I meant to ask, what happened to the dog from this morning?"

"Animal Control showed up this time." It helped when they were actually called—which he'd done personally. "A kid saw Dallas with me at the park and led me here."

"That was lucky, then. I hope someone claims her. Big, black dogs don't get adopted so easily, especially ones with a blind eye. See ya." She waved and got into her car.

Jake sat in his car. "Blind eye? I couldn't tell she was half-blind. Dallas is a good pup. Somebody will adopt her."

The dog deserved someone with a huge yard. Or someone close to a park where she could be trained to catch flying disks or retrieve tennis balls. From the little he'd seen of her interaction with Bree, Dallas had a huge heart. And the loyalty she'd displayed staying with her owner and fighting not to leave her side after she'd been freed, sort of reminded him of his marine brothers.

Would a pup like that get adopted? Or was it amazing she'd been adopted the first time. He'd seen genuine relief on his mystery woman's face when he'd walked up with Dallas. Call it a hunch or good detective work, but he'd bet his next paycheck that Bree wouldn't let Dallas stay overnight in the city pound.

Owens and the rest of the responders were out front, walking toward their vehicles. If he was right about the dog sitter showing up to rescue Dallas, he'd obtain the answers to many of his questions. Official case or not, it wouldn't stop him from finding the murderer.

He'd stared into Brenda Ellen Richardson's death gaze. He was connected to her. He'd also held a half-frozen dog walker in his arms and hoped somehow he was wrong about why she'd been so dang frightened. And especially wrong about why she'd run away.

After a series of calls, Jake finally got the information he needed and the pound location. He circled through a hamburger joint and dealt with his stomach's insistence to be fed. Two burgers and twenty minutes later, he parked in the far corner of the parking lot at the Dallas Animal Services and waited.

Late on a Saturday afternoon, there weren't too many people around. Most of the visitors had a kid or two with them. When a woman driving a really nice ride pulled to a stop, Jake's attention perked up.

Sure enough, less than fifteen minutes later, she had Dallas on a leash and was loading her into the backseat. Jake didn't have to tail the woman closely. They were following the path they'd both taken to get there…straight back to White Rock Lake.

And straight back to Bree.

Chapter Five

"Who's that hunky man? Nice car, but he looks like he wallowed in the snow a couple of times today." Julie brazenly ogled the detective while handing Dallas's leash to Sabrina.

The detective from Brenda Ellen's house? Here? She couldn't turn to look. Maybe he hadn't seen her.

Strong hands landed on her shoulders and long fingers locked her in place inches from his chest. "There you are, Bree. Sorry, I'm a little early."

Oh, shoot. What should she do?

Sabrina hid her surprise as the detective came to her side, tugged her hand from her pocket and locked his fingers with hers. His fingers were warm and his grip secure. His nearness turned her inner thermostat up several degrees. At least he hadn't shoved her face into the picnic table and slapped cuffs on her.

Detective Craig was being gracious and sparing her the embarrassment of an arrest in front of a friend and employer. Julie was just an employer. The only one home who could go pick up Dallas from the pound. And only after Bree had agreed to look after her dogs without charge once.

"Oh, hi, I'm Julie Butler," she bubbled. "No wonder you didn't mind the cold, Bree. Having such a nice guy to warm you back up."

"Sorry to rush you two, but we should probably get

going," he said. "Got to run by my place for some different duds."

Sabrina caught a glimpse of his free hand pointing at his mud-stained pants.

"You two are going out. That's good. Bree shouldn't be alone tonight. Did she tell you Brenda Ellen was murdered?"

"Yes, I was the first person she spoke to about it." He patted her hand. "You're like ice, Bree. We need to get you in front of the car heater."

She'd let him know just how inappropriate he was behaving. Later. Right now, she was grateful not to say another word.

"I should get her home." He kept her hand firmly sealed in his, anchoring her in place.

"Terrible about Brenda Ellen. I'll never feel safe out here again. But Bree, dear, you promised to give me all the details if I picked up Dallas for you." Julie emphasized her fright by dropping her hand across her rather large breasts.

"Another time," the detective said.

"We'll see you in two weeks to sit with the dogs. We're gone four nights and you can bring Dallas with you to the house. If you need to, that is."

"Thanks for picking her up, Julie."

"Ta-ta for now."

Another of her house-sitting jobs walked away. Sabrina acknowledged it would probably be the last time she saw her. If she got away from the police, she'd have to leave all the dogs she worked with.

"Should I thank you, Detective? Or demand a lawyer? Very clever of you to track me down through Dallas. How did you know I wouldn't leave her in the pound?"

"I have to admit I was stuck the first couple of hours, thinking more about what would make you run from the police. But the forensics analyst said black dogs were less likely to be adopted. Then she mentioned the pup was blind in one eye—totally missed that. She seems normal enough."

"She is," she said, defending the puppy.

"I didn't think you'd risk an adoption. Care to answer a couple of questions before we call a lawyer?"

"Well, as you can see, I'm extremely busy right now." She pointed to Dallas, who was doing her best to get off the cold ground. Her scrambling included jumping and slapping her large front paws against Bree's chest.

"Busy leaving?" He pointed to the suitcase just inside a row of bushes.

"Oh, I haven't been home yet. I needed to wait close by for Julie."

"And is home close, since you seem to be walking everywhere? Wait, you ran away five hours ago and haven't made it home and couldn't wait it out at the diner. They put an officer on the place. So you really are cold. I'll be glad to give you a lift so we can chat where it's warm or we could just head directly to see my captain."

"I'm sure we can clear this up right here." She sat at the picnic table, where she'd been waiting since Julie texted.

"I need to see your ID." He extended a hand from the end of the table.

She felt like Jack facing the giant in the fairy tale. "I, um, I lost it about three weeks ago."

"No driver's license? Convenient. Can you remember the number? Or let's try a simple question. One not too taxing on your elusive memory. What's your real name?" He crossed his arms, acting as if he didn't expect a real answer. "Think you can manage that?"

She had barely met him this morning, but she could already tell that the slight curve of the left side of his mouth meant trouble.

"I beg your pardon?"

"Beg all you want, but until I find out who you are—" he paused, digging into his back pocket and then swinging a pair of handcuffs on the tips of two fingers "—you're under arrest."

"For what?" Of course she knew, suspicion of murder, fleeing a crime scene, impeding an investigation. They'd pile on the charges and detain her. Then they'd find out that everyone she cared about in Amarillo thought she was dead. As soon as the police discovered she wasn't, she'd be charged with the murder of whoever was in the clinic fire. And she shouldn't forget about the embezzling and fraud charges that would be sure to follow.

Yes, she knew the answer to her own question…even if this cute detective didn't.

"Fleeing the scene will get us started. I'm certain you're wanted for something, since you're pretty good at avoiding your real name." He gestured for her to hold out her hands to be cuffed. "You know we're going to find out from the prints. Right?"

She held both her hands in front of her, hoping they'd be loosely snapped over her thick gloves. No such luck. He pulled the black fur down, his thumb caressing her pulse.

Did he feel her heart racing?

He took the leash, put a hand on her head and guided her into the backseat of his car. He pulled the shoulder strap and buckled her inside, then gave Dallas a kiss-kiss sound and a gentle tug on her leash. The big, smiling Lab jumped across her, did a couple of turns and settled her head in Bree's lap.

"I hate to ask, but could you get my suitcase? It's on the other side of the bushes."

"Yeah, I saw it."

The door shut, the locks clicked and she was alone while the detective retrieved her stuff. As soon as his back was turned, she tried the door.

Childproof locks. She was stuck. Caught. Going to jail. She stroked Dallas's soft fur, loving the comforting companionship. Somehow she just didn't feel alone when the dog was around.

"Well, girl, I'm not certain what's going to happen now. It breaks my heart to send you back to the pound."

Dallas answered with a sweet sound just like she understood and was commiserating. Brenda Ellen had adopted Dallas four months ago and, honestly, probably never should have. The businesswoman traveled almost twice a month and was gone at least a week for each trip. "I've spent more time with you than she did. Isn't that right, sweetheart?"

Sabrina dropped her cheek to the top of Dallas's head. She was such a loving dog. The trunk opened and closed. It was time to explain everything to Detective Jake Craig. He was her last hope.

"Any chance you're as hungry as I am?" she asked when he was inside the car and had adjusted the rearview mirror to see her.

"I grabbed a burger across the street from the pound while following your friend."

"Oh."

That new look crossing his face lifted one side of his tightly closed mouth, but it clearly indicated pity. She'd learned to recognize it very quickly, hating each time she'd received it over the past six months. But today, right this very minute, it seemed like a sign that her story may not fall on deaf ears.

"I've got some cold fries." He held them out, his long arm extending over Dallas's head.

"Thanks." She shifted her position and held her hands out to take the carton. "Maybe this will keep my stomach from grumbling."

"You should be glad I've got you in custody."

"You think I should be glad to be on my way to jail?" She hated the prospect of being framed and having no one on her side trying to discover the truth.

"Who said anything about jail? Right now I just want some questions answered."

When her family was notified she was alive, they'd be bombarded with questions and accusations, too. They'd only be happy for a moment, learning to hate her very quickly. They'd believe if she could lie about her death, she could lie about a murder.

They'd match her prints since they were on file with the state because of her business. He'd be questioning her right up until they discovered she was a dead woman. But she wasn't—Brenda Ellen was. How had things gotten so out of control?

"Couldn't I just answer your questions here?" she asked, hoping.

She gulped. The dry, cold fry didn't want to go down.

"I don't think that's a good idea." He draped his arm across the seat and stared. Stared straight into her eyes without blinking, without darting those hypnotic deep brown spheres anywhere else. "See, I know your secret, Bree."

This man did something to her. Stirred something she hadn't ever experienced before and couldn't name. Roughly along the lines of instant trust, because he was gaining intimate knowledge without any words. If he searched her inside as deeply as his stare indicated he would, what would he find? An innocent woman had died because of her, didn't that make her guilty now?

She swallowed hard, needing to break the silent interrogation he'd begun. "So you know I love working as a dog walker and moonlight as a serial killer?"

"You're a funny gal." He turned the key and faced her again after putting the car in Reverse. "I know that Brenda Ellen Richardson wasn't the intended victim. You were."

Chapter Six

The silence in the backseat surprised him. Jake expected lots of tears from those magnificent amethyst eyes. Along with a healthy dose of denial and persuasive words attempting to get him to release her.

Dallas whined and nudged the fry container from Bree's lap so she could drop her head there. A moment later Bree buried her face in the pup's fur and he heard a few long intakes of breath as she slowed the tears to a stop.

"I probably shouldn't have sprung it on you like that," he admitted, but gauging her reaction had seemed important. Not so much now.

She wiped both her eyes with the edge of her coat sleeve. "Oh, my gosh, stop being so nice to me and let's just get this done. Haul me to jail so I can tell them everything."

Another unusual reaction.

"Why don't we just start with your real name?"

"It's Bree."

"Do you know who's after you?"

"Can't we just go to the police station, Detective? I don't think the man who killed Brenda Ellen is going to give up as easily as the rest of the police."

"You're with me now and only ten minutes away from a holding cell. I think you're safe enough." Jake put the car into gear and pulled away from the curb. "I've got a hunch you're running from someone. I can help, Bree."

"I know you think you can, Detective. But I seriously doubt you will. I don't think anyone will believe me."

Something twisted in Jake's gut. How many times had he said those words to himself? Why bother explaining what had happened when no one was going to believe him. He'd been convicted without a trial by his family, but he hadn't put up a defense, either.

"Why don't you try me?"

Bree's eyes came to life when they met his in the mirror. He could see the indecision and decided to listen. He turned off the main road and pulled into another parking lot north of the boat ramps, facing the water that was calm after the snowfall the night before.

"I don't know how to start."

"I'd say the beginning. We might need to go for the short version and who's trying to kill you."

She shook her head. "That's just it. I don't know who. They tried to kill me in Amarillo and instead I took something they want back."

"Drugs?"

"No. At least I don't think it's about drugs. I grabbed a list of names and money."

"Where is it now?"

"You see, they were trying to frame me for embezzlement. I don't know how or why except that the man who ordered my death said there was no choice, that it was a direct order from the higher-ups. I grabbed the briefcase and ran."

Still keeping him at arm's length. He knew she'd deliberately not told him everything. He could hear the hesitation in her voice and recognized the deliberate selection of her words.

"How long ago was this?"

"Six very long months." She sighed and looked out the window.

"And how come they haven't found you before now? And why now?"

"I've been working as a house and pet sitter. Personal recommendations and referrals, so I don't actually work for a company."

"Off the grid. So how did they find you?"

"I've been trying to find the 'higher-ups' and have spent a lot of time searching on Brenda Ellen's computer."

Tears again. He was glad there was a seat between them. If there hadn't been, he'd probably have an arm around her shoulders or he'd be patting her back, attempting to comfort. He could relate. He'd been there. Responsible. Blaming himself. Wondering what he could have done differently.

"I never intended for anyone else to get caught up in this mess. I can't believe she's gone."

"Thing is, it *did* happen and the actions can't be changed. But you can help catch the man who strangled the life from Brenda Ellen Richardson."

"How? By going to jail? Who'll clear my name then?"

"You need to tell us everything, Bree. How can I help when you won't even trust me with your name?" He wanted to crack this case wide open. He couldn't deny the anticipation of that happening and could really get into rubbing it in his partner's face. At least for a minute or two.

Through the back window, a truck slowed and reversed. On a busy day at the lake, it might have been an innocent enough action. In the ice and snow, when the streets were basically deserted, a warning jump-started his adrenaline. It suddenly turned, speeding down the incline, and headed straight toward them.

"Hold on!" Jake threw the car into Reverse, trying to get out of the way.

Too late. The car's tires spun, barely moving them while the truck grew into the size of a monster vehicle in his side mirrors. He braced himself for the collision.

The impact slammed them forward and the truck didn't stop. Jake kept his foot on the brake, turned the wheel, pulled the emergency brake. Nothing stopped them.

"We're going into the water. Unlock the doors!"

Bree was right. The truck had the power and traction to ram them a second time, jolting them forward. There was nothing between them and the water. He pushed the button, lowering the front windows.

Dallas barked. Bree yelled. Jake released his seat belt and pulled his weapon and cell. He tossed the phone in the back. "Call 911."

Five more feet and they'd be in the lake. He released the wheel and got a firm grip on his Beretta. He turned, fired at the truck, connected. The car tipped into the water and he no longer had a shot.

"They're going to kill us."

"Stay calm. The safest place for you is here. The car's not going any farther."

"You don't know that. Get me out of here."

"Trust me, Bree. Stay here. I'll be back. I won't let anything happen to you. I promise." He tugged his heavy overcoat off. It would weigh him down in the water.

"You can't—"

Jake didn't hear the end of her sentence. The front seat was filling quickly and he had to secure the area before he got Bree out of the car. He launched himself through the passenger window and heard the gunfire before kicking hard and away from the car.

He surfaced and fired two rounds. The truck backed

away. It didn't make sense. They had the weapons to kill them. Could have rammed the car underwater completely. They were gone in seconds. No license tags to memorize and they'd probably ditch the truck a few miles away. He looked back to the car. Bree was in the front seat, calling to Dallas to come to her.

The frightened pup had crawled to the back window and wouldn't budge.

"Get to shore, Bree. Come on." He stuck his hands through the window and gently tugged on her arm.

"Oh, my gosh. She's scared to death and won't come to me." She locked eyes with him. Pleading.

"I won't leave the pup."

Bree put her cuffed hands in his and he pulled her through the window while the car shifted, sinking a bit deeper into the lake. He steadied her slim figure on the slick rocks until she could stand on her own.

He shook his head, all the while knowing he had to get the traumatized puppy. He holstered his weapon. "They might come back, so stay close to the car. I don't think it's moving again."

"Don't worry. I'm not going anywhere. You'll probably have to carry her."

The doors were still locked, keys in the ignition. He tried the lock button, electrical was gone. "Dallas, come on, pup." He tried coaxing her with kissy sounds, but like this morning at the body of Mrs. Richardson, nothing worked.

"She's blind on her right side, Detective. I don't think she can even see you."

That might partially be the reason, but most likely, the animal was just scared. As scared as the woman climbing up the grassy shore? "I told you to stay put, Bree. You keep moving and I'm coming after you instead of the dog."

"I'll be freezing in the snow instead of freezing in the water. Trust me, Detective, I have nowhere to go." She raised her cuffed wrists to him, emphasizing her captive status.

Restraints hadn't dissuaded some of the men he'd captured before. He hoped she spoke the truth because, for the life of him, he couldn't abandon the dog. He held his breath and climbed back inside the vehicle. This was the first time he'd been grateful to be issued a huge tank of a car, instead of a newer economy size.

Jake shrugged out of his suit jacket and took a couple of deep breaths to prepare for the icy submersion. He maneuvered his long body into the backseat almost as soon as his feet crossed through the window. He broke the water's surface, grabbed Dallas and then lost her when her body hit the ice water. He spun in the water to get out and caught movement on the driver's side of the car. The men who had run them into the lake were approaching through the bushes.

"Look out!" He slammed his hand against the roof, scaring the circling pup trying to get back to the dry rear window.

He pushed the dog under the water and she popped up outside the car. He followed as fast as his legs could push him through, hearing Bree's screams under the water. When he came up for air, she was still yelling at the man who carried her across his shoulder up the small hill to the road.

"Watch out!" she screamed.

He turned away from Bree's abductor and straight into something slamming into his ribs. He'd been a second too late all day, but not anymore.

The rocks were slippery under him, but he scrambled to get through the frozen reeds to the shore. He caught the piece of wood when his attacker tried to ram it in his gut. He shoved back, sending the man slipping backward on the ice.

Jake followed and got an uppercut under the man's chin. A left. Another right. The man stumbled back with each hit. Jake tugged the mask at the top of his head, showing a chin that could barely grow hair. The kid couldn't be more than twenty years old. He still held the branch in one hand while he yanked the ski mask back into place. Jake recognized the crazy, wide-eyed, out-of-his-element look.

The kid blinked, panted hard and dropped the branch. *He's going to run.* Jake was ready to dive and knock the young man to the ground, but the kid pulled a gun. He began firing—wildly. Jake heard a bullet connect with metal, and one ricocheted off a rock. And the third...

Bright shards of light exploded, obscuring his view of anything else and sending him to his knees. He hit the water, plunging face-first into the icy lake. He fought to stay aware. Bree's "no" echoed between his ears along with the thumping of his heart. There was a sharp shove against his ear. Was the floating a sensation or was he really on top of the water?

Shot. Conscious but unable to react. Was this it? Had he survived six years in a war zone to come home and drown in two feet of water?

Hell, no.

Chapter Seven

Jake was dead.

Bree would never forget the twinkle in his eyes when they first met in the diner and how he'd seemed too shy to ask for her phone number. Or how he'd rushed into the house chasing Brenda Ellen's murderer. Or how he hadn't embarrassed her in front of Julie before arresting her in the park.

A good man was dead because of her running. How many more would die? *It has to stop.* "This has to stop," she shouted into the darkness surrounding her. She sniffed one last time, rubbing her nose on her drenched, smelly coat, then kicked out against the car trunk.

Her abductors—and Jake's murderers—had been parked for several minutes. She was petrified but determined to be strong. She'd faced the unknown before. She'd faced Griffin and escaped. She could do it again with a little luck.

Footsteps. A pop. Jarring light shining in her eyes.

"Get out."

"I, um, I can't. My legs are cramping and I can't move."

"Do you think I give a flip?" As much as he tried, the man who'd shot Jake couldn't disguise that his voice was high-pitched and his eyes darted questioningly all around him. It was plain to see he wasn't in charge.

His gloved hands fisted on her collar and the handcuffs, using both to jerk her from the small trunk. Her legs protested and she fell to the concrete floor. It made no difference. He wrapped a hand in her clothing and hair at the back of her neck and dragged her across the filthy floor. He pulled her into a chair on the other side of the expansive abandoned room and began taping her to it.

The man who had carried her over his shoulder from the lake was smoking a cigarette, leaning on the roof of the compact. She wouldn't cry. Not another tear. No matter what they did to her. "You won't get away with this. The man you let drown was a homicide detective. There will be a citywide manhunt for you."

"Like anybody saw us." The younger one laughed as he sliced the end of the tape and stuck his knife back inside his boot.

"Wait," the man in charge said, flipping his cigarette into a pile of rubble. "Our little friend here must be cold in that wet coat of hers. Let me help her a minute."

"She's handcuffed, Larry. We can't—"

He waited until he was in the younger one's face and flipped open a switchblade close to his ski-mask-covered nose. "What did I say about names?"

Bree swallowed hard, her throat dry and sore from the frightened tears she'd shed as she bounced in the trunk. The blade came closer. He polished the flat side just below her collarbone, the long, sharp edge just an inch away from her throat. She dared not look down, afraid that he might cut her and everything would be over.

He guided the knife down her arm, slicing her coat like butter when he came back to her neck. Across, around, down her sleeve and slicing on the way back up. She felt the tip only a couple of times on her right arm as it snagged in her sweater. If he broke the skin, she couldn't tell in her state of mind.

He yanked the coat remnants back over her shoulders. The pieces would have fallen, but he continued, asserting his power by threatening her with each slice.

Her coat lay in shreds around the chair. The man who had shot Jake came closer and wrapped the tape around her chest, forcing her close to the chair. She could barely take a deep breath and definitely couldn't move. She could no longer tell if she shivered because of the cold or shook because of the adrenaline firing through her body.

It took her a minute after they'd both walked away, but she finally got her voice. "What are we doing here?" she yelled to the men.

The man who'd attacked Jake glanced up from the back of the car, but only for a second. He seemed nervous, young, inexperienced, while the older guy, who he'd called Larry, had that dare-me-to-hurt-you look. The same evil gleam she'd seen on Griffin's cohort's face at the animal clinic.

"What do you want?" she asked Larry and his underling. They'd ignored her since taping her to the chair. She hated not knowing why they'd kept her alive. It honestly surprised her since they'd killed Brenda Ellen in such a horrible way.

Not much time had passed since the lake. Her clothes were still wet. Each minute seemed like five while she froze in the drafty warehouse. Colder now that he'd taken so much delight in cutting her coat. Remembering the blunt side of the blade against her skin made her shiver more.

Shafts of light filtered inside from windows high above her head, too high to climb out—if she could get free. It proved the sun was still shining. But the time didn't make much difference. Not really.

No one knew where she was, and no one knew she was in danger. Jake hadn't called his department or asked for backup after he'd found her.

These men could kill her and leave her body anywhere. Her parents already thought she was dead. Absolutely no one would know. She had to get free and, if nothing else, turn herself over to the police to stop more innocent people from dying.

Jake Craig was a hero who died trying to save her. He had a family. Brenda Ellen had parents. Those families deserved the truth. Their deaths weren't going to be in vain. The tears for a man she barely knew threatened to spill, but she couldn't lose control. She'd cry later.

The two men were masked and she couldn't identify them if she did manage to escape. They'd changed cars and she'd bumped around in the trunk for a short drive across downtown.

Escaping didn't seem possible. But could she convince them to release her?

Money!

"You don't know where the money is, do you? That's why you're keeping me alive."

"Shut up. Just shut it. I won't be tellin' you again," the terrifying Larry said, punching a fist in her direction.

Facing this man was nothing like confronting Griffin in their offices. She'd been scared six months ago but able to fight. Tied and feeling helpless, she was more frightened of these men, who stood twenty feet from her. Still near the second car, they argued. Jake's murderer kept looking at his watch and then checking his cell phone.

They're waiting on instructions.

She twisted against the duct tape that barely shifted against her wet clothes. And then the handcuffs jingling made her think of Jake's body floating facedown in that water. She wanted to shriek, shout, use some of the self-defense she'd learned to hurt the man who'd killed Jake. It was an unreasonable desire, but his death seemed unreasonable, too.

She barely knew the detective, but his needless death had pushed her further than she could handle. *Get a grip on yourself and get out of here so their deaths aren't just a number!*

"You can have the money. All two million of it. You don't have to turn it over to Griffin. Have you thought of that?"

Both men stared at her. The younger started to talk, but the other hit the side of his head.

One phone call would get them their money. She'd left the briefcase with the only person from her family who knew she was alive. It would be easy to meet him—but not to save herself.

All she needed was to use one code word and her uncle would bring the police to the meeting. She might go to jail, but she was a witness to the murder of a police detective. She could put these men away for life. Jake's death would mean something.

"It's finally time," Larry said.

The younger guy dialed the phone he'd been holding. The mean one yanked it away, stormed across the warehouse and stuck it in front of her face.

"Hello, Sabrina." That smooth voice was her partner's—her former partner.

"You stinking coward. How's your leg, Griffin? Rotting off, I hope."

"I'm afraid I'm better than your policeman," he said without skipping a beat.

She swallowed hard to hold off the tears. Two people had died today because of her. She wouldn't give Griffin

Tyler the satisfaction of knowing how scared she was of these men.

The prearranged phone call confirmed what Jake had surmised about Brenda Ellen not being the intended victim. Who was she kidding? She hadn't needed any confirmation. It was her fault and she'd make up for it. Somehow.

"We have a slight problem, hon," Griffin said sweetly.

"So what?" She recognized the phony coaxing he used to talk to his clients. It had made her eyes roll six months ago. Now her stomach rolled instead.

"Always the smart aleck. We need the briefcase you stole from me."

"I don't have it."

"Look, Sabrina. These men *will* hurt you and still get their money back. So you might as well tell them."

"You don't understand. I really don't have it, Griffin. These buffoons left my stuff in the trunk of the car. Now it's with the cops—at least part of it is. The rest is hidden in Amarillo."

Hope bubbled inside her while Griffin screamed unsavory words at the masked men. "Get it back. You know what will happen if we don't. I'll instruct the others to move ahead with her family. Do whatever it takes."

Griffin disconnected and the screen went black.

"What is he talking about? What does 'move ahead with my family' mean? My family has nothing to do with the money. They can't help you. They think I'm dead."

"Too late now. Maybe you should have thought about that before you took off with the payoff." Larry flicked another cigarette over his shoulder as he shoved the other guy into a corner. He spoke too low to decipher any of the conversation.

It appeared that the men chasing her had men chasing

them. Griffin's voice hadn't just shaken with anger—he'd sounded afraid.

"Wait! I can get the money back." She could get almost all of the money from where it was hidden. But if something happened to her family… She was sinking in the deep end and needed help. Maybe she could get the police involved by exchanging the suitcase for her family. Maybe. Most likely not, but if there was a chance, she had to try. "Just let me go and I'll give you the money when I get it back."

"You said it was with the cops," the younger one whined. The mean one hit him along the side of his head again.

"Don't listen. She's going to say anything to get us to let her go," the leader said. "But it won't work."

"Do *you* want to waltz into the police station and ask for it? How do you think that will go over?" she said.

"Maybe better if you hadn't killed that cop." Larry punched the younger man standing in front of him.

Again, the thought of Detective Jake Craig being dead made her take a quick couple of breaths to stop the tears. In spite of the handcuffs, she really liked the man. He'd been smart and genuinely seemed to like Dallas.

"I keep telling you, man, I didn't kill him. The damn dog pawed at him and flipped him over. I saw the annoying SOB stand up in the water before I got in the car."

Thank you, God. Jake was okay. He was going to kill her if she escaped, but he was alive.

"I know how to get my suitcase back," she said to them. Both stared at her. Their dark eyes eerily reflected the sunlight. She wanted to gulp again but didn't allow herself. "You can exchange me for the money."

"How? I ain't calling no police station," the younger guy declared, shaking his head.

"There's a phone in my stuff. If the police have it, some-one will give it to the detective and you can demand an exchange."

"What if they don't answer?"

"I don't know. Maybe someone will hear the phone ring and give Detective Craig a message. We can at least try." She wanted to plead, coax, nudge or do whatever to convince these men to get Jake involved again. He'd help. He had to help.

The man who'd carried her to the truck prodded the other. "This might be our lucky break. We still got the phone she was holding?"

"That's his," she said quickly. "He'll recognize the num-ber straight away. Won't that help?"

"We got one shot at this. Get that phone out of the car," the mean one instructed.

The younger guy ran into the far corner of the ware-house. It was dark, but she heard the click of a door open-ing and saw the small pin of light from inside the car.

The one giving orders came back to her and leaned so close she could smell his rancid cologne. "You better hear what I'm about to say and understand that I'd have stran-gled you as quick as that other bitch if Tyler had let me. I will, if you cross us, and you probably will, anyway. No hesitation and no regret."

"If you're going to kill me, then why should I get the money back for you?"

"I know what a softie you are for them dogs you baby-sit. I swear to you I'll kill 'em all if I don't get that cash back." His gaze turned excited as much as his voice shook with evil delight. "Then there's your family. I could have fun watching that younger sister of yours beg a little. No tellin' what she might do first."

There was no doubt in her heart that this killer wasn't

exaggerating. He would follow through on his oath. He wanted to kill her and everyone else in his path. It didn't matter what or who. Everything about him shouted that he enjoyed killing.

"I, um, I can get you the money, but I need the phone from the police station. I hid part of it in Amarillo. But if I don't call, they'll send it to the police with a letter."

He turned away, repeating most of the words Griffin had muttered minutes before. He spun, reached out and began crushing her larynx. The tape held her upper arms close to her chest. She tried raising her hand, ineptly knocking at his side. He was going to kill her and there was nothing she could do. He squeezed just enough to keep her from getting a full breath.

"If you double-cross me, sweetheart, there's nowhere you can hide. Do you understand me? I know where your family lives, Sabrina Watkins. I don't only work for your weak-hearted vet friend. The people who call the shots are worse than you can imagine I am."

"Stop, man. Don't jump the gun. We need her." The second man pulled at the hand while she barely wheezed air into her lungs.

The madman released her and stomped away. She sucked blessed air, all the while coughing and feeling like a vise was still latched around her throat. A bottle of water was soon at her lips and tipped, pouring into her mouth. She coughed and choked, letting most of it stream down her chin.

The calm murderer wagged his finger in her face, resting the bottle on her shoulder. "Talk to your cop and convince him you're dead if he don't help. You should know my partner's not foolin' around."

Yes, she did.

"And you should also know," he whispered, "they's already got someone watching your house 24/7. As soon as they get the call, your family's sittin' in another warehouse like this one with guns at their heads. So don't think you can warn the police or nothing. 'Cause we'll know and your family's dead."

She'd been scared plenty of times over the past six months. The worst had been the day it had all started and she'd listened to them planning to kill her. This was much more horrible. If she died, that was one thing. But the maniac in the corner would seek revenge on her family, make them suffer before killing them.

She'd worried about her family's well-being before but never thought Griffin would kill them. Maybe rob their house, looking for a sign of where she was staying. It was the main reason she hadn't contacted them. Giving these monsters the money was her only choice. She couldn't let anything happen to her family.

Now she had to convince Jake to help her.

"We aren't letting you out of our sight." The mean one stormed toward them. "You tell that cop nothing. We get the phone, get rid of him—again—and we take you back to Amarillo."

"That…that won't work." Her brain scrambled for a reason and could only tell them a version of the truth. "The person who's keeping the money…"

"Yeah?"

"They…um, I convinced them to help me but I swore I'd turn the money over to the police. We need Jake to get it back."

Both men cursed. Bree shut her eyes as a fist loomed close to her head.

"Come on, man," the younger guy murmured. "She can't be beat up."

Bree opened her eyes and Larry was jerking his forearm free as he retreated to the car.

"Don't get any ideas, princess." The younger guy gently slapped her cheek. "All I want is the money. Then he can do whatever he wants."

Chapter Eight

Jake waited in a chair in Captain Kennedy's office. He was ready to face his boss, ready to explain the events of today and not look like an imbecile. He hadn't been the only detective to initially miss the dog sitter's involvement earlier in the day, yet he was the only one called back to the office to be held accountable for her kidnapping.

He'd been patient with the razing, the errands, the grunt work for his fellow detectives. He took his work seriously and would let his supervisor know that he did—even while holding a shivering puppy in the crook of his arm.

There was something special about this pup. Sad eyes. A loyal spirit. He'd connected with her this morning at the death of her owner. Giving her up wasn't an option. He'd decided to keep Dallas and wouldn't send her back to the shelter after she'd saved his life. So he held her in spite of the wet-dog smell and her shivering in her sleep. One officer at the desk had offered to take Dallas off his hands, but he'd shaken his head. Maybe his deadly look had discouraged anyone else from making another attempt.

He'd reported straight to the captain's office upon his return and had been waiting for at least half an hour. There hadn't been much for him to take care of at the scene. Owens had arrived and ordered a patrolman to escort him back. Other officers had returned and were already breaking for coffee.

"You've screwed this case up enough for a review board hearing," the captain said, slamming the door behind him and startling Dallas to a low growl. "They'll contact you when they're ready to convene. Contact your union rep, but until then, you're suspended. Your liability will be determined in regards to the escape of a prisoner and destruction of city property."

Jake stood, shifting the forty-pound pup that was getting heavier by the minute. He soothed her between the ears and used the motion to keep his own cool. He wasn't used to making mistakes. He definitely wasn't used to reprimands ending with a suspension.

"Technically, at the time, she wasn't a prisoner, just an uncooperative witness. Destruction of city property? If you mean the car, I was attacked and rammed into a lake. Doesn't that—"

Dallas interrupted him by barking, clawing at the warming blanket given to them by the paramedics.

"Don't think about setting that dog down in my office. That disgusting mutt stinks," the captain remarked before shuffling through more papers. "You should have gotten rid of it with Animal Control before reporting to me."

"Came straight here just like you requested. She saved my life, sir. I have no intention of sending her to the pound."

The captain tapped a pen, clicking the button with each touch to his desk, never looking up. Giving thought to his decision about suspending him or annoyed at the delay? Jake couldn't tell.

"I would like to explain why I—"

"Your actions today have reeked of insubordination. You disregarded direct orders and if I have any say, you'll be gone for good. I'd start looking for a job somewhere else. Maybe back in the Podunk town you sprouted from."

Again, the captain had addressed him without a direct look. The pen had waved in the air by the captain's ear, but he'd kept his gaze on the folder he'd opened. Jake swallowed hard and forced himself to loosen his hold on Dallas before he upset her further.

"I followed the lead I was assigned." Maybe Owens hadn't reported all the facts? "We'd never have known about the suspect. Or that she was the intended victim."

"So you say. If you'd followed procedures, she'd be in holding." The captain dug in his desk drawer but continued to click the pen annoyingly. "For all you know, this woman was working with the murderers and escaped."

"I saw them abduct her. We'll be lucky if she's still alive."

He slammed the drawer and finally looked Jake in the eye. "If alive, we don't need your inexperience to find her and treat her as a wanted felon." He stood, leaning forward on his desk. "Her prints match a woman who was assumed dead in an Amarillo fire. Now that we know Sabrina Watkins is alive, she's wanted for murder. But that's none of your concern."

"Assumed dead?"

"Amarillo identified her remains in the fire of her business. She's cunning and has resources enough to switch dental records. Her business partner accused her of embezzlement and the next day the building was in ashes." He sat and returned his attention to the file.

"This case feels more complicated than a murder/robbery. Are you certain—"

"You're suspended and it's no longer your concern. Leave your badge." The man didn't bother looking him in the eye while suspending him. He dialed the phone and requested Personnel.

Reprimands were never easy to take. Mistakes were made and corrected. You looked the commanding officer in the eye like a man, assuring him you understood. With your salute, you assured him you'd learn from your error and it wouldn't happen again. But what did you do when a man refused to look at you?

Jake reached for the door with his free hand. *This isn't the military, but I still don't retreat,* he thought to himself.

"If given the opportunity, I'd be a good Dallas homicide detective." An unlikely harrumph surfaced from behind him. Jake pivoted in time to receive the older man's glare.

"There are plenty of officers who put in their time and are waiting for a chance in this department. They know how we do things and have more experience guarding our citizens." He looked back at the paperwork on his desk, using the pen to point to a table by the door. "Leave your badge and weapon."

"Can't help you with that. Must be at the bottom of the lake with the car." His biceps burned from holding the pup in his arms, but denying the captain his moment re-energized his determination not to complain.

"Incompetent fool."

Jake's badge *was* in the car, inside his coat pocket, nothing foolish about its location. His weapon, however, was in the small of his back, under his suit jacket. Keeping his firearm did amount to insubordination. It belonged to him and he wouldn't give it up. His instincts told him he'd be needing it to save Bree Watkins.

Oorah.

He'd halfway decided to help her when she'd cried into the pup's fur just before they'd been forced into the lake. Now that he was suspended there was no question. His gut told him she was in trouble and someone had to help. If she was still alive, he'd find her and straighten this mess out.

Never leave a man behind.

"I put in my time, Captain. Eight years to be exact. Six of them overseas in a war zone. If there weren't a lady present..." He shifted Dallas, who barked on cue. "I might have shown you a bit of the experience I obtained guarding our citizens."

If there'd been a chance of being reinstated, it was none to gone now. The slamming door sent the remaining people in their office running. He stomped to his desk like a sullen child, again upsetting the pup. He nuzzled her with his chin before tying her to his chair.

Alone, he stowed his few personal items in the same box that he'd brought them to the office the previous week. Dallas patiently waited, wrapped in the remnants of the emergency blanket, her sleepy eyes drooped to a close for another nap. He could relate; it had been a long day.

An annoying cell phone rang. Muted, like in a desk. He ignored it and finished stowing his things. He sat on the corner of his desk, scrubbing his face and wondering what he could do to find Sabrina Watkins. Nothing official. That was for certain. He'd made no friends at the station. With the exception of Sharon in Forensics. He'd asked for a heads-up about the fingerprints, but—shoot, he didn't have his phone.

"That's it, Dallas." The pup's head sprung up at her name. "I can trace my phone. Bree or her abductors might still have it."

The annoying cell tune played again. Another look around the desks and he saw the screen light up inside an evidence bag. It was part of the contents from Bree's suitcase.

Late on a Saturday afternoon, there had been few officers at the station. He took a step toward the break room to locate the officer handling the evidence. *What if they miss the call? What if it's her?*

The only person in sight was the captain, who had his ear to the phone, back to his door. By the looks of it, he was shouting and ticked off—probably because Jake had dared to question his authority. Telling him the suspect's phone was ringing would do what? Would he listen to reason? Send someone to rescue her?

Jake lifted the evidence bag. It could be anyone calling her. Anyone from her life, leaving a message or a clue to what was really going on.

Hell, that's my number calling.

No retreat. He broke the seal and answered.

"Who is this and why do you have my phone?"

"Jake. Thank God, you're alive and okay. I can't believe it's you."

Bree's voice sounded relieved but nervous. He'd encountered numerous hostile witnesses afraid for their lives. He recognized the vocal patterns. He thought he'd been finished with surprises today.

"Where are you, Miss Watkins? Can you talk? Do you know who abducted you?" He lowered his voice and moved back to his desk, keeping a close eye on the doorway and stuffing the evidence bag into a file cabinet.

"They want the money located in my suitcase, Jake. If you'll bring it to Brenda Ellen's house, they promise to let me go."

A quick glance showed him there wasn't enough money to kill over. A couple of hundred had already been bagged. Something was off. "I don't know what you're talking—"

Bree screamed. It sounded like she'd been slapped and the phone had fallen to the floor.

"You bring the suitcase where we met this mornin' or you'll find another dead dog walker," a man shouted.

"Wait, there's nothing—"

The line was dead.

No one in the station had witnessed the call and the captain was still occupied with his own conversation. Jake slipped the phone into his jacket pocket. The suitcase had been emptied. Mostly personal items. Clothes, a toiletry bag and dark hair dye—making him wonder about the natural color of Bree's hair.

Constantly scanning for the officer's return, he quickly searched the lining of the case. Nothing.

Then he dumped the toothpaste and makeup from the smaller bag. A lining had been sewn inside. A little tug and it was gone. Hidden between two pieces of cardboard was a large stack of hundred-dollar bills. He stuck all of it in his pocket and replaced the personal items to cover his discovery.

No time to count. He scooped Dallas under one arm and the box in the other, then left the building.

What the heck are you doing, man? Put the money back before someone notices. You're breaking your oath to uphold the law. Are you keeping your promise to a dead woman? Or did the amethyst eyes take over more than your brain?

He didn't have to think about it. Bree Watkins was innocent and needed his help. If his gut was wrong, he'd be the one dumping her in his captain's lap along with her two buddies who'd sent the department car into White Rock Lake.

Inside his truck, the questions of how he'd accomplish this feat without assistance crossed his mind a time or two. A rescue with no team. No backup. No plan.

"Aw, don't be scared, pup. Come here, girl." He patted his leg and Dallas crawled onto his lap, swiveling her head to view him from her left. "There's always the marine corps if I don't go to jail. Either way, I'll get you a good home."

But before that, he had to find Bree. He'd seen the desperation for someone to believe her in those special eyes. He felt the setup in his gut. It was all too convenient. Her genuine look of hopelessness as that brawny son of a bitch carried her away strengthened his resolve to get her back. If they'd wanted her dead, they would have shot her in the lake.

There had to be something he was missing. They knew he was a cop. The stack of bills wasn't enough to risk a ransom drop. There had to be more to the story. He needed details from Bree.

The phone company didn't want to cooperate, but he coaxed until they verified his phone was near the Lakewood area. He'd make good time back to the murder scene. Bree's abductors wouldn't know what he drove so he passed by the house, parking diagonal with a good view of the perimeter. The sky had darkened while the sun dropped behind more forecasted snow clouds. He waited a good fifteen minutes. No activity anywhere on the street.

Dallas whined when he moved her off his lap. She was probably hungry, thirsty and needed to pee. But she'd have to wait in the rear seat of his truck. He had a single-handed rescue to execute.

Chapter Nine

Bree's captors had taped her to the dining room chair in the same way they had at the warehouse. Brenda Ellen's home was eerily empty. She didn't know why she'd hoped police or anyone else would have been here. Her friend and employer had mentioned that her parents had retired to the Hill Country near Llano, Texas, and they didn't travel long distances.

"Remember what I told you. We'll be close by. If your cop buddy thinks about throwing you in jail, he's dead. Then we start on your family. We'll be watching." The man who'd choked Brenda Ellen was dangerously crazy and determined to get the money. He would have killed anyone here.

Somehow, she had to convince Jake to take her to Amarillo. No, she could get to her uncle on her own. She just needed her phone to call, then Uncle Jerry would know it was okay to give her the money. *Please have the money, Jake.* She'd been instructed to leave with the cop, bring him with her and prevent him from seeking help from other cops. Maybe she could escape if the keys to the car were still in the kitchen. She could borrow Brenda Ellen's car without the police realizing it was missing.

Jake didn't have to help her. He was safer if he didn't.

Now that she had a plan, waiting was miserable. Her

wrists were sore, her legs weak. She had eaten only two fries since she'd met Jake that morning at the diner. Even then it had only been some toast and coffee to tide her over until she could cook her own here.

This morning seemed so long ago.

The interior of the house was pitch-black. The blinds and drapes covered the windows. It had been different this morning, full of light and the promise of a soft bed for two weeks. Bree wanted to cry, recalling once again that Brenda Ellen was gone.

No, she hadn't just died. She'd been violently murdered. Her own throat ached, her stomach growled again and she desperately needed water. At the moment there was nothing to do except think and pray. She heard the click of a doorknob turning in the silence of the empty house.

"Detective Craig?" Her whisper came out dry and hoarse.

He silently moved through the kitchen and dining room doorway, raising a finger to his lips to silence her. Then he replaced his hand under his handgun. She'd seen actors imitate "clearing the room," as they put it. Experiencing a strong man like Jake coming to rescue her sort of made her insides jump around like an excited Chihuahua.

"They left right after they phoned you. We're alone." Did she sound convincing? She didn't want to get him killed. Two souls on her conscience were enough.

"Are you injured?" he whispered, kneeling at her side with his back to her, weapon ready to defend.

Natural posture for a police officer. It wasn't just for her. *Remember that.* She'd been so alone, having dreamed too often that someone would swoop into the picture and save her. The delight that he'd come to her rescue stemmed from that wishful thinking—not reality. He was just doing his job.

"No." She cleared her parched throat. "I'm a little shaky, but what about you? I thought he'd killed you. I just need you to cut me loose and we can get out of here. Did Dallas stay with you? Is she back at the animal shelter?"

He didn't acknowledge her. He stood and pressed his back to the wall next to the staircase. There was a stark white bandage just above his ear. He must have sliced it when he'd fallen into the lake.

Poor little Dallas. The thought of the puppy roaming in the snow saddened her heart.

She remained silent while he searched the house. There was no way for her to prove they were alone. The crazy murderer could have returned to the house, lying in wait to kill them both. She wouldn't put it past him. Her only hope was that those men needed the money and knew they wouldn't recover it if they killed her.

"The house looks clear," he said as he stepped from the stairs. His gun disappeared behind his back and he pulled his pocketknife, slicing through the silver tape strapping her in place.

"I hope you have the key to these." She jangled the cuffs, hearing them clink in the dark. "A girl loves jewelry, but this is a little much."

She couldn't get to Amarillo if she was handcuffed. *Please have the key.*

"Good to see you haven't lost your sense of humor. The cuffs stay until I get some satisfactory answers. I've already broken enough laws without freeing a wanted fugitive trying to escape."

"Wanted fugitive?"

"Dallas P.D. wants you for questioning about your employer's murder. Along with this business of identity theft, embezzlement and arson. Then there's the body Amarillo P.D. assumed was you when your business burned." Dark brown eyes, even darker now, kept searching the room and sliding to the door to the backyard, watching for the enemy. If he knew what these men were capable of, he'd want to leave as quickly as possible.

"Shouldn't you be reading me my rights or something? If that's the case, I may as well ask for a lawyer now."

His eyes narrowed, bringing his brows into a straight line. "But I didn't Mirandize you."

Her eyes had adjusted to the dark long before his arrival. She noticed the sharp angles making up his intense face. "What does that mean?"

"I'd like to hear what happened directly from you before I make up my mind. Right now I think we should get someplace safe."

Nowhere was safe until the money was back in Griffin's grubby paws. Jake lifted her to her numb legs, continuing to hold her elbow when she stumbled, encouraging her to the edge of the kitchen.

"Wait. Please. Did you bring the phone and the money from my suitcase?"

He shook his head and she couldn't breathe. It was worse than being choked. And just like that, her knees were on the carpeted floor. Tears blurred her vision and she couldn't prevent the incoherent babbling about thinking he was dead or getting him killed. It all ran together in her head and especially across her lips.

"No one's going to harm you," Jake said, now on his knee beside her. "I can call for backup. You're safe now."

"We can't go out there yet." She shook her head and took hold of his hand. "Please don't." She lowered her voice to a whisper so they couldn't be heard. "If they can't kill you or me…they'll kill my family." There was no doubt in her mind everyone she loved was in danger. No one would be safe. "They want their money back."

He leaned in close to her ear. "I assume they're listening. Just remember I'm on your side. How much did you steal?"

"I didn't—" Jake knew they were listening. "That monster will kill anyone who gets in his way. He likes hurting and killing. I have to get Griffin the rest of the money and I need my phone to get it. You have to help me, Jake."

Jake wanted them to hear what they said. She could see it in his eyes and the slight nod of his head.

"I need more than that you feel threatened, Bree," he said louder. "Do you want to have this conversation here? Okay. Who are these men? Where did they take you? Why does the Amarillo P.D. think you're dead? What's so important about this particular phone? There's nothing stored on it. I checked."

"I must use that number to call the person who has the money. If I use any other phone, he won't come. There aren't any exceptions. No one will ever find the money." She covered her face with her cold hands. The handcuffs jingling snapped her attention back to Jake before she spilled all her secrets.

Stay calm. Griffin's men already knew too much. Then what would they do? Force her to make a call to her uncle on the off chance they wouldn't kill everyone she loved? If the deep furrow between Jake's brows meant he was confused, that was good. She'd almost told him her uncle's name.

"Let me get you somewhere safe and you can start from the beginning. Maybe I'll actually understand some of this," he said, lifting her to her feet and guiding her to the door.

"Do you have a way to get the phone, Jake?"

"That might be possible." He gently tugged, attempting to get her outside—she stayed put. "You told me to bring the money from your case, but there was only a few grand. Not enough to kill over."

"I only brought one bundle for emergency. I think there was around two million in the briefcase. I didn't stop to count. I was in a hurry at the time."

"No wonder they want the money back. Let's go." He twisted at his waist and took another look around the room. "You need police protection while they sort this mess out."

"I can't go to jail." His gun was right at her fingers. She knew how to use it. She didn't want to hurt or betray him—he'd already sacrificed so much for her. But she couldn't let him take her to the police. He wouldn't believe her story. Why would they? She sounded crazy and just didn't have a choice.

"It's better if we sort through—"

The gun shook in her hands. She was more afraid she'd pull the trigger by accident than what would happen if he took it away. The straight edge of his hand chopped hard on her wrist, numbing her fingers, which dropped his weapon. He snatched it before she had feeling again.

"Weren't you ever taught not to play with loaded guns. Don't be foolish, Miss Watkins." He stashed the pistol behind him again.

"I think you'd try to get away if it were your family they were threatening," she said, to focus her thoughts on what was important.

"I wouldn't try. I'd succeed. Are they threatening your family, Bree?"

He held out his hand and she placed both of hers in his grasp. He pulled her close, wrapping an arm around her waist, keeping her on her feet. Still cuffed, her hands were between them, separating their chests. She could feel the rapid beating of her heart and his. She didn't miss the sharp intake of his breathing as her body connected with his.

His eyes had dropped to her breasts. Her nipples—hard from a damp bra and the cold—poked through the thin cotton turtleneck. Any man would have taken a look, right? Her coat and sweater had been sopping wet. The man who'd thrown her over his shoulder had scared her half to death by using a knife as long as her hand to hack the coat off her arms since the handcuffs were in the way.

How could she be so aware of everything around her and so unfocused where her family was concerned?

"Hired thugs are on their way to abduct my family in Amarillo right now. If I don't get the money to them in three days, the man you fought with is going to kill my little sister. They could be hurting them already. Please don't put their lives in danger by taking me to jail."

"Let's go."

"Jake, please," she begged. It was the only option left for her. "Please give me the phone and let me go."

He yanked her closer. "Why don't you tell me the truth?"

She tugged his shirt collar until he bent low enough to get her lips close to his ear, then she whispered, "They're listening to us through a phone that's taped to the edge of the table. If we don't prove that I have the cash, we're both dead. Right now. They told me not to say anything or they'd shoot you. I swear."

His warm breath brushed her ear, sending the wrong type of message to her body, before he whispered, "Trust me, Bree. I can get you out of here safely, but you can't lie to me again."

Jake stood tall, giving her a moment for her head to catch up to his words. It had been so long since she'd been this close to a man... No, wait, she was light-headed from dehydration, lack of sleep and too much stress. The adrenaline of being abducted and rescued was doing weird things to her insides. Jake Craig had nothing to do with it.

He glared intently through the sliding door into the darkness of the backyard. "It goes against my better judgment," he said firmly, loud enough to be heard. "I'm already in hot water with the captain. I took some of the money that was with the phone."

He put a finger over her lips. Then slipped his hand into his pocket and showed her the money she'd hidden in her bag. He removed several bills and slapped them onto the dining table. "I could only grab a couple of thousand or they'd realize something was wrong with the inventory."

"You're going to help me?"

"Nothing's holding me here. I can help you get past the cops and protect you from the men who abducted you. I just want a piece of the action. Have we got a deal?"

If she hadn't known it was all an act, she might have been fooled. The quirk of his eyebrow and the slight rise of the corner of his mouth would have convinced her he was sincere and just in it for the money.

But after the day they'd shared, she knew this man was much too honorable to succumb to a bribe.

Thank goodness the men listening at the other end of the phone had no clue.

Chapter Ten

Jake didn't let go of her as they left the house. Greeted by Dallas at the truck window, Bree's face lit up. He unlocked his truck door, ready to let her scoot across the seat. Instead, she faced him, blowing on her fingers, her dark eyes darting around as if she was thinking hard on her next words.

"I need to call my family as soon as possible," she finally said.

"I need more information before I allow you to call anyone. Get in."

"Hi, Dallas." Bree's voice changed. No longer sounding worried, she made kissy noises and leaned across the seat to pet the dog.

The pup left the warmth of the emergency blanket stretching from seat to seat, trying to get to his suspect. Bree lifted her, kissing the pup between her ears. He'd acted the same way while the captain handed down his suspension. Rubbing those silky ears between his fingers, the news just hadn't felt as bad.

The officers he'd been working with resented his promotion, but he'd screwed up more than a couple of times today. So maybe he'd been expecting bad news from the captain. Just not a suspension.

Jake took his notebook, which had been drying in

the cup holder, and wrote "R U bugged," then showed it to Bree.

"No. They were using one of their cells on speaker-phone to listen. He said they'd be watching through bin-oculars."

He pulled the phone from the console and began to dial.

"What are you doing?"

"Calling the police to pick these guys up. They've got to get inside the house again if they intend on grabbing their phone."

Bree hit the cell from his hand and it tumbled to his feet. "If these two are caught, there are more in Amarillo to do the killing."

"What the hell are you involved in? Drug running? What money are they talking about?" His hands shook a bit. He was tired, but he'd noticed the tremor had shown up more this past week with the additional stress of the promotion.

"I've been trying to figure that out for six very long months. Are you okay, Jake? You look kind of weird."

"What?"

"I said, I've been thinking it has something to do with money laundering. But I have no idea what."

He popped his neck, relaxing, preventing the anxiety or stress from interfering with his work. "Did you get a look at their faces? Any chance you can identify them? Do you remember the vehicles they used today? Anything special about where they held you?"

"Can you interrogate me after we get moving, Jake? It's freezing in here." She brought her hands under her chin, shivering. "They're also watching. Remember?"

He'd noticed at the house she'd been cold and hadn't given it a second thought. He'd been too busy making the decision to cross yet another line for this woman. Why was he trusting her and willing to deceive the very men he'd been working with hours before? Did it go back to the attraction he'd felt at the diner? It couldn't be. There's no way he'd give everything up again for a woman. Just no way.

"Sorry." He cranked his truck, turned the heater to high and jerked his jacket from his shoulders to drape around her. "What happened to your coat and gloves?"

"They were wet and he…um, the one called Larry, cut off my coat." Her voice changed as if she'd made up her mind to say something that wasn't the complete truth. "I'd be warmer if I could put my arms through the sleeves." She shook her latched wrists in his direction, then dropped them back to cradle the pup in her lap.

"I've got a key at my apartment." *And police headquarters and in my pocket.* "We should call 911 and leave an anonymous tip that we saw strangers at the crime scene. That sort of thing. At least let the department know something's up. They might get prints this time."

"Please, Jake. We can't do that. Somehow, they'll make sure we go to Amarillo. If I don't, they'll kill my family. Are you taking me there? Will it cause you more problems?"

"I was suspended today and have broken several laws in the past couple of hours. I don't seem to be too concerned about causing myself problems."

"Suspended because of me? But you're the one who found me and— Why would they suspend a good detective?"

"It's complicated. This murder was actually my first and last case for the Dallas P.D. Your turn to share some details about what's going on."

"I'm so sorry that I've wrecked your life."

"You don't get to wear that title, Bree. My ex-wife claimed it a while back."

She covered her face with her hands, acting ashamed. "Have I endangered even more people? Do you have kids?"

He shook his head, glad for the first time in years that he and Jennifer hadn't pursued children. He hadn't wanted to be an absentee father. And now, if they had, he'd wonder if they were even his.

The more pressing issue was to get Sabrina Watkins to tell him the entire story. Start to finish—or near finish. It was clear she didn't trust him enough to share yet. She kept dodging his questions.

It was a long drive to Amarillo and eventually he'd get it out of her. *Gain her trust. Then you can help and maybe get your job back or some other type of employment.*

"You were flying under the radar by house-sitting. That was a good idea with characters like that searching for you. You'll need new civvies and a coat before we hit the road."

The snowfall was heavy again. He'd listened to the weather off and on today. Dallas wouldn't see much more, then the temperature would warm up and most of the roads would be clear by late morning.

"I appreciate everything you've done. You've saved my life twice today. But after you take these handcuffs off, don't you think I should leave? You shouldn't get more involved. It's already cost you your job and almost your life. Maybe you could exaggerate my escape abilities and let your supervisor think I conked you on the head or something."

He rubbed the lump under the bandage on the right side of his head where he'd been "conked" for real that afternoon. He hadn't meant to draw her attention to it, but her intake of breath and immediate touch proved he had.

"What happened to your head? Did you hit it on something?"

"The bullet grazed me. If it hadn't been for the pup

pawing at my ear, I might have completely passed out and drowned." He watched for a vehicle that might be tailing them. Those two goons might try to follow, but he was determined not to be a step behind this time.

"You've been shot and suspended and it's all my fault." She dropped her forehead to the passenger window.

He could only see her shoulder and matted hair. "I think we need to clean up before we drive five or six hours. Even Dallas is smelling like a sewer."

"Do you think that's a good idea? They could be right behind us."

"I've been driving in circles to make sure we weren't followed. We're clear. My apartment is just around the corner." He wouldn't gain her trust if she knew he'd been close to taking her to the police station. Dang if he knew why he'd changed direction. "Tell me about Dallas. Why would anyone adopt a half-blind dog?"

"You've met her." She raised the head of the pup and kissed her fur. "First, she's absolutely adorable and doesn't let the blindness slow her down at all. I volunteered at the shelter and introduced Brenda Ellen to her after she lost her first dog. She brought her home the next day."

"So you really like dogs." He slowed the truck for the last stop light before his complex.

Bree didn't allow the handcuffs to encumber her. He watched her stroke the black fur, keeping Dallas calm and silent. His dad always said you could tell a man's true character by how he treated his animals. If that were true about this woman…maybe it was the reason he'd sided with her.

"I'm glad you kept her," she said softly.

He parked at the rear of his lot with easy access to leave in a hurry. He'd half expected that his fellow officers would have the place surrounded. He'd stolen evidence in order to save this woman's life.

"Listen." He held her arm through his jacket and she raised those violet eyes questioningly at him. "Stealing evidence isn't the most honorable thing I've done. Probably not the most dishonorable, either."

"You're saving my family. What could be dishonorable about that?"

His mind was made up and he needed to be honest. "You've got two choices. Either go to jail now. Or turn the rest of the money and evidence over to me and go to jail in Amarillo."

She sat straighter, stiff, looking petrified. "I see."

"I'm a cop. What did you really expect?"

Almost spilling Carl's coffee and the woman who had shyly giggled at his awkwardness seemed like a distant memory. *Be honest.* Okay, his physical attraction to Bree had influenced his decisions earlier in the day. But he couldn't admit that to her. He could barely admit it to himself.

"I'm not certain," she whispered. "A lot's happened today that I was unprepared for and I'm so tired it's hard to think straight. I don't want anyone else to get hurt."

"We'll make certain your family's safe. It'll work out, Bree."

"I'm sure you think so."

"I'll be with you the entire time. Nothing will happen to you, but I need to know everything."

"I understand. Now? Or can we go inside first?"

They got out of the truck. Dallas was in Bree's arms and he wrapped his jacket around her. She shrugged it away, along with his arm as he tried to take the forty pounds of Lab to his door.

Inside, she set Dallas on the floor, untied the makeshift silver leash and held her hands out for him to remove the cuffs. He reached into his pocket for the key and a sound of disgust escaped her lips.

"I could have lied to you about why I'm taking you to Amarillo," he said as he pocketed the cuffs again.

"Thanks for reminding me that I'm a fugitive. I know what to expect now." She rubbed her wrists and then pointed down the hall. "Is the bathroom this way?" He nodded and she ran the short distance. Hand on the knob, she hesitated. "Do you need to come in with me?"

"It has to be this way, Bree. I promised to uphold the law." He'd sworn several oaths over his lifetime. Did he still believe he could keep all of them?

Her hands dropped against her sides as she faced him, visibly defeated. He hated what he had to do, what she must think of him. He admitted, "I don't have a choice."

"Neither do I. No one ever asked me if destroying my life was okay. They didn't ask if I wanted to give up everything I'd ever known. Or if I wanted to lose my family and have them think I was dead. And they didn't ask if it was okay to blow up my business and destroy everything I'd worked for since high school. I'm hiding from men who want to kill me for the reason that I was a convenient scapegoat. I completely understand about not having a choice."

He could argue with her, but why? Because he'd wanted her phone number that morning? That path was off-limits now. Why? Maybe she was the first woman inside his apartment since the divorce. So what? Maybe he'd brought her here because he couldn't let her out of his sight.

Again, so what? She was an attractive woman who he happened to be helping with a problem.

Stop lying. She's a suspect who might be as guilty as those men who'd abducted her. How was he lying to himself? A victim of circumstances or a lying con artist? Did it matter? No more questions. No more ifs. He'd save the Watkins family or put Bree in jail.

Across the room, Dallas circled as if she was about to curl up and sleep. "I should probably walk you before you settle down." The pup squatted instead. Too late again. He was finished being a step behind. Time to act like who he was.

A marine.

Chapter Eleven

"If you're hungry, I make a mean hot turkey, pastrami and Swiss sandwich." Jake had his head in the fridge. There wasn't much else to offer. A cold beer wasn't exactly what a freezing woman should drink. He didn't even have frozen dinners left to heat and serve. He'd been guzzling the coffee swill at the department for a week, avoiding the grocery store, occasionally getting a good cup from a diner.

Bree's soggy shoes squeaked on the worn linoleum. "Are you certain staying here long enough to eat is a good idea? They said they'd be watching us until we had the money. I don't think stopping off for a change of clothes and a hot sandwich is what they had in mind."

He checked his watch, eight o'clock. He hoped MacMahan could get the gear together in two hours. He needed a list and a moment alone. That's all the time they could spare before they should be on the road. "I have to make a quick call."

"When can I call my family?"

"It might not be a brilliant idea, but we both stink to high heaven because of that lake dunking. I don't plan to ride in that truck with you for five or six hours in these clothes. Now, are you hungry? I happen to be starved." He pulled the sandwich stuff from the shelf, then pulled the skillet from the dish drain, keeping an eye on his frustrated prisoner.

Bree Watkins glared at him as she crossed her arms and headed toward a kitchen chair. "Dallas and I don't have a problem with the smell."

Dipping the knife in the butter, he acknowledged that she wouldn't let the call to her family wait for long. He also realized an exasperated sigh had come from him. Her family could be in danger or they could be the ones behind everything. He had no way of knowing and needed time to weigh his options. Time to think of a plan instead of react to the problem.

He'd ignore the request for a phone call until he made a decision. Turning from the bread, he pointed the butter tub in Bree's direction. "I'm in charge and I do have a problem with smell. That's a brand-new truck sitting out there. And we really do stink. Now strip."

"I beg your pardon?" Her shock erupted as a nervous giggle.

The same cute sound from early that morning that had been so damn attractive. *Stow it, marine.* One more time, he debated sharing why it was important to wait on the supplies he needed. He'd be prepared this time.

"I'll wash your clothes while you shower. How did you think we were going to clean up?"

"I... That can't possibly be a good idea. What if they come here and I'm—"

"Soapy?" He laughed, unable to stop himself. The look on her face was priceless. "We weren't followed. Promise. If you're worried about getting on the road, you should probably get moving."

She stood and Dallas jumped off the couch to follow. Bree picked her up and Jake held out his hands to take her.

"I'm serious about the stench. The paramedics warned

me about an infection." He pointed to his bullet graze. "Do it for me. After all, I did save your life."

"I can't believe you're trying to guilt me into compliance. Oh, my gosh! Hanging around here can't be a good idea." His "prisoner" huffed down the short hallway. He and Dallas followed close behind. He got his hand on the door, stopping her from closing it. Guilty conscience or not, it seemed to do the trick.

"What now?" she asked, facing him, trying to close the door. "You are not coming in this bathroom with me."

"I need your clothes and you aren't locking me out."

"In your dreams, Detective. I am not taking my clothes off in front of you." Her words were commanding, but she took a step in retreat when he cupped his hand around the door.

"You can hop behind the curtain and hand them to me before you turn the water on. Nothing lecherous about that."

"I, um, I'm not sure I trust you that much."

He crossed his arms like she had in the kitchen and made himself comfortable leaning against the doorjamb, keeping the door open with his foot. Hoping that he looked innocent, with no ulterior motive. In reality his thoughts were just like any other red-blooded marine when confronted with the possibility of a naked woman. To make the situation worse, he'd been attracted to Bree since the first shy giggle drawing his attention to the corner of the diner.

If today hadn't happened, finding her would be a primary objective. But right now, his objective was to get them cleaned up, gather some gear and be gone.

Bree toed off her wet shoes. Funny, he was supposed to be a detective and hadn't noticed that she'd been wearing a tight-fitting sweater all day. Purple, close to the color of her eyes. Granted, she'd been in a heavy coat most of the time. But in the bathroom light, her eyes were the deep amethyst he'd admired first thing.

Dallas sat on the floor between them. He picked her up and took a long sniff of the puppy. "You smell terrible. That lake water left all of us stinky grimy. You have to clean up, too, girl. Now don't look at me with those sad, puppy-dog eyes. It won't be so bad."

"It's completely embarrassing and wrong. I haven't known you twenty-four hours and this is... I'd never do this."

"You're taking a shower and we're doing nothing improper. I'll keep my eyes closed. See?" He clamped his eyes shut, concentrating on sounds.

The shower curtain holders slid opened and closed. Her body shifted. Even if he opened his eyes, he'd only see her silhouette behind his cheap blue curtain. He assumed the wet jean material was being peeled from each slender thigh and tiny foot. Yeah, she had feet the appropriate size for someone of her short height. The plastic shifted again, a plop on the bath mat. Then the purple sweater dropped from over the rod.

It would be wrong to open his eyes and watch the rest.

What's wrong were the images in his head. Actually, there was nothing wrong with the images there. After being loyal to his wife and being stationed overseas for six years, his imagination was pretty darn good. Naked, sleek muscles with water droplets hugging every curve...

Eyes open, he put the pup on the floor and bent to scoop her clothes into a pile, immediately wishing he could throw them away instead of wasting time in the wash cycle. The shower came on. His body reacted. A woman he was attracted to was on the other side of that curtain.

She's my prisoner. Sort of my prisoner. I'm not a cop anymore.

He couldn't lie. He wanted Sabrina Watkins with a fierce part of himself he hadn't dealt with in a very long time.

The curtain moved again. The pup had nudged it aside. He saw the outline of Bree bend at the waist to help her inside the tub.

"So you decided on a bath, too? Good girl."

"Clean towel is on the hanger." He pointed to the rod over the toilet. "My robe's on the back of the door when you're done."

"I'll only be a few minutes."

"Great."

There wasn't a window in the bathroom and probably no way for Bree to escape while his back was turned—especially naked—but he couldn't risk it. She had managed to get past him twice today, not including the abduction. He marched to the kitchen, dropped the stinky clothes and obtained a screwdriver from under the sink, where he kept a small tool kit.

Removing the doorknob only took a couple of minutes. He was silent enough that he didn't think Bree heard him. Bright laughter from the shower in spite of the desperate way she must feel made him wish she really was the first *woman* in his shower instead of the first prisoner.

As soon as she finished in the shower, he'd start the washer. He got everything ready, and noticed how tattered the sweater was. Unlike the jeans, which looked barely worn. It didn't make sense. *Dammit.* She'd said he'd cut the coat off. He'd sliced her sweater and she hadn't said a thing.

Not one word. And he'd forced her into a shower without thinking about any possible trauma she might be suffering from the abduction. He dialed a number he hadn't been able to dial in months.

Mac had been a marine specialist and a good friend who

mustered out three months before him. Jake didn't know if he'd answer with only an exchange of phone numbers over the past two years.

"Hey, Craig, buddy. Where have you been keeping your lonesome self?"

"It has been a while, Mac. I'm texting you a shopping list."

"For girls? I've been waiting for this. I heard you got divorced." His friend laughed.

"Afraid you're going to continue to wait for that party. You still in private security and able to supply friends?" He walked to the bathroom, wanting to push the door open and…and what? The shower was still running. He could hear a few words addressed to the dog.

"How long do I have to fill the order?" Mac asked.

Jake pivoted to the kitchen, away from Bree. "ASAP. I'd like wheels up by 2200."

"You'll be limited to what I have on hand and how long it takes me to get to wherever you live. You need a clean vehicle?"

"I'm good on that front. Something's better than nothing. I'll text you the address."

"Thought you had a whole police force at your back, man."

"Yeah, not so much. The quicker the better." Bree's clothes were pretty ruined. His blood boiled. The rips in the back of her sweater were probably from that psycho cutting her coat off. And he'd seen the small wounds on her right arm. *Son of a bitch.*

"One more thing, Mac. There are a few items for a friend. No laughing. No questions. Shop anywhere that's open."

"You need any help with this op, Jake?"

"Not this go-round, man. This is something I have to

do on my own." He couldn't let anyone else risk anything. He didn't know why he thought he could trust this woman, but he couldn't ask anyone else to.

"Okay, but you'll owe me a favor sometime and you better plan on departing at 2230."

"Not ever a problem. Thanks, Mac." He disconnected and texted the list he'd been mentally preparing. He also flipped on the Weather Channel, hoping they'd rotate through what the weather was like in the Texas Panhandle. The snow front had come from the northwest all week, but he hadn't heard anything about the forecast.

"Jake, I need you." She couldn't mean what first entered his mind.

He dropped the phone and sprinted to the bathroom, curious. The wet dog aroma hit him as soon as he entered the misty shower and he knew why she'd called for help. Bree contained a shivering Dallas next to her in the tub.

It was hard to concentrate on anything other than her creamy skin that had a dozen or so freckles. She had excellent muscle tone. Just right for a woman, proving that she worked out somewhere. Wishing that was all he could see, he focused on the squirming dog with a paw on the edge of the tub instead of the perfect derriere covered by one layer of terry cloth.

"She's through playing, but I still need to rinse my hair. You forgot to leave extra towels."

Bree was wrapped in one of the four that he owned. He held his hands out but was met with a vigorous shake of dog and tiny shocked squeal from Bree. He needed to act fast, before that corner holding her towel in place became unsecured and he could see more than he needed. Or should.

"Are you going to wrap her in your dirty shirt?" Her

perfect lips raised in a clever smile. "You wouldn't want her to get *stinky* again. Would you?"

"Just a sec." The clean towels were still in the dryer. He grabbed them and got back in the tiny bath just as Dallas jumped from the tub and began shaking.

He dropped the towel on top of the pup and rubbed. "What's the idea?"

"I had to set her down. My towel was slipping. Then she jumped. Watch out, she's slippery when wet."

Slippery tile was much easier to handle than the slippery slope that would happen if he caught a glimpse of more than bare shoulders and knees. There's no telling where he—or they—might fall.

Bed was the most probable conclusion.

Chapter Twelve

Bree stared at Jake's king-size bed. It looked inviting and absolutely huge. Since he'd barely let her out of his sight, she was stuck standing in the hall alternating her view between bed and bath. It was either envying Dallas, sound asleep and curled in the middle of a large mattress with soft pillows, or Jake's jean-clad backside as he dried the tile with a washcloth since he was out of towels.

Sometimes the bath view made her forget she was in trouble or that the man on his knees had threatened to turn her in to the police. Duh, he *was* the police. He'd changed his dirty slacks for an old pair of work jeans. Slung low on his hips, frayed holes in both knees and, of course, no shirt.

She tightened the belt around her only garment and switched to staring at the bed. His fluffy robe was nice and warm for all of her body except her feet. Those were covered with a pair of his woolen socks that looked and felt like marine issue.

"Don't you have a pair of sweats I could put on? You could shower and we could be on our way in fifteen minutes instead of a couple of hours waiting on clothes."

"I told you—"

"I know, you've got it covered. Just be patient." *Easier said than done.* "Dallas seems to love your bed." Tired and dead on her feet, she wanted to sink onto that pillow top, dive under the heavy comforter and not move for three days. She'd go without food to just lie in one spot and not have to think about anything.

"You ready?"

She must have phased out leaning on the door frame because Jake stood in the hall holding a sofa cushion in one hand and pointing toward the bathroom with the other. "Aren't you going to shower?"

"Yep. And if you think I'm letting you wander the apartment...forget it." He pulled his handcuffs from his back pocket.

"Now, come on, Jake. Where do you think I can run dressed like this?"

"I turned my back on you twice and you disappeared on me. Twice. It's not happening again. Have a seat." He dropped the cushion in the doorway. She tried to pass and he took her left wrist gently, stroking the scratches she'd received while trying to free herself at the warehouse. "I wish I could keep it loose, Bree, but I'm afraid they don't work that way."

She knew and understood his dilemma. He rubbed a thumb across her pulse point, where the same handcuffs had rubbed her raw. The soothing circles of his fingers worked magic, but all too soon he put his arm around her and helped her sit. Then reaching behind her shoulders, his warm breath caressed her ear as he leaned to connect the second handcuff to the pipe under the sink.

The tickle made her tweak her neck close enough to the hero of the day she could kiss him. She wanted to. It would be the most natural thing in the world to lean just a bit forward...

Her eyes fluttered open as she caught her movement. Jake had met her halfway and their lips explored each other. Excitement mixed with longing and wonder, then an "oh, no, what am I doing" moment took over.

Their kiss was everything the connection she'd shared with him in the coffee shop had promised. And then some.

The sound of the handcuffs closing around the sink's drain caused her to pull back too far and bump her head on the wall. How embarrassing. She'd kissed him and he'd cuffed her.

"Ah…am I supposed to cover my eyes when you undress? Don't you feel a little awkward?" She wasn't clear if she spoke about the upcoming shower or the rising anticipation his touch had caused. She didn't close her eyes, keeping them completely open and noticing the day's growth of stubble on his jaw.

The lines etched into his face—were they from smiles or worries? His closeness made her curious to know which. His nearness mixed with a simple desire to want anything other than what was actually happening to her.

"Are you kidding?" He laughed. "I've been showering with other people for eight years. Six of those years were in a tent in the desert. Sharing a shower with one person is super easy."

He stood and unbuttoned the top button to his jeans as if she was another soldier. Her free hand smacked her eyes she covered them so quickly. She wanted to be casual about watching. If he weren't so darn cute or hadn't just kissed her and moved on like it was nothing, maybe it would be easier to watch him undress. She heard the loose jeans fall to the floor, the hamper lid as it dropped shut, the tub curtain pulled to the side and swished back into place. She was glad one of them didn't have a problem showering in front of others and wished she'd been brave enough to peek. She dropped her hand but kept her eyes shut, leaning her head against the hard wall.

Someone calling her name brought her back from the edge of a nightmare starring Larry in his black ski mask. His knife was about to cut more than her sweater.

"You were snoozing hard and fast there. Sorry to wake you, Sleeping Beauty, but can you toss me that towel on the sink? I can get it, but I'd be in my altogether."

Bree could see more through the opaque curtain than she'd imagined possible. The outline of his tall, lean body for one. She reached above her head for the towel and tossed it in his general direction. She'd seen his shoulders while he walked around bare chested. Well, not completely bare—it had the cutest amount of hair right where there should be.

"Thanks for taking such a quick shower." She gulped.

"No choice. All the hot water was gone." Behind the plain curtain, Jake shook the water from his hair, much like Dallas had earlier.

Bree admired his outline as he gingerly dabbed at the spot above his ear where he'd been shot. She was very grateful he wasn't asking her to answer questions. She was certain she'd forgotten how to speak.

Oh, my goodness. He stepped over the side of the tub with the towel splitting open across his thigh. Her eyes had to be popping from their sockets. She couldn't force them to close, her free hand refused to rise to her face and she was definitely no longer sleepy.

"I decided to save time and live with the stubble." He scratched his sexy jaw with his nails, creating a sound only stubble on a man's chin can make. She knew what his stubble against her cheek felt like, and darn it, she wanted to feel it there again.

Water droplets still clung to his tanned, hard chest. How could a man be so tan in the middle of winter? She wanted to know more about him. Why had he left the marine corps and how could he be so darn confident putting a plan into action to help her?

"I'll be back in a sec to unlock you."

There wasn't much space in the doorway. As tempting as he was to look at, she shifted and practically hugged the pipe with both arms. He passed behind her and she began to relax a little.

Then his towel shot over her head, landing in the tub. She dropped her face in her hands and heard roaring laughter behind her from his bedroom. He didn't shut the door.

Holy moly.

Chapter Thirteen

Bree expected the police or Larry and his cohort to pull up at any minute. In her opinion, they'd been at Jake's apartment too long. They had enough money to buy anything they needed and didn't need to waste time doing laundry.

But here she sat, nice and clean, full from a very good sandwich and cup of instant hot chocolate, waiting on her jeans and shoes to dry. An exhausted Dallas was curled on the couch cushion as her host gathered things for their trip.

Jake had finally let her call her family. She'd tried several times. No answer. Her heart pounded each time it rang, uncertain of what she'd say or how they'd take the news that she was alive.

Would they forgive her? Understand why she'd thought it was necessary to hide? And more than anything, were they okay or had Griffin's men already harmed them? The same questions she'd been asking herself while she'd been gone. She needed to get to Amarillo, find the answers and put an end to this story.

For the umpteenth time, she counted the cars in the parking lot and on as much of the street as she could see. The newest parked were easy to spot since another snow flurry had begun. There were two cars in the lot with snow melting on their warm hoods. But she was more curious about the tire tracks next to Jake's truck, where a car had come and gone.

Being mindful of her surroundings and if anyone followed her for any length of time was a way of life for her now. It hadn't prevented any of the events today, but she must have seen those men at some point. Where? They must have found her location and followed her around. Otherwise, how would they have known she was supposed to work for Brenda Ellen?

Sitting here, wearing only a robe, she was vulnerable and unprepared. But finally warm. Jake brought her an ancient handmade quilt as an extra layer before he joined Dallas on the couch.

Poor little Dallas. Even at six months old she slept a lot, but she needed to run and play. Maybe it would be better to leave her behind somewhere? It would be so hard to part with her, though.

Dallas had played in the warm shower like any Labrador who loved the water. Handing her over to Jake to be dried had been strangely intimate. She still wasn't certain which had been more embarrassing—him watching her throughout her shower or her watching him during his?

Actually, it hadn't been too intimidating undressing in front of him for some reason. She trusted that he'd kept his eyes shut. Trusting him was actually rather easy. Jake was the one who'd gotten soaked when Dallas shook the water from her fur. A lighthearted moment before he'd pulled off his shirt and tossed it in the hamper.

But she hadn't been laughing when he'd kissed her and handcuffed her to the pipes. Not only didn't he trust her to stay in the apartment, he didn't trust her to be cuffed to something comfortable in another room. And was totally avoiding any contact or repeat of their kiss.

"Does it make sense to just sit here? The longer we

wait, the harder it's going to be to get my family back. I can't call my uncle again until I get a replacement charger since you left mine in my suitcase." She took a deep breath before facing him, determined to stand her ground and move forward.

"You can't panic when we're delayed. Trust me. I made a couple of phone calls while you were in the shower. I'm not dragging my heels waiting on your clothes. I'm waiting on a marine buddy who's bringing some equipment.

"We should be on the road in a half hour or so. Anything about the weather?" he asked.

"Sorry, I had the sound down and was watching outside."

She tugged the belt of his terry-cloth robe tighter and hugged the collar closer to her neck. Under the robe she wore nothing. She'd chosen the hard footstool so she wouldn't fall asleep. She should be exhausted and terrified, but relaxing when she couldn't reach any of her family didn't make sense. She could only leave messages for her uncle, too.

Four paws in the air, Dallas stretched, laying her head on Jake's lap. Bree could easily be envious again. Of the soft cushions, not Jake's lap.

"When will your department notice the money's gone?" Bree asked as the clothes and tennis shoes tumbled dry in the background.

"They'll probably miss the phone Monday morning, but the money? No one found it before you called. You're lucky I hadn't been escorted from the building. A little earlier or later and I wouldn't have been able to help you."

"I feel terrible that you've lost your job. Do you think you can get it back?" She did feel bad. But if he hadn't been suspended, would he be helping her now? She had to count her blessings when she could.

"Maybe." He shrugged, the white of his undershirt outlining his solid, broad shoulders. "Maybe I don't want it saved. I haven't decided. It's been an awkward promotion. I've known from day one it wasn't a great fit. They groomed another patrolman all last year. My military service fast-tracked me and, unfortunately, there was only one opening. It might have worked out in the long run, but it would have been a very long, lonely run to make. Enough about me, I need facts, Sabrina Watkins. You ready to tell me your story now?"

Had he just shared personal feelings with her? Was he trying to gain her confidence in spite of securing her to the bathroom floor? *Does it matter? You've got nowhere to go and no one to ask for help.*

"Do you know the guys who abducted you?" he asked. Leaning back, he stretched his neck from side to side before raising a water bottle and tossing two aspirin into his mouth.

"I can't identify them. They kept their masks on the entire time they had me in a car and an old warehouse. But I'd recognize the one called Larry. I don't think I'll forget his eyes. He had the same glare of the man who told Griffin I had to be killed. I'm praying he's not the one who has my family."

What was she going to do? She rose to wander the room, unable to be still. There weren't any boxes sitting in corners, but there were stacks of things that had been unpacked and just left.

"Now who's Griffin?" he asked. "You've mentioned him before."

"Is your friend ever going to get here?" She walked back to the balcony door, searching the lot again. Should she mention those tire tracks or ask him to let her in on his plan? *Trust works both ways, fella.*

"He's getting our supplies. Talk."

"Our families were friends in Silverton. Griffin Tyler is a bit older, got his veterinary license and started his own business in Amarillo. I owned a pet grooming and boarding business. Very small, but he asked me to join forces with him almost four years ago."

"So that's the business they took from you?"

She nodded. "They ended up setting fire to the building, after I stabbed Griffin with a scalpel."

"In self-defense?"

"He was trying to kill me."

He smiled. Even in the dim light from the hallway she could see the shine of his teeth. "What made you think they were trying to kill you?"

In spite of the conversation, Bree was very conscious she was undressed and couldn't leave. As much as she wanted to avoid discussing what happened on the day that changed her life, she couldn't steal his keys that he'd left near the door and just go. He'd catch her as she fought to keep the robe together while running down the sidewalk.

"The gun for starters. I know a lot of long-haul truckers, my dad's friends," she continued. "I'd groom their dogs when they stopped in Amarillo. I usually worked two Sundays a month. That day, I finished early and decided to check on the animals we were boarding for the weekend. My assistant had gone to a wedding or baby shower and couldn't get by until much later. That's when I overheard them talking. The evil guy—his eyes gleamed when he spoke about killing—he was there telling Griffin what their orders were."

"And you saw his face?"

She shivered when the image of the man popped into her mind. "I can't forget what he looked like. The nightmares keep it fresh. I've never remembered things so vividly before. There was just something evil about the way he looked when he mentioned killing. I hate the nightmares."

Jake looked as though he sympathized and understood. Did he have nightmares from his experience in the military?

"So you…" He urged her to finish while stroking Dallas gently between the ears.

She searched the titles of books stacked in the corner instead of Jake's face. She shouldn't wonder about his dreams or what his life was like. She had too much to think about as things stood. "I knew I needed to get out of there fast. I ran for my van, hoping they hadn't seen me. Then I remembered the animals. If they were going to 'torch' the place, like they'd discussed, all the animals I was boarding would die. I couldn't let that happen."

"Just like you couldn't let Dallas stay at the shelter and risk no one adopting her?"

"It took three months to talk Brenda Ellen into taking her home and if I wasn't there, they might have…" She didn't want to think about the animals she hadn't gotten homes for—there'd always be too many. "Why did you think I'd come back for her?"

"Don't know. An impression from the connection you two seem to have with each other." His voice was low, like he almost didn't want to admit that she could care. "So where did the money come from?"

More reality. She hadn't shared the details of that night with anyone, but they were as clear as ever. She'd written them down so she wouldn't forget. Everything was in her electronic journal that she hoped would be impossible for anyone to find.

"Griffin must have heard me moving pet carriers. He caught me just after I loaded the last cat and forced me back to his office. We fought. I grabbed an open briefcase.

I escaped in my grooming van, leaving it in front of another animal clinic."

"Why not go to the police and explain what you overheard? You could identify the guy and they could have protected you." His east Texas twang became more prominent.

Just like when he'd been irritated with her earlier. Which part had upset him? Not going to the police? Or not identifying a potential killer?

"I overheard Griffin say that someone in the police department would help with the cover-up. The evil guy wasn't too pleased with a cop's involvement but said it would help when they blamed me. I was so confused. I drove around in the van with three dogs and a kitten, too scared to talk with anyone. I just kept driving around in circles."

It was doubtful a confident marine would ever feel as scared as she had been that night. She could see the framed commendations stacked on a bookshelf instead of hanging on the wall. Maybe she'd ask her own questions about his past one day. But right now, they had to concentrate on putting Griffin and his cohorts in jail.

"The fire was huge and could be seen for miles. Griffin made a statement for the radio claiming he'd confronted me about embezzling and that the police were searching for me. The next day, I was…my remains were positively identified in the fire. That meant they'd not only switched the dental records but had killed a woman. It sort of confirmed they had someone on the police force. I didn't know who to trust."

"I'd think the same thing. It's amazing that you managed to stay under the radar so long. How did you get from Amarillo to Dallas? And how in the world did you end up as a dog sitter?" He smiled and sort of laughed at the last words.

"You wouldn't know this, but I started my business

by pet sitting and dog walking. Some of us didn't have money for college or fancy careers and made the best of very difficult times."

He rose from the couch, carefully moving Dallas's head as he got up. In a heartbeat he stood in front of her and tilted her chin to look at him. "I didn't mean to insult you. We just met this morning, but I can tell how much you love animals. It's a good fit."

She had been momentarily hurt. Right up until she looked into his concerned eyes. *Remember that you're alone and vulnerable. You have to stay strong.* She had an uneasy feeling and searched the parking lot. Snowflakes fell, melting as they hit the warmer blacktop or refreshing the piles of snow from the previous two days.

"There was more than money in the briefcase. A list of names I've been checking. All of them have pets and lived around Lakewood. I thought I heard the evil guy say the higher-ups were in this area, but I haven't found any connection. All I accomplished was getting Brenda Ellen killed and you suspended."

"Don't do that to yourself. Nothing good will come from it. There's no retreat and no going back." Jake stared somewhere over her head.

At first she thought he'd stopped speaking because he'd seen something. But she quickly realized he spoke from experience and had changed his mind about explaining.

"Let me think a little while about what you've told me," he said finally. "We can talk more in the truck."

"Is there an all-night store nearby? We need dog food for Dallas. She needs something more suited for her than lunch meat." She joined the puppy on the couch, needing her unconditional comfort. The dryer buzzed.

"It's been taken care of." He followed her to the couch

and stroked Dallas on the crown of her head. "You know, we can ask my pal to take care of her."

Strong, lean, long fingers...so close to her breasts and a robe she felt compelled to flatten across them was all she could focus on. If the circumstances had been different... She shook her head, answering his question about Dallas and saying no to her attraction. Jake's extra care with her pet touched her deeply. "I'm probably being selfish, but I'd like to keep her with me. She's been through so much, I don't know how she'll react if I leave her behind."

"Got it."

Maybe he considered the Lab his now? If it was his intention to send her to jail, she couldn't keep a puppy. Either way, he treated Dallas in a loving manner. And unfortunately for Bree, it was very attractive. She had to remember that Jake Craig intended to put her in jail and she couldn't let him succeed.

Jake answered his house phone by just listening. No words, then he set it back on the charger. "Can you two go to the bedroom for a minute? Mac's here." He withdrew his gun from the holster and stood at the door, ready for the worst. "We've got what we need now and will be leaving in five."

Bree kept the bedroom door cracked a fraction, trying to listen after Jake let his friend into the apartment. They spoke too low. She couldn't get a glimpse of what the other marine looked like, just the large black bag Jake set on the floor and the five or six bills that he counted into the other man's extended hand.

The puppy whined. "Shh, girl, we'll be okay."

We have to be.

She didn't know Jake well and he'd just admitted that he probably wasn't returning to law enforcement. Could she really trust that he wasn't after the money?

Whatever his motives, she had to take advantage of his help to free her family and waltz around the hot attraction that sizzled with each look.

Chapter Fourteen

Jake berated himself for not checking the weather before leaving Dallas. Once they'd gotten north of Fort Worth, it had begun snowing hard. He hadn't thought too much about a snow flurry at the apartment. He'd driven through them before. No big deal. They had food and a full tank of gas.

Two hours north and he was barely moving twenty miles per hour down the highway. They followed the few drivers brave enough or foolish enough to keep pushing forward. But now even those cars were exiting to a closed gas station.

"Need some coffee?" Bree stretched awake from the sound sleep she'd needed. "Oh, they don't look open."

"Afraid we're stuck here awhile."

"But we can't stop. We don't have time."

"I can't see the road any longer. Not to mention the ice already on the bridges." He was physically tired of driving through the crosswinds hitting the truck. And when he was this exhausted, he could lose control. He wouldn't let that happen. He knew how to avoid that dark place.

"But—"

"Look, I want you to get there ASAP. I don't feel comfortable helping you escape from the Dallas P.D., but I realize this is the best solution for you, me and your family. I also want us to get there alive. Everyone's pulled off of 287." He slipped his gloves on, immediately regretting the harshness he'd used to speak to her. "I'm going to check with the truck driver we were following. See if he received word about road conditions or if he was just tired of fighting this wind."

He pulled the keys. Dallas popped her head up when the cab light came on. "Stay."

"Do you really think we'd try to go anywhere?" Bree asked.

"I was talking to Dallas."

"Right. Want to cuff me again?"

He closed the door without letting the wind slam it shut. It was tense enough in the truck just driving. He didn't need the wrath of a woman to aggravate the situation. The snow didn't fall as much as it slammed against his exposed skin. He quickly zipped his jacket and pulled the collar up around his neck.

"This dang wind makes this morning's walk in the snow feel warm."

In the military police, he hadn't been in the middle of many blizzards and sure hadn't faced them in east Texas, where he'd grown up. That gut-wrenching instinct told him this wasn't a normal snowstorm. He had a very bad feeling they'd be stuck until morning. If not here, then along the road away from any town or cell reception.

The wind gusted enough to blow him sideways as he walked. He wasn't a lightweight and had to shield his face with his hand to see the vehicles in front of him. The tire tracks of the car that they had pulled off with were almost gone. As he passed, he noticed the man inside was alone and bundled into a sleeping bag in the backseat.

Jake jogged as best as he could to the big rig and tapped on the door. The driver gestured through the closed window for him to go around to the other side. When he got there, the door was cracked open and he climbed up. He was greeted by a very large man holding a wooden bat.

"A. B. Mills. You need something?"

"Jake Cra—Crain." He caught himself before using his real name. "I was wondering if you had news of road conditions into Amarillo?"

"Slow going and icy bridges to Wichita Falls. Not much movement west on I-40 right now. No rescue vehicles can get through the storm. Everyone's hunkered down and there's talk they'll close the highway. You might have better luck waiting it out till morning. That's my plan."

"That's what I thought."

"You in the car or the truck?" A. B. Mills never put the bat down. He just kept tapping or twisting it in his palm, sending a very loud message not to mess with him.

"Truck. Guy in the car's already camping there."

"In a hurry to make Amarillo?"

"As a matter of fact, yeah. Family emergency."

"Your truck got four-wheel drive? If so, get you some weight in the back end and you won't slide around as much. Slow and steady. You might hit I-40 in five or so hours."

"Thanks. I better get back and let my…wife know."

"Just pick you up a couple of logs or something like that. Good luck."

"Thanks again." Jake braced himself for the blast of cold.

He and Bree weren't completely unprepared to stay on the side of the road. They had coats and gloves. But the only blanket belonged to the dog. There was no extra gas if they stayed put and ran the truck's heater to stay warm. Being one swing away from striking out was wearing a bit on his nerves.

He'd come up with a plan, got MacMahan to bring him every piece of electronics he could think of…but hadn't followed through each time he'd begun to check the friggin' weather.

Walking between vehicles was so cold, the truck seemed like a hothouse to him by the time he sat inside. Dallas was curled in a tight ball and his prisoner shivered. He quickly started the engine and put the heater on high.

"Sorry about that. I should have left the truck running."

"I don't blame you. If you'd left the keys, you might be hitching a ride with one of the other drivers."

"Is that a warning that you need to be handcuffed to the steering wheel from now on?"

"Not hardly. As much as I want to do this on my own, I know I can't. Did the trucker know anything?"

He repeated the information he'd received and Bree visibly reacted the way he felt. "We can't wait here all night. Jerry's usually in Amarillo every Sunday. We'll miss him if we're not there. He's a trucker. He leaves tomorrow night."

"Whoa, wait a minute. Who's Jerry and why do we need to meet up with him? The plan's to collect the money from your uncle."

"Uncle Jerry hid the money. That's why I needed the phone. He's the only person who knows I'm still alive."

"You gave a truck driver almost two million dollars to hide? Man alive." He threw his cap and gloves onto the backseat. "You really think he's just going to hand it back over?"

"He's my mom's brother." She rubbed her hands together in front of the heater vent. "He kept the money safe."

Should he explain human nature to her and how unlikely a prospect it was that this man still had the money? "Is there a particular reason you waited until now to tell me?"

"Maybe because of the way you're reacting. Are we staying here or driving?"

"Going. But it won't be fun."

"As if any of today has been?"

"You have a point." He understood her sarcasm better than anyone else who'd been a part of their day. He slammed the truck into Drive. The spinning tires emphasized more than just his frustration. "The ice is going to be a problem."

"Would you like me to drive? I was raised here in the Panhandle. I'm used to it."

He shot her a look like she might be crazy. She wasn't watching him, just the road. She was serious. Maybe she wouldn't attempt an escape. That didn't mean he'd let his guard down. This woman had a habit of slipping away from him when he turned his back. Or worse, she'd slipped under his radar and broken his personal perimeter.

"I'll tough it out. Is there anything else I should know before we get to Amarillo?" Jake's foot itched to go faster, but twenty to thirty miles per hour was all the truck could manage without sliding across both lanes.

"I'm not sure." Bree clicked the radio to AM and pushed the scan button. It landed on excited, rapid talking. Spanish news.

He didn't speak Spanish and opened his mouth to tell her, but she shushed him, turning the faint station irritatingly louder. Dallas perked up, paws on the seat. Bree coaxed her over the top and had her head quickly dropping onto her lap.

Bree turned the radio off and leaned back. She was deep in thought somewhere and wasn't eager to share what she'd deciphered.

"Did you understand any of that?" he asked.

"I can pick out the major words and assume enough to fill in the blanks."

Patience wasn't his virtue, but he waited. Both hands

on the wheel to keep the wind from blowing the truck into the ditch. There hadn't been any lights in the past mile. Visibility was down to almost nothing. No headlights. No taillights. No points of light indicating a small town.

"What's the verdict?"

"As best as I can understand, there's a whiteout in Amarillo. All the traffic's been diverted off Interstate 40 and they're warning people to get to safety."

The rear of the truck slid back and forth for several seconds as they passed over another iced bridge. "Maybe that's what we should do."

Bree seemed to handle sliding across the highway well. She gripped Dallas with one arm and the safety handle with her other. If she was panicky, there wasn't any outward sign.

"We can't turn back. Please. We have to keep trying or they'll—"

"Kill your family. I know. But if we're in an accident, there's even less chance of helping them. Our best shot is to call the local cops and get your family to safety."

"You know that won't work."

"I know you *think* these men—whoever they are—have someone on the payroll, but every cop in Amarillo can't be. The odds of something like that happening—"

He saw the fright in her eyes and released his right hand to cover hers. A second, maybe two, and they were careening onto the grassy median. Black ice under the fresh snow or another gust of wind sent them onto the icier shoulder and began the spin.

Jake pumped the breaks and steered into the turn, but it didn't help. They were out of control and could only pray nothing like a ditch, concrete barrier or parked car got in their way.

"Brace yourself."

BREE HAD BARELY wrapped an arm around Dallas to hold her steady before latching onto the shoulder strap. The truck spun and she closed her eyes, unwilling to watch their out-of-control fate. The sickening feeling lessened as the truck slowed to a stop and she realized they'd come out unscathed.

They hadn't hit anything, hadn't rolled over and were barely in a ditch. Jake released the steering wheel, put it in Park, rubbed his neck and extended his arms to the ceiling as if he was on a long-overdue break.

"You and Dallas okay?" he asked while stretching his neck from side to side.

"I think so." The pup was shaking but stayed in her lap. "My heart thinks it's still spinning in circles, though."

Jake's laugh was full of tension but warmed her.

"We're turning back and that's the last word. It's too dangerous, Bree."

He sounded final and she couldn't think of a thing to change his mind. The only thoughts filling her brain were of those maddening, murderous eyes and what they'd do to her family.

The truck inched forward, Jake slowly gave it gas and, miraculously, they weren't stuck. If it were possible to go slower than he'd already been driving, he did. The snow obscured everything in front of them and she had no idea how Jake could see well enough to keep on the road.

"We'll return to the parking lot and call or use the trucker's CB for assistance. Worst-case scenario is we wait until the peak of the storm passes."

"Maybe the storm's not as bad west of here. We could go back to Decatur and try west to Lubbock, then north to Amarillo?"

Jake released a long sigh filled with the frustration she felt down to her frozen toes.

The shrill ring of an old-fashioned telephone had her and Dallas jumping in their seats. She seemed to be sitting on the receiver, but it wasn't possible. Both phones were on the dashboard, where he'd tossed them after talking to the trucker.

"How did you get a cell past me?" he accused. "Hand it over. Now."

"I didn't and I don't have one. It has to be them. They're watching us, just like they said, and they know we've turned around."

"That's impossible. There's not another car around for miles. Nothing's moving on these roads."

He guided the truck to the shoulder of the highway and cut the engine. She set Dallas back in her dog bed between them, unbelted and had to dig through several items under the seat. It was hard to see, but the phone lit up when it rang.

"Here it is."

"Got it." He took the cell from her extended hand. "Look, Bree. Whatever I say to them, remember I'm on your side. I give you my word. If they can call us, that means we can call the authorities to get your family protection."

His fingertips and palm absorbed her racing pulse without calming her in the least. She knew the voice on the other end of that ring. And also knew that Jake couldn't keep that promise no matter how much he tried.

Griffin's men already had her family or they would have answered their phones. Three cells and a house phone wouldn't all be out because of the blizzard. She knew they had been abducted.

"This is Craig," he answered on speaker.

"You go back, her family dies." The voice from her

nightmares coldly commanded. "The phone stays with you or her family dies. We'll stay in touch."

He disconnected.

The screen lit again and Jake mumbled some words she'd like to shout in the face of the man who haunted her.

"What is it?" she asked. Fearful tears blurred her vision and prevented her focusing when he flipped the phone around for her to see.

"I assume this is your family?"

She wiped her eyes, wanting to stay hidden behind her palms, but she had to answer. The small image took shape. She nodded, recognizing the small porch leading up to the old front door that her mother painted red at the beginning of each new year. Red for prosperity and good fortune.

But in front of the door, her family were on their knees in the snow. Hands zip-tied, no coats or winter protection and completely helpless with three guns pointing at their heads.

"The snow is barely covering the ground. The radio said it's been snowing hard since three this afternoon. When Griffin found out I didn't have the money...he said he'd do this."

Jake touched the screen of the cell. "Dammit, password protected. I can't call them or turn the GPS off." He flipped the phone to remove the cover.

"Please don't. They need to know exactly where we're at. We should get moving. Now."

"I still think we should call the Amarillo P.D."

"Detective Craig, what made you decide to help me? Not very long ago you said you didn't know if you wanted your job back or not. So why are you helping me?"

He tapped the steering wheel with his long index fingers, either trying to create a reason or carefully planning his words. She knew exactly why she'd stayed with Jake.

Her choices were limited. She either accepted his help or went to jail. His reasons weren't that clear-cut. At least not to her.

"Is it that tough a question?" she prodded.

"I want to be honest," he said.

"With me or yourself?"

He made a grunting *hmm* sound and continued his search out the windows. "Do you need my jacket?"

"No, just your answer." She recognized the confused, questioning, furrowed brow. Too many people looked at her the same way. As if she were foolish to want her own business instead of attending college. And then again when she went into partnership with Griffin. "I'm not crazy and I have a logical reason for asking. I want to know your motivation."

"Not following. Who said you were crazy?"

"You see, Detective—"

"Jake."

"No, right now, you're being the police detective who feels obligated to get help from his brothers in arms. Thing is, *Detective,* you've already ruled out that would work, or you would have turned me over to the Dallas P.D. So can we stop going over the same failed idea and come up with a plan that might actually have some merit?"

Even masking his words by his hand and mumbling in a low growl didn't keep her from deciphering the expletives probably common to a marine.

"My gut's normally right. I make a decision, then I run with it. No second-guessing myself." He scratched his chin, then the top of his head, acting a little confused. "I made up my mind while leaving my captain's office I would help you. A few minutes before you asked."

"So we're agreed that the police aren't the wisest course of action?"

"As much as I hate to admit it, yes. You're stuck with me."

"Thanks, Jake. So if we're not returning…"

"Got it." He cranked the engine and eased back onto the highway.

During their time in the median, not one car had passed. There wasn't a light within sight. The weather situation was probably worse than what Jake feared. But there weren't any alternative solutions.

"I wasn't kidding about driving," she said, calmer than she felt. "This isn't my first blizzard and I've driven lots of trucks."

"I've spent a few days in a bad climate or two. Harsh weather. Drastic temperatures. Wind blowing sand so hard you felt like each pellet was piercing your skin." Jake eased the truck across the highway. Slow and steady toward the exit.

His voice had grown harder, far away, sad. She didn't mean to make him relive his battles in the Middle East.

"You can count on me until we get everything straightened out. No more questioning where our loyalties lie. Your family's in danger and we'll work together." He didn't hesitate or argue that the overpass was too dangerous. He edged the truck forward, maintaining control, and got them headed north again.

"Thank you, Jake."

"These bastards plan to kill all of us. You know that, right?"

"Yes." She could barely say the word.

"You're right about the police. Going to them isn't an option. But once we get the money, we'll be in charge. We need a better plan."

Chapter Fifteen

"That one! That's his rig." Bree shouted, unfastening her seat belt and preparing to jump from the truck. "Just pull up behind him and we can knock on the door."

It hadn't been that long since Jake had knocked on A. B. Mills's door. He remembered the baseball bat clear as a bell. "Hold on. Let's make sure no one's watching him. Or us."

"But no one knows about Jerry."

"You didn't think anyone knew you were working for Richardson, either. Let's take this one step at a time. You told him you'd call. We'll gas up and see if anyone pulls in acting suspicious."

Jerry Riley's rig hadn't been there too long. Where the other trucks they passed were covered in snow, his looked like it had parked recently. He was also parked across the street. They'd searched two truck stops for her uncle and each time they'd called he hadn't answered. But he'd warned them that might be the case. Spotty cell coverage and the basic fact that he needed both hands on the wheel fighting the dangerous fifty-mile-per-hour wind gusts.

Before Jerry answered his phone, he'd been at a rest area, safe from those winds that could turn a truck his size over. After learning their family was in danger, he agreed to fight the winds and meet them in Wichita Falls.

With the parking lot full to the brim, Jake drove to the pumps, amazed that dozens of trucks had enough room for their doors to open and nothing more. No space between their engines and the back of the next trailer.

Jake filled up and Bree stood next to him dialing. "No answer."

"You folks look tired. Come a long way?" A squeaky voice said behind him.

The roar of the wind and loud flapping of the metal canopy must have hidden the approach of the young man. Jake was momentarily taken back to a sandstorm in the Afghanistan desert, searching for his enemy. He shook it off, but his hand had already landed on his weapon.

The bright orange jumpsuit with the gas logo emblazoned front and back indicated a legitimate attendant. At least for the time being. "I can take care of this if you folks want to wait inside. It's not a problem."

"No, thanks. Where can we park when we're done?" he asked, still watching for cars or men watching him. The visibility was just too low to see anything moving more than thirty feet away—nothing was clearly defined.

"Well, if you're staying for the duration, we've got a row going in the back. There's room for four or five more cars end to end. All the motels are booked up. They was the first to go last night when we got word they was shutting down the highway."

Being blocked in would never work. Bree looked anxious that he would even consider staying here, pinned down in the car jungle. "We just need a short break. The wind's fairly bad."

"You know the highway's shut down from here past Amarillo. Highway patrol won't let anything past 'em." The attendant removed the pump and stowed it.

"We're not driving too far," he lied, and saw the confusion on the kid's face. "We were running on fumes and thought we should fill up. Patty here just had to make sure her mother was home safe yesterday, but I couldn't stay there another minute."

"Gotcha." The attendant pointed to the street just north of Jerry's rig. "If you ain't staying, I gotta ask that you park off the premises. We're keeping things as orderly as possible, but the lot's not good for anyone who wants to leave before they give the all clear."

"We completely understand. Any idea how long they think the storm's lasting?" Bree asked. "Um…my mom's satellite was out and we weren't getting reception on these." She held up the phone he'd stolen from the police.

"Could be the rest of today. Amarillo had over a foot of snow drop on her overnight. Sun might help, but we have to wait on the bridges and drifts to be cleared. Storm's headed northeast, but they're still not advising travel south of us yet. If that's everything, I'm going back inside to some warmth." The kid waved his gloves and disappeared on the other side of the truck.

Dallas howled at the kid as he disappeared around the corner. Jake took a long time staring toward the highway, hearing nothing except the loose canopy that might fly free at any minute. If someone was out there watching, he'd never know.

"No luck getting your uncle?"

They moved the truck closer to Jerry's. Bree shook the cell and dropped it on the seat. "It's a cheap little prepaid phone from a truck stop just like this place. He's probably asleep in his rig."

Jake parked, careful to leave enough room in front of his truck in case they needed to leave in a hurry. "You stay here with the doors locked."

"But—"

"But nothing. We limit our risks. There was one thing we both agreed on earlier. I'm giving the orders." He killed the engine, snatched the keys and jumped out, avoiding further discussion.

"I don't think I really agreed to anything," she said as the door closed.

The wind slammed him into his fender before he crossed the street. The closer they'd driven to Wichita Falls, the more local weather reports they'd picked up on the radio. The wind was gusting somewhere between fifty-five and seventy miles per hour and yet the storm was creeping through the area. He believed it. Visibility was down to almost zero.

Traveling to Amarillo right now was a stupid idea, but he knew Bree would steal his truck or steal another, taking back roads around the barricades before waiting or giving up. He went to the passenger side of the rig and climbed on the rail, but before he could catch a glimpse inside a quick yank had him falling on his butt in the drift.

When he looked up, a giant of a man stood steady in the whirling snow. "Hey, boy. This is your third look at my rig. What do you want?"

"Are you Jerry Riley?"

"You Craig?"

The answering grin confirmed he was Bree's uncle. When Jake responded with a firm nod, the giant grabbed his gloved hands, pulled him to his feet and pumped his arms until he thought they might come loose from their sockets.

"I was beginning to worry. Where's my girl? Is she all right? I heard the phone but couldn't answer it in these high winds while driving and then had to get some grub. I can't wait to see her and make sure she's okay. Have you told her parents she's alive yet?"

Jake didn't crane his neck to look up at very many people, but he did tilt his head back to look Bree's uncle Jerry in the eye. The wind was so bad they both had to raise their voices to be heard. Someone could be standing ten feet away and listen to parts of their conversation without being seen.

"I'd like to keep this as low-key as possible, sir. I'm not sure you should see her right—"

"Uncle Jerry!" Bree bounded into Jerry's arms. He lifted her off the ground without the wind or snow bothering him at all. The man planted his feet and wasn't budging.

"Oorah. Good to see you, little lady."

Jerry Riley wasn't just built like a marine, he *was* a retired marine. *Oorah*. Jake let them have a private moment, taking advantage to search the perimeter he could see. Maybe he shouldn't allow a conversation that he couldn't hear, but he couldn't have prevented it. He kept his hand on his weapon, expecting to be charged or fired upon at any minute.

If he had been the person tracking them, he'd verify what just transpired before an attack. But why would they assume the money wasn't in Amarillo as she'd said? The phone Larry had left in his truck to track them—or the GPS phone as they'd begun calling it—was still in the front seat. There was no telling what would happen once Larry and his sidekick noticed they were in Wichita Falls for an extended period. One thing he'd had drilled into him since entering the corps, you could never predict when your opponents would strike.

"Let's get moving," Jerry said. "These old bones don't like the cold too much. So you do what you gotta do and I'll be ready to go in fifteen. Just need to move my rig into the lot."

"Wait." Big man or not, Jake pulled him to a stop by grabbing his arm. "We just need the package."

"Jerry can help," Bree said.

"We agreed," he spoke to her, "that he'd take the GPS phone to Amarillo when the roads open. We advance from the south highway and get to Amarillo without them knowing. We take them by surprise and keep the leverage. It's the best plan." He turned to Jerry, whose face was a blank slate. "I appreciate the offer to help, but you know I'm right."

"Sabrina, darlin', can you check on Charlie for me? He refuses to do his business in the cold."

"But—"

Uncle Jerry's suggestion didn't receive as much debate as Jake's did when she disagreed with a decision. One look at his niece and she performed an about-face and climbed into the warm truck. He caught a glimpse of that perfect backside encased in tight jeans and…yeah, he could do with some heating up himself.

The door clicked shut and before Jake could fully focus on Jerry, a fist connected with his jaw. The second time alone with this marine and Jake was making snow angels on the side of the road.

He moved his jaw back and forth to verify it still worked, and paused, debating where to hit this man to bring him down. Then Jerry extended his hand to help him back to his feet.

"I could ask what that was for, but I think I know." If he'd caught someone looking at his niece the way he'd just looked at Bree, they wouldn't be standing, either.

"And I'm betting you don't know why. It was to make a point I haven't stated yet."

"Okay, I'm biting." And wanting out of the blizzard that

was knocking them both into the side panel of his trailer. "Am I just tired or is the wind blowing harder?"

"I know Sabrina wants to get the money and take off. But I just caught you unawares because you're not just tired, you're exhausted. So, you either take me with you and I do the driving around those barricades. Or you stay here until the bulk of the storm passes, 'cause that ain't your imagination about the wind."

"I can't take you with me, Jerry. And unfortunately—" he rubbed his sore jaw "—there's no way she's going to stay put."

"I thought you'd say that. And, yes, I know my niece. The same young woman who's been hiding for six months instead of endangering her family. They've reported seventy-five-mile-per-hour winds blowing snow and small vehicles across the road. There's no physical way to get to our family without encountering this storm. None. And for who you're going to face, you'll need all your strength when you arrive. I guarantee that driving in hurricane-force winds isn't just tiring, it's downright stupid."

"What do you suggest? They're tracking us via a GPS in a cell. When it doesn't move, the guys following us are going to come looking for it."

"Let 'em find it. Give me the keys to your truck, climb on up in my sleeper with Sabrina and hand me that pug, Charlie."

Jake pulled the keys from his pocket. "I should go get Dallas."

"If Dallas is a dog—and knowing that niece of mine, it is—I'll take care of it. Lock the doors and get some sleep."

"First, I need to flush out some wolves."

Jerry rubbed his gloves together. "I've been ready for a good hunt for six months."

Chapter Sixteen

The wind whistled down the chimney flue, pushing a small puff of smoke into Griffin Tyler's living room. As many times as he'd hired professionals to fix the problem, his eyes still watered when he lit a fire. He tossed another log into the opening to build up the flame and warm the room. The bourbon no longer helped as he sent the last shot down his gullet.

Five years of "favors" were beginning to take their toll on him. And now those idiots had killed another woman. They should have killed the right woman in the first place, then life would be easier.

"I hate that bitch!"

No one heard him scream his frustration. He needed to be free from owing "favors." But that should be soon. Constantly working or creating ways to launder the larger and larger amounts of money showing up each week was wearing thin.

The second phone he'd nicknamed his "favor" line vibrated on the bar behind him.

At first money laundering had been an easy way to pay off a gambling debt. Not too difficult to list fictitious surgeries. Animals would come in, he'd write up the bill and he'd be paid in cash. Several grand a week he could handle. Larger amounts of money caused problems when Sabrina began asking questions about unnecessary boardings or animals that weren't there. She was gone and he had a new clinic that cost much less than the books showed, and here he was again on the verge of losing everything.

"I really do hate that troublesome bitch."

If Sabrina hadn't stolen his briefcase, he would have disappeared six months ago. He should be somewhere tropical, free of the money-laundering operation and this stress. Free of the threats from murderers and men who would never let him stop. He might escape if he got to the two million before his silent "partner" and if he could disappear during a blizzard.

The phone rattled on the granite countertop again. The wind shook the windows. Three in the morning and it hadn't eased up for twelve hours. He'd have to get the roofer to verify the shingles were still attached.

He dreaded answering. There could only be two people on the other end of the call—Leroy or Leroy's brother, Larry. Those weren't their real names, but he hadn't cared to learn the real ones. Larry and another no-name lowlife were following Sabrina and her cop. He didn't want to hear from them until they found the money, but the damn blizzard was screwing with everything. In particular, the deadline to return the money.

"Hard to believe this started with a string of bad bets on a few football games." He stood from the lounge chair and poured himself the remaining bourbon. The phone vibrated again.

Nothing in Amarillo was moving—not even the police. He could only assume that Larry was reporting that they'd stopped, too. He'd have to answer the blasted thing.

"Yes?"

"Something's up, man. They're in Wichita Falls talking to some old fart. We can't get close enough to hear," Larry whispered into the phone.

"What do you think I can do about it?"

"The boss said I should check in with you and you'd handle it. That's what I'm doing. I can take my orders from him, but I'm thinkin' that's not exactly what you want me to do."

Griffin understood the threat. Any problem and the hired muscle would eliminate him right along with Sabrina and her new boyfriend.

"Where are they?"

"Same place as every other car that could make it this far, man, a truck stop."

That's why it was difficult to hear Larry speak. The background voices and distorted music coming from overhead speakers nearly drowned out Larry's voice.

"Does the man have a dog? She could know him from her pet grooming business. Or they could be asking a stranger about the freakin' whiteout between there and Amarillo. Are they still talking to him?"

"It looks like they're headed inside and the old guy's heading to his big rig. Hold on—"

Griffin put the call on speaker and leaned on the bar, waiting. He'd stayed awake specifically to handle this mess.

"The old man's looking through stuff."

"Stay with them and keep back. Call me when they start moving again. If anyone gives them anything, make sure it's the money before you move in. I don't care what it takes, you have that money back here in twenty-four hours."

"Do you still want the woman brought to you?" he asked.

"No, let's let the police take care of the problem you

created yesterday. Let her take the fall for the woman you killed. That's only if you aren't forced to kill her alongside her new boyfriend. I really don't care. Just get me the money."

He clicked the phone off and tipped the rest of the bourbon down his throat, hearing the fire pop behind him. He could finally get some sleep. He set the tumbler in the bar sink, feeling the past six months of stress lifting from his shoulders. It was nearly over.

"Hello, Griffin."

The maniacal voice came from the dark near the kitchen.

"Leroy?" He was early. Most likely preventative insurance to make certain the money got back into their hands. "I wasn't expecting you until Monday."

He shrugged. "We ran into a situation that needed your input." He crossed to the back door and shoved it open.

Three people stood in at least two feet of snow that had blown onto his porch. They were bound and gagged and he recognized them immediately. Sabrina's family.

"They can't be here. Are you crazy?"

"Some people have said so." He yanked Darlene through the threshold and her parents followed.

Half frozen, pure hatred burned into him from the glares of the bitch's parents. Confusion and tears from her sister. Griffin didn't care. There was no reason to offer them comfort or feel pity for them. Now that they knew of his involvement, they'd have to be killed as soon as Larry arrived with the money.

Watkins should have shot these men before allowing them to take his wife and daughter. The man holding a gun on Sabrina's family didn't come inside. He scurried away like the scorpion he was, hiding in the dark until he could prey on his victims.

"What's the problem?"

"The boss is closing down this branch of operations." Leroy's heavy-lidded eyes were dark slits in his squinty face.

No more favors? "When?"

"I thought that would make you happy," he mocked. "You'll know when soon enough. You got a place to keep these three awhile? A secure room? Maybe a cellar?"

"I have a storm shelter out back. Once it's locked, there's no getting in or out. The key's by the back door."

Watkins made a muffled protest or something. His wife's tears continued to fall. The two of them knew they were going to die and had no idea why any of this was happening. Just like they had no idea Sabrina was still alive. It helped having friends in the Amarillo P.D., who switched the dental records.

Leroy whistled and his apprentice scurried back through the door. "Put these three in the storm thing in the backyard. Key's by the door."

The three were shoved through his kitchen at gunpoint. He caught himself opening his mouth to protest, but he couldn't show that he cared. And he didn't. Not for the reasons someone might think.

The only reason he'd protest is that the Watkins family would probably be shot in his storm cellar and be left to rot there. If he got the money before Leroy, he would be out of here so fast.

"Larry called. Did he get the money?" Leroy asked, sitting on the arm of the lounger.

"He thought Sabrina would have it soon. Once he gets it, he'll call again."

"Right."

The fire crackled and popped in the background, and the wind still shook the windows during its bigger gusts.

He was at a loss. What kind of a conversation was he supposed to have with a hit man for gamblers? He stood there like an idiot. He hadn't had too much contact with Leroy since the fire and still didn't know the true identity of the woman who died instead of Sabrina. He didn't want to know. The less he knew about the operation, the better.

He'd do his favors until they shut him down or until he could skip town with the money. Whichever situation presented itself, he'd take advantage. He always had.

"Want a drink or something?"

"Do you have a beer?" Leroy asked, standing and following him to the bar.

Griffin moved to the small fridge behind the counter and grabbed an import. "So how long do you think until they're through with me?"

He stood and was met in the face with a gun barrel.

Leroy shrugged. "Now?"

The urge to run was great, but for some reason he couldn't move. The bottle dropped, shattering at his feet. Leroy threw back his head, laughing. He focused on the finger squeezing the trigger and—

Chapter Seventeen

"You're really okay waiting here?" Jake asked one last time.

"Jerry's a professional driver. If he says he can't drive your truck to Amarillo, then we're forced to wait. I'm not thrilled about staying in the sleeper of his rig, but I admit that neither of us has slept in two days. He made a good point about how ineffective we'd be rescuing my family. It's hard to argue with him, but that doesn't make the worrying go away."

Jake had compromised with Jerry. Logic told him that the guys in Dallas were following. He wanted a chance to flush them out, to see if Larry or Griffin Tyler would call, asking why they were delayed in Wichita Falls. The GPS phone was in his pocket and they were inside the convenience store where the signal was stronger.

"Ten more minutes and we're hitting the hay." So far the phone hadn't rung and he hadn't spotted anyone interested in them. But he couldn't shake the feeling that someone had eyes on his back. "I admit your uncle isn't exactly like I imagined."

"What did you expect? Some grumpy old fat man who drove a truck?" She laughed exactly like she had at the diner the day before. "I'll have to tell Uncle Jerry. He gets a kick out of proving people wrong. He's not shy about working out in public—rest areas or places like this. If there's room, he exercises."

"I didn't expect him to be…a marine."

"If I'd told you that about him, would that have made a difference?" she whispered, pulling one of the last packages of powdered doughnuts off the shelf.

The conversation seemed almost normal—or as normal as his life got. Bree was excited to see her uncle, but Jake had a creepy feeling tying his guts in knots. A feeling like he was being watched. It was bad enough that he wanted to put his back against a wall and come out fighting.

He'd dealt with the strain of going against orders—sort of. Going against his principles by breaking the law was worse with his conscience. But if he'd followed his instincts those last four months in the marines, he might have… He couldn't play the "what if" game any more than Bree should. He'd given her the same advice that he lived by. That's how you got through the beginning days and the only way it got easier as time dragged on.

"Jerry just wants to help," she said in a low voice.

If she spoke much lower, he'd have to bend to her height to hear. The truck stop was crowded with people and chaotic noise. The café was packed with stranded motorists camping in every available corner. No one was leaving. The same was true for the store. The shelves were being depleted of food since the highway had been closed for going on eight hours.

It was worse than an airport with stranded travelers.

"We stick with the plan. If we're stuck here while the road's closed, he's right, we should get some rest. He'll keep watch so we can."

"He could come with us and leave the phone with one of his friends."

"Do you trust them like you do your uncle? We stick

with the plan and take control of the situation by getting your family to safety. Then we go to the police. That's the deal. We can't fight an unknown enemy. Agreed?"

She abruptly nodded and picked up some oversize gloves. "You're one proud marine, Jake Craig. Too proud, if you ask me."

The feeling of being watched intensified. He kept his head down looking at a portable heater for a car, pretending to read the details but looking around him at all the possibilities. He'd have no problem recognizing the kid who'd shot him.

There were a lot of people around, but most were staying put, not wandering the aisles. Not many—if any—had arrived after them, either. Maybe the fear of being caught off guard again was just making him paranoid. There was a strong possibility that Larry and the kid hadn't made it as far north as he and Bree. He needed to make her understand that it wasn't his pride unwilling to accept help.

He tapped her shoulder and she raised her purple eyes to his. Her skin was clear with a spattering of freckles across a straight nose. He wanted to stroke the bruise he'd heard Larry give her before pure rage that anyone had flawed her skin rushed through his veins. He had to cap it and let the anger go.

"If I were you, I'd probably be listening to my uncle, too. You've known him longer. But you have to trust that I know what I'm doing." And won't make any more mistakes like the previous day. "What we're doing isn't for public knowledge. I'm willing to break the law to help get your family to safety, but if we accept help from your uncle, then he could go to jail. I don't think you want that."

"It's nice to see a familiar face, that's all."

"I know how you feel." But he was looking for a young, chunky face that could barely shave. Sifting through all the noise for a rough voice he'd heard only once on the phone. And hoping that the GPS phone would ring so he could get Bree away from all these witnesses and just kiss her senseless.

He had to be as tired as Jerry had proved with that punch to think about kissing her in the middle of all this chaos.

"Do you? How?"

"Hmm?" He shook his head. He'd forgotten what she was asking. The man two aisles over turned his face to avoid eye contact or so he couldn't get a look. Time to go. "Let's pay for this stuff."

"What's wrong?"

His arm was around her shoulders and he got a good grip on her before she could react. He didn't resist sliding a finger over her bruised cheek. Then he tilted her chin toward him to keep her from searching the room, leaning close to her ear as he whispered, "I think the guy in the black coat and stocking cap a couple of rows behind me has been shadowing us around the store. We're paying for our snacks and walking outside. Can you do that without being weird?"

"Sure."

"Good. 'Cause I don't want him to have any idea about what hits him when he rounds the far corner."

"He's coming over here," she said, her lips inches from his.

If they hadn't been in the middle of a hundred people, stuck in the middle of a blizzard whiteout with two murderous bastards on their heels…well, he might have kissed her then and there.

"Pardon me?"

Jake spun around, keeping Bree behind him. The guy

was young all right, but his face was drawn and more slender than the man who'd shot him.

"What?" Jake snapped. His adrenaline was on overdrive along with every sensual cell in his body that he knew about and some that he didn't. The guy's face looked embarrassed. "Sorry, you caught me off guard."

"I'm the one who's sorry, man. I guess I've hit up everybody else in this place, but I'm trying to hitch a ride west when the storm breaks."

"Can't help you there." Bree tugged on Jake's sleeve and he dug some bills out of his pocket. "This might help."

"I don't want no charity, man."

"Someone gave me a break once. Pass it on when the time's right."

He smiled, took the money, said thanks and left. Jake barely heard him. The GPS phone was vibrating.

"THIS IS CRAIG."

Bree listened to the one-sided conversation, glad Jake didn't lose his cool telling Larry the murderer they were staying in Wichita Falls. The conversation only had two or three sentences. Jake kept her against his back while, she guessed, he kept an eye out for a man on a cell phone. That's what she would have been looking for if she could see over the rows of items for sale.

"Come on, let's get out of here," he said, guiding her elbow to the counter.

They zipped their jackets while the cashier totaled their doughnuts, milk and gum. Her heart was just beating normally again when they pushed their way through the door. Each step was a struggle. Not only did they have to walk through the snowdrifts, but each time one foot was off the ground, the wind gusted to blow her to one side.

They got to the rig and her uncle took the dogs to the

truck so he could keep watch. He had everything ready for them to rest in the sleeper section.

"I have had serious bed envy over the past couple of months. And let me tell you, none of them looked as good as that thin mattress and old, thick comforter." She pulled her jacket off, then her shoes, and had every intention of stripping the uncomfortable wet jeans off, too.

Warmth was definitely more important than modesty.

"Bed envy?" Jake asked from the driver's seat, where he was peeling his hat and gloves off.

"I've been sleeping in a different bed every four or five days for several months."

"Or not sleeping in one at all when you sat at the diner. I get it."

"I wanted to crawl into yours so badly last night." Too late she realized what she'd implied. "Not that I meant while you were in bed, 'cause you weren't while we were there. Dallas was and that's why I was even looking."

"I understand, Bree." He smiled and rubbed his jaw, then used his nails to scratch near his sideburn. "Think Dallas will be okay with Jerry? She seemed to like Charlie good enough."

Short, manly nails rubbing against manly beard stubble on a manly, square jawline.... Her insides turned to mush. He stopped and looked at her as if she might just be crazy. "I'm sorry. What? I must be really tired."

"We both are. Is that door locked?" He was taking his time getting his boots unlaced and off his feet.

She was ready to shimmy out of her jeans and put her head on a pillow. Once her eyes were closed she wouldn't put her foot in her mouth so easily. At least she hoped not to step all over her words.

Jake leaned back against the window and closed his eyes. Now was her chance. She quickly unzipped and scooted and pulled, peeling each leg out of the denim. Now she wouldn't get the bed soaking wet. She rotated to get between the cab seats and took a quick glance toward the driver's seat.

Hot brown eyes burned her skin as he looked her over from her hip to her ankle and back again. "That probably wasn't a great idea."

"Nope." Jake's Adam's apple visibly moved.

Why she was paralyzed she didn't know. He took another long, smoldering stare, not bothering to hide it. How was it possible for brown eyes to look so hot? Or for her skin, so cold a few moments before, to feel on fire when he hadn't touched her at all?

"Night." His voice was low and hoarse. And, more than anything else, sexy.

"Good night, Jake."

She moved her left foot toward the bed and a single finger circled her right hip bone, stopping both her movement and her heart. The same nail she'd envied moments before skimmed the length of her leg like a butterfly. So soft she wondered if she was imagining it.

Her heart jump-started again, pounding, questioning what should come next or if *anything* would come next. Her mind told her to wrap herself tight in those covers and forget he was in the sleeper cab. But her body had reacted to him from the first moment she'd seen him twenty-four hours earlier.

It was too soon. Then why was his finger still taunting her skin? Was he asking permission? Wondering what she'd do?

She wanted the answer to that question, too. Unable to move forward, unable to tell him to stop. She barely knew him. But she'd lived more in one day at his side than she had in the past two years alone.

She captured his hand closing in on her hip again. He didn't pull away. She didn't push him away. She closed her eyes, breathing deeply and letting the warmth of his palm soak into her skin again.

Then she laced her fingers through his, not letting go as she lay between the covers and tugged him into the sleeper with her.

Chapter Eighteen

"I don't think this is what your uncle had in mind when he told us to get some rest." He smiled at her, staying on his knees, giving her time to reconsider.

Their first kiss at his apartment didn't encourage her to reconsider. She wanted to take advantage of the storm and their break in this madness.

"Shh. Don't talk. Don't think."

Exhausted from listening to her head and pushing her heart aside, she slid her fingertip across his lips until the fire returned to his eyes. She dragged her nails down his sweater and warmed her hands against his tight undershirt against his abs.

He crossed his arms and a moment later the soft wool was tossed to the front seat. "There's not much room back here."

"I think we'll fit."

Her hands tugged a moment at the white cotton, but he delayed her, reaching to the small of his back. He unhooked his gun holster and laid it to the side of the pillow. Shifting, he straddled her legs, removed his shirt, belt and moved to his jeans.

"Wait." She took his hands away from the zipper. "There's something I've been dying to do."

Back in his apartment, he'd casually walked around

shirtless. This moment wasn't her first glimpse of his muscles and tight abs or the first time she'd longed to get his hot skin next to hers. But it was her first contact and she planned on enjoying it. She wasn't disappointed. His heat shot through her palms as she slowly caressed each curve and hard contour.

Jake could have melted those snowdrifts if he'd just taken his shirt off. The burning under her hands intensified with each pass across his chest. There wasn't an ounce of soft on him.

It would have been easy to let her eyes close and just feel. Let his hands have their way and start the intimate exploring. But watching *his* eyes close and hearing *his* sharp hiss between *his* clenched teeth as she ran her fingers along the top of his jeans…it made the anticipation of his exploration even more intense.

She was glad the diesel engine had the entire truck humming as much as her body. The small vibration hid the quiver shooting through her. She didn't want Jake to feel guilty or question this moment later—today, tomorrow or days from now. He wasn't taking advantage of her emotions or their fatigue. Whatever happened later between them happened. She had no illusions.

But she also knew the risks of not loving when you could. What if she went to jail and never had the opportunity to love again? What if something went wrong with the rescue and she wasn't around at all?

Making love was her question to ask. Her choice to make. Jake had already given his consent. She unzipped his fly, feeling his power as she peeled the jeans down to his knees. She saw him stretched to capacity and they hadn't truly touched yet. He leaned forward, his arms to either side of her, demonstrating the control he had by kicking out of one pants leg and then the other. He didn't touch her. She longed to arch her back or wrap her arms around his neck, pulling him to her breasts.

After the jeans joined the other clothing in the front seat, Jake pushed back to his previous straddle. His last article of clothing did little to hide his desire. The jolt of longing kicking its way through her insides was driving her crazy. The man who had saved her more than once today, leaned to one side, tugging slowly at the comforter she'd been hiding under.

It was still her choice to move forward or pull the covers back to her chin. She allowed them to glide past her hips. He used the back of his finger, dragging it along the bottom of her T-shirt, then along her ribs and the curve of her breast. She thought she'd died right then and there, but he drew more circles on the inside of her arm, across her belly, along her neck—everywhere except where she wanted him the most.

"Your turn to lose the shirt," that deep voice said, thick with lust. "Need help?"

Was it just lust?

No.

Jake Craig could have seduced her in the shower, could have coaxed her to his comfortable bed. Instead, he'd fought icy roads and high winds to get her closer to rescuing her family. Even now, he skimmed the outside of her shirt, raising the edge, skittering across her skin to make her ache with need.

This humble marine turned detective had given up so much to help her. He'd pushed forward through a blizzard. He might have threatened her with jail, but he'd sent a detailed shopping list with her sizes for new clothes. And every step of the way, he'd listened to her opinion and thoughts.

There was a strong possibility she was falling for this guy and they had kissed once.

Remedying their lack of kissing should be easy. She put her hands on his shoulders and brought his hard body down to hers. But Jake had his own idea and slid one hand under her waist, arching her back to expose her neck.

A sigh escaped her when their hips finally connected. It wasn't enough. The weight of him felt protective and she wanted more. Her fingers seized his flexing biceps, wanting to push them aside and have him crash onto her.

He teased her flesh by tipping her head back and caressing her jawline with his lips. He got closer, his kisses hotter, but when she turned her lips toward him, he'd dart to the flesh on the inside of her arm. He continued his playful toying down her neck and across the tops of her breasts.

How long did he think she could take this exquisite abuse?

"Ready to lose this shirt yet?" he asked.

Her shirt came off with the barest break in his torturous touching. He was building a bonfire and she was the wood. Each stroke added another bit of fuel just waiting for a spark. His hands skimmed over her nipples, almost ignoring them, making them ache for a wild grasp right until the palm of his hand scorched her belly.

And then…the shyest of touches on the outside of her panties. Her heart pounded at just the thought. If his hands weren't skimming, touching or cupping, his lips were. She didn't want to be on the edge of this flame by herself and did a little of her own skimming, but the place Jake was taking her was within her grasp.

"Go on," he whispered into her ear. His lips continued down her jaw and he dipped his head toward her shoulder.

Her hands darted out to bring his face to hers. As her body exploded, his lips enveloped hers. Strong and just right. Everything about it was as perfect as she'd known it would be.

If the two of them had been smoldering since their chance encounter at the diner and he'd built her bonfire on top of the embers, then their kiss was the ignition switch.

There was no slow left for either of them. Wild, demanding kisses and strokes that left them with the covers tangled around their ankles. The chill in the air didn't matter. Encased in Jake's heat, Bree could only think of getting closer to his burning skin, becoming a part of him completely and staying there. The more she thought about it, the warmer she became.

He shifted to his side to lean on his elbow. His eyes were dark, and the furrow was back between his eyebrows. He lightly rubbed that serious spot on his forehead.

"You're thinking again."

"I feel like I've been waiting a lifetime to see you naked. You are so damn beautiful, Sabrina Watkins."

"And that makes you worry?"

"It's hard for me to remember we've only known each other twenty-four hours." *And that you should be handed over to authorities.*

"Does that make a difference?" she asked, dragging a finger across his chest. Making him forget even more.

"Maybe it should, but it doesn't." He twirled a strand of her hair around his pinky, leaving it curled as it unwound and dropped next to her tiny ear. He could spend hours taking her body to different sensual levels.

"I know," she whispered before dragging his mouth back to hers. He was ready to kiss more than just her luscious lips.

Before he got crazy with Bree again, he needed the condom from his jeans that he'd picked up inside the truck stop. He'd known—or hoped—this would happen as soon as Jerry suggested grabbing some shut-eye together.

Reluctantly, he backed away from the woman in his arms and dug through his jeans. The snow was still coming down and the wind still moved the truck from side to side. It was the first time he noticed the curtains for the sleeper. He flipped on a small mounted lamp, pulled the curtains and created an intimate cocoon.

The awaiting butterfly still needed to shed one more layer. The frilly black bra hadn't been replaced by something practical from his list. It was hers. The one she'd been wearing since they'd met.

Crazy that it had been one day.

Crazier still was the way he wanted this woman. He wanted her with a fierce hunger and couldn't understand why. He didn't need to understand. She clearly wanted his body, as well.

The back of her hand skimmed across the front of his skivvies when he returned. He pressed toward her fingers, straining to be skin to skin. He used his hand in much the same way and received a sigh and tingle from Bree. Her hands roamed his body and he let his hands roam, too. He lightly traced the lace cups and her pulse leaped in her throat.

Watching her come to life and enjoy his exploring had taken him to a level of sensuality he hadn't experienced before and didn't want to rush. But this was definitely torture.

Time to unsnap the bra and kiss more of Bree's skin. He slid the cups down, releasing the most perfect pair of breasts he'd set eyes on. His mouth followed what his eyes had devoured in a heartbeat. His lips locked on her cool nipple, making it pebble while the other warmed in his hand.

He looped his finger in the material at her hip, a gentle

tug on one side of the thong and—without intending to—the delicate sides snapped. Bree giggled. And his mouth jumped into a smile at the sound.

As bold and comfortable as he became with Bree, she became with him. She matched him touch for touch, stroke for stroke, kiss for kiss. Her body's need was matching his, too. No question about it as she reached for the condom.

Bree surprised him with long, gliding strokes before rolling it on. The tension and heat rose within him and her, if her breath was any indication. She lay back on the mattress, ready, waiting.

No more waiting.

The small space had its advantages. It might not be the sexiest place to make love but he didn't care. He braced himself with one locked arm and slid the other to the small of her back and lifted her, sliding home. Her eyes closed and her mouth opened on a long sigh as she surrounded every inch of him.

Lying next to her, exploring her body…all fine and good. None of that compared to connecting to her. Being complete with her. Rushing to a place that only the two of them could get to together. No, it was more than just *good*.

Why he wanted that connection and with this particular woman—well, he wasn't wondering about it too much. He needed to be closer, dropped to cover her, feel soft skin next to his.

Finishing would be easy, but he'd make sure Bree was satisfied and then satisfied a second time. With slow, even strokes, he loved her. Her hands gripped his shoulders and her body met his, thrust for thrust. The pace picked up, as did their breathing. A moment later her body tightened and she cried out. He caught her hands in his and kept on going.

Inside her was a warm cocoon of its own. She wrapped her legs around him and kept him close. If the wind hadn't hidden the rocking motion of the tractor, then no one would have had any doubts of what was happening inside. The small berth locked the world out, intensifying her softness, her smell, his need. With a few last strokes, they both cried out in fulfillment.

He rolled to his side and caught her to him, barely catching his breath before the scent of his shampoo in her hair made him stiffen again. He wanted more than one morning in her arms. He'd thought he was crazy before. Now there was no doubt.

The magical first moment was over and he waited for reality to burst back on the scene. Waited for Bree to move away. But she didn't.

When her breathing slowed, she faced him, pulled his mouth to hers and he kissed her lips like the first and last time all melted together. She curled her fist against his chest and in two shakes was asleep.

How could he have thought sharing sex would lessen the need for her? Once would never be enough. It wasn't even enough for the moment. There needed to be a *lot* more moments between them. He used the back of a finger to softly caress the darkening cheekbone where she'd been hit by her abductors. He skimmed her breasts and her breathing hitched, wakening her from her light sleep. His hand wandered over her tight belly and then lower.

"We should probably get some shut-eye," she said with an anticipated sigh. "You were...um...pretty tired before the workout."

"Tired before you took your pants off and I saw how little that tiny thong actually covered." He tucked a strand of almost black hair behind her ear and remembered a box of dark hair dye. "I was thinking I should probably know what your real hair color is."

There was one way to satisfy his curiosity and to start another *moment*.

"I've dyed it darker than…oh…"

They could sleep soon, but first, he needed to see for himself.

Chapter Nineteen

Something was different.

Jake woke to darkness and a warm body in his arms. That *was* different. He hadn't had a woman in his bed since before his last tour began. But there was something more.

He was with Bree in the sleeper of Jerry's big rig, behind a heavy curtain. Light snuck through the edges a little brighter than it had when the sun came up.

Storm raging, at different times, they'd pulled most of their clothes back on to be ready to go. He missed the warm smoothness of Bree's skin under his fingers and missed her nails lightly scraping his flesh.

Lying next to her still felt good. She fit. He needed someone who fit. Maybe… The "maybe" dangled in front of him, taunting. Challenging him to jump forward and grab it. Those kind of thoughts were for someone with a future. They wouldn't have one if he didn't clear her name. Even then, the woman in his arms knew nothing of his past. Nothing about the nightmares of war. And he knew nothing about how to tell her.

Now, he needed to concentrate on what had changed.

The diesel still hummed. The noise level from the wind wasn't as loud. He'd swear that the swaying had died down to almost nothing. Both cells vibrated at his head. He'd kept them close in case they rang, but they were both out of his reach unless he moved the sleepyhead off his shoulder. The limited space in the sleeper kept him from claiming Bree's lips first thing like he wanted. He settled for her forehead.

"Bree, time to go." He stretched as best he could and pulled a curtain back to him, filling the small area with bright sunshine.

No snow blowing sideways.

The wind hadn't just slowed down. It had barreled to a racing halt.

"You okay?" Bree asked, pushing up and leaning on her forearm. "Holy smokes, is that the freeway? The storm's over. You're right, it is time to get moving."

Different. He liked different. He patted the bed around his head, searching for the closest phone to answer. She reached over him, her breast flattening against his chest, starting a desire that couldn't be finished...at the moment.

"Here." She handed him his cell. "It's Jerry."

He sat and slammed the phone to his ear, ready to join the game again. "Yeah?"

"Someone's got eyes on your truck." He put it on speaker for Bree to hear as she gathered their shoes in the front seat. "I'm not inside the vehicle. I'm walking the dogs between the third and fourth row of rigs to keep an eye on things. How long do you need?"

"I'll be right out."

"Unwise. They can see my tractor. I don't think they know you're inside. You should keep it that way. Start by getting Sabrina away from the windows."

"Three minutes." Jake disconnected and grabbed Bree under the arms to yank her back to the sleeper—surprised face and all.

She scooted to the opposite side, shoving her feet into

the rubber boots she'd retrieved. "What are you going to do? What happens in three minutes."

"I'm pulling my shoes on and making certain you understand the rules." He pushed his head through the black sweater. He'd be a sitting duck, easily spotted against the snow, but he had nothing else.

"What rules?"

He laced his boots quickly while looking only at Bree. "You aren't going to want to follow my orders, but your uncle and I both need you to stay put. Here. Safe."

"But I can help—"

"I'm better going solo. I'll verify if the men watching the truck are Larry and that young sidekick of his. If they are, I can deal with them. And don't forget, your uncle's out there, too. The last thing we need is to worry about you."

"I've been taking care of myself since this thing all blew up."

"And that's turned out great. You're a distraction if I have to worry about protecting you. Remember, it's you they're after. You're the only person who can give them what they want."

He could tell that his words were getting her peeved. She sat Indian-style with her arms closed around her. An apology was on the tip of his tongue. It was the truth. She was a lovely distraction but a distraction nonetheless. And he couldn't do his job if he was distracted.

"They shot you."

He shifted to her side, pulled the curtain back to the center so no one could see her and kissed her like he'd wanted to when they'd first woken up. He had to rein it in before he had them back under the covers, naked and forgetting about the world.

"Nice jab, but it was just a graze. Won't even leave a

scar as a reminder." He leaned his forehead against hers, tempted to kiss her again, but he needed to get to her uncle.

"Do you have other reminders?"

Several images of early this morning clamored for time in his mind. He didn't think he was likely to forget any part of this weekend adventure and he didn't want to think about the scars he did have from the past eight years. That was a part of him he was determined to forget.

The past was the past. *Former* marine. *Former* life. The scars were there, old wounds that had healed. It was dangerous to go down that path. And dangerous if he kissed her again. What he needed was to get outside and watch the men who thought they were watching him.

"I've got to go. Can you peek through the curtain and take a look at the man leaning on the SUV?" She peeked out as he pulled the laces tight on his second boot. "Recognize him?"

She shook her head. "Jake—"

"I really need that promise, hon." Her purple eyes were going to be his downfall. If one tear fell, he'd…he'd handcuff her to the steering wheel, that's what he'd do. "Promise me."

"I…" The violet orbs darted back and forth between his. "I'll promise you if you promise not to get *grazed* again."

"It seems I've given you a false impression about my capabilities, darlin'. I had a run of bad luck yesterday, but I'm pretty good at what I do."

He withdrew his weapon from its holster and tossed the worn leather in the seat before checking his ammo. Then he bent as low as possible for someone over six feet tall and shifted to the passenger seat to dial her uncle.

"Jerry, got a ninety-second distraction?"

"Oorah." Jerry disconnected.

"What do I do if things don't go like you've planned?" she asked.

"Did I say I have a plan?"

Raised voices from the parking lot. There was his diversion. "Is our Peeping Tom on the corner moving away?"

"Looks like it." She leaned forward and kissed his cheek. "Seriously, Jake. Please be careful."

Somehow that felt as sexy as anything that had happened earlier. Okay, maybe not anything. He slipped out the door and sloshed to level ground where the snow wasn't as deep as the shallow ditch next to the road. There were snowdrifts taller than his head next to buildings.

The whiteout might have ceased, but it would still take hours to get the roads clear of the mess it had left behind. Running through this snow was like running in a thigh-high ocean surf. A terrific workout, but tiring.

What they needed was a chopper. Expensive, but he didn't see any way to lose the men tailing them. Or a way to get to Amarillo fast. They were running out of time to save Bree's family.

If they hadn't already.

There wasn't any real running through the snow, but he moved as quickly as he could, darting behind a post to reassess his opponent. He should have asked Mac for some winter camouflage so his dark jacket didn't stick out. But the closer he got, the more familiar the man watching his truck became. The same young hitchhiker he'd given a hundred-dollar bill to earlier that morning tried not to be obvious about his actions, but he was definitely watching the truck.

His phone vibrated. Jerry. "You stand out like a tick on a white dog sloshing through that snow. You recognize that fella?"

"He's not one of the men who attacked us at the lake, but he's watching the truck, all right."

"I'll be close."

Jake chased several things from his mind. He liked Bree's uncle Jerry. He also liked Bree—a lot. Maybe too much in such a short period of time. Heck, they already shared a dog. He pushed those thoughts aside and concentrated on his surroundings.

There were more tractors and trailers than he could count. All had their engines running—just like Jerry's. Instead of parking front to back in a straight line, these rigs were side by side. If he could get to higher ground, up top, then he'd be able to see all the movement in both this lot and the truck stop across the street. He pulled himself up between the cab and trailer.

Once he had a good grip, he used his upper body strength. On the roof he dropped to his belly, apparently not the only one with the idea to get a bird's-eye view. A familiar black jacket was perched on the opposite end, five trailers away.

No time to warn Jerry or Bree about his plan—if he could call taking this man down no matter the cost a plan. He pulled his weapon. Once he stood and ran, there wouldn't be anything other than adrenaline pumping through him.

If he could take him alive…great. But that action wasn't high on his priority list. From where the guy was lying, he didn't think Jerry was visible. And where Bree sat on the passenger side of his tractor wasn't.

Surprise was all he had going for him. Jake slid on his belly from the front of the trailer roof to the back, keeping his weapon above the snow and ice. His hands were frozen, but he couldn't pull the trigger wearing gloves. He blew on his right fingers, rubbing and warming before he stood.

The man still hadn't seen or heard him. He could thank the diesel engines for drowning out most of the noise. A couple of quick inhales and he took off, thankful he wore the military boots that kept him from sliding around as he pushed from one trailer to the next. He jumped the first three-foot space between trailers easily enough, the second wasn't so tough. But after Jake landed the third, the man rolled to his back at the sound.

One more to go.

Shots. He heard the ping of metal midair between four and five. He landed and dropped flat. More shots, but this guy wasn't a good aim. Must be the kid who grazed him at the lake.

"Give it up, kid. Didn't you learn that you can't hit the broadside of a marine?"

The kid scrambled to his knees, scared. He wasn't wearing the ski mask. Sure enough it was Larry's sidekick with the unshaven double chin. Jake jumped to his feet and leaped to the silver roof before another shot came a little too close.

The length of a trailer and a three-foot opening was all that stood between him and taking this wannabe murderer to the police. Right after he supplied Jake with any information he might have about where the Watkins family was being held.

"Come on, kid. You know you aren't getting away from me. Everything badass that you've heard about marines… imagine that and add a little more…then you'll get me." It was the part of him he wanted to bury and never resurrect, but the kid didn't know that.

The kid's gun hand shook and it wasn't from the cold. "Y-y-you c-can't do n-n-nothin' to me. Y-y-you're a c-cop," he stuttered.

Jake wanted to feel sorry for him. But he didn't. This

kid had joined forces with a murderer and abducted Bree. He still hadn't gotten the full story about what they'd done to her. Neither of the creeps deserved mercy from him.

Think calm. Try not to kill him.

"You shoot me, kid, you're a cop killer. You know what they do to cop killers?" He watched the kid's face go paler. "That's right, it's the death penalty."

"They ain't ever gonna c-c-catch us."

Jake shook his head and purposefully smiled. "Look around you, kid. No one's going *anywhere* soon. How are you going to get away?"

Jake walked slowly to the edge of the trailer, faking the confidence he lacked. He hadn't caught a good look at the type of weapon the kid was using or had any idea how much ammo he carried. They were squared up with about ten feet separating them, three of which had a thirteen-foot drop to the ground.

The kid wasn't moving anything except his eyes. He seemed nervous but frozen in place as much as the ground.

You want this guy alive, a voice nagged at him.

He wants you dead, another shouted.

Taking him into custody wouldn't be easy. Jake wanted him alone. Wanted to give the kid a dose of his own medicine. The trailer shifted just as he was about to make a move. An extra thump or rocking motion shot up his back about the time the kid's mouth slightly rose at the corner in a smirk.

The kid raised his weapon. Confident.

Fire.

"Behind you, Craig!" Jerry yelled from somewhere on the ground.

Larry. The kid's partner stood at the back of the silver trailer. Gun in hand. Aimed at Jake's chest.

Chapter Twenty

Fire.

Jake's weapon didn't waver. He didn't need to cover both men. Larry was the threat.

"Take care of the dog walker before someone else comes around," Larry commanded.

Jerry disappeared around the back ends of the trucks. He hoped one of his "partners" would think now was a good time to call the cops. Naw, Bree wouldn't, but Jerry might. They could keep Bree hidden and out of the police questioning.

"Big, tough m-marine fell for...for the stuttering routine." The kid swallowed hard, his Adam's apple bobbing in his thick neck.

Clearly accepting the orders, the kid dropped clumsily off the orange rooftop and out of sight.

"We got a problem, man," Larry said. "All we need's the girl and the money."

You need this guy alive. Jake knew why he stood there listening to a criminal, but what was Larry's reason to talk it up with a cop? What did they hope to gain?

"So maybe you should shoot that gun in your hand instead of treating it like a toy. Or I could shoot you and resolve both our problems."

Larry shrugged, trying to look tough by smiling, like

every stereotypical bad guy Jake had seen in the movies and rarely encountered on the streets.

Jake wanted to punch the smile right off his face, leaving a mark a hell of a lot worse the one on Bree's cheek. He'd settle for dislocating the man's jaw. Then he'd dare *Larry* to try to look like…whatever.

"You think you're smart? Thing is, ya shoot me and you know you'll never get her family back. No chance my brother will let 'em go unless you do what I say."

"Yeah, I know. It's the one reason you aren't dead already. So your point, Larry?" It was tempting to pull the trigger and end the smug arrogance of a confessed murderer, but the cop in him was stronger than the shoot-first-and-ask-questions-later. *Alive. You need this guy alive.* He'd keep the man alive and lock him away in jail.

"The point is," Larry said, "I have what you want and you won't shoot me. So drop it."

Barking. A familiar howl. Dallas and Charlie.

"Get 'em off me. Stop." That had to be the kid. "I'll kill her, old man. I'll kill her."

Larry's eyes darted toward the sound of the scuffle. Jake stared at the gun barrel as it drooped. Slightly, but that was enough. Jake squeezed the trigger microseconds before Larry. No longer aiming at a stationary target, Larry missed, then dropped flat to the top of the icy silver trailer, dodging Jake's shot.

Jake jumped to the orange trailer, dug his toes into the ice, keeping his footing on the roof. *Alive. You need this guy alive.* If he hadn't been repeating the line, he would have emptied his clip. But he didn't fire. To his right he caught a glimpse of someone with long, dark hair rolling in the snow, fighting with a man in a black jacket. Just a glimpse as he refocused on Larry, to his left, who was getting to his knees and standing.

Jake raised his arms and leaped across the trailers, smashing Larry to his back and sending both weapons flying. The crash thrust them skidding across the trailer. Jake latched on to his opponent's jacket. He dug his steel-toed boots into the icy silver roof to slow their slide. His feet caught on a roof reinforcement, stopping them from plunging over the side.

Larry threw his arm across Jake's windpipe, pushing, acting unconcerned that they both might teeter over the trailer's edge. Hitting the ground headfirst—snow or no snow—could be deadly.

"What now, cop?" he said, clenching his jaw and shoving harder.

Another impasse. They'd have to roll to their sides and let go of each other in order to get to their feet. How could he take this maniac alive?

The double-chinned kid backed around the corner of the semi, shoving Bree. Her arm was twisted behind her back with his gun pointed straight at her temple.

Jerry was nowhere in sight.

"Let him go or I'll kill her!" the kid shouted. "But don't drop him. I mean—" Bree stumbled into a snowdrift and the kid began kicking, connecting with her side. She curled into a ball, protecting herself. "I won't stop till you let him go."

"Don't kick her to death. He gets it," Larry said. His face was too close not to miss the "I win" glare in his eyes. "We need her."

The arm crushing Jake's larynx cautiously lifted. Jake rolled and pulled himself back until both of them could grab the side of the truck and catch their balance. They moved apart, rolling in opposite directions and scrambling to their feet. The instant he stood, he saw the challenge in Larry's eyes. His opponent already had a switchblade palmed.

Jake wasn't worried about the aggression. He was through treating these men like they were worth any kindness. Every strike he inflicted wouldn't begin to pay back for what Bree had endured.

Larry thumbed the lever and the blade popped into place. He lunged.

One defensive move at a time, Jake's years of military training took over. Once let loose, there was no stopping the return of the machine he'd never wanted to evoke into action again.

Chapter Twenty-One

Bree's side was on fire from the kicks to her ribs. She halt-ingly unzipped her jacket without anyone noticing and withdrew one of the guns she'd taken from Jake's black bag. She couldn't see either man on top of the trailer, but she could see her uncle's signal telling her it was time. Hopefully, Jake would benefit from the distraction and be able to save himself. And her. She uncurled and rolled under the edge of the trailer. As soon as the bastard who'd just kicked her leaned down to grab her, she stuck her gun in his face.

"Drop your gun." She spoke softly so only the kid—as Jake had called him—could hear.

When he did, she moved until she could pick it up, then shoved the gun into her pocket. Her uncle came from be-hind her with packing tape he'd retrieved out of his bot-tomless pit of road supplies. But her uncle didn't move fast enough. The kid started running, yelling and flail-ing his arms.

"Larry! Larry! Larry!"

"I'll get him." Jerry came out of hiding. "Find those guns. The cops will be here any minute." He ran through the snow, gaining on the kid.

Bending to look for those guns, the pain in her ribs shot through her like an ice pick. She'd almost felt sorry for the kid, but not so much while she clenched her jaw and got control of her breathing back. Finding those guns was easier said than done. "I don't think anyone's going to find them until this snow melts," she mumbled.

The trailer rocked at her back. Jake fought with Larry again, just as her uncle had predicted. She backed up in the knee-deep snow until she could see the men on the rooftop. A crowd had gathered outside the store across the street and were headed this way.

"Jake! I can hear the police." The siren wailed in the distance. She couldn't be delayed trying to convince them her family was in trouble. They had to get out of there. She looked up in time to see Jake's boot catch Larry in the chest, rocketing him over the back of the trailer toward her.

He landed on his back at a weird angle. They needed him for answers.

"Bree, stop!"

She was already at Larry's side to see if he was dead. His eyes popped open, his hand latched to her arm and toppled her to his chest. Before she blinked there was a knife, nicking her throat.

"No playing this time, princ—"

A loud gunshot stopped Larry's words and knife. Jake tugged on her to get her going. He'd jumped down so fast she hadn't seen him. His mouth moved, but she couldn't understand him through the fog. Larry's eyes were open, a bullet wound to his chest.

"I'm going to be sick."

"Do it over here." Jake pushed her behind him into a snowdrift. "As soon as the crowd gets brave enough, they're going to investigate that last shot. Where's Jerry?"

As much as her stomach objected to the picture fresh in her mind, she didn't lose her cookies. "After the kid, who was running toward the freeway."

She took a step to pass Jake and was enveloped in his arms instead. His gentle touch to her neck was a sharp contrast to the man she'd seen fighting on that trailer. The same man who had shot Larry dead to save her. He tilted her chin, using the pad of his thumb to create those soothing circles.

"Are you okay?" He tilted her head farther. The wet drops of blood where the knife had broken the skin were whisked away.

"I'm fine."

"If we weren't in a hurry…"

"But we are. Where's my uncle and that other murderer?" Bree couldn't think of him as a young man who'd fallen under the wrong guidance. That was for a jury to decide. Right now, she needed to help her family and he was the key. Their only clue.

They took off. Jake had her elbow securely in his strong hand. She wanted to remember his hands from early this morning—gentle, loving. The firm grip was comforting, but it had also pulled the trigger pushing them farther from getting the money to Griffin.

They skirted the oncoming crowd. The police cars made it to the truck stop. She ran, barely keeping up with Jake as he searched for her uncle. Then they both saw the hitchhiker trying to get their attention.

"He's going to kill him. They're behind the trash." His hands were full trying to contain both dogs.

"Stay here," Jake instructed, looking at them both.

"This is my fight," she said to his back, following.

Her uncle was pinned on the ground. The kid hit his arm with a pipe. As he raised it again, Jake grabbed it, hurling the pipe into the bags of excess trash spilling from the receptacles.

The younger man turned his anger on Jake. "I'm not

going back! They promised." He pommeled Jake, who kept retreating, leading him farther away from Jerry.

With the hitchhiker on her heels, she ran to Jerry. "Are you all right?"

She helped him sit and listened not to his explanation but for sounds of another fight.

"I think my arm's busted." He cradled his left wrist in his thick hand. "The boy caught me by surprise. I turned right into that pipe and went down like a sinker on a fishing pole."

"Can you stay with him?" she asked the man holding their dogs. She and her uncle had "hired" him to dog sit with the promise of a ride to California when they'd concocted their plan to keep Jake from being shot.

"Take one of these things, will ya?"

Dallas squirmed out of his arms and into hers, licking her hands, glad to see her. She set her on the ground and put her leash back in the young man's hand.

"I love you, Uncle Jerry." She rose, ran in the direction Jake had led the fight and listened for sounds. When she didn't hear any, she backed up to the corner of a small building and waited.

She should have stayed with her uncle. Things had moved so fast. Her first thought had been to help Jake. How in the world could she do that? Screaming for help was the last thing she could do. The police were in the parking lot. People in the crowd had to have seen them running from Larry's body.

Her stomach lurched at the image of the bullet hole and blood on the snow.

"Where's the money?"

At first she thought the person was asking her. Then she realized the kid Jake chased was around the corner of the building.

"Man, I told you. She said Amarillo. That's all I know," Jake lied.

He knew the money was in his bag of black op equipment. If she could get the gun she had into Jake's hands, then he could capture the kid. She pulled the gun from her pocket and knelt on the ground.

"I don't know what to do. Where's Larry?"

"Want me to take you to him, man? I can do that."

She looked around the corner, straight into Jake's jeans. She could almost tug on his hand and place the gun in his fingers. He took a step forward, his hand out of her reach.

She stood, leaning against the stucco building, holding the gun in both hands just like she'd been taught. But she'd also been taught not to point a loaded weapon at a person. Life or death made it different. She'd get the kid to drop the knife, Jake would be safe and they'd find out about her family.

"Hold it," she said, barreling around the corner, gun aimed at both men.

"Ahhh!" the kid screamed, knife raised, lunging for Jake.

"Stay back, Sabrina!"

Jake's defensive moves were textbook perfect. He countered the downward thrust of the knife with a sweeping block of his forearm. He caught the kid's wrist in his hand and shook. Pinned in the snowdrift, their legs barely moved as Jake released the kid's opposite shoulder to grab the arm with the knife.

The kid pressed forward, wild-eyed and hysterical. He yanked his arm free from Jake's grasp, violently shoving and wildly wielding the knife from side to side. "I'll kill her. I'll kill her."

Jake growled and blocked the descent of the blade. Bree realized she still aimed the gun at them both. She shoved it back in her pocket, knowing she wouldn't shoot. They couldn't risk killing their only lead to her family.

Each assault from the younger man was countered by the more experienced ex-marine. The kid's wielding of the knife became more frantic and chaotic as he tried to get past Jake.

Their attacker kept crying out, "I have to kill her. I have to kill her." His words hypnotized Bree at the building corner. She was unable to move or cry out or help. Her uncle came around the corner and darted forward without hesitation, broken wrist and all.

There was a final sweep of Jake's arm, the knife disappeared, a scream and then the kid threw back his head and collapsed in the snow. While Jake and Jerry looked at his wound, trying to stanch the blood, she ran over and took the young man's face in her hands. His eyes focused far from her. She shook his coat collar to get his attention, losing whatever bit of decency she had left.

"Who are you working for? Where's my family? Tell me!" Her uncle could have died. What if Jake had died for her?

"You won't get—" He coughed. A bead of dark red blood dropped from his nose. "They promi…"

She stumbled back into Jake's stable body.

Her uncle checked for a pulse and confirmed what was evident from the glazed, open eyes.

"They're…dead. Both dead?" She started breathing and talking fast, unable to block all the unanswered questions filling her head.

"It'll be okay," Jake said, from just above her ear, leading her back toward the truck.

"Can't you see he's dead? Did he say where my family is being held? Who he works for? Why did you kill him? You killed them both. It's all your fault."

"*My* fault?" Jake answered, leaning on the truck, breathing a little hard. "Damn, why didn't I stop to interrogate him? Oh, yeah, he was beating your uncle with a steel pipe. Then he was determined to kill you and me with a knife. I saved your uncle. And I saved you. Totally unnecessary if you'd stayed in the truck."

She knew she was wrong and still the fear bubbled to the surface in the form of spiteful words. "What about my mother, father and sister? What if these two have to report to Griffin? And when they don't? What happens when Griffin knows his men are dead. It'll be all over the news before we can possibly get near Amarillo."

"Try to calm down, Bree. You're in shock." Jake pulled her face to his shoulder, muffling the sounds of her sobs. "We'll find a way. Don't give up. Right now we've got to get out of here."

"Give her the black dog," Jerry told the hitchhiker. "Bree, you and Jake need to get out of here before the police head this way."

"Are we getting out of here, too?" the hitchhiker asked, setting the dogs in the snow.

"All in due time," her uncle answered.

"Dallas should stay with you," Jake told him.

She shook her head. "She's *my* dog. You can't give her to anyone."

Burying her face in the dog's cold fur, she had little faith they'd succeed and paid no attention as she was pushed into the truck. The engine started, Jake barreled through the snow away from the crowds, two dead bodies and the police stuck trying to determine what had happened.

"I don't know how my uncle thinks he's going to talk his way out of jail."

"If you'd stayed in the truck—"

"You'd be dead," she answered quickly.

"Dammit, Bree. You broke your promise to stay in the truck. Don't blame me for having to clean up the mess."

"You really expected me to just sit there and not fight for myself?"

"Yes."

"Then I'm not sure why you're even trying to get away or continue to help me. It's hopeless."

"We aren't beaten yet, Bree. I've seen hopeless, and this isn't one of those scenarios."

She tucked Dallas into the dog bed in the backseat. She couldn't look at Jake, no matter how encouraging he was attempting to be, so she dropped her face into her hands. Yes, he saved her life with his accurate shot, but at what price? "They're dead, aren't they? My family. All of my family's gone and it's my fault."

"Never think that. Griffin knows he needs them alive to get the money back."

"It's a long way to Amarillo. We can't just snap our heels together and get there in an instant. And then we have to find them. And rescue them. Driving, it's three and a half hours on a good day. Just admit that it's impossible to save them."

"I promise you, sweetheart, we're getting to your family before anything happens. It's only two hours by chopper. They won't be expecting us. We'll have leverage and surprise on our side."

A hint of the look she'd seen while he'd fought crowded the features she adored and had kissed so hungrily less than an hour ago. She couldn't possibly be attracted to the fighter he'd unleashed on those two men, but she needed those killer instincts to win this battle.

"Just tell me what to do."

Was there a fighter left in her? She'd been running so long, afraid of failing, afraid of no one believing in her.

Had the past years of building her business against the advice of her friends and family meant nothing? Could she remember what it was like to fight for what she wanted?

Chapter Twenty-Two

Sometime during one of his encounters today, Jake's side had been sliced by a knife. Not a bad wound, but enough blood to show through his sweater. Bree had accused him of keeping the cut a secret, but he honestly didn't remember it happening.

No helicopters had been available and it had taken a lot longer for a charter pilot to get there than he'd hoped. He'd been anticipating the police finding them before they could get the runway cleared and their plane in the air. Five thousand dollars later, they still had a good hour before reaching Amarillo.

All he wanted to do was nap. His sore jaw reminded him he needed to be alert and at his best. But the look in Bree's eyes wasn't restful. His clean T-shirt was off, his side had been washed and he waited while she searched through the pilot's first-aid kit for antiseptic.

The atmosphere inside the cabin was still freezing. Bree had stopped talking, using gestures instead of words. At least with him. He didn't like it, wanting to wrap his arms around her and haul her to his lap. He wanted to forget the faces, his actions. Wanted her to believe everything he did was to keep her safe.

"Finding this plane is better than a noisy helicopter." He

settled for random conversation instead. "Easier to stretch my legs."

He extended his long limbs into the aisle as Bree rested between their seats on one knee, cleaning his wound. The plane pitched in the air and she wobbled. When he reached out to steady her, she jerked away.

"I don't feel right using any of that money for this plane."

"We didn't have much of a choice. It was the only charter available and Ernie wanted three thousand cash up front before he'd fly." Her delicate fingers were warm and soothing against his skin. Her gentle touch was worth the alcohol sting on the laceration.

She balanced in the aisle and worked in her seat as the plane sped forward. A picture of her bare thigh and the thong he'd torn came to him. He'd love to get his hands on that black lace bra again.

"I think you need stitches." She had the gauze and tape in hand and ready to go when the plane dipped quickly and she lost her balance heading nose first to the floor.

Jake steadied her around her ribs, forgetting that she'd been kicked by the kid. Their pilot recovered with a few curses and a message of "Sorry, folks." Bree twisted from his grasp.

"Are you in a lot of pain?" he asked. He didn't think it was just her injury keeping his hands off her. He'd seen that disgusted look before.

"Only when I lean hard on something."

"Or if someone grabs you." He looked at his injury. "I'll be fine with no stitches. Tear some of that tape into half-inch strips."

She began and he gritted his teeth before pulling his wound closed tight. "If you…um…put the tape on and…

yeah, draw it together. Just like that. Now the gauze. Great. See, no stitches needed."

"You still need a doctor."

"I'm all caught up on my shots." It wasn't his imagination—she got away from him as fast as possible. "I've had many a scratch taped like this. No trips to Emergency for me when I was growing up."

"You can't be serious." She sat and pulled Dallas onto her lap. "Why would your parents do that?"

"My grandmother, actually. She took care of me summers. Stitches were equivalent to being stuck in the house. So she'd tape me back together, I'd go play outside and she had peace."

"My grandmother's the reason I started my business. I'd walk her dog and bathe it. My uncle moved back after his discharge and her dogs did wonders for him. Charlie was amazing helping him work through his PTSD. When I got older, I house-sat. My granny connected me to friends in Amarillo for summers. Seemed natural to expand my business instead of attending college or working in a coffee shop."

He caught a silent tear on her cheekbone. He could see the withdrawal in her violet eyes as she pulled back from his touch. "Look, I'm sort of getting the impression you'd rather I keep my hands to myself. I thought we were past that but—"

"We moved past it way too fast. No offense, Jake, but I don't know you at all. So maybe we should back up a little."

"You want to pretend this morning didn't happen?"

"I wish I could pretend none of it happened."

"None of it?"

"Why would I want to remember those two men being killed?"

Or him killing them. "I get it."

"I know you did what you thought was best."

He needed out of here and he didn't see a parachute handy, so he was stuck a foot away from the first person he'd let close since returning from overseas. He'd let a dang puppy break through his defenses and she'd tugged her owner right along with her.

The plane dipped and Bree almost lost the pup out of her hands. "Whoa there, girl."

Dallas squirmed and jumped to his lap, barking a couple of times and ending on a short howl. She climbed Jake's chest and started licking his chin. "That dog going to jump around the whole way?" Ernie asked.

"I should have left her with my uncle. I wasn't thinking straight."

He knew exactly why she'd brought the pup. Comfort. "It's okay. Maybe we can pay Ernie to dog sit."

"Or find another hitchhiker. That was so bizarre. Jerry asked what he was watching, gave him the once-over and then said, 'Boy, I'll give you a ride clear to California if you just hold these dogs for me.'"

"You left your uncle's truck. Before I was almost shot. Why? You promised you wouldn't. I knew I should've used the handcuffs to keep you there."

"I really couldn't sit there letting you fight for me and take all the risks. Besides, I wanted to help you keep your promise that you wouldn't get grazed." She drew a line through his hair above his ear, mirroring the bullet burn from the day before.

He jerked his head away from the pleasant stroke. "No touching works both ways."

Her face changed from relaxed to what-am-I-doing in a heartbeat. "The chubby...guy was following my uncle. I thought he was in trouble. I couldn't stay safe while you were both fighting."

"That's exactly what you should have done."

"Our impromptu plan got you safely off the trailer roof," she defended.

Did your plan include shooting Larry? Even unspoken, the question hung between them. Her eyes darted worriedly back and forth. She knew what he'd almost asked. She bit her lip and drew in a long sigh. She also knew his answer. If she hadn't been in danger, he wouldn't have shot him.

Whatever had taken place in their dark corner of the whiteout this morning had vanished. Just like his ex-wife had needed him for her own purposes, Sabrina Watkins did, too. His place was either as a long-distance husband or the hired help.

He wasn't looking for a permanent relationship. Hell, he wasn't looking for *any* relationship. So what was the big deal about losing this one before it had really begun. *You've only known her for two days.*

"I can hold Dallas while you rest."

He stroked the pup's soft fur and rubbed her tummy when she stretched her paws into the air. "She's fine where she is. You've already discovered I don't share well. Now it's the pup's turn to learn who's boss."

He closed his eyes and was met with another death stare chiseled into his memory. He'd seen too many deaths to count. But he knew. He'd always know the number of people who had lost their lives on his watch. Larry and the kid may have been murderers and trying to kill them, but Jake hated having their deaths on his conscience.

You killed them both. It's all your fault.

He jerked awake, unable to get her words out of his head. He and Jerry had tried to help the kid after he'd deflected the knife into his abdomen, but nothing could be done. He'd washed and washed again before they'd gone wheels up. He would never get all the blood off.

His hands were clean, only figuratively stained. Bree knew it and should keep her distance. She rested her head against the window. He missed her head on his shoulder.

"I should have sent you to jail. You would've been safer."

She rotated to face him within the confines of her seat belt. The plane still pitched in the wind. "Maybe those men would be alive if you had. Should I wish that you'd never gotten involved?"

Did she think he'd enjoyed taking their lives? "You can say whatever you want. But maybe you should also know that if there were other choices, I would still make the same decisions I made today."

She looked shocked. Surprised that he would stand by his actions. The actions that had killed two men and probably began a statewide manhunt for them both. But he'd also meant making love to her, picking up the evidence cell and speaking to her at the diner.

He stared into her rich amethyst eyes and knew he'd be a happy man waking up next to them every day. Could he make that happen? Make her understand? Maybe see that he was more than a way to rescue her family?

"I get it, Bree. I'm a means to an end. Been there a lot over the years. No hard feelings." He reached into his bag of gear, tossing Larry's cell onto the seat. "We have the money. We have a phone to contact them. All we need is a car when we land and a place for the exchange."

"And a giant miracle."

"Miracles are for amateurs." The machine was back.

"Ah, folks, I think we may have a little problem." The pilot pointed to just off the runway as they landed.

Bree leaned around Jake, who had been checking his gear and keeping Dallas silent with a stern look and snap of his fingers. The snowplow had cleared a small area for planes and next to it were two police cars.

"You just had to do things your way." Waffling between fury and desperation, she could only stare through the plane windows.

"Wasn't me. Think about it. If I'd called the police, I wouldn't have fled the scene of a double homicide." He removed the gun at his waist and zipped it into the bag. "The police are normally smart, Bree. Add two and two together and they ended up with Amarillo. It's not a big leap from my truck to a plane headed here."

He was right. The desire to admit he was correct brought the words to the tip of her tongue, but she bit her lip instead. It was over. There wasn't a possibility they'd be together. Ever.

She'd failed her family.

Ernie slowed to a stop. "The tower's telling us to open the door and throw out any weapons we might have. Then exit one at a time. I'm supposed to go first, then open the rear door for you guys." He showed his empty hands in the window, opened the door next to him and got out.

Bree unhooked her seat belt, took Dallas into her arms and kissed her between the ears. "I'm going to miss you so much, you sweet little puppy."

"You'll see her again."

"I don't know how I'm going to survive in jail without pets. I've always preferred four paws to the two-legged variety." If they couldn't arrange a ransom exchange… She couldn't think of her family. She'd be a hysterical mess by the time her feet touched the ground.

"We'll convince them to help with the rescue of your family. You have enough evidence here to prosecute. We convince the police to back us up while we get names and an exchange site. It'll happen. Trust me."

"If they don't go for your idea, well, thanks anyway. For everything, Jake. My gratitude isn't nearly enough for what you've lost helping me."

The outside door opened. She shifted to the nearest seat, ready to climb down. He darted behind her, holding her elbow in spite of the no-touching rule. "It's not over. There's still a chance to free your family."

She climbed through the opening and made kissing sounds for Dallas to come to her. She looked at Jake one last time, wishing she hadn't pulled away and hoping he knew she didn't blame him.

"Thanks for trying, but it's time to give up."

She expected to be thrown to the ground, searched and hauled off to a horrible little interrogation room. She hoped not to cry or be hysterical during the entire interview, since she knew there was no hope of a rescue for her family.

Ernie was placed in a police car and driven away. Dallas was on her leash, walking in circles, looking for a place to go in the snow. Two officers held guns on her, and after a minute, Jake tossed his black bag to the ground and stood next to her, his arms folded behind his head.

Dallas whined. She didn't like the snow at all and wanted to be held. After this trip, she would be completely spoiled. "May I pick her up?"

One of the officers shrugged.

"I don't get it," Jake said. "What's going on?" Jake didn't favor his side. If she hadn't known about the laceration along his ribs, she wouldn't have been able to tell.

"We were given orders to wait."

A police car arrived and a familiar face flicked a finger at the officers to follow him. "Bring them inside."

The officers escorted them into the hangar. Officer

Wilder took the leash from her and gave it to the man who'd dropped Jake's bag at his feet. "Walk the dog, get it some water and then wait in the car, Powell."

Jake positioned himself between her and one of her former clients. He was probably as confused as she was at the strange treatment.

"When I heard the news that Sabrina Watkins's fingerprints had been found at a crime scene I spit out my coffee."

"Do you know this cop, Bree?"

"I know his wife better, but yes, this is Kyle Wilder. I used to board his dogs when his wife forced him to take a vacation."

"Detective Craig?" Kyle extended his hand. Jake let it hang in the air. "Thanks for getting Sabrina back safely. I have an officer who's going to escort you to Wichita Falls as soon as the roads are clear."

"I don't understand," Jake said along with her.

"You left two bodies and the WFPD wants a statement. Numerous witnesses stated it was self-defense. Then I think the Dallas P.D. wants to clear up the confusion regarding a suspension."

"That I get, but you're taking Bree's rising from the grave all in stride. Are you arresting her?"

Kyle raised an inquisitive eyebrow while nodding toward Jake. "Other than being wanted for questioning in the Richardson homicide, why would I detain her?"

What?

"You let her go and she'll be dead as soon as she's out of your sight." Jake placed his body between her and the officer again. "Is that your game? You the cop who switched the dental records?"

"Funny you should mention that, Detective Craig. Since the explosion last summer, I've been working with state investigators on a joint task force." He sat on the edge of a table next to the wall. "They've suspected that Griffin Tyler has been involved in racketeering and money laundering for a while, especially after Sabrina's suspicious death. We found a couple of our officers who were a little too cozy with Tyler and have our eye on them, too. If you're willing to testify, we might be able to drop any charges that apply."

"You've got the wrong—"

"Jake." She tried to tug him to face her. She took a step next to him when he refused to look anywhere but at the man he considered a threat. "I'm standing right here and very capable of speaking for myself. I'm not guilty of anything except running."

"Are you willing to cooperate?"

"I'm willing to do anything. But first, I need to find my family. Griffin is holding them hostage in exchange for money I took when I left."

"That explains a lot." He looked at Jake. "Doesn't look like the roads will be clearing anytime soon. I assume you want to see this through?"

Jake stuck his hand forward and Kyle shook it.

"Where's your task force?" Jake asked. "Once we place the call, we'll want to move quickly."

"You're looking at it. Things are a little different out here, Detective."

Jake pivoted and thrust his hand into his hair. Then his eyes locked with hers and he grabbed her shoulders. "Do you trust me?"

"Yes." And she did. If they'd been alone she would have admitted how sorry she was for thinking the worst of him. He'd defended himself and her. Anyone would have done the same.

"My idea's simple. Draw them out, see if we can't get

a confession and find out who they're working for," Jake said to the officer.

"You don't know?" Kyle asked her.

"I didn't know—"

"She wasn't—" Jake began at the same time, but her hand on his arm stopped him. She did her own questioning glance to see if he'd let her continue.

"I survived because I overheard them planning to blow up the clinic. I've tried to put things together—like a list of clients who don't exist or have never had pet surgeries. I'll turn over everything just as soon as my family's safe."

"I'd have to go through the department to obtain the equipment necessary for what you're suggesting."

Her heart stampeded. "But the officer Griffin's working with could find out and warn him."

Jake lifted his black duffel holding the money and electronics onto the workbench. "I can help with that."

Chapter Twenty-Three

They'd made the call. Bree's family was alive. And they were waiting in the pitch black fifteen miles southwest of town at an abandoned ranch for the exchange. Might as well have been on the moon for local response time. Why did criminals always have to meet in the dark? They'd waited all afternoon in the airport hangar updating Wilder, waiting on officers he could trust.

Jake didn't envy Wilder's part in the rescue. He was on foot, waist deep in snow, waiting for a signal to move in and make the arrest.

"You were right about not giving up." Bree was in the passenger seat, gripping the bag of money like a lifeline. "I know this is coming late, but I really appreciate everything you've done. We'd all be dead if you hadn't made the decision to help."

"Just follow the plan this time." He would not let his guard down. "If that lunatic hadn't insisted you be the one carrying the money, you wouldn't be here at all."

"I recognized his voice. It's the guy who was with Griffin at the clinic. I've had plenty of nightmares about him trying to kill me."

He knew all about nightmares and didn't want that for Bree. His hand covered hers without discussing it with his brain first. His brain would have reminded them that there was a no-touching policy in effect. "I'm… It'll be okay. Just follow the plan. You get to your family and run. Leave the rest to me."

He wanted to comfort her. Wanted more. His family. Her family. The whole package.

Dead Larry's phone rang.

"Yes?" Bree answered, as they'd instructed.

"That's on this road? Okay." She disconnected. "We drive to the feed lots we passed at the corner, get out and wait."

"Did you get that, Wilder?" he said, for the benefit of the transmitter he shared with the cop. He'd only had two. When Bree ran and she was out of sight, he wouldn't have contact with her.

"It'll take me ten or twelve minutes on foot," Wilder answered.

"Got it." Jake put the Jeep in gear and battled the snow-covered road. "Remember. Don't move forward until your family does. You drop the bag and get to cover."

"Got it."

"I have confidence in you, Bree." He couldn't tell her just how much. Wilder could hear everything they said. Instead, he squeezed her hand again when he pulled to a stop.

They parked and got out, waiting in front of the dark-ened vehicle.

"Wilder?" Jake whispered, barely moving his lips.

"At least five minutes away."

Three bodies turned the corner, close together as if their legs were— "They're not going to be able to run. Their legs are lashed together as if they're in a three-legged race."

"They'll run. Follow the plan," Bree said with confidence.

"Right. The only cover is in the lot with the cattle. They're tied together. You can't get them through the pipe fence, so you'll have to bring them back to the car. If something goes wrong, run up the road through the pens. Walk slow now. Run later. You've got the knife in your pocket, right?"

She looked up at him. "Should I go?"

He wanted to shout no but nodded yes. He wanted to kiss her, but she'd already opened the door and taken the first step away. Where was the "machine" when he needed him?

BREE WALKED SLOWLY, the snow crunching under her boots. She slowed even more, wanting to meet her family as close to the drive into the feed lot as she could. The wind hummed through the electrical wires high overhead. Another front was moving in from the south behind her. She could smell the cattle to her left, hear them moving toward the fence where they expected to be fed.

"That's far enough." A shout came from somewhere behind the buildings. It was the voice she'd never forget.

Her family stopped. She stopped and dropped the bag at her side. She'd soon be face-to-face with her nightmare.

"Open the bag."

She unzipped the duffel and a spotlight shone on her from the top of a grain silo. She left the bag in the snow. "Here's half. I want my family back."

"You were supposed to bring me all the money."

"And you'll get it if you just let them go."

"Sabrina Watkins." The voice was closer, in the direct path of where she intended to run. "You and your boyfriend have cost us a lot of time and money. Our entire operation here is…kaput."

She saw the outline of a gun in his hand as he walked toward her. Kyle had told them Larry had a brother. She could see the resemblance, especially in their horrible, evil eyes.

"Stay back, boyfriend," he shouted. "I think we'll do this the hard but fun way. Pick up the money and walk to me."

"What?" This wasn't the plan. How could she get her family out of here if she was with him? But Jake was there. He could get her family out.

Waving his gun like a flag, he stomped the ground. "Sit!" he screamed, and pointed at her family. They tumbled into the muddy snow, tied like they were. "See, dog trainer? I'm a good trainer, too. They obey or the punishment is my partner shoots. Now pick up the money and come with me."

"No! That's not the deal," Jake shouted. "The rest of the money's hidden. We'll tell Tyler where to pick it up."

"Tyler's dead. He can't find anything." He waved over his shoulder, pointing to Jake. "I think your boyfriend likes you."

Three quick shots were fired. "Son of a b—" Jake dove to the far side of the Jeep.

"Pick up the money, Sabrina."

"You'll leave my family alone?"

"Maybe." He raised the opposite hand into the air. Her family cringed. Her father covered her sister as best he could with his body.

"All right. I can take you to the rest of the money." All she had to do was make it into the cattle lot. They couldn't shoot her family if they were trying to shoot her. She picked up the bag and looped it over her shoulder.

Her nightmare lifted his arm, attempting to grab her. She sidestepped, scooting through the snow and getting a couple of steps ahead of him. "Let them walk to the Jeep."

"Sure."

They stood as she got even with the cattle. Thank goodness, her father encouraged them to shuffle faster. She walked backward, watching her family and staying more than a lunge away from their captor.

They were very close to Jake by the time she was at the gate.

Run! JAKE'S FIST hit his leg again and again. He pulled his knife from his boot, ready to cut the ropes and get Bree's family to safety. He inched around the fender, trying to spot the man who'd fired at him.

"Wilder, from the angle of those shots, cover the top of the silo." Bree was at the gate and out of time. *Run!*

"I'm crossing the south pen. Damn snowdrifts and manure."

"I'm sending the family out in the Jeep and following Bree."

"Roger," Wilder acknowledged. "There's a truck headed in from the north."

"I didn't think it would be easy. I'll get the family. You get the shooter." Jake had his knife in hand and sprinted the remaining ten or so feet to Bree's family.

Rifle shots echoed. "He's either a lousy shot or—"

"Bree made a break. She didn't get away from him…." Wilder trailed off.

Jake had to focus on one rescue at a time. Get the family out. Think of nothing else or he was useless. A shot hit the Jeep. The shooter would correct his aim soon.

"Pick up your daughter and keep running as best you can. I'll carry your wife."

Jake didn't have time to verify if Watkins understood or not. They all kept running. He met them, cut their ropes and lifted Bree's mother off the ground by her waist, very glad she was about the same size as both her daughters.

He had the three of them on the safe side of the Jeep before he cut and removed their ropes completely.

Jake yanked out his bag of gear and pushed Bree's sister into the back of the Jeep. "Stay low. Drive. Don't stop. Don't look back. We'll meet you at the police station. Address is in the GPS."

"Is Sabrina really alive?" asked Bree's mother. "Was that really her?"

"Yes, ma'am. Sorry, I can't explain."

"Thank you," Watkins said, and began backing down the road as a truck sped into view and gunned its engine.

"Anytime now, Wilder. Anytime." Jake picked up his rifle and ran to the cattle fence. It was the only cover he had and that might make it harder for the shooter to actually hit him.

"I think I have the shooter. I warned you about my marksmanship."

"I'm taking out the truck so they can't follow the family. Cover me if nothing else."

Jake sprinted along the path he'd cleared to the road as the truck gained speed to follow the Watkins family. He dug deep, blew out his breath and fired at the front tires until he heard the blowout and the truck swerved into the far barbed-wire fence.

"Do you have eyes on Bree?" he shouted over the continuing gunfire behind him.

"Negative. There you are, you son of—" A lone rifle shot, then another, then something fell and clanked against the metal of the silo. "Done. My team's in place around the perimeter. They can't get out of the lot."

Jake left the men in the truck—alive, dead or unconscious, he didn't care. Wilder could take care of them. "I'm heading after Bree."

Chapter Twenty-Four

"Shut up and keep moving."

"Which direction?" Bree asked.

The man she'd been so petrified of for six months, who had haunted her dreams on a regular basis, shoved between her shoulder blades and cursed when she fell.

He grabbed her coat and hauled her back to her feet. "Fall again, bitch, and I might as well blow your head off."

"Tell me which way to go and I won't fall." For once she didn't cower. Afraid, definitely. And she had no idea if anyone was following to help her out of this mess. But she knew the police were out there. This monster wouldn't get free to haunt someone else. There was still a chance she could survive. She just had to figure out how.

With the faint yellow glow of the mercury lights, they followed the road used to load and feed the cattle. There were tire tracks from earlier in the day that were quickly getting slick without the sun to melt the snow.

Thinking they would be fed again, the cattle pushed toward the fence, jumping on one another's backs, bucking, mooing.

"Cut across that pen to the left."

This was her chance. She could go through the pipe fence, but her abductor would have to climb over. She'd have precious seconds to disappear among the cattle. She followed his instructions, sliding through the icy pipes, pushing her way through the cattle as fast as they'd move out of her way.

"I swear, girl, if you make another move, I'll shoot you through the head," he said, perched on the top row.

She stopped as best she could with the cows pressing against her. Even if the man fired and missed, she'd be crushed between these huge animals. He entered the pen and shoved his way to her side, sticking the gun against her temple.

"You might not care much about your own hide, but think about your family and friends. I *will* get out of here and I *will* slice all their throats." He shoved her head and then shoved the cows.

The cows squeezed her between them, crushed her toes and clamored to get closer. Crossing the pen was exhausting and disgusting in the slush and manure. They were at the mercy of which way the cattle swayed for the longest time. Then the herd sort of turned the opposite direction. Maybe…

A long shadow fell across the backs of the cows. Someone was cutting across the pens on top of the fence. She pointed to the opposite corner and said, "That way's open."

Very few cows were between her and the field where they'd been heading. She picked up her pace, hoping whoever followed could get to her soon. *Please, please, please, let it be Jake.*

"What are you looking at?"

Her nightmare spun to look behind them and she ran. Something hit her back and tangled her feet, tripping her. She caught a glimpse of Jake at the side of the pen where they were headed.

"Drop your weapon, Leroy. Don't move and stay where

you are." Jake's voice shouted across the pen. "Lot seventy-seven, come in silent."

Would Leroy know he was telling the police where they were?

"Or you'll shoot? Your girlfriend's on the ground, Detective. Spook a cow and she's dead." His boot went square on her stomach, keeping her pinned down in the icy mud.

Her feet were untangled, but Leroy had his gun pointed at her. They were in a corner with fewer cows, but he was right. One little spook and she'd be trampled.

"I think it's your turn to drop your weapon."

"You got nowhere to go, man. The police will have this place surrounded in a matter of minutes."

The cattle had noticed Jake at the rail. They'd all be clamoring on top of each other soon. She pushed at Leroy's boot, desperate to get off the ground. *How?* She couldn't see Jake and her knife had been taken away from her back at the first gate.

What had her self-defense instructor told them to do if caught on the ground? Pull the attacker's clothes to get them off balance. She began tugging at his jeans, then rocking her body back and forth. As soon as his foot shifted, she twisted from under him and rolled to the other side of a cow.

"I'm free, Jake!"

Someone fired. She scrambled to her knees and headed away in the direction of the fewest cattle. She found an open spot, stood and pushed between anxious cows heading in all directions because of the gunfire.

And anxious because of a fight. She climbed to the top of the fence in time to see Jake land two good punches to the other man's jaw. He stumbled backward, but Jake stayed on top of him. With a punch to his gut, the man fell against a large white cow and that evil grin she'd seen at the clinic slithered onto his face. It seemed like a lifetime ago but she recognized it.

"He's got my knife!"

She watched a repeat of this morning's fight with that young kid. Every slash of the blade was perfectly countered by Jake. His arm dripped blood from a gash but he didn't slow down. And then the move that had killed that crazy young man in Wichita Falls was repeated.

This man fell, crazed eyes squinting shut, never crying out. Jake dropped to his knees and Bree jumped from the fence to run to his side.

"Oh, God, Jake. Are you all right?" Her voice was low and scared.

They made it safely to and over the fence in time to watch several police cars sloshing through the snow. They sat on the curb of the feed trough, waiting. The cattle followed to the fence behind them, noisy and wanting to be fed. They seemed unaffected by the fight.

Totally unlike her.

"You're bleeding. Is Kyle still listening to you through the microphone?"

"I lost the earpiece after the first punch to my face. It's somewhere out in the muck." Jake shook off her hands from his arms. "God, I thought he'd shot you. Thought you were dead." He gently trapped her face with his long fingers and she covered his hands, keeping him close. "I'm not sure where this relationship will lead, Bree. But I don't want it to end."

"This is crazy, Jake. We met yesterday morning. You don't have to say that because we had an interlude."

"You what?" Kyle Wilder asked as he walked up. "Are you about to kiss that witness, Detective Craig?"

They split apart. An officer brought a first-aid kit to look at Jake's arm and Kyle backed her out of the way. "It will complicate my case if you're having a fling with the detective."

"We barely know each other." She didn't believe that. They'd connected somehow. Or was it just extenuating circumstances?

"Good, because a relationship with a suspect would just be another bad mark in his file." Kyle had lowered his voice so the other officers couldn't hear.

"To think we have a relationship is stupid. I just met him yesterday." It didn't matter if she felt something or not. After everything Jake had done for her, she wasn't going to let him get into trouble for kissing her—or sleeping with her.

Kyle guided her down the road to a car ready to pull out. "Get in, Sabrina." When she hesitated, his grip on her arm prevented her from running back to Jake. "I'm not asking."

"Why are they arresting him? You said—" She twisted free and took a step toward the officers escorting Jake to another police car. "Are we both under arrest?"

Kyle caught her arm again and snapped a cuff around her wrist. "I've been instructed to get you into protective custody and out of Amarillo. You're the key to bringing these scumbags to justice. Now get in the car."

She wanted to explain to Jake how she felt. "Can't I see him for a minute?"

"We have to obtain your statements separately. I can't let you see your parents, either."

"I...I don't understand, Kyle."

"This money-laundering scam is huge and you're the key to putting them in jail. They're cleaning house. My men found Griffin Tyler shot through the head in his home. They've been trying to kill you for six months. Do you think they're stopping now?"

"What if I refuse? I mean, Jake's done a fantastic job of protecting me and—"

"Will he be able to protect all your family? What if he does jail time for his actions at his precinct?"

"If I go with you he'll be cleared?"

Kyle nodded. She got in the car and he closed the door.

Police protection scared her more than when she'd been held at knifepoint by Larry. She rubbed the place on her neck where the blade had cut her. But why? She had no reason not to trust Kyle. What worried her was not seeing her family.

And not telling Jake how much he meant to her. Maybe she hadn't answered him, but she could clear his name and guarantee that he got his old job back. She could do that much for the marine who'd defended her so completely.

JAKE DIDN'T LIKE sitting in the backseat of a police cruiser. Locked on the wrong side of the glass, he could only watch as Kyle Wilder drove Bree away from the scene. An officer took him to the station and put him in an interview room. He had a lot of explaining to do to his captain, the Wichita Falls police and, right now, to a special task force rep in a nice, clean suit.

Jake still stunk from rolling in the feed lots. The only thing clean on him was the bandage where they'd dressed the knife wound on his arm.

"Detective Craig, the state of Texas would like to thank you for your help. I'm going to get your statement and make arrangements for your travel back to DFW." He set a pad and pencil on the table.

Jake stood and leaned on the table, looking down on whatever officer was attempting to be nice to him. "Where's Sabrina Watkins?"

"Miss Watkins is no longer in Amarillo. She's been secured."

Secured? "When can I see her?" Jake sat, trying to keep a lid on the fury coursing through him.

"I have no information. Nor, if I did, would I be able to share it with you, Detective."

"So where's my dog?"

"Pardon?"

Jake knew the drill. He'd done it too many times himself. They wanted his recollections as fast as he could get them written. He pushed the notepad an arm's length away.

"Kyle Wilder sent my pup, Dallas, with an officer when we landed at the airport. She could be at the pound for all I know. And that's not going to happen. I'll make my statement when you find my dog." Bree's dog that he'd keep until she said otherwise. He laced his fingers behind his head. The tape on his side pinched his skin, but he kept a straight face. "Don't shake your head and tell me I'm not in a position to make demands. Come on, man. Just find my dog and get me a hamburger. I'm starved."

The officer scooped up the pen and paper and left. Ten minutes later, Dallas bounded through the door.

"There's my girl." *At least one of them.*

When the time was right, he'd demand to see Bree. And if he couldn't—if he could hang on to the pup, he was certain they'd find each other sooner or later.

Chapter Twenty-Five

The jumping Chihuahua in Bree's stomach had twenty pals join him. Testifying had nothing on the nerves she was trying to get under control. Facing Jake after five long, lonely months waiting to testify might be harder than walking that snow-covered road with a gun to her head. That night she'd known Jake would come after her. Today, she had no way of predicting how he'd react to her just showing up.

This house with the rolling hill country backdrop was a far cry from Jake's one-bedroom apartment.

"So, this is the place. I'll wait for you if you want," Mr. Soku, the driver, said with a foreign accent.

She'd had plenty of time to share her doubts about arriving unannounced. Her fear had just come pouring out to her driver.

"I can't do this, after all. Can you turn—" A bark and familiar howl stopped her. *Dallas.* She didn't even need to see the puppy to know who beckoned to her. "I'll call when I'm ready to go. It might be as soon as five minutes."

"I'll be close by, Miss Sabrina. Much good fortune to you. I wish you luck finding your happy beginning."

"Thank you so very much, Mr. Soku." She paid him and got out the driver's side door he opened, standing in the deserted street as he drove away.

Dallas barked from behind the fence. Mr. Soku honked

from the corner, leaning out his window and gesturing that she move from her spot. She couldn't or was afraid to take a step. What if Jake rejected her? A vehicle turned the corner and she had to get out of its way. There wasn't a sidewalk so she quickly walked down the driveway to the porch.

A door slammed and she wanted to look behind her, but that petrified feeling had her glued, facing the bell. If she turned away, she'd keep right on walking. *Chicken.* She pushed the doorbell and waited. There was scratching at the door, more barking and a bit of howling.

"May I help you, ma'am?" asked a deep, sexy voice from behind her.

Jumping Chihuahuas, she'd missed that voice. It started all sorts of bubbly good things inside her.

"Hi, Jake." She turned to greet him, hand extended, hoping he'd smile and not turn her away. Could she run in this tight sundress and heels to catch Mr. Soku? Had it been five minutes?

The tall marine-turned-homicide-detective-turned-state-investigator gulped. He gulped again and looked around as if he was embarrassed to have her on his steps, let alone near his house. "I didn't recognize you as a blonde and in that— That's some dress, Bree. What are you doing here?"

"Oh, no. I'm sorry. I should have called." She darted down the single step, hearing the little howl behind the door. It broke her heart as much as the confused look on Jake's face.

His hand darted out, catching her bare upper arm. It was blazing hot outside and just a couple of minutes in the afternoon sun had her skin heated. But Jake's touch shot a flame through every inch of her being.

"Wait. They told me you were coming to see Dallas."

She had come a very long way to see *Jake*. Months of wondering and debating. She stepped back under the shade of the porch and searched his dark eyes. "You look great, Jake."

As soon as he got through the door, he ignored Dallas until she sat in front of him. "Good girl. You ready to eat?" The dog was twice the size she'd been five months earlier. All legs, she bounded to Bree before chasing around the corner, sliding on the wooden floors after Jake.

Bree stayed in the entry hall, unsure about where to go and completely convinced this had been the wrong thing to do. They'd known each other for less than two full days. He'd moved on with his life while hers had been in limbo waiting in protective custody.

Jake stuck his head around the corner. "Coming?"

"Your home's very beautiful."

"I got a good deal on it. The owners were downsizing and left a lot of the furnishings, and Dallas needed a yard." He scooped dog food into a dish. "Come on, girl. You know the drill. Sit."

The Lab plopped down, her long tail sweeping the floor as it wagged behind her.

"You're so good together. I'm glad you decided to keep her."

Jake's face scrunched up in confusion. "You thought I'd give her away?"

"No." She shook her head. She wanted a do-over. Maybe if she ran back to the front door and he answered it, she could get the speech out she'd practiced all morning on the plane. Jake gave Dallas one last stroke and stood, making Bree crane her neck to look him in the eye. "I'd forgotten just how tall you were. You all healed?"

Her dress spun with her as she turned to go. She'd never come back. Never see him again. She couldn't do this more than once. She remembered the slick new heels just as her feet slipped from under her and she fell into Jake's arms. He set her in the kitchen chair faster than she'd thought possible. In a matter of seconds, he faced her from across the table and quirked an eyebrow in her direction.

The warrior who had risked everything to help her and rescue her family materialized as he tossed an envelope onto the table. "I got the papers. You're suing for joint custody of Dallas? You came to take away my dog?"

"What? I didn't—I was joking when I said I might. I'd never take her away from you, Jake. You're right. She's your dog now." She loved the puppy who had brought them together, but she loved Jake more. "I never had any intention of taking her away. I had this weird conversation with an attorney, but I didn't go through with it. I was going to use the story as an icebreaker...not a deal breaker."

"So it was a joke?"

"They shouldn't have done anything at all."

"That's different, then. You know, I can let you have as much time with Dallas as you want. Anytime you're in town." He stuck his hands in his pockets, shoulders sort of drooping.

She stood, swaying in the stupid, sexy shoes she'd worn just for him. She kicked them to the side and bent down next to the dog.

Dallas nudged her snout under Bree's hand, looking for some loving. Suddenly, it was like they hadn't been apart. If only finding love was that simple.

"I really came here to tell you I was wrong."

"About?" He shot a hand through his hair and brought it back to scratch the stubble on his jawline.

She grabbed the edge of the table, knowing what would come next—a surge of longing for him. That simple gesture just made her weak in the knees. "Shoot, Jake. There's no tippy-toeing around why I came. I wanted to see you. I missed you."

"And Dallas, don't forget." He was teasing her. The twinkle was back in his eyes.

"I missed you both. I wanted to call more than once, but the prosecutors wouldn't let me."

"I didn't know how hard to push. The last time we were together you told Wilder we didn't know each other. That to think we had a relationship was stupid—your words, not mine. And to think we had more than a one-night stand—also your words—was completely foolish."

"I told him that so you wouldn't get into any more trouble. I was also very wrong. Our two days together got me through the last five months."

Jake's fingers brushed a tear from her cheek and he shifted her into the circle of his arms. He heated her core and sent shivers up her spine at the same time. No man had ever made her feel anything close to these sensations. His lips were close and just waiting...so she kissed him. He tasted cool, like iced tea and lemon. His arms circled her back and pulled her close to his chest.

Dallas whined and jumped on them both, making it impossible to kiss through their laughter. "No need to be jealous, girl." Bree stroked the black, wiry fur.

"I wanted to turn you around and do that from the moment I saw you in the street," he said into her hair.

"I thought you didn't recognize me?"

He latched those brown eyes to hers. "I'd be able to pick you out of a crowd at a hundred yards. I couldn't believe you were finally here."

Jake shrugged out of his coat as he dialed his cell. "I need to send a text canceling tonight. You see, this crazy chick I knew suggested I get therapy."

"I did not. I just said working with Charlie helped my uncle."

"It didn't take me long to realize how much Dallas was helping me deal with stress. I found an organization that helps military vets find the right pet and I volunteer."

He faced her and pushed his hands through his hair. A sure sign that he was nervous regarding whatever he was about to say. She barely knew him, but then she also knew him so well.

"Bree, the time I spent with you—" He took her hand into his palm, using his thumb to draw those concentric circles that drove her mad with desire. "They were the best hours of my life. I've missed you every minute since."

He tipped her chin and tilted her world with his smile.

"You're crying again and I haven't even gotten to the good part," he whispered near her lips.

Sure enough, tears leaked out of the corners of her eyes. "There's a better part?"

"I know it's early and I'll give you all the time you need. But I fell all the way when you ran into my life. Being apart has only convinced me that I love you."

His lips descended and captured hers. Captured and wouldn't release. He wrapped his arms tight and held her as tenderly as their first kiss. He taunted and kept their lips devouring each other until Dallas jumped on them again.

"Definitely the best part." She leaned her cheek against his chest. "That's what I came to tell you. I love you. I thought I was crazy. I kept telling myself it couldn't be real. It was too soon. Or just one of those whirlwind adventures. Maybe a bond I felt because of the intense situation."

"Me, too." He hugged her to him, keeping her close, his breath tickled her neck. "I kept thinking we'd see each other somewhere throughout all this process. But the police kept us separated in Amarillo and then the state authorities threatened me within an inch of my life not to compromise the case again. They offered me a position with the Texas Racing Commission. I couldn't turn them down."

"I wanted to call so badly. Kyle Wilder assured me they'd give me your address after I testified. The prosecution placed me in protective custody, locking me in a safe house in the middle of nowhere. It made Amarillo look like a metropolitan city. I've had a lot of time to think. But my feelings about you haven't changed."

"The state prosecutor kept telling me I couldn't see you. And when I called your uncle last month—"

"You talked to Jerry?"

"Yeah, but he didn't know where you were. Said the family got one letter, but had no idea what was really going on."

"One letter with no real details was all they'd allow."

"No one could have convinced me I'd fall this hard or fast. Or that I'd start missing you before we said goodbye. But I did...." His voice trailed off as he nibbled on her neck. "I hope you're staying for a while. Maybe a week or two? I warned them I'd be taking off as soon as I knew where you were."

His burning lips left a smoldering trail across her collarbone. She pulled back to see his eyes reflecting the desire she felt.

"As for your petition for custody." He paused to kiss her, leaving a burning trail from the backs of his fingers running along her exposed skin. "If you want to spend time with Dallas, we're a package deal. You're stuck with the both of us. Move in with me."

He lifted her, twirling her through the kitchen, laughing and playfully taunting Dallas.

"Sounds like perfect joint custody." She kissed his furrowed brow that she'd missed every day. "Remind me to call Mr. Soku at the cab company. He wished me luck finding my happy beginning. I want to tell him it worked."

* * * * *

A sneaky peek at next month...

INTRIGUE...

BREATHTAKING ROMANTIC SUSPENSE

My wish list for next month's titles...

In stores from 17th January 2014:

☐ Undercover Captor – Cynthia Eden

& Rocky Mountain Revenge – Cindi Myers

☐ Blood on Copperhead Trail – Paula Graves

& Rancher Rescue – Barb Han

☐ Tennessee Takedown – Lena Diaz

& Raven's Hollow – Jenna Ryan

Romantic Suspense

☐ Cavanaugh Hero – Marie Ferrarella

Available at WHSmith, Tesco, Asda, Eason, Amazon and Apple

Just can't wait?

Special Offers

Every month we put together collections and
longer reads written by your favourite authors.

Here are some of next month's highlights—
and don't miss our fabulous discount online!

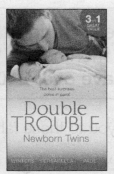

On sale 7th February   On sale 17th January   On sale 7th February

Save 20%
on all Special Releases

Join the Mills & Boon Book Club

Subscribe to **Intrigue** today for 3, 6 or 12 months and you could **save over £40!**

We'll also treat you to these fabulous extras:

- 🌹 **FREE L'Occitane gift set worth £10**
- 🌹 **FREE home delivery**
- 🌹 **Rewards scheme, exclusive offers…and much more!**

Subscribe now and save over £40
www.millsandboon.co.uk/subscribeme

Discover more romance at

www.millsandboon.co.uk

- ❤ WIN great prizes in our exclusive competitions

- ❤ BUY new titles before they hit the shops

- ❤ BROWSE new books and REVIEW your favourites

- ❤ SAVE on new books with the Mills & Boon® Bookclub™

- ❤ DISCOVER new authors

PLUS, to chat about your favourite reads, get the latest news and find special offers:

- 🔵 Find us on facebook.com/millsandboon

- 🐦 Follow us on twitter.com/millsandboonuk

- ❤ Sign up to our newsletter at millsandboon.co.uk

The World of Mills & Boon®

There's a Mills & Boon® series that's perfect for you. We publish ten series and, with new titles every month, you never have to wait long for your favourite to come along.

Blaze.
Scorching hot, sexy reads
4 new stories every month

By Request
Relive the romance with the best of the best
9 new stories every month

Cherish™
Romance to melt the heart every time
12 new stories every month

Desire™
Passionate and dramatic love stories
8 new stories every month